The AMERICAN ADVENTURESS

Also by C. W. Gortner

The AMERICAN
ADVENTURESS

A Novel

C. W. GORTNER

WILLIAM MORROW
An Imprint of HarperCollins*Publishers*

P.S.™ is a trademark of HarperCollins Publishers.

FIRST EDITION

Designed by Diahann Sturge
Vintage art deco pattern © Daniela Iga/Shutterstock

Library of Congress Cataloging-in-Publication Data

Names: Gortner, C. W. author.
Title: The American adventuress : a novel / C.W. Gortner.
Description: First edition. | New York, NY : William Morrow, [2022]
Identifiers: LCCN 2021039661 | ISBN 9780063035805 (paperback) | ISBN 9780063035812 (ebook)
Subjects: LCSH: Churchill, Randolph Spencer, Lady, 1854-1921—Fiction. | LCGFT: Historical fiction. | Biographical fiction.
Classification: LCC PS3607.O78 A84 2022 | DDC 813/.6—dc23
LC record available at https://lccn.loc.gov/2021039661

ISBN 978-0-06-303580-5

22 23 24 25 26 LSC 10 9 8 7 6 5 4 3 2 1

For Vicki,
Sister, mother, grandmother, friend,
and angel

The AMERICAN ADVENTURESS

PART I

THE MILLIONAIRE'S DAUGHTER

1866–1874

Strong women make beautiful women.
—CLARA JEROME

ONE

1866

Miss Jerome. How many times must I tell you? It is unacceptable for you to abandon your desk in the middle of a lesson. Return to your seat at once."

Miss Green's voice cracked across the classroom. I stood on tiptoes at the window, straining to see past the snowfall. There was no clock inside the room, but I innately sensed the passage of time, of which there was entirely too much at school.

Papa was late.

"Miss Jerome! Must I repeat myself? To your seat. *Now.*"

Turning around, I found her glaring at me, her flat bosom puffed out against her black bodice with its ruffle of tarnished lace.

"My father is coming to fetch me," I said, causing my sister Clarita to gape in disbelief.

"Mr. Jerome is not here yet, is he?" Miss Green replied. "Honestly, the nerve. You flout every civilized norm."

I didn't move, keeping my eyes on her. I had found it was an effective trick. If I stared long enough without fear, she wouldn't know what to do.

"Jennie," hissed Clarita. "Just do as Miss Green says."

I didn't spare her a glance. Clarita—pretty, blue-eyed, blond Clarita—was two years older than me and obedient to a fault, which made her Mama's favorite. I found her lack of character tedious, not to mention annoying, especially at times like these.

"Yes," added Miss Green. "If you please."

"I do not please." My voice rang out, bringing every pencil in every girl's hand clattering upon their desks. "My father pays my tuition and I can do as I please."

Miss Green's flush turned virulent. Clarita shrank into her seat.

"Your father pays your tuition for you to learn proper manners, to be educated as a young lady should, not to leap up from your seat whenever you please and defy those with your best interests at heart. You will recite today's poem in French. This instant."

I let another moment pass before I made my return to my desk beside my sister's. I remained standing, as it was another of her inviolate rules. Students must stand when called upon to declaim. But I lifted my voice higher than required, to emphasize my impeccable French:

> *Je suis belle, ô mortels! comme un rêve de pierre,*
> *Et mon sein, où chacun s'est meurtri tour à tour,*
> *Est fait pour inspirer au poète un amour*
> *Eternel et muet ainsi que la matière.*

Aghast hush ensued. Miss Green's fingers clenched about her ruler. She'd wielded it before, if never on me. Instead, she vented her thwarted fury on the other girls, and those closest to her now cowered, as if bracing for her assault.

Beside me, Clarita let out a desperate exhale.

"That—that is not the poem you were assigned," Miss Green managed to say.

"No, but I like it better. Shall I translate it?" Before she could respond, I did:

> *I am fair, O mortals, like a dream carved in stone,*
> *And my breast, where each one in turn has bruised himself*
> *Is made to inspire in the poet a love*
> *As eternal and silent as matter.*

Her entire person went rigid. "Enough. Wherever did you find such unsuitable verse?" She spoke as if I'd chanted a Negro refrain, which I also knew, as my childhood nanny, Dobbie, had taught me many while I was growing up.

"In my father's library." I looked at Clarita for confirmation; she averted her eyes. "We often visited Paris when we lived in Europe, and Papa acquired many books—"

"She's never been to Paris," my sister exclaimed. "She wasn't even born when my parents resided in Italy. She's always making up fibs to make herself seem important." Clarita swerved to me. "Tell the truth for once. You stole that book from Papa's library, though Mama strictly forbade it, as it's not suited for a girl of twelve—"

"It most certainly is not," cut in Miss Green. "I daresay, it's unsuitable for a girl of any age. It was written by a foreign degenerate."

"You're familiar with Monsieur Baudelaire's work? I thought you mustn't be. My father owns an exclusive French edition. I don't believe it's published here."

She took a menacing step toward me. "Jennie Jerome, I've endured these antics out of respect for your parents, who entrusted me with your education. But you've trespassed beyond my tolerance. You will never recite such abomination again. And you will stay after class to translate the poem by Mr. Arnold that you were assigned. Am I understood?"

"My father is due at any moment—" I started to protest, but I wasn't so sure now.

Papa might laugh and deride Miss Green behind her back for her petty spinster ways, but her academy was one of the most prestigious educational establishments in the city, coveted by families like ours, if not attended by the Four Hundred, the elite authorized by Mrs. Astor to fill her ballroom. For years, Mama had campaigned for inclusion on the Astor list. She'd not be pleased to hear I'd again earned chastisement that would be bandied about by the other girls—and for reciting a poet I'd indeed been forbidden to read.

"Mr. Jerome shall be duly informed." Miss Green stared at me. This time, no matter how boldly I returned her stare, she was not backing down. She flicked her hand clutching the ruler, dropping me into my seat.

Clarita hissed, "You're impossible. *Why* must you challenge her at every turn?"

"Because I can." I kept my voice low as one of the simpering perfect girls in the front row stood up to recite Mr. Arnold's insufferably dull poem. "Just wait until Papa hears of this. He'll box her ears."

"And Mama will box yours. Don't think she won't."

I did not think it. But a boxing on my ears was a small price to pay.

The rest of the hour was interminable. I slumped in my seat—"Miss Jerome," barked Miss Green, "has your spine melted?"—wondering where Papa could possibly be.

Only a few months ago, he'd inaugurated his Jerome Park Racetrack in Bathgate to resounding success. Papa adored horse racing; he owned over twenty purebreds, including ten Lipizzaners he'd imported from Europe. When he wasn't working at his trading firm or attending musical engagements, he spent his spare time overseeing his racetrack, the first of its kind in New York, which had attracted society in droves.

For our new mansion on Fifth Avenue, in addition to a private theater, where he held concerts for a select audience of six hundred—"two hundred more," he'd reminded Mama, "than the Astor ballroom"—he'd had an adjacent three-story stable built, equipped with gleaming walnut stalls. I loved to go there with him. Clarita and I were both expert riders; Papa had insisted we learn from an early age, saying the only sight more beautiful than a woman on horseback was a woman at the piano, so he'd ensured we did both to perfection. He'd promised to fetch me early today for a carriage ride, but every time I braved another glance at the window to see the snowfall increase, I grew more despondent.

Had he forgotten? With so many things on his mind, he'd neglected to remember his promises to me in the past. I always forgave him. How could I not? But today, my resentment overwhelmed me, for his tardiness meant I must contend with Miss Green.

By the time the lesson ended and the girls were gathering their satchels to depart for the day's final course—music, in which I also excelled—I'd forgotten my punishment, until Miss Green said, "Miss Jerome, you are not yet excused." Her cold smile held a hint of teeth. "Sit back down and open your notebook, please. I believe you still have a poem to translate."

Clarita shot me a withering look as she sashayed out with the other girls. I scowled back at her, flinging open my notebook.

Leaning over it under Miss Green's baleful stare, I began copying out the poem by Mr. Arnold, which I'd barely learned. I didn't care. I hoped I'd earn enough of her reproof for her to actually use that ruler on me, all I required to have Papa remove me from her academy, where I wasn't learning much anyway. Mama had had Clarita and me tutored by governesses for years; she'd enrolled us in Miss Green's Academy only so that she could boast of it in society. She thought it would make her a lady of proper standing— yet another of her bids for Mrs. Astor's approval, should the news reach Mrs. Astor's unyielding ears.

"Mrs. Astor is also a petty tyrant," I muttered aloud.

Miss Green said, "I did not hear you, Miss Jerome. Ladies do not mumble. Say what you must clearly or refrain from speaking at all."

I lifted my eyes to her in hatred.

"Yes," she said. "Silence in your case is preferable."

Oh, she was enjoying her petty victory. I scrawled out the poem in French, without caring to amend any mistakes. "Done," I announced.

"So quickly?" She didn't move to review it. "Again, if you please."

"Again?" My voice lifted in furious disbelief.

"Yes. And if you question me, you will do it a third time."

At that moment, I heard the jangle of harnesses outside. As I bolted upright, Miss Green held up her hand. "You will stay here. I shall attend to Mr. Jerome forthwith."

She swept from the classroom, her bell-shaped black skirts brushing against the narrow doorframe. I might have ignored her and followed, only I knew that no matter what, Miss Green would inform Papa. While he might have waved it aside as something of no account, once he learned I'd purloined a book from his library, it would be another matter.

When the familiar sound of his footsteps came down the passageway, I stuffed my notebook into my satchel. I wasn't pleased. Had he arrived on time as promised, I might not have found myself in this predicament.

He wore his black greatcoat with its lynx-fur collar, his mustachios perfectly waxed despite the snow. His dark blue eyes were piercing in his face, with its strong nose and prominent jawline; as he removed his top hat, his fair hair fell in disarray over his forehead. My father never used pomade.

My heart sank when I took in his expression.

"Jennie." He sighed. "Again?"

I made myself shrug.

He motioned. "Come. Clarita is attending a musical recital after school at one of her friends' homes. I'll send a carriage for her later."

"Oh." Clarita was always attending some function after school; Mama had inculcated in both of us the need to cultivate our social contacts, but I preferred to avoid the endeavor whenever possible. "How tiresome. None of her friends play the piano as well as we do."

"That may be, but they at least know how to comport themselves. Your sister Leonie would never try her teachers so, and she's younger than both of you." As I trudged after him, stung by his rebuke, he went on, "Jennie, you must stop antagonizing Miss Green. She's beside herself in despair."

"Because I recited a poem in French?" I took my cloak from the peg in the hallway. "She did assign us a poetry lesson."

He pinched my cheek. "You know precisely what I mean."

My smile faded. "Are you going to tell Mama?"

"What choice do I have? If I don't see to your discipline, Miss Green warned that she'll have no alternative but to issue her complaints directly to Clara."

"*Discipline?*" I echoed. "Whatever does she think you should do? Take a crop to me? You don't even whip your horses."

"I don't believe in whipping children or animals, so we'll have to come up with something less drastic." His mouth quirked under his mustachios as he repressed a smile. "Piano practice for the rest of the month with Mrs. Ronalds, perhaps?"

He took up the reins of his crimson calash with its two harnessed black horses stamping their hooves in the cold; he preferred to drive by himself, never mind that he made a spectacle of it, as no gentleman should be seen managing his own carriage.

I wasn't surprised to hear Fanny Ronalds had returned to stay with us. She'd become a frequent guest, his dear friend who shared his passion for music, and a talented singer and pianist in her own right, though I hadn't failed to noticed how Mama maintained a rigid smile in her presence. Once, as Mrs. Ronalds waited in the foyer for Papa to bring around the carriage, I overheard my mother say, "I don't blame you, my dear. I know how irresistible he can be." I hadn't been sure what she meant, but Mama didn't share Papa's enthusiasms, so I'd assumed she forgave Mrs. Ronalds for doing so in her stead.

"That is why I was late," he now said. "I went to fetch Fanny at the station. She's come to stay with us for the holidays. She's eager to see how you've progressed in your study of Liszt. I told her, you practice every evening, but she'll want to hear proof for herself."

I flung my arms about him. "Oh, yes. Mrs. Ronalds can be *so* very strict."

He grinned, snapping his whip in the air. The horses leapt forward, jolting me as I clung to him, for I always sat beside him on the elevated seat. The snowfall turned heavy, enfolding the city in a white shroud, powdering his broad shoulders under his coat.

"Hold on, Jennie. I don't want you falling off, on top of everything else."

He didn't have to warn me. I knew how fast he drove, regardless of the weather. As he raced into the unpaved avenues that had begun to link the city, pedestrians leaping out of his way, shaking fists and cursing him for his recklessness, he finally let loose his laughter. "Baudelaire! Of all things. You truly are the daughter after my own heart—my own *fleur du mal!*"

TWO

Our red-brick mansion with its arched oblong windows and gothic-spired upper tiers sat on the corner of Madison and Twenty-Sixth, near the Fifth Avenue Hotel, whose luxurious appointments had made the district fashionable. Most of the avenue itself was unfinished, strewn with horse leavings, but the squalid tenements had been demolished, the impoverished inhabitants relocated, and the opening ball to inaugurate our mansion had been Mama's supreme achievement to date.

She'd flung open the gilded doors to her garish red-silk-papered drawing room and magnificent cream-and-gold ballroom to welcome society, champagne flowing from sculpted-ice fountains atop overladen buffet tables, liveried servants armed with eau de cologne spraying the air to revive the faint or overglutted. The ball lasted into the early-morning hours. To her delight, every invitee but one attended: Mrs. Astor sent her regrets. I remembered how Mama stood as if in confusion amidst the detritus, exhausted maids clearing away the platters.

"Disdained, again. What will it take for them to recognize us, Leonard?"

She was so distressed that Papa, who rarely had patience for anyone's disdain, said, "My darling. Everyone else recognized us. Must we abase ourselves to the few who did not?"

Mama's face had shut like a trap. Abasing oneself was intolerable, but she did it anyway, at least in my opinion. Researching every school until she pounced on Miss Lucy Green's Academy, where it was rumored—falsely, as it turned out—Mrs. Astor had enrolled her daughters. Cajoling Papa to offer a donation to repair the academy's dilapidated music room, prompting Miss Green to shift our names to the top of her waiting list, though she must have regretted it once she had me under her tutelage.

Recalling her comment today, I glanced at Papa as he pulled the carriage into the stables and his footmen rushed to attend us. I started to ask the question when Papa waved the footmen aside, saying to the grooms, "See that the horses are rubbed down thoroughly. I don't want them catching a chill. If they so much as sneeze, I'll sack the lot of you."

Then he turned to me. "Horses are sensitive creatures," he said, and I recited his next words by heart: "You must tend to them as if they were girls. Like you tend to me."

"You?" He snorted. "A girl who acts like a boy." But he grinned as he gestured to the back door into the mansion. "Don't forget to remove your boots in the foyer. You know how your mother detests us tracking muck on her carpets. She's in the drawing room with Mrs. Ronalds. Go and greet them." As I nodded, suddenly apprehensive, he added, "And for pity's sake, don't say anything about today. I'll be there shortly."

He turned away, impatient to see to the horses, as no matter how well-trained his staff was, he wasn't about to leave it to them.

Removing my lace-up boots and coat, I slipped my chilled feet into the soft-soled shoes left for us to use indoors. Usually, Dobbie would come downstairs to assist me, but we had company and Mama no doubt had charged our nanny with putting Leonie to bed for a nap. I paused by the mirror in the black-and-white foyer. My eyes stared back at me. Crystalline blue that could turn gray, slightly tilted at the corners—my mother's eyes, only lighter in color, overpowering my strong-boned face and wide-lipped mouth.

Clarita was all milk and honey, taking after my father's Scotch ancestry, while Leonie and I more closely resembled Mama, with our slightly sallow complexions and darker hair. My mother was considered a beauty, if tall for a woman, or what was politely termed "statuesque," but her resolve to remain as expressionless as possible detracted from her appeal. Mama detested her assertive nose, which Papa declared worthy of a Roman coin—hardly a compliment for Mama, who'd refused to let herself be painted or daguerreotyped in profile. I peered at my reflection, wondering if my nose was too long also, then sighed and made my way upstairs. I had no patience like Clarita did for gazing into the glass, seeking out imperfections I must correct.

Female conversation issued from the drawing room. Or discourse, for only Mrs. Ronalds could be heard, her refined Bostonian accent detectable as she regaled Mama with gossip. I was glad of her arrival; being agreeable to our guests was one of Mama's inviolate rules, so she'd not take me too much to task once Papa informed her of my insubordination today.

Still, I faltered when I entered the red-wallpapered room—so red, it seemed to be ablaze, though it was, according to Mama, the height of fashion—and I found Mama on the settee in her violet day gown, flounces up to her cameo-pinned collar, her expression stolid as Mrs. Ronalds broke off mid-chatter to exclaim, "Jennie! How lovely to see you!" as if we'd been separated for years, although she'd just been here last season after her annual European sojourn.

I curtsied as Mama had taught me.

Fanny Ronalds laughed. "Oh, please. After all this time, we can do without formalities, yes?"

I smiled in return, avoiding my mother's regard. Mrs. Ronalds was airy as a froth of meringue, with inquisitive blue eyes, upswept ringlets of gold-brown hair, and a supple figure in a fitted pink silk dress. She presented a stark contrast to Mama, festooned to her chin, and my heart expanded at the warmth in her greeting. Mrs. Ronalds exuded vigor and joy; she was never given to melancholia.

"And how was your day at school, my dear?" she asked as I

pecked her powdered cheek. Turning to Mama to do the same, noting the dry cast to her skin—she abhorred cosmetics, relying solely on a regimen of soap and stringent lemon juice—I heard my mother say, "How else? I'm afraid she earns only contempt these days for her high-handedness."

I paused, frozen at the thought that somehow word from Miss Green had already winged its way through the snowbound city.

Mrs. Ronalds laughed. "Is she not studious or accomplished enough? I scarcely think it can be the latter. Jennie has the finest touch on the piano of any girl I know. And I'm certain she'll demonstrate equal skill in the ballroom, when the time for her debut comes."

"In the ballroom and on the piano, perhaps," said Mama as I sat on a nearby chair, careful to not reveal the wool pantalettes under my skirts. "But her attitude . . . it leaves much to be desired."

Mrs. Ronalds laughed again. "She is her father's daughter, you mean."

"Entirely." I heard the weight in Mama's pronouncement. She might not know about my latest insubordination, but she hadn't forgotten Miss Green's prior grievances.

"Well." Mrs. Ronalds took up the Wedgwood pot from the table before them, her charm bracelet emitting a chime. "She should show some spirit. The century is more than half over; women can do more these days than assign seating arrangements or pour the perfect cup of tea."

As she proceeded to do just that, letting another of her astonishing modern notions linger in the air, a slight grimace crossed Mama's face.

"Will you answer Mrs. Ronalds?" she said, as if daring me to admit my contrariness. All of a sudden, I wanted to oblige. Fanny would no doubt find the incident amusing. She was very familiar with France, often traveling there; she'd hardly think reciting Baudelaire was a crime.

"My day was fine," I made myself say instead. "I'm not learning very much anymore."

Mama said, "Not for any lack of effort on Miss Green's part."

Mrs. Ronalds made a commiserative sound, even as she gave me a secretive smile, conveying that she hadn't learned much at school either. But my pleasure at her camaraderie was pulverized by Mama's next words: "I fear a change of scenery has indeed become pressing. Time abroad, away from all these distractions, should set matters on their proper course."

"Abroad?" I echoed. "In the dead of winter?"

Mama returned my stare. "It snows just as well in Paris as it does in New York."

"And with far less manure underfoot," added Mrs. Ronalds. "Winters in New York are so primitive, while Paris is delightfully civilized any time of the year."

Paris . . .

I grappled with a sense of menace lurking under the conversation when Papa entered. Kissing Mama's cheek and Mrs. Ronalds's hand, he declared, "Whatever have I done to deserve the extraordinary fortune of being surrounded by so much beauty?"

"Earned too much money?" quipped Mrs. Ronalds.

Papa laughed, moving to the sideboard by the billiards table at the end of the room.

Mama said flatly, "Speaking of which, your solicitor came by. He said it was urgent."

Papa didn't pause in his stride to pour himself a measure of brandy. "Solicitor? Oh, you mean that villain who calls himself my lawyer. Really?"

"Yes." From under her spread of skirts, she extracted a parcel. "He asked that you arrange an appointment with him as soon as possible."

With a frown, Papa retrieved the parcel from her, taking an armchair by the fireplace to examine it, his crystal tumbler balanced on his knee. As he consulted the documents, I glanced at Mama. Her expression did not change; she might have handed him her tally of the monthly household accounts. But Fanny Ronalds looked suddenly uncomfortable, rising to her feet to excuse herself when Papa said quietly, "He should not have left these with you, Clara. It is not your concern."

Mrs. Ronalds stepped to my side as Mama replied, "I insisted he do so. It seems I have been left entirely too unconcerned about our current state of affairs."

"Jennie, dearest." Mrs. Ronalds put a hand on my shoulder. "Let's go upstairs and see you changed for supper, yes?"

I couldn't move. I couldn't look at her as I watched Papa's expression harden, his gaze fixed on Mama, who faced him from her seat with equal resolve.

"It is not as dire as my lawyer would make it seem," he said at length, but I heard the falter in his voice, a hesitation that shifted my gaze to my mother.

"Is it not? Then do explain it to me, Leonard. An ignorant wife like me, thinking all is well in our home . . . Tell me how accusations of war profiteering do not concern your family?"

"Not here," said Papa flatly. "Not before our guest."

"Jennie." Mrs. Ronalds's fingers dug into my shoulder.

"Fanny already knows." The calm in Mama's voice frightened me. I knew from experience she was never angrier than when she adopted that particular tone, but I'd never heard her direct it against Papa. My parents were unfailingly cordial with each other, especially before Mrs. Ronalds. "What else was I to do? He arrived here in a panic. You'd gone to fetch Jennie, and dear Fanny had already arrived. Naturally, I relied on her counsel. She understands the need for discretion, as we must so often practice it in this house."

The color drained from Papa's face. I flinched when, without taking his eyes from Mama, he said, "Jennie, please go upstairs with Fanny. Your mother and I must have our privacy."

I didn't want to leave. There was definitely something amiss, and it had nothing to do with my insubordination. Those papers from his lawyer. Was Papa in trouble?

Mrs. Ronalds guided me from the drawing room. I looked over my shoulder at my parents, sitting apart from each other, eyes locked as Mrs. Ronalds shut the doors on them. "Now," she said. "Upstairs. I will try to explain."

AS SOON AS we reached my bedroom, which adjoined Clarita's, Mrs. Ronalds closed the door between them and gave me a pained look.

"I'm so sorry about that. Your poor mother is distressed, but I have every confidence that Leonard will set the situation to rights. A dreadful inconvenience, but he's dealt with such inconveniences before. You needn't worry. It's not your concern—"

"That's what he told Mama," I interrupted, forgetting my manners. "What is it?"

"A tiresome legal matter," she replied, but I could see by the way she tugged at the rings on her fingers that it had to be more than that.

In all the time since she first arrived, four years ago as Papa's invited guest to sing in our private theater, Fanny had exhibited nothing but poise. She'd helped me with my piano lessons and taught me how to train my voice for intimate recitals, an expected accomplishment for girls like me: to sing with skill but never abandon, for we were not actresses nor should we ever be confused as such. One evening after Clarita and I had retired, she swept into our room in her evening gown and furs to sit by our bedsides (we shared a room then) and sang a refrain from an operetta she'd performed in London. I'd never forgotten this spontaneous serenade, something our mother would never have done. Mama never sang in public or otherwise. She had no ear for music, other than as background accompaniment to her balls.

Now seeing Fanny Ronalds at a loss for words disturbed me more than I'd thought possible. Because she was always so voluble, with her charm at the ready—to me now, her silence foretold calamity.

"It's serious, isn't it?" I asked.

"I'm afraid so." She perched on the edge of my bed, patting the space beside her. As I sat down, smelling her rose attar, she reached over to tuck a lock of my hair behind my ear. "You mustn't ask him about it, Jennie. Your father would never want you to worry about such things. You are so precious to him. He would be very ashamed if he ever lost your affection or respect."

"He could never lose my affection or respect," I replied hotly.

"I'm relieved to hear it." She folded her hands in her lap. "You're nearly thirteen, practically a woman. Or perhaps already . . . ?" She let her intimation fade. It should have astounded me. It was an intimate matter that Mama would never have given voice to, much less admitted she had cause to query.

I averted my eyes. "Last month."

"Well, then. You are a woman. Not entirely, but soon enough. You will learn that being a woman can be complicated." She smiled to ease the discomfort her words must have roused on my face. "I wish this were easier. You aren't old enough yet to understand, but your mother only has your best interests at heart."

I'd heard these words before, only today in fact, from Miss Green. "What precisely does that mean?"

"It means Clara must concern herself with her daughters' reputation at this time, as every mother must do in moments of crisis."

My voice quickened. "Is it a crisis?"

She lifted her shoulders in a gesture of resignation. "For your father, perhaps not. For your mother, it most certainly is."

"Mama mentioned time abroad. Paris . . . ." I searched her eyes. "Is that what she intends? To take us away from Papa?"

"From New York," she clarified, and she grasped hold of my hand, stopping me before I could lunge to my feet. "It is necessary, Jennie. For all your sakes."

"No." I wanted to thrust her aside and barge downstairs, crash into the drawing room and inform my mother that I would never be separated from my father—*never*, no matter how necessary she deemed it.

Mrs. Ronalds kept my hand in hers. "You mustn't become an inconvenience yourself. Your mother indeed wants only what is best for you and your sisters."

"What is best for her," I spat out. "She hates New York. She hates that she isn't received as one of the Four Hundred. That Mrs. Astor rejected her because Papa makes his money in the trade and our family isn't distinguished enough."

"No one here is distinguished enough. But they must pretend they are. How else can they do so, if they don't exclude others? Only in Europe will you find distinguished families. Here in America, we are all parvenus."

I bit my lip. Tears welled up inside me. "I don't want to leave."

She embraced me. I felt the whalebone of her corset under the slippery silk of her gown, the pressure of her hands at my nape, and longed to lose myself in her, to forget this day had ever occurred. "It won't be for long," she said. "You'll see. I'll travel there with your father to visit in the summer. Paris is so delightful . . ."

THREE

Whatever had gone on between Mama and Papa resulted in Mama's early retirement to her room with a headache. Fanny took her place at the table, relating amusing anecdotes as Papa's smile strained his mouth and he drank more wine than usual. Clarita seemed oblivious. She'd returned from her recital to boast that she'd performed better than the other girls—which wasn't any surprise to us—and then, pleased to see Mrs. Ronalds here, rushed upstairs to change her dress, ignoring my hissed attempts to draw her aside.

After showing off her skill at the piano for Mrs. Ronalds, Clarita declared herself exhausted, leaving me to mope in my room while Papa and Mrs. Ronalds departed for an evening engagement. Seven-year-old Leonie, defying her own strict bedtime because Mama had retired, joined me. We read aloud from one of her storybooks until she fell asleep, sprawled across my quilt, and Dobbie came in to retrieve her.

Our nanny harrumphed. "Don't you be staying up late now. Every time Miss Clara retires early, you think you can keep the lamp burning, with your nose buried in a book for hours on end. And not your school books, neither. Borrowing books from your father's library, indeed."

Papa had told Mama about my behavior today and Dobbie had overheard it. She'd raised us since we were children; nothing that transpired in our house escaped her. In truth, she was fearsome in her ability to ferret out any secrets we might try to hide, and when she returned from putting Leonie to bed to ease me into my nightdress and tuck me between my sheets, she said, "And don't go

fretting over things that aren't your concern, neither. Leave whatever needs doing to Miss Clara." She always called Mama that, in
her Georgia drawl, which years of living in New York had failed
to erase. I bit back my retort that Miss Clara was ruining my life.
As much as I cherished Dobbie, and I knew she loved me, she'd not
condone a word against my mother. And so I lay awake listening
to the clock in the hall striking the hour before I eventually fell
into a shallow sleep.

The next morning, Mama appeared at breakfast with her chignon upswept, although I'd hoped her headache would incapaci-
tate her for the rest of the year. Mrs. Ronalds was still in her room,
Papa said; they had attended the opera and returned late.

"Dobbie." Mama lifted a glazed smile as she sat before her plate
of toast with fruit jam and single cup of tea, "please see that a tray
is brought up to Mrs. Ronalds."

"Yes, Miss Clara." Dobbie hurried out to assign a maid to the
task. We didn't keep a housekeeper as most families did because
Dobbie had taken charge of overseeing the household, since only
Leonie required her daily oversight.

As Leonie dug into her oatmeal and Clarita fidgeted with her
hair bow, I kept my gaze downcast, avoiding the misery on Papa's
face until he cleared his throat.

"Girls, I have a surprise for you."

My younger sister looked up, oatmeal on her chin.

"Leonie," said Mama. "Your napkin, please." She shifted to
Clarita. "Darling, you can fix that bow later. Pay attention to your
father." And then I felt her turn to me. "Jennie, is something wrong
with your breakfast? You've been staring at those eggs as if they
might hatch."

I raised my chin. I despised her so intensely in that moment, I
was certain she must have felt it, but she only returned her regard
to Papa.

"Your mother and I . . ." He cleared his throat again. "We agree that the time has come for an extended stay abroad. In France. To complete your education."

"But Jennie still has a year left at Miss Green's . . ." Clarita faltered. "Unless . . ."

I shot a glare at her.

"Jennie can continue her education in Paris," said Mama, as if it were a given, as if going abroad for "an extended stay" happened all the time. "It's a cultured city, and lest you forget, my darling, you will graduate from Miss Green's Academy at the end of this term. We must enroll you in a proper finishing school."

To my chagrin, Clarita gave an incredulous gasp. "In *Paris*?"

Mama smiled. "Yes. All three of you will come with me to Paris."

My sister darted a look at me; I could see it in her eyes, the abrupt understanding that while she'd been outdoing her friends at the recital, something momentous had taken place without her. She might feign shock, declare anything she found disagreeable as "horrid" or "unspeakable," but she wanted to know everything anyway. I had no doubt she'd besiege me on our way to school, and I took savage pleasure in the fact that I held the upper hand. It served her right, for being such a tattler.

"Jennie?" Mama's voice cut at me like a blade. "Have you nothing to say?"

I swallowed. I had plenty to say, but nothing would change her mind. My sole resort was to beseech Papa, and I intended to do just that. Later.

"No opinion?" Mama sipped her tea. "Well. You usually have something to say, so we shall assume this unusual reticence must mean you are pleased."

"Is Dobbie coming?" asked Leonie. She adored Dobbie, as Mama's social aspirations left her with little time to oversee my younger sister's care.

"Naturally. Dobbie must be wherever we are. Who else can look after us?"

As if Dobbie had a choice, I seethed. As if any of us had a choice. Papa added, "Arrangements have to be made. A residence secured, passage booked for the spring, so until then . . ." He attempted a smile, sending a bolt of hope through me. Spring was months away. He might resolve his troubles by then. We might not have to leave at all.

"Now, finish your breakfast. You mustn't be late." Mama turned brisk. "Just because we're going abroad"—she directed her warning in our general vicinity, but I knew she intended it for me—"doesn't mean you can fail your studies here. I want perfect marks for the end of the term. Finishing schools in Paris are very demanding. I'll not have it said that my daughters lack the requisites to further their education. Is that understood?"

Perfectly. If failing my term would result in my staying behind, I would fail every class with resounding success.

PAPA HAD HIS head groom take us in the hansom to the academy. He didn't accompany us, kissing me distractedly on my cheek; he was carrying a briefcase filled with, I assumed, those troublesome papers. I also smelled the acrid tang of tobacco on his person, though he never smoked this early in the day. He didn't promise to fetch me when school let out. He did not allow me a moment to voice my grievances.

As our hansom rattled down Fifth Avenue, I gazed out the window to the snowdrifts shoveled aside for traffic; at the townhomes that had begun to sprout up everywhere, glazed in winter's carapace. Pedestrians hurried down the sidewalks, bundled in layers, while urchins perched on bales of sodden newspapers shouted out the daily headlines. Vagrants—far fewer now in our district—scurried to evade the policemen patrolling on horseback. The day was overcast but no longer stormy, frail sunlight drifting down like confetti.

A knot filled my throat. New York. My home. I'd been born across the river, in my parents' first house, in Brooklyn. Everything I loved was here—in this raucous, dirty, and, as Mrs. Ronalds called it, primitive city that to me was like no other on earth.

Not that I knew any other. My parents had resided in Italy for a year when Papa took a diplomatic assignment, but I hadn't yet been born then. They returned to Brooklyn, where Mama gave birth to me. It was during the outbreak of the Civil War when Papa made his first fortune in trading, even as the South crumbled. President Lincoln's assassination plunged the entire city into mourning, the avenues lined for miles with mourners waiting to view the president's casket in City Hall before it continued on its funeral procession to his native Illinois. Much of the conflict itself hadn't affected us; however, upon the war's end, Papa declared it had been very good for business. His investments in newspapers and railroad stocks had soared, earning him millions.

To me, that was enough. No city could compare because New York was our talisman. Even if I knew nothing else, I didn't care to revise my opinion. Under any other circumstance, France would be a thrilling prospect, the center of culture and our model ally, whose manners, cuisine, and fashions we emulated. But this wasn't another circumstance. This was my mother's act of sabotage against Papa.

Clarita broke into my thoughts. "Why the long face? I should think you'd be over the moon. Every girl at the academy will be green with envy. They all want to go to Paris."

I turned to her. "Do you think I care what those silly girls think?"

She tugged at her fur-lined gloves. "You certainly seem to care when it comes to poetry, always showing off how much better your French is. Or was that scene yesterday not designed to incite envy? Honestly, Jennie. You didn't fool me for a second. None of the girls had heard of Baudelaire. I spent the entire afternoon at Abigail Gould's recital fending off questions about who he is and why you recited him. They all thought it very scandalous."

"Abigail Gould is a goose. Of course she doesn't know who Baudelaire is. The only thing she knows is the dressmaker of her latest frock, if that."

Clarita smiled. It wasn't a nice smile. "Paris has better dressmakers. And I assure you, Abigail Gould won't enjoy them."

I stared at her. I'd been mistaken. I thought I'd seen comprehension in her at breakfast, but she hadn't sensed anything untoward. To her, Paris was a weapon to wield over her rivals. The Jeromes hadn't been deemed worthy of the Four Hundred, but now their daughters would further their education in France. Even Mrs. Astor must be obliged to take notice.

"You're a fool," I said. "You don't know a thing, either."

My sister shrugged. "Why should I care about what doesn't concern me? And I rather think you're the one who's being foolish, moping over something every girl in New York would cut off her right arm to attain."

"Then they'd be more ridiculous, wouldn't they? With one arm and no common sense."

Clarita's eyes dimmed. "That's a horrid thing to say. Why are you so upset?"

I returned my gaze to the window. "I don't want to leave Papa."

"We're not leaving him. He'll come visit us, of course. He must stay here to oversee his business; it is what men do. But he knows we must prepare for our future."

I went still.

"Jennie." She sighed. "Mama says this is the most important time in our lives. You can mope all you like, but I want to be ready for what comes next."

"What comes next?" I muttered, though I already knew.

"Why, marriage, of course. We must attract a suitable husband. Take our position in society, with a home and children of our own."

I saw my scowl reflected in the window. "And we'll find all of that in Paris, will we?"

Clarita reached for the door latch as our hansom halted at the academy gates. "If we don't find it in Paris," she declared, "then we would be fools, indeed."

MY OUTLOOK DID not improve over the next months. Papa was out all day on business or tending to his racetrack; he missed supper at home at least three times a week, a rarity for him. Whenever he was present, he had a pained look, as if he nursed an inner wound. Yet as often as I resolved to approach him, I lost my nerve, recalling Mrs. Ronalds's words: *You mustn't ask . . . Your father would never want you to worry.*

I trudged about with such ill humor that Mrs. Ronalds had me sit at the piano in the music room every afternoon after school to practice. She had me sing French chansons to refine my diction as she extolled the marvels of Paris, where all the important people in society attended the city's famed Opéra, its numerous theaters and concert halls, as well as the rounds of galas at the court of Louis-Napoléon III and his Spanish empress, Eugénie.

"It sounds crowded," I said sourly, for only with her did I dare voice my discontent. "I don't see how we can possibly be expected to make an impression there. Mama barely speaks French. She can't even entice Mrs. Astor to attend our functions here."

Mrs. Ronalds gave an airy wave of her hand. "The French adore Americans, especially American women. Your mother may not speak the language well, but she'll have no trouble making an impression, with such accomplished daughters at her side."

"I thought we were going to further our education." Suspicion underscored my voice. "Do finishing schools in Paris also hold balls for the emperor?"

"All of Paris is a finishing school. Books are the very least of it as far as one's education is concerned," she replied. "And don't frown, Jennie. It will leave lines on your face. Do you want to look like your dreadful Miss Green?"

I had to smile. Mrs. Ronalds had a way of making my worst imaginings seem less so, as though the enterprise were a carousel for which we must gauge the proper speed to leap onboard and be ferried to an enchanted realm. Despite my aversion, I found myself starting to wonder about Paris, about what awaited us there; about, as Clarita said, what came next. Mrs. Ronalds took pains to assure me she and Papa would visit.

"I maintain a residence in London, where I spend part of the year," she said. "It's a mere crossing of the Channel to France. Leonard won't abide separation from you for long, so you mustn't let him see you so down-in-the-mouth. He does notice, my dear. It grieves him."

"Then why?" I asked in an anguished whisper, for Mama was in the drawing room, reviewing fabric samples for the slew of outfits we must have made for our two-week journey across the Atlantic on the steamer ship.

Mrs. Ronalds lowered her voice. "Because he must. Remember what I told you. Do not ask. Do not cry. He must allow it for your mother's sake. His situation here . . ."

"What?" Fear tightened my chest. "What is so awful about his situation?"

"Only that it's liable to get more unpleasant before it improves, if your mother is obliged to witness it." She smiled. "As I've said, you mustn't worry. Your father is very resourceful. He will overcome this setback, as will you, my dear. You are his daughter, after all. His *fleur du mal*."

"He—he told you about that?" I darted another glance to the closed music room doors. When she had a mind, Mama could hear through walls.

Mrs. Ronalds inclined to me. "Leonard and I are the best of

friends; we confide utterly in each other. I hope you know you can also always confide in me, too, dearest Jennie. Whomever is beloved by him is equally so by me."

The discomfiting intimacy in her words made me avert my eyes and return to the piano, fumbling through my attempt to master Chopin's Nocturne opus 9.

Secrets. All around me. Secrets everywhere I turned.

Perhaps I should be like Clarita and shut my eyes and ears to what didn't concern me.

It might be the safest way to survive whatever came next.

FOUR

1869–1870

"Jennie, look! Mama had it made for me. Isn't it divine?" Clarita stood poised in the doorway of our white-paneled drawing room in our flat on boulevard Malesherbes, her confection of ringlets framing her bare throat and upper shoulders. "No crinolines"— she swept her hand over the narrow drape of her canary-yellow gown—"only a train. And a much higher waistline." She thrust out her chest, as if it weren't apparent. "It's called *empire*. Eugénie has made it fashionable again, after it went out of style with—"

"Josephine Bonaparte," I said from the piano bench. "I know my history. You might, too, and not because a dressmaker told you, if you'd deigned to pick up a book since we got here."

My sister grimaced and stepped into the room tugging at her train, which I knew was the exact regulation length of four yards. Anything longer was reserved for the nobility.

I forced out a smile. "It's lovely." I had to refrain from asking how much it had cost. The question would sound petty and envious, though the effort of withholding my resentment curdled in my mouth. I couldn't bring myself to admit that my sister was radiant, her naturally pink complexion highlighted by the gown's unusual color, its high waist and stiff collar fringed with lace lending her the illusion of a slimmer figure than she had.

Our mother had been nothing if not relentless when it came to asserting her advantages once she gained the empress's notice.

Eugénie's grandfather had been American, so upon hearing of Mrs. Leonard Jerome's arrival with her daughters, she invited Mama to her *les Lundis* salons at the Tuileries, where Mama wasted no time in making the required impression. Despite her appalling French, she was soon plunged into a ceaseless round of social activities, leaving me astonished at her transformation from dour matron to lady-about-town. This evening marking the apotheosis of her efforts, as Clarita had turned eighteen and would make her debut at an imperial ball.

"Do you think it suits me?" Clarita plucked at the collar. "I wasn't certain, but Mr. Worth assured us it's the height of style."

"He would, wouldn't he?" My smile slipped. No doubt Mr. Worth, Eugénie's favored couturier, had charged his weight in gold for the assurance.

Clarita scowled. "You can stop pretending you're happy for me."

Wincing at her chastisement, I moved to the bay window overlooking the boulevard, one of the emperor's innumerable renovations. His minister Haussmann was tearing down every medieval remnant in the city, converting ancient rubble into ample streets, decorative parklands, and ornamental buildings to glorify the reign of Louis-Napoléon III.

I had to concede New York paled in comparison, even if everything in Paris wasn't as it seemed. In our two years here, I'd seen the beggars huddled in soon-to-be-demolished doorways, the legions of threadbare seamstresses trudging to work in suffocating ateliers to satiate the appetite for attire. Certain districts must be avoided for fear of contagion—unnecessarily in my case, as I was never allowed outside without Dobbie. But Paris was still stunning in its beauty, especially as the summer dusk draped the boulevard in velvety light and people partook of the lively cafés and restaurants. Not for the first time, I thought I should count myself fortunate, even if, thus far, my sister was having all the fun.

Clarita let out a sigh. "It's not forever. In two years, you'll make your debut—"

"Is your sister moping again?" Mama's voice cut into the room. "Has our pianoforte ceased to yield entertainment?" She stood regarding me from the doorway, dressed in a colossal blue gown. No innovation by Charles Frederick Worth for her. Mama had grown very plump—another unexpected development for a woman who until now had been abstemious—and the high-waisted, slim-skirted silhouette popularized by another Napoléon's wife would have done her figure no favors.

"I'm not moping," I said. "I'm bored. While you and Clarita are out visiting friends and getting fitted for dresses, I'm here all day, practicing the piano and studying history and grammar under that insufferable Teutonic governess you hired."

"It is what girls of your age must do." My mother unfolded her lacquered fan—a personal gift from Eugénie—and waved it about her, though the day's heat had waned. "Cultured women make for attractive prospects. In time, you shall see as much."

Returning to the piano, I blew air impatiently out of the side of my mouth, eliciting my mother's arched brow of disapproval. But rather than deliver her expected reprimand, she clapped her fan shut and deposited an envelope into my lap. I stared at it, frozen for a moment as I recognized the handwriting.

"Your father sends his love. All is well with him. You'll be happy to see that Mrs. Ronalds added a postscript for you, asking you to write with your news. She claims they haven't had a letter from you in six months, which I find highly unusual."

I looked up at her. "Did they not say when they're coming to visit?"

Mama might have rolled her eyes had it been something ladies did. "I'm afraid not. Your father has been delayed again. Something to do with his business."

My hand clenched the envelope. "Can't he spare us any time at all?"

"Lest you've forgotten, his business is our livelihood. Since when do wives question their husbands' affairs?"

I put the letter aside by my music book, taking a moment to compose myself and not reply that her questioning of his affairs was the reason we were in Paris. Reading his letter now would ruin it for me, as I thought I must be the only one who missed him. Mama didn't behave as if their separation posed any hardship, while Clarita was too excited about her own impending prospects to care. Leonie would still sometimes mention Papa in passing, but she'd been enrolled in a convent school, so she was kept very busy and often acted as if she'd forgotten we had a father at all. It incensed me, that they could carry on as if living abroad had become a permanent arrangement.

"I'll write tonight," I said, for it was true I'd ceased my barrage of letters in the desperate hope Papa would take note of my silent displeasure at his prolonged absence.

"Do so. Next week, you'll have no spare time. Monsieur de Persigny is taking us for a sojourn in the Bois de Boulogne."

"To ride?" I couldn't curb the enthusiasm that crept in my voice. Monsieur le Duc was one of Mama's new friends, a gallant gentleman of a certain age, with a cloud of silvery hair and an impressive mustache. He spoke flawless English; more important, he owned a magnificent stable he'd set at our disposal after Mama mentioned we had neglected our equestrian skills, never mind that Clarita preferred to spend all her free time pinning curtains to her hem to practice dancing with a train. For me, the opportunity to ride was always welcome, allowing me to exert myself at something other than the piano or promenades with Dobbie to the Bon Marché.

"Yes," Mama said. "He's invited us to ride and partake of supper at his townhouse. You must therefore finish your practice, dine with Leonie, then write your letter. I'll need you at your best.

Monsieur so admires you on horseback." She turned to Clarita. "Come, my child. We mustn't be late for Their Imperial Majesties' entrance. Eugénie must be the first to congratulate you on your splendid toilette."

Clarita hastily kissed my cheek. "Wish me luck," she whispered. "I'm so nervous!"

"Why? You've met the empress before. But, *merde*," I said, citing the French theatrical charm for good luck.

My sister scowled. "How crude." Then she swanned to the door, her train rustling behind her.

Mama glanced at me. "Remember what I say. Be patient and prepare. It is what women must do. Your time will come sooner than you think."

After they departed, the flat yawned about me, filled with the ornate furnishings Mama had acquired, yet feeling desolate as I took up Papa's letter. It brimmed with his habitual affection and glaring neglect of any mention of a forthcoming trip, while Fanny's exuberant postscript was full of queries as to how I fared.

Exhausted from her day at school, my sister made for poor conversation, excusing herself after supper to go to bed. Dobbie saw her to her room before returning to help our maid, Marie, clear the dishes. I went to pace the drawing room, trying in vain to shut out images of Clarita in her Worth gown waltzing the night away in the Tuileries.

I'd accompanied Mama once to the Monday salon and been impressed by the palatial magnificence, if not the banal recitation of poetry. Eugénie—clad in a sumptuous pink silk gown, her red-gold coiffure set with so many jewels she basked in her own aura—had greeted me warmly. She asked about my studies, expressing delight at my propensity for the piano, confiding that she, too, had played as a girl, but that royal duties had left her no time to practice. Her suggestion that I return to play a duet with her plunged me into hours of preparation, but her invitation never arrived. I couldn't help but think Mama had ensured I didn't steal any attention from Clarita when she made her debut. Perhaps now that my sister had done so, my own invitation would be forthcoming.

Dobbie cleared her throat behind me. "Brooding in the dark won't make the time pass any faster," she said, with that sharp instinct she had for deciphering my moods. "And you still have a letter to write."

"Oh, Dobbie." I heard the tremor in my voice. "New York feels so far away. I don't even know what to tell Papa anymore. I feel as if I'll never see him again."

Dobbie harrumphed. "It's a wonder that after all this time you're still wasting your breath trying to lie to me. This is about your sister. She went off to the ball in a nice new dress and left you behind."

"The nice new dress must have cost a fortune. Papa probably can't afford to visit us after seeing to all of Monsieur Worth's bills."

"And how are the bills any concern of yours?" Dobbie fixed me with her stare. "You lack for nothing. Didn't Miss Clara have a riding habit made especially for you?"

"Only to impress Monsieur le Duc. He so admires me on horseback, didn't you hear?"

Dobbie pursed her lips. "I'll hear no more of this nonsense. Your father will visit when he's good and ready, so don't go complaining to him about bills. It's not for you to question. If Mr. Jerome has something to say about it, let him do so—to Miss Clara."

As I stepped past her toward my bedroom, she took my hand, cupping it gently. "Just write to your father and tell him how much you miss him, child. Before you know it, he'll return word that he's on his way. Time might seem eternal to you now, but believe me, it passes quickly nevertheless."

In my room, I lit a candle at my escritoire and attempted to compose a cheerful letter, detailing my dubious achievements. But my discontent kept seeping in, causing me to blot out lines and then crumple up the entire page to start over. Finally, I wrote two letters, addressing one to Mrs. Ronalds, imploring her to encourage Papa to pay us a visit. As I sealed both envelopes and left them in the foyer for Marie to deliver to the post office, another surge of frustration overcame me.

Be patient and prepare . . . Your time will come sooner than you think.

Easy to say, but for me, waiting was becoming intolerable.

FIVE

Your daughter is such a beauty. I believe she'd make an unforgettable impression at court, Madame Leonard. Have you seen to her arrangements yet?"

Seated on one of the duc's roan mares, I overheard his laconic compliment and then Mama's distinct pause before she said, "Jennie has two years left before she can make her debut, monsieur. A mother must exercise restraint, especially when the child lacks it. I've quite enough on my hands with Clarita."

Persigny chuckled. "Yes, I understand Clarita had a very successful evening at court. Is your lovely Jeanette chafing to do the same?"

He called me that: Jeanette, a French twist to my name that I actually enjoyed. Pulling back slightly on the reins, I tried to pretend that I was engrossed in my riding while maintaining a safe enough distance to eavesdrop.

"She is." Mama was riding today to my surprise, as she'd never been fond of it. In times past, she would have stayed on the terrace, tea at her side. But Clarita had begged off, claiming her feet ached from dancing at the ball, so Mama felt obliged to join us. Ensconced on the sidesaddle, she restricted herself to a ponderous gait, betraying her inexperience. "I fear my husband overindulged her as a child."

"Well." I heard the duc's mirth. "With such a daughter, how could he not? Am I to understand you've made no arrangements on her behalf?"

"Monsieur, trust me." Mama let out a taut laugh. "She'd be utterly impossible to manage if I didn't maintain a firm hand. When we received His Imperial Majesty's invitation for Clarita to join the hunt at Compiègne, Jennie was fit to burst. You have daughters of your own. Must I remind you of the struggles we must undergo to see to their welfare?"

"Alas," said the duc. "I fear I'd require such reminder. My daughters' welfare is currently managed by my estranged wife at our country château."

Mama laughed again, this time with a disturbing affectation that cost me every bit of effort to not look around. It seemed to me that while she uttered complaints of me, she ought to pay mind to her own behavior. Had I not known better, I might have suspected she engaged in an illicit flirtation with Persigny.

I nearly reined to a halt when she abruptly said, "And her ears are too keen for her own good. Jennie, do you mean to ride today or to listen in on conversations that aren't yours to hear?"

Finally braving a glance over my shoulder, I saw Monsieur smile through his mustache. "She might not be of age, but she's learned keen ears are essential at court." He beckoned me to their side, his gaze admiring as I pivoted the mare with a flick of the reins. "Do you never use the crop, mademoiselle?"

"My father doesn't believe in it. He says it spoils a horse's spirit."

"I see. You must miss your father very much."

I thought of denying it, then thought better. "Very much so."

"And no doubt, he must miss you. But he'd want you to enjoy your stay in our belle Paris, oui? A girl of your charms must find much to delight her here."

As his blue-gray eyes lingered on me, I sensed a disturbing challenge, as if he wanted me to voice my dissatisfaction with the very situation my mother had described.

"I fear I haven't seen much of the city, monsieur," I said at length. "I'm not of age."

His smile widened. "Then we must remedy the deficit. I believe Her Highness Princess Mathilde would make an exception for one so mature for her years. She holds a salon for painters, writers, and musicians. Somewhat eccentric, but you are a talented pianist. Perhaps a recital for her can help you to experience more of our splendid city."

I looked at my mother. She didn't appear pleased. Princess Mathilde Bonaparte was the emperor's first cousin, whose separation from her aristocratic Russian husband had left her extremely rich. After the empress's, her salons were the most coveted in Paris, the princess being renowned for her patronage of artists. My sister had campaigned to attend these salons until Mama diverted her by arranging her debut.

"Monsieur," said my mother at length. "Your suggestion is very much appreciated, but I fear Jennie isn't prepared yet to pay her respects to Her Highness."

The duc didn't take his eyes from me. "I must disagree. I believe that not only is she prepared, but she would be well-received. Her Highness has a fatal weakness for music. Please, allow me to arrange it. It would be my honor, if mademoiselle so desires it."

"Oh, mademoiselle does!" I exclaimed.

Mama's stolid expression turned dark, but surely she had to realize keeping me cloistered in the flat wasn't serving anyone. Clarita had made her debut and was about to embark on the royal hunt at Compiègne—an achievement that in due time would secure her the advantageous match our mother demanded. It was implicit that beyond the vanities, we must attain the exalted position that would deflect the sting of her rejection in New York. What did it matter if I had two years before I turned eighteen? Attending a salon wasn't a debut, so I could do both.

Around us, the autumn leaves of the chestnuts in the bois rustled in the evening wind, lamplighters racing out to ignite the sconces along the pathways for those returning to the stables. I heard and saw it all, but my entire focus was on my mother, as she appeared to contemplate the offer.

To my relief, she finally said, "If Monsieur thinks it an honor, who am I to refuse? I trust a piano recital will prove inoffensive enough."

"Entirely, *mon chère* Clara," said the duc. "I have the utmost confidence that Mademoiselle Jerome will enchant everyone."

ON OUR WAY home after supper at the duc's palatial townhouse on Place Vendôme, where we were chaperoned by his liveried servants, Mama went so quiet that I braced for her recrimination. She must have felt as if I'd left her no option other than to consent; as I started to squirm on the carriage seat, she directed a long, pensive look at me.

"You should be forewarned that we often can only mislead men once into doing what we desire."

"*Mislead?* I did not mislead anyone."

She gave a wry chuckle. "You tarried so close, I could hear you breathing; and the moment Monsieur de Persigny turned his attention to you, you seized advantage in it. Not yet of age, indeed." Her amusement faded. "You don't understand that the power we wield must be exercised with extreme caution. Otherwise, it is we who can fall astray—and women are always far more harshly judged for it."

Was this praise from her? I wasn't entirely sure.

"Be that as it may." She returned her gaze to the window. "You'll need a new gown for the occasion. Perhaps something by Monsieur Worth, in moiré silk."

SIX

My new gown's sole distinction, to my eyes, was its watery lavender hue. When Dobbie and Mama unpacked it from the box sent by the atelier, which I hadn't been allowed to attend in person, to my disappointment, my measurements taken at home, I gave a dejected groan.

"I thought it would have an empire waistline, like Clarita's."

Mama motioned me to undress to my shift. "This style is perfectly current. As we've discussed, it's a recital. I'll not have you appear in unsuitable toilette for your age."

Once she saw me into the gown, I was somewhat assuaged. Dobbie smoothed out the crumpled folds of the voluminous bustle, enhancing the fabric's iridescence. The bodice was still too high for my preference, but the narrow sleeves banded in rose-bud velvet, with trailing lace cuffs, were very flattering, if impractical for playing the piano.

Mama surveyed me. "The color is ideal. And the fit is flawless; Worth always does impeccable work. You're slim enough that we needn't tighten the stays too much."

"Especially not if I must spend all my time on the piano bench," I grumbled.

"What of her coiffure?" Mama gathered up my thick, loose dark hair in her hands. "Ringlets in satin ribbons?" she suggested to Dobbie, who nodded, because, what else could she do? She was now both housekeeper and ladies' maid; Mama was too extravagant, but she'd not gone so far as to hire extra servants other than Marie.

In truth, Dobbie was capable enough, but not even she knew how a girl should style her hair for a princess's salon, other than it should never be unadorned.

"*Ringlets?*" I said in dismay. "I'm not a schoolgirl anymore."

"Jennie." My mother's voice took on an edge. "I'll have you know this dress was not without its cost. You will do as I say or I shall cancel the—"

Her rebuke was cut short by a sudden clarion call from the foyer: "Clara, darling! Are you receiving uninvited guests?"

Mama went still, her gaze on Dobbie. "Is that Fanny Ronalds?" she said, as my heart leaped in my chest.

Dobbie nodded. "It would appear so, Miss Clara."

"But we received no advance word—" Mama held out her hand to detain me before I bolted forth in my new gown and bare feet. As she took a moment to adjust herself, Fanny materialized in a travel suit of light gray wool, a feathered bonnet cocked on her upswept hair.

"My dears. You must be so surprised to see me!"

"I'll say," I heard Dobbie mutter under her breath.

I strained to look past Fanny, anticipating Papa behind her, whipping off his top hat with a grin. When no one else appeared, disappointment overwhelmed me.

"I had no idea you were in Paris." Mama's smile was glazed. "Jennie, wherever are your manners? Come at once to greet Mrs. Ronalds."

"Oh, my sweet girl." Fanny's embrace nearly made me weep. "Have I interrupted preparations for her debut? How can this be our little Jennie, already so grown-up?"

"Not a debut," said Mama. "A recital. We just received her new dress."

"It's superb." Fanny held me at arm's length. "The color is perfect for her."

"I was telling her as much myself. Dobbie, please see tea is served in the parlor." Mama stepped aside as Fanny unpinned her bonnet in the mirror and gave me a wink.

"I know this is very unexpected," she said. "Please don't make any fuss on my account. I was in London for an engagement. It's been much too long."

"Two years," I reminded her, though I was very glad to see her. She hadn't aged a day, her exuberance a gust of fresh air in Mama's overstuffed room.

"Has it really been as long as that? Time can be so devious. Well, I'm here now, and I intend to hear absolutely everything of how you're getting on. *Everything*, do you hear me?" She wagged a finger at me, rousing my reluctant smile. "You've been remiss in your correspondence. Poor Leonard thinks you've forgotten him."

"How is Papa?" I burst out. "Is he coming, too?"

She paused. Only for an instant, but I detected her reluctance as she reached into the tasseled bag dangling from her wrist to extract an envelope. She handed it to Mama. "I thought I might as well deliver this in person, rather than post it from London."

Mama's smile didn't waver. "Thank you. I am in your debt, as always. I was starting to wonder when Leonard would see fit to address our obligations."

"He's doing much better. I'll tell you the latest over tea. I'm simply desperate for some refreshment. The crossing was so tedious. Will Jennie be joining us?"

"No," said Mama, before I could answer. "Dobbie, please see Jennie out of the dress and directly to her practice. Her recital is tomorrow," she explained to Fanny, escorting her to the parlor. "Princess Mathilde has invited her to play at her salon. I wasn't at all in agreement at first, but my friend the Duc de Persigny can be so persuasive . . ."

I stared after them, not knowing what to feel. While Fanny's appearance pleased me to no end, I'd heard covert resentment in

Mama's tone. I had no doubt Fanny had delivered much-needed funds from Papa, confirming my suspicion that Mama was over-spending. But if he couldn't visit because our stay here was proving too costly, why didn't he insist on our return to New York?

Dobbie assisted me out of the gown. I'd ceased to care about it, longing to find a way to listen in on the conversation in the par-lor even as Dobbie made sure I proceeded directly to the drawing room. "I want to hear Liszt," she warned. "And don't you move from that bench."

She planted herself on a chair at the doors, removing her house shoes to massage her feet, which she'd never do in Mama's pres-ence. As I went over the pieces for my recital, my focus wasn't on the music.

All I could think of was this latest news from New York I wasn't supposed to hear.

AT SUPPER, MAMA apologized for the lack of variety, even as Fanny declared she was content with a bowl of consommé. When ten-year-old Leonie returned from school, Fanny took time to peruse her notebooks, expressing her delight with Leonie's progress, as well as her fluency in French, much as she'd expressed delight in the news that Clarita wasn't present because she'd gone with the court for the annual royal hunt at Compiègne.

Mama offered Clarita's room in her absence. Fanny declined, saying she had booked a hotel. I noticed Mama's relief; while they were cordial as ever, I could now see theirs wasn't a true friendship and had never been. I was no longer a child. Paris had taught me enough, albeit at a remove, to understand that Mama was more in-timate with Persigny, just as Papa was with Fanny. Perhaps married people grew complacent with each other and had to find comfort elsewhere.

This unsettling thought went through me as I hoped for a moment in private with Fanny before she departed. As Marie served the coffee, Fanny finally said, "Perhaps Jennie can play something for me. I heard her earlier and she's improved so much, I can scarcely believe it."

Mama nodded. "I'll see Leonie to bed and then join you."

In the drawing room, I began a nocturne, soft enough that we could converse. Beside me on the bench, Fanny swayed. "Oh, Jennie. You could be a concert pianist. Leonard would be so proud." She paused, taking in my silence. "You mustn't be so aggrieved with him." From her little bag, she slipped out a blue velvet box. "A belated gift for your sixteenth birthday. Your father says a young lady should always have her special jewel."

She opened the box to display a diamond-studded star nested within. Tears pricked my eyes when she added, "He asked me to tell you that your hair always reminds him of a summer's night sky, and night skies need stars to show off their luster."

"Is he really doing well?" I reached to the star, thinking of Papa's forlorn expression as our ship had departed New York.

"He is. That dreadful inconvenience dragged on for months on end; the poor man couldn't catch his breath—"

"What happened?" I asked, and something in my tone made her pause. "It made Mama take us, so it must have been serious."

She let out a sigh. "I suppose there's no point in hiding it. Leonard was accused of profiteering during the Civil War. He had to reach a settlement to evade a trial. He was targeted because he's not an Astor or a Vanderbilt, though they certainly made their own profits on the war. It was very unfair. But the worst is now past, and he's doing what he does best: shoring up his resources."

"Papa was accused of a crime, and Mama left him?" I said, enraged.

"Oh, my dear. It's not so simple. Your mother left for several reasons."

"Such as?" I demanded, even as I darted an apprehensive glance at the drawing room doors, in case Mama made her entrance.

Fanny paused. When my fingers on the keys did so as well, she nudged me to continue. "I'm overstepping my confidence, so what I'm about to tell you must never be repeated. Especially not to your mother or sisters."

I missed a chord as I felt something long withheld, a secret I wasn't certain I should know, break between us.

"Clara has decided not to return to New York," she said. "She endured too much there, and she finds Paris more to her temperament."

"Not returning?" I echoed. "But . . . why?"

"I'm afraid these things are never simple to explain. We marry with the best of intentions, only to discover it isn't to our liking. Most of us must make do, because we have no other alternative. Clara, bless her heart, has found one."

"Is she divorcing Papa?" I couldn't believe it, though a part of me had known all along. Mama behaved as if our residence in Paris was a permanent arrangement because it was to her.

"Never. Your mother won't hear of it." Fanny gave me a sad smile. "I pray you never experience it, but an unhappy marriage is so unpleasant. You mustn't fault your mother. Indeed, she deserves our admiration. It's very brave to leave everything behind to start anew."

"Not everything," I said sharply. "She brought us with her."

"Where else should you be? Daughters belong at their mother's side. By mutual consent, it will be a private, amicable separation. They agree to live apart."

"Amicable?" I met her eyes.

"Yes. I fear Leonard was as unhappy as Clara, but as I said, he has his divertissements."

I found myself thinking that Fanny must be one of his divertissements.

"Men aren't so affected by domestic disharmony," she went on. "A wife's lot is more circumscribed, so when matters at home aren't as they should be, it is she who feels it the most."

I had to take a moment, reeling from the revelation. "But if they're no longer to live together, must we stay, too? Will we never see Papa again?"

Fanny laughed. "He's not separating from you. You must complete your education and then we shall see. In the meantime, he promises to visit very soon; his circumstances didn't allow it before, but he sent me here especially after I showed him that plaintive letter you sent. He never wants you to think that you and your sisters aren't foremost in his thoughts. Everything he does is for his family. It's not easy to have three daughters whose futures he must secure, even for a man as versatile as he is."

I couldn't keep up the pretense of playing anymore. Leaning back from the piano, I also didn't look toward the doors. Mama wouldn't appear. Fanny may have sworn me to secrecy, but I was certain Mama was well-aware of what I was being told. She condoned it, seeing as I was the only one who still pined over our absence from Papa. She'd allowed Fanny to assume the burden of informing me of our circumstances.

"You mustn't worry." Fanny took my hand in hers. "None of this has any bearing on you. You and your sisters will be cherished as ever; your parents are in full accord on that account. Chin up, Jennie. The only way to face these vicissitudes is with a smile. We cannot anticipate what fate has in store for us, but we can control how we contend with it."

I lowered my eyes to the box beside me, the diamonds in Papa's gift catching the candlelight in slivers of blue-tinged fire. "Will you come with me to my recital?" I asked, thinking that if I had her at my side, I might be able to do as she advised and not collapse in a heap of woe, knowing how far away my father and New York truly were.

"Of course. Your mother already extended the invitation. I met the princess during her time in Rome, and who better to deliver an account of your performance to Leonard?" She kissed my brow. "There, now. No tears. You have his star to guide you. Never forget that, for him, you'll always be the brightest star in the firmament."

SEVEN

When we entered Princess Mathilde's townhouse on the rue de Courcelles, I heard Mama's envious intake of breath. Opposing colonnaded galleries garlanded in ivy framed a winter garden atrium, overflowing with imported hothouse flowers. Oriental carpets were strewn across the marble floors, her attendees lounging on settees upholstered in velvet damask, exotic pelts tossed across the furnishings like somnolent beasts.

Lively conversation hummed in air redolent with the scent of vegetation. Though I couldn't place the source of the heat, I felt its density at once, wringing sweat under my stays and, I feared, on my brow, made all too visible by my rebellious coiffure.

A battle had ensued with Mama when I refused to submit to her ringlets. To her disbelief, I demanded Dobbie style my tresses like Fanny's, piled above my forehead and coiled at my nape; for the centerpiece, I impulsively set Papa's diamond star.

"How——?" Mama swallowed. "Wherever did you obtain such a bauble?"

"Fanny brought it to me. A gift from Papa," I said, and I was fortunate that Fanny elected to make her arrival at that moment, in a bustled ivory-silk gown of such elegance she immediately overshadowed Mama in her flounced blue velvet.

"Oh!" she cried. "How innovative. Who would have imagined employing a brooch as a tiara?" Fanny beamed at Mama as if she were responsible, obliging my mother to muster a tight smile. "One can hardly ruin a Worth bodice by running a pin through it," she muttered, but her unspoken fury was evident as she ordered me to retrieve my gloves.

Confronted by the guests of the salon, I thought I must look absurd, a girl trying in vain to appear older than she was. Cupping my elbow, Fanny whispered, "See that balding man over there? The one who resembles a walrus with indigestion? That's Gustave Flaubert. He caused a scandal with his risqué novel about a depraved woman. When it was first serialized in the *Revue de Paris*, the government sued him for immorality. He was acquitted after the princess took to his defense. Once *Madame Bovary* was published in its entirety, it sold thousands of copies in several printings."

"I know. I've read it." I found him disappointing. Rotund and dour-faced, he wasn't at all what I'd expect of a scandalous writer, though I did notice how Persigny steered Mama past him, her voluminous skirts threatening to sweep aside the plethora of porcelain figurines perched on marquisate side tables.

"You read it?" Fanny said. "Clara must have been appalled."

"She doesn't know. She rarely pays mind to what I do these days, save for my music lessons. All her attention is devoted to Clarita."

"Count yourself fortunate." Fanny paused. "Oh, there's Carpeaux. To earn his commission these days is quite the feat. His bust of the princess at the Salon des Beaux-Arts gained him imperial notice. He now charges a ransom for immortalizing one in clay."

As we approached this gruff-looking bearded man, whose mane of salty hair was capped by an incongruous red fez to match his outlandish embroidered robes, the stout woman with whom he was conversing turned to us.

I caught a glimpse of beady brown eyes, a necklace of enormous pearls and diamonds encircling a fleshy throat before Fanny breathed, "Your Highness," and swept into a curtsy, her pressure on my elbow compelling me to do the same, though as I felt the pull of my gown across my knees and the weight of the bustle at my rear, I feared I might not be able to rise again.

"Mrs. Ronalds." Princess Mathilde motioned that we should stand, which I did gingerly. "We've been deprived of the pleasure of your company, though I hear London is the better for it. To what do we owe this visit? Shall you be singing for us, perhaps?"

"Not today, Your Highness. Please, allow me to present Miss Jennie Jerome of New York. She's scheduled to play the piano for you."

The princess's gaze shifted to me, giving me the disquieting impression that she had no idea why I'd been scheduled to do anything of the sort.

She wasn't beautiful, though I'd assumed princesses should be. She had the squat Bonaparte build and ordinary features that didn't merit artistic homage. Had she not been in that magnificent parure and striking black-and-white gown, I would have thought her any other woman. I understood in that instant that beauty by itself meant nothing if one lacked the means to exalt it, and in her case, beauty was superfluous. Princess Mathilde held herself with the assurance of someone who never questioned her place in the world.

"From New York?" she said. "Do they play pianos in America?"

The sculptor guffawed. "To muffle the flagrant rifle fire in their streets, one suspects."

"Now, now. We mustn't be uncouth." She did not take her regard from me. "And are you wearing a gown by Monsieur Worth?"

"Yes, Your Highness." My voice was hoarse. I felt as if I might perish of shame as her mouth twitched.

"The star in your hair is very fetching. It gives the ensemble a flight of fancy Monsieur Worth often lacks. Your touch?"

"Her mother's, Your Highness." Persigny's voice sliced between us. As he stepped to the princess with my mother, I was obliged to move aside.

Mathilde Bonaparte's mouth twitched again, this time without a subsequent smile, as she surveyed Mama's colossal toilette. All of a sudden, I wasn't concerned anymore about my own appearance, given the princess's praise and her evident distaste for my mother's attire. A pang of unexpected pity went through me for Mama. As much as she thought of herself as someone of importance, received at court, Princess Matilde regarded Mama as if she saw her exactly for who she was: an overdressed foreigner whom Eugénie may have seen fit to befriend but who wasn't anyone of particular noteworthiness.

"You must be one of those new American friends Her Imperial Majesty is so fond of," she said with a droll note in her voice, confirming my suspicions. "Isn't it wonderful how France and America can remain so devoted to each other?"

"Would that the same could be said of France and Prussia," remarked Monsieur.

The princess's sudden burst of laughter gave her a mischievous air. "Persigny, one day you'll get yourself arrested for that intemperate tongue. Bismarck's grunting at the gate is nothing we need be concerned about. There will be no conflict with Prussia. They are all too aware of our superior power and, given their fractious state, in no position to challenge it."

"Yet they claim to hold the superior army," countered Monsieur. "And are threatening to set their poltroon Hohenzollern-Sigmaringen on the throne of Spain."

"An abomination we've objected to in the most vehement terms. Rest assured that Wilhelm of Germany and his lackey are in no doubt that we'll never permit an insignificant Prussian to rule over Spain, much less with a Spanish-born empress here."

"But didn't the Spaniards offer their deposed queen's crown to this very insignificant Prussian?" said Fanny, startling me.

The princess's humor vanished. "The dishonor of their conduct toward an anointed sovereign has only been compounded by the outrageous offer." She turned to her salon, where, I realized, every one of her guests had gone quiet, attuned to her conversation.

"You play the piano, I'm told?" Her gaze shifted to me. *"Allez."* She motioned to the grand piano under swaths of drapery in a plant-festooned corner. "Entertain us, Miss Jerome of New York. Talk of politics bores me to tears."

"BUT IT'S PREPOSTEROUS! Surely such an inconvenience can't affect us here." As I heard the rare lift of Mama's voice, I paused at my studies, glancing warily to the ajar doors of the drawing room, where she'd received an unexpected visit from Persigny.

My governess was dozing in her chair, as she often did, since I'd surpassed her limited instruction. Leonie was at school and Clarita on an outing with a viscount she'd met in Compiègne, having returned home brimming with tales of the imperial court.

Her prattle roused my envy. My recital at the princess's salon had elicited her praise, but it was my sole claim to distinction, vanquished by Clarita's triumph at court, where she attracted the notice of an eligible viscount and the empress invited her to ride in her entourage, never mind that she'd never shot a bow, let alone at any living creature.

Inching up from my seat, I eased past the governess, her mouth slack in oblivious slumber. At the doors, I caught Persigny's response to my mother's outburst.

"Mon chérie, the Prussians don't give a whit about our inconvenience. Our troops under the emperor and his son the prince imperial have suffered unsustainable losses at Metz. His Majesty was advised to abandon the field and return to Paris, but Her Majesty declared a Napoléon must never retreat, so he advanced on Sedan. It was a calamity."

"But, *how?"* I glimpsed Mama rising from her settee, nearly toppling the tea service on the table in her haste. "The Germans have no emperor. No empire. His Majesty must bring about an end to this intolerable spate."

Monsieur said, "The spate has killed thousands of our soldiers in the mere span of a summer. The Germans may not have an empire yet, but they're definitely united. They also hold the upper hand. His Majesty had no choice but to surrender to Wilhelm. He safeguarded the prince imperial by dispatching him to England, but he's been obliged to submit to his own captivity. I lament to say, we, too, no longer have an emperor."

At this, I yanked open the doors, eliciting an outraged gasp from my mother. "Return to your lessons at once—" she started to bark. The duc preempted her. "Clara, let the girl hear what will be announced soon enough on every front page. We've lost the war with Prussia. In a short time they'll be coming to lay siege to Paris."

"Siege?" Mama regarded him in horror. "But His Majesty appointed the empress to oversee the state while he was at the front."

"Indeed," said Persigny drily. "Yet seeing as His Majesty is now a captive of Prussia, not even our proud empress can stave off the demand for surrender. Already, there's chaos in the streets. When I departed the Tuileries, Her Imperial Majesty was ordering her women to pack her jewels." He had the temerity to chuckle. "God forbid a common *fräulein* should lay claim to Eugénie's priceless diamonds."

Mama collapsed onto the settee. "But this house . . . my Italian paintings. My Limoges. What shall I do with all of it?"

"You must take whatever you can and leave the rest. Clara, you have hours, not days. I saw a mob outside the palace. Once they storm the gates, we'll fall into anarchy until whatever means can arise to contend with the Prussians. You're not French. You have daughters to protect and no husband present. There's no reason for you to suffer our fate, not even for Limoges."

"Clarita," Mama suddenly said, as if my sister's absence had only just occurred to her after tallying the incalculable loss of her possessions. "She went with the viscount in his carriage to the Luxembourg. Dobbie is with them. Leonie is still at her academy."

"I shall fetch them." Monsieur leaned to Mama, pressing her hand in his. I couldn't avert my eyes from the undeniable affection between them. "You must prepare while I'm gone. I'll book passage on the train to Deauville. Under the circumstances, the ferries to England will be very crowded, but the Channel will prove an effective barrier against Prussian aggression."

Mama sat as if paralyzed, helpless in a way I'd never seen her before. "And my husband," she said faintly. "Leonard was planning to visit us in October . . ."

"I'll try to send word, if I can find a wire office willing to telegraph America, which is by no means guaranteed. In any event, Mr. Jerome will doubtless be apprised before you've set foot in England."

"But where shall we go? We have no accommodations readied." Mama clasped his hand, making me want to shout that we could stay in a hotel and book passage to New York, where we had our mansion waiting for us.

"Mrs. Ronalds keeps a residence in London, does she not?" he said, and when Mama winced, he added, "Clara, this is no time to stand on pride. If I can't notify New York, you can do so from London. Then your husband can see to your arrangements."

"I can't," said Mama. "I can't go back. I was so happy here. Everything was so perfect."

"Alas, perfection never lasts." The duc lifted his eyes to me. "Jeanette, please tell the maid to start packing. And might I suggest a chamomile infusion for your mother's nerves?"

As I turned about, Mama said tersely, "The linens. Tell Marie to pack all of them. They're hand-embroidered with Chantilly lace. We are *not* leaving our linens behind."

MONSIEUR WAS TRUE to his word. Clarita arrived an hour later, her bonnet askew as she exclaimed that she and her viscount had nearly been waylaid in the Luxembourg by rabble spewing hatred against the empress. A nun brought Leonie home soon after, informing Mama that the Academy of the Blessed Heart was closed for the foreseeable future. While Dobbie oversaw our packing, our maid, Marie, appeared distraught when Mama ordered the Italian landscapes in the drawing room transported personally by her to Deauville, though how she was expected to accomplish it was left unexplained.

By dusk, we were in Monsieur's carriage, our trunks in an accompanying cart guarded by footmen. Before we left, Mama snapped at Marie to lock every window and door before she left the house. Poor Marie, who must have had concerns of her own with her city poised for siege, gave dejected assent.

At the *gare*, we arrived among hundreds of others, clutching children, mounds of luggage, even cowering dogs—all clamoring for a seat on the trains. Mama went pale at the tumult, but the duc's footmen, bearing our trunks, carved an indomitable path through the vociferous masses. Once our reservations were confirmed, we were escorted to a first-class compartment on the train, courtesy of Monsieur de Persigny.

Only after we were seated, breathless from our flight, our hand luggage piled at our feet, did Clarita give voice to something none of us had considered.

"What of Monsieur le Duc? Will he be joining us in London?"

Mama had the wherewithal to sound offended. "He's an important statesman, with his own affairs to attend to. I did not inquire as to his plans." She turned resolutely to the window as the train lurched from the station. Pulling down the shade, she said, with more defiance than conviction, "There will be an accord. Prussia can't possibly conquer France. And once there is, we shall return home."

I felt Clarita's fingers lace about mine. At my other side, Leonie had fallen asleep against Dobbie, her wide-eyed amazement at our exodus having given way to exhaustion.

"The viscount was so gallant," murmured Clarita. "I'm certain that, given time, he would have proposed to me."

I didn't reply, lowering my gaze to our entwined hands.

With Mama's French dream shattered behind us, we now faced the unknown.

EIGHT

1872

"I'm so tired of this dreary existence." Clarita heaved a sigh as we sat on a park bench overlooking Fanny's Sloane Street townhome. There wasn't a private garden, only this gated green for residents, but after days of confinement in the house, from which Mama had refused to stir since learning of Louis-Napoléon III's mortal illness after his release from captivity and exile to England, I'd insisted we must partake of some exercise. Leonie was restless; at thirteen, she'd gone from a schedule of studies to aimless boredom, so as she made her rounds of the green with Dobbie, Clarita and I, having walked the paths arm in arm, held vigil from a nearby bench.

I wouldn't admit it, but I agreed with my sister. London must have had its charms, despite its perpetual shroud of acrid fog, but we'd experienced very little of them.

"Come now, it's not so terrible," I said, as she reached into her pocket to retrieve the much-read and crumpled sole missive from her viscount. "You're only miserable because you fear your beau will forsake you, now that we know the empire won't ever be restored."

"He already has forsaken me. He sent this letter a year ago, expressing his relief that I made it out of Paris. I've not had a word from him since."

"What can you expect?" I said, unable to curb my impatience. Much like Mama, my sister regarded the chaos in France as an inconvenience designed to upset her plans. "His country has been at war. He must have more pressing concerns than furthering his courtship of you."

"His family owns a château in Avignon," she said sourly. "He wasn't at the barricades."

"Well, then you needn't worry. With the siege over, your gallant viscount could rush across the Channel at any moment to bend his knee."

Clarita jabbed my side with her elbow. "Your prospects have been thrown into disarray as well. We're coming up on two years since we left Paris, without any assurance of what will happen next. We can't stay here forever as Fanny's guests."

"We'll return to New York, of course," I said.

"*New York?*" she exclaimed. "Do you want to find yourself relegated to invitations from the sons of robber barons because we're not received in society? There are no titled prospects in New York for girls like us."

"As I understand it, there are no titled prospects there for any girl. Let Papa sort it out. That's why he's here." I nudged her back. "Who can say? In the meantime, you might meet a gallant English lord desperate to woo you."

"I haven't seen one at any of those endless tea recitals we've been obliged to perform for London's upstanding matrons."

"Our recitals have been quite the success. Lady Camden told us no young ladies in all of Britain can play as charmingly as the Jerome sisters."

"Lady Camden is an eighty-year-old dowager with two married sons. Unless we wish to marry her piano, how does such praise do us any good?"

I laughed, refusing to let her mood affect me. Ever since Papa had arrived, I was determined to look on the bright side. I'd been overjoyed to see him, so handsome in his fur-collared greatcoat, enveloping me in his arms and whispering, with a choke in his voice, "How can my beautiful little girl have become such a beautiful young woman?"

"Nearly three years is how it can be," I'd replied, causing him to throw back his head in laughter.

"And I see Paris failed to instill any moderation in that obstinate character."

But my joy at our reunion had been subsumed by Mama's brooding. Fanny's residence was well-appointed, if cramped for five women and two servants. Papa had taken a hotel room, while Clarita and I shared a bed behind screens in the parlor and Dobbie made do with a below-the-stairs cot alongside Fanny's maidservant. Leonie and Mama squeezed into the guest room. When Fanny graciously offered to book her own hotel suite for whatever time required, Mama replied, "There's no need for extra expense, my dear. We'll not be here long."

But we'd been here much longer than anticipated, though I kept expecting Papa's announcement that we must go home. With Paris destitute from the siege and subsequent revolt, surely returning there was out of the question. And as my sister had declared, we couldn't stay in London indefinitely. Thinking this while Leonie skipped past, Dobbie chiding her for exposing her ankles, I caught sight of a carriage drawing up to the house. When Papa and Fanny descended, I jumped to my feet.

"They're back."

"From another visit to one of her friends' country estates, no doubt," said Clarita. "At least they seem to be enjoying themselves."

"What of it? Fanny extended her stay especially for us. If Papa must cross the ocean to see us and Mama refuses to join them, would you deny him his pleasures?"

The harshness in Clarita's reply froze me where I stood. "Jennie, you will be turning nineteen next January and have yet to make your debut. That should be Papa's concern, not his pleasures."

Her insinuation outraged me. "My debut was delayed for obvious reasons. His sole concern is our comfort, though he should be in New York tending to his business."

"Why should he, when he can enjoy just as well what he likes here?"

I stared at her. "Whatever is that supposed to mean?"

She let out a tight laugh. "Don't pretend you don't know." Her declaration dropped between us like a chunk of stone. "Papa and Fanny are lovers; they've been so for years. Though he's married and she's a divorcée. It's shameless how they carry on, right under Mama's nose."

"Mama left him," I said, my voice catching.

"Wouldn't you?" Clarita retorted. "It is not how marriage is supposed to be. Between his business affairs and Fanny, he drove her out of New York—"

"Not another word." I had to take a step back, lest I lost control of myself and slapped her. "You will not speak like that of him again. He is still our father."

She clenched her jaw. "And you always take his side. Go. Be the first to hear whatever news they bring. Perhaps we can look forward to our own pleasure of playing yet another duet at Lady Camden's tea next week and hope we don't turn into spinsters at her piano."

I stalked across the street, coming upon Papa and Fanny in the foyer as she removed her wrap. "Jennie, dearest." She kissed my cheek. "I hope you didn't miss us too terribly. I fear our trip took longer than expected."

I failed to muster a smile. Until this moment, I had yet to fully accept it, but now it was undeniable. Fanny and Papa couldn't be anything other than what Clarita claimed. And it had been going on for years. I remembered how Papa had delighted in telling the story of how he'd teetered himself over Niagara Falls, refusing to right himself until Mama declared she was undeniably falling in love with him; now, he was openly traveling with his mistress. While Mama may have been willing to accept it until it became intolerable, it perturbed me that one day I might find myself in her same shoes. With marriage an inevitable expectation—indeed, the only expectation required of me—how would I know if the man I wed would be true? How could I predict an entire lifetime together? And if he displeased or betrayed me in some way, could I be as bold as my mother had been and leave? I'd never had much admiration for Mama, but in that moment it came to the fore. Her resolve to carve out a new existence for herself made me wonder if maybe I'd been too quick to judge her, too easily distracted by Papa and Fanny's magnetic glamour, while in truth, Mama had been the solidifying influence in our lives all along.

My sole consolation was that if she'd found a way, perhaps other women did, as well. Perhaps this type of arrangement was more common than those romantic notions that Clarita believed in so fervently.

"Where did you go this time?" I asked, flinching inwardly at the harshness in my tone, the residue of my anger at my sister and resentment of them for enjoying what was, for us, a very trying time.

"To Paris and Wiesbaden." Fanny handed her wrap to her maid. "Leonard, may I be the one to inform Clara? She'll be so delighted, the poor dear, after all these terrible upsets."

My father nodded, keeping his gaze on me as Fanny proceeded into the drawing room, where Mama sat ensconced like an effigy. As soon as Fanny disappeared, I turned to him.

"You went to Paris?" I demanded.

"Your mother requested it," he replied. "She worried that her maid never arrived in Deauville with her artwork, so I offered to look in on things. The reports of widespread destruction concerned me, but it appears the new Third Republic is intent on restoring law and order, so it ought to be safe to return."

"Return? I thought we were going back to New York."

"I'm afraid Clara will not hear of it," he said uncomfortably.

"Then let her return to Paris without us. Papa, surely we've had enough time abroad."

As he raised a hand to his chin, I saw his beard was threaded with silver that I'd failed to notice before. "I'm afraid we no longer have our home in New York. I had to lease it to the Jockey Club. I didn't know how long I'd be away. All that extra space—it's ideal for their social events. Your mother's ballroom will host more parties in a season than the entire time we lived there." He took in my stricken expression. "I'm sorry, Jennie, but my situation, your mother's household in Paris . . . It was unavoidable." He gave a dry chuckle. "I made certain to maintain access to my stables, however. When I return, I'll rent a room at my gentleman's club. I don't need more than a clean bed at night."

Our home. Our beautiful house—his pride and joy. Our entire life, ravaged like Paris.

"Why?" I heard myself say, tears choking me. "*Why* did you let her leave?"

He swallowed; I saw the movement above his starched collar. "I had no choice, Jennie. Clara couldn't abide it. The Four Hundred. My business . . . It became too much for her."

"And Fanny," I said. He flinched. "She left because of Fanny."

"No." His voice was flat. "She knew who I was. What she couldn't abide was our lack of standing in society, or what she deemed a lack. It never concerned me. I never cared whose ballroom didn't receive us. I still don't."

I gulped back my sorrow.

"And neither must you." As he cupped my chin, I finally let myself see the weariness under his façade, the toll of the sacrifices he'd made for our sake. "Jennie, never let anyone make you think less of yourself. Promise me."

"Yes," I whispered. "I promise." Though I had no idea what he meant.

"And never think I will leave you. You'll always have a home with me, no matter what."

"But not in New York." I wiped at my eyes, ashamed by my outburst.

"Not for now. Your mother wishes to acquire her own flat in Paris. I've begun the negotiations on her behalf. Her belongings are as she left them; her rented house was untouched, though the district is uninhabitable." He stepped to the foyer looking glass, tucking his fob chain into his waistcoat, but his gaze was remote, as if he were looking much farther away. "I've also located a boarding school in Wiesbaden for Leonie. After I see her there, I'll return to Paris to conclude the purchase of the flat while your mother takes you and your sisters to Cowes for the summer."

"Cowes?" I'd never heard of the place.

"A maritime town on the Isle of Wight. Fanny knows of the perfect cottage to rent for your stay. After the season, the best of society repairs there for the royal regatta."

I snorted, despite myself. "Mama detests boating."

His mischievous smile surfaced. "When she hears Eugénie and her son the prince imperial will be in Cowes as guests of Their Royal Highnesses, there'll be no objection. Nothing is more certain to incite Clara than the chance to offer her comfort in person to her empress."

NINE

1873

J ennie, stop fidgeting. You'll spoil your décolletage," rebuked
Mama as we prepared to board the launches that would transport
us across the port to where the royal guardship *Ariadne* glimmered
like a fantastical whale, strung with banners and candlelit lanterns.

"As if I had any décolletage to spoil," I muttered to Clarita.
Casting a quick look past my sister to where Mama was presenting
our engraved invitations, I plucked the enormous satin rose from
the froth of lace on my upper bodice and tossed it into the sea.

Clarita chuckled. "Well, there's a solution. You can now greet
Their Highnesses of Wales, His Highness the Duke of Edinburgh,
and the duke's new bride, Grand Duchess Marie, with your shoulders as bare as the day you were born."

After I'd hooked my train onto the pearl buttons of my opera-
length gloves, we boarded the launch. I ignored Mama's outraged
stare. She'd insisted on affixing that ridiculous bauble to my bodice to refresh the look of my dress, which I'd worn before, while
refusing to countenance my plea to put Papa's diamond star in my
hair instead.

This gala was the culmination of our whirlwind summer—our
formal introduction to the heir and his brother, who'd wed the
Tsar of Russia's only daughter. I'd made my debut in this very
gown a few weeks past, at a ball hosted by the Prince of Wales.
He hadn't been present, but many of his friends who shared his
penchant for the theater and other pursuits were. After Clarita

and I dazzled them with our piano duets, we were inundated by invitations to dance. We'd spent the evening reveling in our popularity and disregarding the envious glares of the other young ladies, though Mama had advised us not to favor any gentleman in particular but rather ensure our cards were filled by a variety of applicants.

"Furnishing your own décolletage was wise," Clarita now whispered in my ear as I gazed in awe at the looming guardship. Hundreds of guests were milling onboard, roaming the ample decks under the magical colored lanterns as the evening breeze billowed the standards of Russia and Britain. "That gentleman with the oversized mustache who was so taken with you at your debut should also be here tonight."

"Who?" I had to force myself to tear my gaze from the ship. All of a sudden, anxiety flooded me at the thought of being presented to the royal heir, though I'd be just another stranger in a queue and not expected to do more than curtsy.

"Don't be coy. I saw you returning his stare when you thought no one was watching."

"Oh, him." I shrugged. "He was rather peculiar. He may have admired me from afar, but not once did he ask me to dance. And then he just disappeared. Perhaps he was simply taken with the novelty of seeing an American girl hold her own in society."

"He was smitten. He couldn't take his eyes off you. I made inquiries. Do you know who he is?" Clarita paused for dramatic emphasis, which was unnecessary, as she'd already impressed me with her skill. Her time at the imperial court had not gone to waste; to my amazement, my sister transformed into another person when garbed in her Worth toilette, her ringlets framing her cheeks and smile polished while the gentlemen lined up to fill her card. From what I'd seen, we wouldn't depart Cowes without her finally setting aside her absurd penchant for the forgetful viscount.

"You never said a word to me about inquiries," I said.

"I thought it best to keep it to myself. I'm certain he must be here, as he holds the requisite pedigree. The second son of the Duke of Marlborough, no less."

"A rare titled lord, at last. Perhaps tonight, he'll be smitten by you instead."

"No." She drew out her denial with a hint of regret as the launch reached the ship. "I have it on excellent authority that you are the only girl he cares to see."

THE BRITISH HEIR was a plump man of modest stature, with jovial pale blue eyes and a bushy beard. As we curtsied before him and his wife, Princess Alexandra, who sparkled in silver tissue and pearls, then proceeded to do the same before his brother, the ginger-hued duke, and his petite Russian bride, I felt his eyes linger on me. When I braved a glance over my shoulder, Edward of Wales winked. I went still, meeting his amused stare.

"The prince," I whispered to my sister. "He just gave me a very indiscreet look."

"Naturally," said Clarita as Mama hustled us to the upper deck, protected by a velvet palanquin, where the dancing would be held. "It's well-established that no woman is safe from his attention, despite the fact that he has a beautiful wife."

"She's very much so. How unhappy it must make her."

"Why? Because she's beautiful or because he can't be satisfied by it?"

"Both," I said, again taken aback by my sister's sophistication. Had I not known better, I might not have recognized her, with her careless gossip and disregard for propriety, given her disapproval of Papa's relationship with Fanny.

I abruptly wished Fanny was still with us. She'd left Cowes after seeing us settled in Rosetta Cottage, a charming Georgian home with wild-rose trellises winding up its stone façade. She had to close up her London house in advance of her return to Boston; she would then proceed to Paris, where Papa was overseeing the purchase of Mama's new flat. I still couldn't reconcile myself to what had happened, though my parents had made their decision. It lurked like a dark pool in my heart, which I feared falling into. All of a sudden, marriage had adopted an entirely disconcerting hue, tainted for me by an unpredictability no one ever spoke of.

Having bid a forlorn goodbye to my father when he departed for Germany with Leonie, knowing he'd take passage to New York from France, I hated saying farewell to Fanny, too, until the summer turned out to be eventful enough to distract me.

"Her Imperial Majesty wishes to greet you," Mama now said breathlessly, tugging up my bodice. "I'll not have her submitted to this unseemly display. Since when does an unwed girl show her shoulders in public?"

I almost reminded her that Eugénie had introduced the fashion at her court, as evidenced by the women all around us, flaunting the bustled skirts and cinched low-cut bodices that she had popularized. But I refrained as we came before the empress.

She was no longer the benevolent goddess I'd met in the Tuileries. In mourning for her husband, who had died very recently of a lingering illness, she wore unrelieved black taffeta, which emphasized the tragedy of a woman whose glorious past had been tarnished by chaos, now dependent on Queen Victoria's charity as she made her exile in England. She sat surrounded by the few loyal women who'd fled with her from Paris, under a noticeable pall as Clarita and I curtsied before her.

"Your Imperial Majesty," I murmured. "I'm honored to see you again."

She leaned forward in her chair. "Can this be . . . ?" She sounded dubious.

"My second daughter, Your Imperial Majesty," said Mama. "Jeanette. You may recall you were so kind as to invite her to one of your *Lundis*."

At the mention of her salons, the empress's eyes grew dimmer. "Ah, yes. I believe she played Liszt for me."

"I did," I whispered, touched by her recollection. I suddenly wished I could console her. She appeared so lost in her dark corner on the ship, when once she'd been the brilliant locus around which an entire world revolved.

"I did not recognize you at first," she went on. "How quickly time passes. You've become such a lovely young woman. Like your sister." As I curtsied again at her compliment, Eugénie said, "You must enjoy your youth. It fades before we know it."

I had to blink back tears as Clarita took me by the arm and we left the empress. "How dreadful," I said. "The poor woman has lost everything."

"Except for Mama's undying affection." Clarita's fingers tightened on my elbow. "Chin up, Jennie. Smile. What did I tell you? He's here."

Glancing up, I caught sight of him among a group of gentlemen. His protuberant eyes, a watery hazel-green, were fixed on me. In his impeccable black-tail frock coat, with its white satin waistcoat and a flamboyant red cravat knotted at his throat, he appeared too slim, not as tall as I seemed to recall. He was not conventionally attractive, with those large, low-set ears and high forehead, his receded hairline parted in pomaded symmetry, and delicate features overpowered by a preposterously large mustache, waxed to dagger points above his thin-lipped mouth.

"Must he stare so? He's not at all as I thought."

"He may not be the most attractive gentleman present," retorted Clarita, even as her smile materialized when those about him turned toward us, "but he's certainly the most eligible. Go. This is your chance." To my shock, she pressed her hand to the small of my back, nudging me forward.

The men swarmed toward us at the same time, eager to request places on the dance cards hanging on ribbons from our wrists. Only he didn't move, his gaze on me as I heard Clarita reel off each inquiring gentleman's name as if she'd known them for years.

Just as I thought he meant to stay there, staring, he took a step forward. His lips brushed my fingers. When he looked up at me, a disconcerting frisson, akin to contact with an overheated bath, slipped under my skin. "Miss Jennie Jerome, I believe?" He had a staccato voice, not unpleasant, but clipped, as if pleasantries made him impatient.

"You have me at a disadvantage, sir. You know my name, yet I do not know yours."

"Randolph." The hint of a smile surfaced under his mustache. "Spencer-Churchill."

If he meant to impress me, I made certain not to show that he had succeeded. "A pleasure, Lord Randolph." Behind us, the orchestra tuned their instruments. I started to turn to his companions; I'd danced with several of them at my debut and wasn't about to forgo the pleasure of doing so again.

His next words halted me. "I would like to dance with you, Miss Jerome."

I turned back to him. "Naturally. My card isn't full yet—"

"All evening." He ignored my proffering of the card.

"*Every* dance?" I started to laugh when I saw his expression. So somber.

"If you would allow it, yes. Every dance."

"Sir, you must realize—" I paused, all of a sudden intrigued. "You must know an unengaged lady should never permit a single gentleman full charge over her card."

"I do. I don't believe you care a fig for such trivialities. Or am I mistaken?"

"Not at all." With that, I untied my card, letting it fall to the floor. He took my hand. He wasn't wearing white gloves like his friends, and the gemstone signet ring on his index finger was a cold indent against my palm as he escorted me to the floor for the first waltz.

He moved with practiced elegance, his hand at my waist imperceptible. As we whirled past those seated around the floor, I caught a glimpse of Mama, her gaze narrowing at me from her place beside the empress.

"I fear Mrs. Jerome will not approve," he remarked.

"Of me?" I laughed again, not caring this time how he interpreted it. "My mother rarely approves of anything I do."

"Have you always been so rebellious?" He gazed into my eyes with startling candor. "Or is it a habitual trait among American women?"

"Is it not among English ones?"

"Unfortunately, no." He bowed at the waltz's conclusion. "It is why I took notice of you at your debut. Alas, you were too overwhelmed by other admirers."

I couldn't tell if he meant it as flattery. As abrupt regret at my impulsiveness overcame me, he said, "Whiskey?" and retrieved two tumblers from a servitor, though I'd never tasted the stuff. To drink anything stronger than champagne, Mama declared, was not a feminine quality.

He seemed to sense as much, challenge in his gesture as he handed me the glass. "You'd think His Highness would procure finer quality," he said as the fiery liquid scorched my tongue. "But Bertie has the most banal tastes when it comes to spirits and food."

"Do you know His Highness well?" I thought he must, to refer to him thus.

"As well as anyone can, I suppose. Our families are, you might say, friendly. In our circle, one can't afford not to be friendly with the heir." Before I could respond, he went on. "You must have experienced the same in France. Courts are alike everywhere."

I almost replied that I had, but in that moment, I didn't want to feign what I didn't know. He might have made inquiries about me. "My sister Clarita attended the French court. I was still too young. Though I played the piano for Her Imperial Majesty."

"Ah. Our woeful empress." He finished his whiskey with a contemplative air. "By such precarious twists of fate do civilizations fall." He paused. "You were in Paris when the calamity occurred?"

"Yes. It was terrible." I had to set aside my glass, though I'd taken only a few sips. The whiskey was going right to my head. "We escaped on one of the last trains. Mama's benefactor, Monsieur le Duc de Persigny, was kind enough to assist us."

"Persigny?" He broke into sudden laughter, startling me again as he took me by the arm and we returned to the floor for a quadrille. I couldn't ask more during the exuberant dance, but as soon as we finished and moved aside, I said, "Why would the mention of Monsieur cause amusement? He was very gallant in our hour of need."

"No doubt. He was always renowned for his gallantry. But he was no duke. Believe me, I should know. My father is the seventh duke in our line."

"But everyone in France referred to him as . . ." I went quiet as Randolph bent to my ear, an elfin schoolboy with a tawdry secret. "Persigny's title was fictitious. His father was a tax collector, and he himself made his living as a journalist. Only after he was involved in the first coup to set Louis-Napoléon on the throne did he assume the title, which he claimed ran dormant in his family. He never presented evidence to support his claim, but he was such an ardent champion of the Bonaparte cause that once Louis-Napoléon assumed power, no one dared question it. The empress, however, held him in the highest contempt. He led the opposition to Louis-Napoléon's marriage to her, one of his few failed campaigns on his emperor's behalf."

I regarded him, stunned. "My mother and he were very good friends. She was devastated to hear of his sudden death last year. He helped arrange my sister's introduction at court and my invitation to Princess Mathilde's salon. And Mama and the empress are on the very best of terms."

"As I said, courts are alike everywhere. Eugénie had to accept her husband's dependence on an impostor, along with his numerous other indiscretions."

A woman like Mama. I had to restrain myself from glancing at the empress, realizing how little I'd known about the goings-on in her perilous world.

"Mama will be devastated. She's always thought so highly of him."

"Then we mustn't ever tell her. If there's one thing the British know, it's how to keep a secret. I wouldn't wish to be seen in an adverse light. Her goodwill is very important to me."

I met his eyes. "Why?"

His reply was assured. "Because I intend to see much more of you in the coming days, Miss Jerome. If you would allow it."

I hesitated for a moment that felt much longer. He'd upended my expectations of what a titled lord should be. Daring and irreverent—I'd never met anyone quite like him. Without realizing it, I also was starting to find him more attractive. He was that rare man whose charm didn't reside in his looks; it came from his character. He was not ordinary at all.

"I believe I might," I said.

I let him enclose my hand in his and escort me back to the dance floor.

TEN

The following afternoon, Randolph fetched me in a carriage, which, to my delight, he drove himself, like Papa. Dobbie accompanied us as my chaperone, but my stout nanny in her green turban and red shawl seemed to amuse Randolph. While he took us through town to the Solent, he asked Dobbie about her childhood in Georgia, before she'd entered our service.

"I was raised on a plantation," she told him matter-of-factly. "My parents were born slaves. They were freed before the end of the war, and we moved to the east. My mother had always done housework and I was expected to do the same. I met Miss Clara at her debut; I helped her find a missing bonnet and she later offered me a position when she became engaged to Mr. Jerome."

Randolph appeared horrified at the mention of slavery, while I felt myself flush red with shame at the realization that we'd never bothered to ask Dobbie much of anything, save for where we'd happened to misplace our combs, much as Mama must have inquired after her bonnet at her debut.

Dobbie seemed unperturbed by the awkward silence that ensued until we reached the coastline and he offered his hand for her to descend. Then she shook her head. "I'll sit here and enjoy the view." Randolph turned to me; as I climbed from the carriage, Dobbie added, "Not too far down that promenade, mind you. I want both of you in my sight at all times."

He chuckled, tucking my arm in the crook of his as I opened my parasol. The day was overcast, storm clouds hovering on the horizon, but to protect one's complexion outdoors, much as to have a chaperone for one's reputation, was indispensable.

"Your nanny is quite remarkable," he said. "Nothing escapes her notice, does it?"

"Nothing. Dobbie raised us. She knows us better than we know ourselves." I glanced at him. "Like Mama's, her approval is not easily won."

"Well, I trust I've begun my way towards it." He nodded as if to himself, looking ahead and lending me the opportunity to assess his attire—a crisp linen suit, with a scarlet cravat pinned by an opal brooch, and a straw boater. His brown leather boots polished to a sheen, his rounded collar stiff with starch. I thought he must have had an influential woman in his childhood, to take such care of his person.

"Did you have a nanny as a boy?"

He extracted an enamel case from his jacket pocket and lit a thin cigarette. The smell of the smoke as he exhaled was aromatic, tinged with sweetness. "Governesses." He grimaced. "The English governess is an unfathomable relic. Stolid and unyielding, lacking in any warmth or wit. Nothing as exotic as your Dobbie."

"Dobbie was strict with us, too. And in America, colored nannies are not exotic."

"No, they wouldn't be, would they?" He drew on his cigarette, pacing to the edge of the promenade overlooking the Solent. "Tell me about America. I've never been. Bertie—His Royal Highness—visited New York years ago. I remember how enthused he was when he returned, saying how much he admired its spirit. He declared that in America a man could be whoever he wanted to be. He's had an incurable fondness for Americans ever since."

"Well, I don't know about the rest of America, but New York is a marvelous city." Without ado, I told him about how Papa raced his hansom through the streets, flinging up mud at outraged passersby—"Oh, how they bellowed!"—and of our mansion, built with his wealth. I rhapsodized over our winters, with everything laced in ice, and unbearably humid summers, when we repaired to Newport to ride horses for hours on end. Before I realized it, I'd confided my disdain for the Four Hundred's refusal to accept us in their ranks—and my envy of Clarita, always ahead of me—but I managed to stop myself before I explained why Mama had removed us to Paris. I didn't want to imply my parents had separated.

I found it too easy to talk to him. He didn't interrupt me once. He lit several cigarettes in succession as I prattled on, his eyes never wavering from mine, as if he were truly interested in whatever I had to say.

"How I carry on," I exclaimed. "You must be exhausted by it."

"Not in the slightest. You have no idea how fascinating I find you," he said. "Snobbery is endemic here, too. One of our less laudable gifts to your nation. People in my circle: they cling to their status as if it were the only thing of importance. My mother and five sisters are all frightful snobs. And my older brother—"

He grimaced again. "George is Marquess of Blandford and stands to inherit our estate, but seeing as he was born to it, rather than make himself useful, he spends his time conducting useless scientific experiments and quarreling with his wife, Albertha, who's very unpleasant. At least your family made its fortune through enterprise. I admire it. Everything we own is descended from an illustrious lineage that must never be challenged, no matter how the world may shift around us. If the fall of the French empire should teach us anything, it's that we too can be discarded if we fail to adapt. But change in our world is tantamount to anathema."

"Oh," I said. "Do you have any ambitions for yourself?" I imagined even an aristocrat must do something to occupy his time, even if I had no concept of what it might be.

"I'm afraid you'll think me terribly idle. I did not excel in my studies, so once I completed my education my father determined I must stand for Parliament. Our seat at Woodstock is traditional and my brother has no inclination. As the heir, he needn't, so the obligation has fallen upon me, though I've been avoiding it." His voice drifted into discomfited silence. "I'm twenty-four years old and have done nothing important with my life."

"Would standing for Parliament mean a political career?" I asked. "You might be good at it. You have a way with words."

"Do I?" He sounded surprised.

"I think so. Not that I know a thing of politics, but I assume politicians must be seen to speak with authority. If you wish to create change, wouldn't it be a way to start?"

He reached for his cigarette case again, then paused. "I'd never considered it before. I've always seen it as a burden I should be desperate to evade . . ." He gave me a tentative smile, making him appear less like someone without purpose and more like the inexperienced young man he was at heart. I liked this questioning of himself. His otherwise unimpeachable poise was disconcerting, as if he looked down on the world and found nothing of interest to him.

"Would you enjoy being a politician's wife?" he said.

I burst out laughing. "We've only just met!"

"Yet how can it be that I already know?" He folded my arm under his, holding it close to his ribs. "Jennie Jerome, you make me feel as if a future might be worth the effort, after all."

"I'M NOT SURE it was an actual proposal," I told Clarita. We lay in our bedroom, the open window letting in the balmy night. The threatening storm had abated, but its lingering wind soughing in the rose trellises, scattering petals across our sill, reminded us that summer neared its end and roused the specter of our uncertain future.

I'd spent the entire afternoon with Randolph, who took Dobbie and me to tea at one of the establishments in town. The sight of my nanny arched eyebrows among the patrons when Randolph insisted on sitting her with us at the table, waving aside her protest that she could wait in the carriage. I understood that he was attempting to make clear his lack of prejudices, to give her her due as my nanny, but he put her in a somewhat difficult position, obliging her to take tea under that barrage of downcast stares. I started to protest that she should wait outside, but Randolph refused to hear of it. Dobbie went stony as she took her seat, and then he leaned to her to say, "Our empire abolished slavery in 1807. You have every right to be with us, so never mind them. Besides," he added more loudly, and rousing her rare, unwitting smile, "perhaps it will set the fashion. Personally, I think every woman should wear a turban to tea."

"He might have just let me sit in the carriage like I told him," muttered Dobbie after he deposited us at the cottage and promised to fetch me tomorrow for another outing. "He's what my pa would have called a hardheaded white man. But I suppose he's not ordinary, neither."

"No," I said faintly. "He is not." She'd perceived precisely what I had, Randolph's extraordinary character, and I, too, was beginning to like him—very much. Mama's terse silence over supper warned, however, that impulsiveness would do me no good.

"If he asked if you'd like to be a politician's wife, it was most definitely a proposal," said Clarita. "Of course, he must still do it officially and seek proper approval, but, Jennie"—she clutched my hand— "just imagine it. To marry an English lord. Everyone will envy you."

"Even you? As the eldest daughter, you are expected to marry first."

"Oh, I'll envy you. I'll *seethe* with it. But if you become Lady Randolph, you can open the doors to society for your sisters; we'll have to visit you for the season, of course, and you shall introduce us to his eligible friends. I should marry before you, by all rights, but seeing as Mama is determined to return us to Paris, where I scarcely think I'll meet anyone suitable, if you must wed before me, so be it. One of us has to make a start."

"Let's not get ahead of ourselves. I'm not sure I want to marry yet."

She gave me an incredulous look. "Why not? He must be in love with you, to have suggested it so soon. Only a man who's madly in love would do such a thing. Don't you love him?"

"Love him? How on earth would I know?"

"Well." She put her hand to my chest. "Does the sight of him quicken your heart until you feel as if you can barely breathe?"

"After one evening of dancing and an afternoon at tea? That's two sightings. Three, if you count my debut, which was only from a distance."

"Fine, so you've not seen him enough. But, how do you feel when you are with him? Can you imagine spending the rest of your life with him? Love will grow over time. I daresay, few women are in love when they first wed, but the sentiment inevitably develops."

"Do you think Papa and Mama were ever in love?"

"They must have been." She paused. "Is that what your reluctance is about? Are you worried Randolph won't be constant after you wed?"

I averted my eyes. "He's not given any indication of inconstancy thus far, but it hasn't been much time. I suppose Papa never did at first. It seems to me that marriage can't always be relied upon."

Clarita sat up straight. "Jennie, you can't go into marriage anticipating the worst. What happened between Papa and Mama, it's not as if that's the rule."

"No?" I plucked stray petals from the bedspread. "How can you be so sure?"

"Because no one would ever marry if it were," she declared. "You're just nervous because he's your first. It's normal to have doubts, but don't let them impede your common sense. The son of a duke doesn't come around every day."

I had to smile. "Neither does a viscount."

"Exactly." She scowled. "I left Paris and look what happened. Do you want to leave Cowes and suffer the same? When the opportunity arises, we cannot vacillate. Women must be more steadfast in these matters."

It seemed to me that by her words, she proved my supposition that men were by their very nature inconstant. I sat in silence before I said, "I suppose so. But . . ." I went on, dampening her eager assent, "Seeing as he is my first and I've not met any others to judge him by, how can I know if he's the one I should marry?"

Clarita tossed back her plait. "Mama didn't leave New York only because of Papa. She brought us to Europe so we could take our proper place in society. She's always said we deserve the very best. Who better than Randolph? You'd be mad to refuse him."

I set my chin in my hands, gazing out into the night. The shimmering moon, wreathed in tendrils of gossamer cloud, reminded me of his opal pin.

"Lady Randolph," I mused. "It does have a nice ring to it . . ."

WHEN RANDOLPH ARRIVED the next day, dressed in a navy-blue frock coat and smart top hat that seemed out of place for Cowes, Mama invited him directly into her parlor.

I waited anxiously in the corridor, longing to press my ear to the door but prevented by Dobbie's unswerving guard. When Randolph eventually emerged, he was pale; glancing past him, I saw Mama give a terse nod. I followed him into the garden, where dusk had begun to fall. She'd kept him with her for so long, we'd lost the opportunity to go anywhere, as an evening excursion was impossible. An unmarried couple couldn't think to be seen out together at night in public. At a loss for what to say as he struck a match to his cigarette, I blurted out, "Will you stay for supper?"

"I'm afraid not." His heels crushed discarded rose petals as he paced, wafting a slightly rotten scent into the air. "I've been summoned home. Some tiresome burden my mother has seen fit to saddle me with."

"Oh." I tried not to sound too disappointed. "Not soon, I hope?"

"On the first ferry tomorrow morning." He blew out smoke. "I may as well tell you. Your mother was clear about her concerns. I tried as best I could to explain, but as you can imagine, it did not go well. It seems she's been apprised of the same rumors as my mother—who's all the way in Blenheim, no less." He scowled. "Blasted gossipmongers. One can't do a thing in this infernal country without someone recording it in a scandalized letter. It's astonishing how impossible it can be to have a simple convenience like gaslight installed, yet the post manages to wing its way to Oxford overnight."

"Are you saying someone wrote about us to your mother?"

"Specifically, she was told I was seen monopolizing your company at the prince's gala for his brother, among other things I'll not deign to repeat." He turned to me. "Jennie, if I asked you now, would you marry me? I can't imagine my life without you. I know it must seem very reckless, but I'll not abide by what anyone thinks. I knew you were the woman I wanted as my wife from the moment I first set eyes on you. Knowing you has only furthered my resolve."

As I grappled with this declaration, which shouldn't have been unexpected yet struck me like a blow, he extinguished his cigarette under his boot and clasped my hands. "If you think it's too soon, I'll understand. Your mother believes it is indeed much too soon; and in truth, I'm in no position to ask anything of you. As Mrs. Jerome informed me, permission from our fathers must be secured. In addition, there's the matter of my current standing."

"Your . . . standing?" I was finding it difficult to speak and breathe at the same time.

"I'm not the heir. I'll be expected to earn my keep if I take a wife. And I will. I told your mother I shall stand for Parliament, with you at my side. And I shall tell my parents the same. Jennie, would you . . . ?" He lowered his eyes. "I fear I shall perish of sorrow without you. And you must think me a terrible fool."

He sounded so disconsolate that I heard myself whisper, "Yes."

"Yes?" He raised his eyes. "Did you say . . . yes?"

I nodded. "I must be terribly foolish, as well."

He took me in his arms. It was awkward. We didn't seem to fit, all knees and elbows until his smoke-tinged mustachioed lips pressed against mine. His kiss was quick, not the prolonged passion of an operatic romance, but the sensation traveled to my very feet. My entire body felt as if it dissolved and was held upright only by my dress.

"I love you, Jennie." He nested my cheek against his shoulder. "I will do everything I can to make you the happiest wife in the world. I promise, you'll lack for nothing. I'll do whatever I must to earn your trust and your heart."

I couldn't say the same in return. I had no breath with which to say it. As he drew back, he said, "If you find cause to regret this moment, I'll not hold it against you. I vow on my very life to keep it between us."

"Between us?" I managed a tremulous laugh. "My mother just demanded to hear your intentions and your mother has ordered you home to explain yourself. I think it's gone beyond our ability to keep it to ourselves."

He chuckled in return. "Indeed. As you can see, I am quite the fool."

"My fool." I caressed his jaw. His skin was slightly rough from his razor, but when I lifted my fingertips to my face, I smelled the lotion he used. Lavender.

"I will write as soon as I arrive," he said. "Your mother told me you'll be returning to Paris next week, so if I can manage to come back to see you before you leave, I shall." He thrust a card into my palm. "My address. Please, send a letter first thing tomorrow, so when I reach Oxford, I'll have something of you with me to brave the ordeal ahead."

I pocketed the card, still struggling to make sense of what had occurred as he turned heel to stalk from the garden. In the encroaching night, he became a silhouette, ghostly in his slightness. Sudden fear seized me that he'd vanish and I would never see him again.

"Don't forget me," I called out.

He paused by his carriage. "You are engraved in my heart. Not even death itself can make me forget you, Jennie Jerome."

Alone in the garden as the wind tugged at my skirts, I thought that of everything that might have happened, he was the last thing I'd expected. I didn't know if I was in love. I had no experience to judge for myself.

But if the aching void in the core of my being as I heard his carriage fade into the distance was any measure, love, I thought, was what it must be.

ELEVEN

1873–1874

We're going to the Marché," my sister announced. "Mama says you must come with us. You cannot sit at that window for hours on end. She'll not abide it."

I didn't look at her, my eyes on the rue de Courcelles, immune to the allure of early summer in Paris. Our return here had only exacerbated my dark mood, though the city was rebuilding itself, society attending the theater and the Opéra, as if the war had never occurred.

Clarita came to sit beside me in the nook. "He hasn't wavered once in all this time."

"It's already been six months. I feel as if it's become impossible."

"It's not. He couldn't come see you before we left Cowes, but he wrote to tell Mama that he informed his family. He promised to abide by his father's request for a period of reflection, but that doesn't mean he'll repudiate his commitment. He's written every week, hasn't he?"

"You know that he has. I share all his letters with you."

"Well, then. You must be patient. These matters simply take time."

"How much time?" I rose to my feet, yanking at the rumpled folds of my day dress. "We're engaged but not allowed to see each other until terms are reached. We can correspond, but no visits. *What* could possibly be so difficult for everyone to agree upon?"

She laughed. "Engagements often extend for a year or more. For someone who wasn't certain she wanted to marry, you've become rather impatient."

I glared at her. "You told me to say yes. You said I'd be mad to refuse him."

"And do you regret it?"

"Of course not," I said, but I had to avert my eyes from her as I paced to the gilded chairs in Mama's new drawing room, her latest acquisition from auctions of the ransacked Tuileries. Moving to the pianoforte, where I'd spent too many hours trying to distract myself, I went on, "I'm just tired of it. I can't attend any soirees because I'm engaged. I can't dance or be seen to favor others." I trailed my fingers over the keys, rousing a discordant chord. "I wonder how anyone manages to marry under these restrictions."

"Papa has given his approval," she reminded me. "He said he always knew you'd make a splendid match."

"Yes, but then he wrote to me in private, saying he always thought if I married for love, it would be a dangerous affair. Whatever did he mean by that?"

She didn't answer, but as I saw her wince, I said angrily, "If you know something, you must tell me. I've told you everything—"

"Enough." My mother appeared in the doorway. "Clarita, you will go with Dobbie to the Marché. It seems your sister and I must have an overdue talk."

Clarita departed, casting a worried glance at me over her shoulder.

Mama regarded me. "I will not hear voices raised in my house. You are not a fishmonger's wife to carry on in this manner."

"I'm not a wife at all," I said.

"At this rate, you may have to grow accustomed to it." Before I could reply to her chilling statement, she drew an envelope from her wrist bag. "This cable arrived from New York yesterday."

"But you told me there was no post yesterday . . ." I started to reach for the yellow paper when she added, "It's from your father. He has withdrawn his approval."

I froze mid-gesture. "Why?"

"It seems His Grace the Duke has requested stipulations that Leonard finds unacceptable." She motioned to the telegram. "Read it for yourself, if you like."

I couldn't. I couldn't move, looking at the wire as if it contained blades.

My mother let out a breath. "I did warn you. He's unsuitable due to his present situation. He may hold a title, but he has no prospects to speak of—"

"He promised to stand for Parliament," I cried out.

"And so he did," she said, cutting off my protest. "I understand he won his seat by a very narrow margin, but how he intends to support a family remains under doubt. MPs are not paid to serve, and aristocrats in Britain are forbidden from gainful employment. Given the circumstances, I'll not subject you to the sordid details."

"I must know the details." I steadied my voice in the hope I'd appear calmer than I was. "Aren't my prospects under doubt as well?"

"If you insist. Your father requests he have a sum settled on him by his family and that you in turn be protected by the terms of your dowry, should Randolph precede you in death."

"Death? How can anyone speak of death when we're not even married yet?"

"Because such are matters of utmost importance in Britain. Apparently, wives there are not accorded the same guarantees as we enjoy in America. Your father will not see you married without the assurance you'll always be provided for."

My legs buckled. Sinking into one of my mother's tiny, uncomfortable chairs, I fought back a wail of despair.

"I realize how hard this must be," she said, with a compassion she'd never shown before, which only made it worse. "But we must defend your interests. Randolph is no doubt sincere in his avowal, but . . ." She paused. "His privilege impedes his reason. He should never have proposed so precipitously. The situation has gone beyond his means to contain it, so we can't allow it to proceed further. He cannot marry without his father's consent, no more than you can."

"It is over then?" Anguish darkened everything around me. "Mama, I . . . I think I must love him, too. I can't bear the thought of losing him."

"I know." She lowered herself into the chair beside me. "I was once very much in love with your father," she said quietly, once more taking me by surprise. She'd never spoken of her personal sentiment. "He was so irresistible and dashing. You might say he swept me off my feet. I was so very young. So innocent. Like you."

"And you married him. Why shouldn't we do the same?" My question was tremulous, as if it might shatter the fragile confidence between us.

"Because your father and I had to learn after we wed that marriage brings obligations. Once the passion ebbs, the hard work begins. Those who are ill-prepared reap untold misery."

"Surely not in every marriage," I said, even as I remembered she and Papa now lived an ocean apart.

"I've yet to see proof to the contrary." She returned the telegram to her bag. "Your father will do what is necessary to protect you." Coming to her feet, she dispelled our intimacy. "I'll not see you turn gray before your time. A visit to Monsieur Worth's atelier is in order. I'm planning a salon next month, and I want you and Clarita to entertain my guests. It's time for you to resume your place in society. Given time, we can put this unfortunate incident behind us."

I felt as if I'd plunged into a netherworld where the ground had turned treacherous, pitted with unseen chasms waiting to swallow me whole.

"Can I at least write to him? Mama, please," I said, as her mouth thinned. "He must be beside himself. If we're no longer engaged, he must hear it from me."

She nodded. "One letter; that's all I can allow. And I must review it. After that, not another word. The most efficient way to erase a mistake is to never mention it again."

MAMA HAD ME rewrite the letter so many times it didn't seem to have issued from my pen at all. She promised to see it dispatched, but after I wept bitterly in Clarita's arms, my sister said, "You must write again in secret. Tell him everything. I'll see that your letter gets to him."

I moaned. "How? I told you, it's impossible."

She took me by my shoulders. "Listen to me. I didn't want to upset you more, but I overheard Mrs. Ronalds tell Mama something when she visited us last month."

"Fanny?" I rubbed at my tear-salted eyes. "What did she say?"

Clarita lowered her voice, though we were in our bedchamber and Mama had retired, fatigued from planning her salon. "Mama was complaining, as is her wont, over the hastiness of your engagement. Fanny confided that she'd overheard in London, through one of those matrons who praised our duets, that the duke chastised Randolph, saying that while you may be a lovely girl, Papa is a speculator. Randolph took offense. They had an altercation. The implication is obvious. The duke thinks the daughter of a self-made man isn't worthy to marry his son."

I let out a gasp. "But Randolph admires that we come from enterprise."

"And he and his father argued over it. The duke then issued his demand to Papa, knowing Papa would never agree. If neither family can reach an accord, there's less dishonor in it. Engagements must fall apart all the time over these kinds of disagreements."

"And Randolph wouldn't know," I said, in rising panic. "He'll think I've had time to reflect and come to regret it, giving Papa the opportunity to withdraw."

"Precisely." Clarita retrieved the stationery from our desk. "Write to him this instant. Tell him you were aggrieved to hear our father so disparaged. He'll understand. No matter what," she added, as I took up the pen, "you must not give up hope. As for how I'll send the letter . . . Marie is not averse to the occasional bribe."

I was sick with worry after Clarita saw my letter off, wondering how Randolph would interpret simultaneous missives that read as if they came from different persons. I wanted to believe he'd see through my ploy, knowing Mama must have overseen my first letter, but I also feared he'd think me inconstant. I might make matters worse, though as Clarita pointed out, with our engagement already awry, nothing I put in a letter could jeopardize it further.

And my sister's support bolstered my determination. Enraged that I'd been reduced to unsuitability because of how my father made his living, I threw myself into the gaiety of Mama's salon, to which she'd invited several artists—none of any particular renown, but promising enough to warrant their invitations. Clarita and I flaunted our new Worth gowns, my sister reminding me that many ladies of quality in Britain couldn't afford Worth's exorbitant prices and had to make do with lesser dressmakers, so wearing his creations signaled more than mere vanity on our part. After we played the piano together, to the salon's applause, I danced with several of the gentlemen—all of which I hoped would reach Randolph's ears.

At the evening's end, Mama gave us a nod of approval. "Now we shall see what is said about us."

As she proceeded to her bedchamber, Clarita smiled. "She hasn't given up hope either. Mama is nothing if not proud. Your marriage must come about on her terms."

Being back in society was the very antidote I needed. Paris was reviving, if more slowly than Clarita preferred, given the paucity of available suitors, but as summer faded into a glorious autumn, I finally came to love the scenic boulevards and rattle of omnibuses over ancient cobblestone, the tarry scent of coffee in the morning and the bluish tint the newly installed street gas lamps cast at night. Leonie came home from boarding school for two weeks and astounded us with her near-fluent German. Together, we visited the Louvre and the fashionable Champs-Élysées; we competed on horseback in the bois and on the piano in the evening, then went on holiday with Mama to southern France, walking arm in arm along the seashore.

It wasn't until the new chestnut trees that had replaced those chopped down for fuel during the siege started shedding their leaves that I realized my distress had waned. It now felt as if meeting Randolph had been a dream, that he'd appeared and vanished just as I'd feared he might when we said goodbye in Cowes.

He hadn't replied to either of my letters.

I did not think we'd see each other again.

Until his telegram arrived shortly after my twentieth birthday in January 1874, announcing his arrival in Paris.

TWELVE

Seated in a prim light-blue day dress in the drawing room, I waited nervously. Mama had declared it most inopportune of him but set Marie to polishing the silverware and dusting every surface and dispatched Dobbie to the finest patisserie in the city. She had the table set with her gold-rimmed tea service with the deposed emperor's initials, which she'd bought at one of her auctions; she claimed it had once belonged to Eugénie.

When I heard him enter the foyer, I sat so erect that Clarita shot me a warning look. Mama accompanied him into the drawing room, engaging in pleasantries as if nothing untoward had occurred. The very sight of him, after a year of absence, stifled my breath.

He wore a fitted gray suit, his coat buttoned at the top to display his patterned vest, a white gardenia in his lapel. His mustache seemed larger than before, but maybe that was because his face was thinner. When his gaze reached across the room to me, my welcoming smile felt taut on my lips. He looked despondent.

The tea was excruciating. He spoke without his habitual wit, imparting the news that he was due to take his oath for Parliament after having spent a month in Ireland caring for a dying aunt, and that his fourth sister, Anne, had recently wed. All expected familial matters, but at the mention of his sister's marriage, he shifted his eyes to me and I had to look away.

Just when I thought I couldn't bear another moment, Mama rang her bell for the service to be cleared and said, "If you like, Randolph, you may take Jennie out for a carriage ride. Dobbie will accompany you. I'm certain you must have much to discuss."

Clarita nudged me under the table. Quickly fetching my bonnet and wrap, I found myself beside him in the carriage on our way to Parc Monceau.

Dobbie followed us at a distance while we walked the paths, passing but not admiring the displaced Renaissance archway by the pond with its swans, the magnificent elms that had somehow survived the siege, and lichen-stained statues standing guard over shaded groves.

He lit a cigarette, trailing smoke in his wake. Unable to abide his silence now that we were alone, I said, "Will you persist in saying nothing?"

He turned to me. "I think you must speak first, seeing as you never answered my letters."

"I most certainly did. I had to resort to bribery to send my private letter to you. The expected courtesy would have been to acknowledge its receipt. Or did you not receive it?"

"Oh, I did." His sudden chuckle outraged me. "Your letter bristled with indignation, though I assured you in my response that I had no part in that situation, other than to defend you and your father most strenuously. And you had to resort to bribery, you say?"

"You think it amusing? Clarita paid our maid, Marie, to dispatch it to you."

"Well, then it seems we were put to the test." He glanced at Dobbie. "I cannot say I wasn't warned. You told me in Cowes that your mother's trust wasn't easily won."

"What does Mama have to do with it?"

"She oversees who receives letters in her house, doesn't she? I wrote to you at once, protesting the accusation. You may blame my brother's odious wife for that particular imbroglio. Albertha delighted in spreading gossip during the season that my father and I were on the outs over my American penchant." He drew on his cigarette. "And while matters between my father and I have never been easy, our disagreement was greatly embellished by those who ought to keep their stupidity to themselves. I also did tell you my family are frightful snobs."

I clenched my hands as he went on. "But you couldn't have known any of it because Mrs. Jerome withheld my letters. Like I said, a test. For all this bother over who's unsuitable to marry whom, in the final say our families are far more alike than they care to admit. While my father requested a period of reflection, your mother instituted it. And here we are."

Fury surged in me. Now that he explained it, it made perfect sense. Mama had kept his letters from me because he was a mistake that must be erased.

"I feel like such a fool," I said through my teeth.

"Then you understand how I've felt this past year. Letter after letter without any answer, imploring you to remember how much I care for you. But when your father withdrew his approval, you didn't pine too harshly over my loss."

I came to a halt. "Meaning what?"

"You went on to enjoy yourself. At your mother's salon and elsewhere. The Jerome sisters are the toast of Paris, which comes as no surprise to me."

"That's very unfair. I was miserable for months and months. I thought I'd never see you again. I thought"—my voice fractured—"I thought you'd forsaken me."

"Never." He reached for my hand. I wanted to resist, but I again succumbed to that sensation of slipping into a warm sea. "I came to see you because I can't forget you for a moment, though the entire world stands against us. I feared you might no longer love me."

I hesitated. I'd never said it aloud and wondered now if I should. Our engagement was over. How could it serve either of us to declare our love?

"I . . . I do," I whispered. "But there are conditions your father has imposed and my father cannot accept. How can we hope to marry?"

"Yes, I'm afraid the conditions are a sore contention, and both our families have dug in their heels. It's rather tiresome, arguing over who will get what upon whose death, but things have been done the same way in every Spencer-Churchill marriage since the cornerstone was set at Blenheim." He chuckled once more. "We could elope and damn the consequences. You can play the piano for sous while I give revolutionary speeches in the hamlet square."

I shook my head in disbelief at his levity, even as I couldn't contain my own laughter. "We'd perish within the month. Our clothing expenditures alone would drown us."

"True." He let go of my hand to light another cigarette. "Yet I cannot believe either of our families wants us to be perfectly attired and miserable for the rest of our lives."

We resumed our walk, closer now, our arms brushing against each other. "I could write to Papa," I said at length. "I might be able to persuade him."

Randolph nodded. "Should he relent somewhat, my father may feel obliged to do the same, though there's no certainty of it."

I didn't know why it suddenly occurred to me. It wasn't a solution I should ever have considered. I had no knowledge, let alone experience, to embark on such a path. Even as I contemplated it, my entire being quailed. But we were in love. We'd suffered enough. We deserved some happiness, and, I reasoned, it would happen anyway, sooner or later, and sooner would guarantee success. There could be no way forward should our families refuse to meet each other halfway. But if we tipped the scales in our favor, everything must fall into place. And we'd have a moment all our own, dictated by us. All of a sudden, I wanted this more than anything. I longed to seize charge of our destiny and no longer be battered by forces beyond our control. I wanted him on my own terms.

"Could we—?" I swallowed, still incapable of uttering the words aloud.

He stopped. He didn't look at me, but he must have understood my intent, for he said quietly, "Jennie, I would leap at the chance. But it's a terrible risk, especially for you."

"Forget the risk. *Could* we?" I heard myself say, to my astonishment. It was as if a stranger spoke through me, someone brazen I didn't know. "Clarita will help us if she can."

He went silent for a moment. "My hotel wouldn't be appropriate."

"There must be inappropriate places in Paris," I replied.

He nodded. "There must be. Are you quite sure?"

"Are you?"

He took another moment before he said, "I suppose we must indeed do something."

MAMA HAD GRANTED me this time alone with Randolph only as an unavoidable concession to his visit. She wasn't about to allow us another such liberty. The subterfuge required to meet him in secret seemed insurmountable, yet once I confided in her, my sister plunged eagerly into the ploy.

I didn't reveal my full intent; I merely told her we needed to meet again in private, to determine if we were resolved to wed. She'd seen how down-in-the-mouth Randolph was and had weathered my own misery, so she assured me that together, we must connive a way.

"We could go riding," she said. "As long as we're seen mounting and dismounting at the stables, Mama won't suspect a thing. Why not meet there? You could have as much time as you need while I make myself scarce."

It was a sound plan I was hard-pressed to reject. But the bois was miles from any hotel, disreputable or otherwise. "He hurt his leg in Ireland. He can't ride until it heals."

My excuse sounded as lame as I claimed he was, but my sister only sighed. "That's unfortunate." She toyed with her plait as we sat in our shared bedroom. "What about a shopping excursion?"

"Dobbie always goes with us on those." I shuddered at the thought of attempting to hoodwink our nanny. "I could never elude her."

Clarita frowned. "Doesn't he have any idea how to accomplish it?"

"He suggested a café in the Marais." I had no choice other than to say something in order to direct our conversation toward his designated vicinity.

"The Marais? But it's so unsuitable, full of drunkards and students. Not at all where a lady ought to be seen . . ." As I felt my breath stall in my chest, she added, to my relief, "Of course, it's also the ideal place not to be seen by anyone of standing, as he must know."

I nodded. "But to actually get there . . ."

"It'll be quite the endeavor, but worth it, if you and he can reach mutual accord. He's come all this way, after all. He must be desperate." She considered. "You could take an omnibus. Not that we ever have, but people do."

"What excuse could I devise for taking an omnibus?" I paused. "Unless . . . We do have that piano recital next week at Madame de Chambard's salon."

"We're not taking an omnibus there. Mama will hire a carriage for us."

"Yes, but Mama isn't going. She's attending an auction and told me Dobbie will accompany her because she may acquire something and only trusts Dobbie to take care of it. Marie will escort us to the salon, instead."

"Marie can't be bribed to look the other way while you board an omnibus. A secret letter or two, yes. Not this."

"What about the carriage we take to the salon? I can . . . I don't know—excuse myself early. Say something didn't agree with me and I must return home."

"Marie will insist on going with you."

"But she'll not want to leave you behind. I'll convince her to let me take the carriage alone and send it back for you, while you keep up the Chopin for as long as you can. No one will doubt my departure due to an unfortunate indisposition."

Clarita gnawed at her lip. "Marie will still feel obliged to inform Mama that you left the salon early, and our butler will certainly know you never arrived home."

I went quiet, turning it over in my head. "What if I claim I suddenly felt better? I could then return to the salon after seeing Randolph to fetch you and Marie."

"Can you meet with him and return so quickly?" she asked.

"I'll have to manage it. Providing I'm not gone too long, what is there to question?"

"Plenty," said Clarita, her eyes bright with excitement. "Still, it might work."

"If it doesn't," I said, "and Mama finds out, providing she hears we're firm in our resolve to marry, she'll have more pressing concerns than how we managed to meet in private."

BY THE TIME I reached the café in the Marais where Randolph sat at one of the outside tables, I was certain the entire city would soon be apprised of my flagrant disregard for the rules set in place to prevent exactly these types of transgressions. I'd feigned a stomachache at the salon, refusing the immediate offer of a bed upstairs and a variety of soothing tinctures, pulling on my mantle, and making my way to the carriage. The hired driver gave me a look when I told him the directions but made no comment, though he must have surmised I was up to no good.

Randolph stood at once. With his hand at my elbow, he guided me into the labyrinthine district, untouched by any renovations and given over to the wretched forced out of their homes in other parts of the city under refurbishment after the siege.

At a pitted entryway into a soot-stained building that I could scarcely believe qualified as an establishment, reputable or otherwise, he paused.

"Jennie, there's still time. We can find another way."

I lifted my chin, even as I felt my heart pounding so hard I wondered he didn't hear it. "Mama will move heaven itself to see us wed, once she hears what we've done."

"More like hell itself," he said. "She'll think me a villainous knave."

"She will. And once we're married, she'll put it out of her mind."

He'd already booked the room; the haggard woman at the reception desk didn't bother to look up when she handed over the key. "Not a minute more," she called out as we climbed a staircase that felt unsteady under my feet. "This is a decent establishment."

"Decent, indeed," muttered Randolph, jiggling the key in the misshapen lock.

The room was small and airless, furnished with the necessities—a sagging bed that looked none too clean, a washstand with a pewter basin, a wardrobe without doors.

Sensing my dismay, Randolph said, "It doesn't get more disreputable than rooms that rent by the hour. No one can vouch we were here."

"It is . . ." Words failed me.

I tried not to think of how he knew of such places. I wasn't entirely ignorant of what came next. One afternoon in London, perusing Fanny's library for something new to read, I'd happened upon a slim volume tucked behind others on the shelf. When I opened it, a cascade of engravings spilled out. As I gathered them in a panic, I'd glimpsed depictions of men and women in a variety of compromising positions, and could still recall the heat that flared in my cheeks. In my haste to return the illicit trove to its hiding spot, I hadn't examined them too closely, just enough to understand, more or less, what I was seeing.

"Dreadful." Randolph broke into my silence. "Not the sort of tale we can ever hope to share with our children."

I smiled weakly, removing my mantle to drape it over the bed's threadbare cover. Of all the things that might have concerned me, a louse infestation came first to my mind.

He unfastened his cravat. That one gesture froze me in place. I'd chosen my simplest gown, with a minimum of accessories, to Mama's consternation, until I whispered my monthly time was on me and she drew back as if I were contagious. Still, I wore a corset, layers of petticoats, and padding for my bustle. The realization that I'd have to either request his assistance or allow him to rummage past my attire mortified me.

I had envisioned something entirely different. Or so I told myself, though in truth the subterfuge required to reach this point hadn't left me much time for contemplating the actual event. Now here I was, with the man I loved, and no idea what to do next.

Randolph paused, taking in my frozen stance. "Please, allow me."

His fingers were deft; again, I tried not to consider how he'd learned to navigate the intricacies of feminine attire. As he began to undo my corset, I stepped away, feeling too exposed in my knee-length camisole, under which I wore the split-legged bloomers that revealed more than I'd ever shown anyone except Dobbie.

"Yes," he said. "That ought to be sufficient."

He started to undress himself. To my surprise, I saw that men had their share of discomforts as well. Braces for their stockings and trousers, and—

"A corset!" I exclaimed, as he paused in his unfastening of the item encasing his waist.

"Why, yes." He looked discomfited. "It's required, is it not?"

His obvious embarrassment at my delight that we were similarly confined dispelled our tension. I helped him remove the corset; beneath, he wore a light cotton undersuit with a convenient row of cloth-covered hooks down its front.

"I prefer yours," I said, motioning to my rigid undergarments.

"Yes, well. This does make using the chamber pot less arduous."
He undid the hooks; as I caught sight of his narrow torso—he
didn't require a corset; he was so lean—I turned to the bed.

Lying upon it, I closed my eyes.

I heard him search within his clothing, then the creak of his
tread on the plank floor followed by his voice at to my ear. "Don't
move. This will hurt a little."

His hands slipped between my thighs, nudging them apart. I
suddenly felt faint from lack of air as his hands were replaced by
something stiff and bulbous, with a slippery pliancy to it. Despite
my resolve not to look, I couldn't help glancing down. His erect
member was sheathed in an odd device, affixed at its base by a rib-
bon, like an odd waxen sock.

"I'm told these contraptions can prevent complications," he explained when I lifted my bewildered gaze to him. "I've never actually employed one."

"Is it uncomfortable?" I thought it must be.

"It's made of boiled sheep gut, so you can imagine. But again,
required."

He kissed me slowly, rousing that sensation of a warm sea. As
his hands roved over me, I finally succumbed to my pent-up desire.
I forgot we were in a room rented for an hour, on a bed that was
none too clean. I forgot that I'd abandoned my sister at a musical
recital to trek across the city to meet a man to whom I wasn't officially engaged anymore.

I forgot that what we were doing could cast me into ruin.

His lips seared mine at the same time as his encased member
probed between my thighs. "Jennie," he breathed in my mouth, "I
love you so much."

"I love you, too," I whispered back, for the first time. And my
release of the words incited his passion. He thrust into me, a sharp
jab. I couldn't contain my gasp. Behind my eyelids, I saw images of

those stylized engravings scattered on the library carpet, the artifice of them that bore no resemblance to the awkwardness of two bodies that didn't know how to fit together.

"Wait," I said. He went still, arched over me on his elbows.

"Does it hurt very much? I can—"

"Let me." I smiled to ease his concern and rocked up my hips. As the pain subsided and his eyes widened to feel himself slip deeper inside, I felt a sudden, exquisite wave that peeled a stifled moan from me. He bucked eagerly a few times, his body quivering, then withdrew so fast that I feared I'd done something to dissuade him, though my sole intent had been to increase our pleasure. Maybe women weren't supposed to enjoy this?

Then he said, "Oh, no." I followed his gaze to see the sheath was no longer there.

"Where did it go?" I asked.

To my dismay, he gingerly reached inside me to extract it.

"I'm not sure." He peered at the crumpled object as if it required a diagnosis. "I think . . . You'd best wash yourself in case. One hopes that jug by the basin has fresh water in it."

"That's it?" I couldn't believe it. It had taken less than five minutes.

He faltered. "For now. I'm afraid I was too excited. It happens."

"Oh. Does it happen often?"

"I sincerely hope not," he said drily.

An unwitting peal of laughter escaped me. He was kneeling before me, that shred dangling from his fingertips, looking appalled, before he, too, started to grin.

"Some lover I turned out to be," he said, and I had to wipe tears of mirth from my face as I sat up and kissed his lips.

"We have much to make up for on our honeymoon. But now, it is done."

"Indeed." He went to fetch the jug. "Time to face the consequences."

HE WANTED TO accompany me to fetch Clarita at the salon, then escort us both home at once to present himself to Mama and suffer her wrath. I refused. I hadn't exceeded the time to draw suspicion to my absence, so it was best, I told him, for me to go on alone and arrange an invitation for him to tea so we could inform Mama together.

"I'll write first thing in the morning," I said. "Will you be at your hotel?"

"Only for three more days." He shot a censorious glare at the driver that scuttled the man onto his seat to take up the reins. "After that, I must return to London."

He remained by the street as my carriage departed. Within it, I winced at the throb in my loins. I had bled, requiring him to fetch water from the proprietress, as the jug contained only a scummy film. Even now, I felt wetness seeping out of me. My mantle was dark, so the stain wouldn't show, but when I entered the salon, where Clarita was already bidding our hostess farewell, I thought my degradation must be plain to see.

On the ride home, Marie frowned as Clarita asked breathlessly in English, which our maid didn't speak, "Tell me everything. Are you still very much in love?"

I nodded. "We are."

"Oh, Jennie. Mama will be beside herself, but if you and he are determined, she can't do anything else but consent, after she states all her objections again, of course."

We arrived to find the flat blazing with candlelight. Clarita lost her fervor when she realized Mama had already returned. "She might have decided to join us at the salon," she hissed as we entered the foyer. "What on earth would I have told her?"

"Girls." Mama's voice issued from the drawing room. "Please, come here."

I went in behind my sister, wishing every lamp in the room

wasn't lit even as I told myself nothing could be read by my person, much as I might fear it.

Mama sat on her settee, her embroidery hoop in her hands. "How was Madame de Chambard? Did you remember to give her my regrets? I wish I could have accompanied you, but I'd been assured the auction would feature a set of porcelains from the Tuileries."

"Did it?" I asked, and I bit my lip. Feigning interest in something I hadn't shown any interest in before could appear suspicious.

"No. All the items were fake. I didn't recognize a single one, so I decided to return here. You must have played your entire repertoire. I expected you over an hour ago."

"Madame and her friends were so charmed by our talents!" Clarita said, in a voice that was much too shrill. "I thought they'd keep us at the piano all night."

"Is that so?" Mama pricked her needle through the hoop. "How strange. I sent a note once I arrived, thinking you'd indeed forget to convey my regrets. Madame replied that she hoped Jennie was feeling better. It seems she was indisposed. A stomachache, I believe?"

Clarita stammered, "Mama, it—it's not—"

"Go at once to your room." She didn't look up, but as I started to follow my sister, Mama intoned, "Not you, Jennie. I still have words for you."

A tense silence ensued, broken only by the hiss of her needle slicing through cloth.

"Where were you?" she finally said. "You most assuredly did not come here."

I saw no reason to equivocate. It wasn't how Randolph and I had planned it, but I'd rather she vented her fury on me first. By the time she saw him, she'd be obliged to contain the worst of it. "I was with Randolph. Mama, we had to—"

She slapped her embroidery aside. "How *dare* you? I was indulgent past any obligation on my part. I allowed him into my house, endured his mournful eyes and dispirited conversation, though he had the poor taste to mention his sister's marriage after his father broke off your engagement—"

"His father did not break it off. Papa refused to consent to the duke's terms. Had he agreed," I said, as she stared at me in disbelief, "we'd be planning our wedding now, not stealing away to meet in secret."

"You will never do so again." She lifted a hand to her throat, as if she were short of air. "I forbid it."

I swallowed. "It's too late to forbid us anything."

Her color drained. "God in heaven . . . What have you done?"

As I returned her stare, she let out a desolate sigh. "You've gone beyond forgiveness. I will carry your disgrace to my grave."

"Only he and I know. No one else."

"Not Clarita? Or did you mislead her, too?"

"She only thinks we met at a café to talk."

"Then I suppose we must be grateful for that mercy." She shut the drawing room doors, then paced to the decanter of brandy on the sideboard for her guests. Pouring a precise measure into a glass, she thrust it at me. "Drink this. Though I highly doubt your nerve requires further fortification."

I gulped, coughing at its potency.

"Well." She arranged herself back on her settee, her anger evaporating as quickly as it had flared. "You've obtained what you desired." When I looked up, she said, "Your father would have surrendered in time; he never could refuse you anything. I was the one who insisted we must stay firm. The duke would see you bound as chattel to his son, without any say over your financial affairs should something untoward occur. I had no wish to put a daughter of mine in such a precarious state. Life will upend us if we don't have the foresight to prevent it—something you've clearly yet to learn."

I finished the brandy, feeling sick to my stomach. "And now?"

"Now we must abide by their terms." She gave me a severe look. "You've foregone the security I sought for you by taking matters into your own hands. Randolph will receive an annuity income from his father's estate for as long as the duke lives, but your dowry payments will not revert to you should Randolph die. I can only hope he'll be worth the sacrifice."

"He is," I said quickly. "We love each other."

Her mouth pursed. "Believe me, without money, love doesn't fill the larder." She sighed. "What is done can't be undone. I'll cable Leonard in the morning to inform him I've had a change of heart. Go and take your rest. You look dreadful."

I went to the drawing room doors and paused. Before I could open my mouth, she cut me off. "Do not think to thank me. Marriage, you will discover, can be for a very long time."

THE CEREMONY WAS set for April in the chapel of the British embassy in Paris. My gown by Worth had lace-covered sleeves and a cloud of rosebud-embroidered veiling. Papa brought me a stunning pearl choker, which Dobbie promptly insisted I keep stored away, lest I take it into my head to wear it before I married. I had other jewels as well, sent by Randolph's mother, the duchess; he presented them to me at our engagement dinner, along with a letter from Lady Frances, detailing the jewels' provenance and every late duchess who'd worn them before. Randolph whispered to me, "She kept these for you from a recent auction of our Marlborough gems"—an unsettling remark that, coupled with the letter, made me feel as if the jewels might be better displayed in a museum. When Dobbie saw them, she stated as much herself, indicating her time in Paris acting as our ladies' maid had not gone to waste.

That night in our bedchamber, Clarita likewise sniffed when I showed her the antique case containing the necklace and bracelet. "Dobbie's right. No one has worn settings like that in ages, though the gems look real enough."

"Burmese rubies and Indian diamonds. Randolph assures me they're of considerable value."

"Then they'll need new settings. Valuable or not, as they are now, they're fit only for Madame de Chambard's salon."

I closed the case. "Oh, Clarita." I gazed about our room, where we'd spent so many nights plotting my future. "This is the last time I'll sleep here as I am. Tomorrow, I shall become Lady Randolph and Jennie Jerome will no longer exist."

"I should hope so. I'm counting on Lady Randolph to introduce me in London's society."

"Our house in London won't be ready for several months," I reminded her. "It requires extensive renovation, so after our honeymoon, we'll be staying at Blenheim."

"A palace. Who would have thought? The girl who recited Baudelaire and whose family wasn't deemed fit to join the Four Hundred will now be the wife of a duke's son."

"And she'll reside in a palace with only one working water closet, according to the duke's son. How do they manage it? Do they queue up every morning?"

"What does it matter?" She flung herself across her bed. "You'll be married, received everywhere. Once you have your home in London, I'll have to remind you every day that your sister was instrumental in helping you become so terribly important."

I spread out beside her, and we lay looking together out the window into the spring night.

"Do you think it odd that his parents won't attend the wedding?" I asked.

"Perhaps it's how they do these things in their family. They did send their regrets, and his brother the Marquess of Blandford is here in their stead."

"Yes, and have you seen how George stands aside and leers, as if he's in on a joke no one knows? He's so different from Randolph, I can scarcely believe they're brothers."

"But you liked his parents well enough when they came to visit us?"

I nudged her. "I barely got a word in edgewise, with Mama commanding all the attention." As Clarita giggled, I recalled the way Lady Frances's hazel-green gaze (Randolph had her eyes) had scrutinized Mama's drawing room and gown, which was more current than the one she wore. While the duchess's smile never slipped, I thought I'd glimpsed disdain in her appraisal and her slight wince when Mama made a point of displaying her painted fan with the comment that it was a personal gift from the empress.

Or was it envy?

"The duke was very distinguished," said Clarita. "Though I expected him to be taller. Randolph has his mustachios. His Grace's put a walrus to shame."

"Yes, he was cordial with me." I felt a sudden chill, reached up to shut the window. "Even if he didn't say much."

"How could he? Mama did all the talking!" Clarita started to laugh, then went quiet as she took in my expression. "Surely you're not *afraid* of them?"

"Of course not," I said at once, but as I looked away, she tightened her hold on my hand.

"You mustn't be, Jennie. There will be a period of adjustment, but what's most important now is how you conduct yourselves in your marriage."

I tried to smile. "I don't know anything about being an English lady."

"Don't let Mama hear you say that. She's spent our entire lives preparing us to be ladies. In French society, perhaps, but it can't be so different. You'll be the most celebrated hostess in London. I have no doubt."

I met her eyes. "Do you truly think so?"

"Silly goose." She embraced me. "You'd better not disappoint me. If you fail to become the undisputed belle of British society, how can I possibly hope to marry above you?"

PART II

LADY RANDOLPH

1874–1880

"Thanks, sir," cried I, "'tis very fine,
But where d'ye sleep, or where d'ye dine?
I find by all you have been telling,
That 'tis a house, but not a dwelling."
—ALEXANDER POPE

THIRTEEN

1874

As our carriage cleared the ostentatious gateway, the horses re-harnessed to it after the local villagers had uncoupled them to pull us through their township in a bizarre welcoming, Blenheim Palace loomed before me in all its splendor, framed by miles of groomed acreage, ancient oaks, and impressive tiered gardens.

"The finest vista in England," Randolph declared. I gave him an appreciative smile, thinking of the verse by the famed English satirist Alexander Pope—"'tis a house, but not a dwelling"—as we approached the monumental Great Court, dominated by an imposing statue of the first Duke of Marlborough, for whose hero-ism in battle his grateful Queen Anne rewarded him with this site. The palace was unlike anything I'd seen, rivaling Versailles in its grandeur, but I couldn't help but compare it with our recent honeymoon at the Château de Petit Val, an idyllic *petit palais* built by Madame de Pompadour and restored by its current proprietors, the American banker Charles Moulton and his wife, who were friends of Mama's. In contrast to the château's elegance, Blenheim seemed overwrought, a massive edifice in which everything was stately yet without any warmth, like a mausoleum.

The duchess greeted us in her old-fashioned crinolines and a lace cap, the likes of which hadn't been seen in Paris in a decade. Taking me on a tour of the high-ceilinged, frescoed enfilade of staterooms enveloped in permanent penumbra—"To safeguard the artwork from sunlight," she explained, even she marched past said artwork without a glance, forcing me to catch glimpses of masterpieces by Rubens and others whom she didn't seem to think merited a remark. I didn't fail to notice, however, the faded blank spots on the damask-papered walls of her immense drawing room, where paintings must have been displayed once, nor the icy undercurrent in the air. May was chilly in England, not like the balm of France, though as I looked around, I saw far too few fireplaces than necessary to heat such a space.

"Since the eighteenth century, this has been the seat of our dynasty," said Lady Frances, as if I were a paying guest. "Its construction took over twenty years under expert craftsmen, with the gardens designed by Capability Brown. It has no like in France or indeed any other nation. When His Majesty George III came to visit, he exclaimed not even the royal family had a house to equal it."

Randolph chuckled. "Mamma, I've apprised Jennie of our illustrious past." He toyed with an unlit cigarette as our tea was literally rolled in on linen-draped carts by livery-clad servants, plates of scones and crumpets, pyramids of sugar-glazed cakes beside Wedgwood teacups and pots—an excess of abundance.

"Randolph, dear," rebuked Lady Frances, "must you?"

He put away his cigarette. It impressed me. I'd seen how much he smoked during our honeymoon. One day, I counted over thirty cigarettes consumed, and at night, his dry cough perturbed me. I'd implored him to reduce his consumption, saying he must safeguard his voice for Parliament, so I took note of the effect his mother's disapproval had on him.

She nodded gratefully. His Grace the Duke was tending to the estate but would return in time for dinner. Other members of the family in residence joined us, including Blandford's wife, Albertha, and the unwed Churchill daughters, Rosamund, Georgiana, and the youngest, nine-year-old Sarah, accompanied by a stern governess of that rigid ilk Randolph had cited in Cowes.

The girl in her starched pinafore gave me a shy smile. When I patted the seat beside me, thinking she looked forlorn, the duchess said, "Sarah will take her tea in the nursery. She's only here to greet you. Sarah, please curtsy for your new sister, Lady Randolph."

I almost winced as the child made formal obeisance. While the governess steered her away, it struck me that I barely knew this family into which I'd wed, an unsettling realization made more evident by the protracted tea, during which Randolph's sisters conducted innocuous conversation while Albertha, whose dowdy caplet did nothing to diminish her zealous gaze, appraised my cream-wool travel suit, part of the new wardrobe Papa had furnished for me. Randolph had forewarned me that Albertha was covetous, but it was his sister Rosamund, her pinched face betraying imminent fear of spinsterhood, who abruptly asked, "How many French dresses did you bring, Jennie?"

"Thirty-four." Randolph laughed. "Not to mention countless hats, shoes, parasols, and linens. Getting all of it into trunks for the trip across the Channel was quite the undertaking."

His careless remark conveyed that my clothing had required a separate ship. Rosamund's lips tightened in a disapproving moue. "As much as that?" She herself wore a brown day dress so plain that it looked as if she'd taken it from her maidservant.

"I'm told Americans tend to prefer foreign styles," remarked Lady Frances.

"It's very vulgar," said Albertha eagerly, though she also appeared as if she'd borrowed that ridiculously outdated bonnet. "Why do they feel they must flaunt their wealth?"

As if I wasn't sitting right before them. As if this overwrought estate wasn't flaunting one's wealth. But as Albertha narrowed her eyes in glee at my discomfiture, I saw it for what it was: envy. For all the vaunted historic grandeur, those faded spaces on the walls spoke for themselves. The Spencer-Churchills had come down in the world, been obliged to sell off valuables, while I was the upstart American who dressed too fine for her own good. And while instinct warned me that I should downplay my finery as paternal overindulgence, I heard Papa's voice in my mind: *Jennie, never let anyone make you think less of yourself. Promise me.*

At the time, I hadn't understood him. Now, I did.

"Americans appreciate quality," I said. "France offers it."

Albertha gasped. "The French are barbarians who exiled their emperor!"

Lady Frances's voice turned razor-thin. "Albertha, you know I detest talk of politics over tea. Please, do refrain from it."

Before Albertha could reply to her chastisement, Randolph drawled, "Moreover, seeing as you've never set foot outside England, you're in no position to judge."

"Everyone says it," Albertha flared. "George—"

"Bah." Randolph waved a dismissive hand. "Honestly. When has George been an authority on anything? Neither of you ever read a newspaper."

"Randolph." Lady Frances shot him a look. "Is this necessary?"

"Yes." He came to his feet. "She's a dull-witted fool."

Tension crackled in the air. Then Albertha lunged up, as well. "You think you can march in here with your rich American bride and insult us? I hope her fine silks and parasols from France are enough to pay your rent elsewhere."

My husband chuckled, bringing an ugly flush to her face. "As soon as our London townhome is finished, we'll relieve you of our fine silks and parasols, have no fear."

"Townhome? In London?" Albertha swerved to the duchess. "How can they afford it? I thought they were only receiving an annuity under the marriage agreement."

Lady Frances went white as her teacup.

"My father," I heard myself say. "He acquired it for us." I refrained from asking how she could possibly have been apprised of our financial arrangement.

Albertha threw me a contemptuous snort. "And a townhome as well. Vulgar, indeed."

My husband said coldly, "One more word and I'll not be responsible for my actions."

She stormed out in an enraged rustle of skirts. Lady Frances said thinly, "You must be exhausted, Jennie dear. So much excitement. Please, allow me to see you to your rooms."

Randolph accompanied us. Once his mother left, after murmuring something inaudible in his ear, he gave me an apologetic shrug and lit his delayed cigarette.

"Welcome to the family. Charming, aren't they?"

"What on earth was that about?" I asked, even as I eyed the narrow four-poster bedstead and wondered how both of us were supposed to fit into it.

"The usual." He exhaled a plume of smoke. "Money. Albertha is counting the hours until my father drops dead so she can pillage the estate. While my brother, as you plainly saw, prefers to let her do the bludgeoning while he keeps himself away, doing whatever it is he does."

"It was . . ." I had difficulty finding the appropriate words.

"Awful. Tedious. Typical. George insisted on marrying her in the mistaken impression that her status would make up for her lack of intelligence. You'd think a daughter of the Duke of Abercorn would have a measure of both. Instead, she's avaricious, shallow, and, worst of all, stupid."

I didn't know what to say. He finished his cigarette and kissed my cheek. "I'll see you at dinner." As he moved to the door, I finally dislodged the knot in my throat. "Dinner?"

He sighed. "Rest after tea is mandatory. We're not expected to emerge from our chambers until dinnertime, regardless of whether we're tired or not."

"But we are in our chamber," I said.

"No." He sighed again. "Mine is in the opposite wing, my child-hood room."

"We're expected to sleep apart during our stay?" I was aghast.

"We can always creep into each other's beds like the forbidden lovers we were." He winked. "Albertha will be so outraged, perhaps we'll give her a well-deserved apoplexy."

Our move to London couldn't come soon enough, I thought, as I yanked at my corset to recline on that musty bed.

My stomach was churning. I felt inexplicably nauseous. I blamed it on the haste Lady Frances had mentioned; it seemed as if time had sped up since Randolph and I were given leave to marry, the preparations for my dowry, the wedding, and our honeymoon pass-ing over me like a swift fog. Only during our stay at the château had I caught my bearings, reveling in our nights together, where we'd made up for our first attempt. He'd been considerate and ap-preciative, murmuring how beautiful I was and how lucky he felt to call me his wife. If he'd still not ignited in me quite the passion I anticipated, imbibed, I suspected, from reading too many French romances, I told myself it didn't matter. As Clarita said, what was important now was how we conducted ourselves.

But as I closed my eyes to seek a few hours of respite before fac-ing his family again, I couldn't stop from wondering if my quea-siness might signal more than I could admit only weeks into my marriage.

"SUNDAY SERVICES TAKE three hours at least, and the teas are in-terminable," I confided to Clarita. "They already frown enough that Randolph and I refuse to attend the services, seeing as neither of us believes in such things, so I can't escape the tea."

We walked in the gardens designed by Capability Brown. She'd come to visit me at my request. After two weeks in Blenheim, I needed my own fortifications and sent word to Paris. Though taken aback, the duchess couldn't refuse once I explained I would require my sister's help for my upcoming move to London and debut season as Randolph's wife. "At dinner, Their Graces insist on formal dress," I continued. "They must cut every joint themselves at the head of the table in that icebox of a great hall, then the plates are passed down to each of us in turn. The food is nearly cold by the time it reaches us from the kitchens and practically inedible after they've seen to its distribution."

Clarita giggled. "And do they always keep those jugs by their chairs? I haven't seen jugs like that since when we were at Miss Green's."

"Only one water closet, remember? The jugs must go everywhere they do. Imagine the disaster should the urge overcome you when you're thirty rooms away. There's no such thing as convenience here. After dinner, we repair to the Vandyke Room for the most insipid pastimes: games of whist or reading poetry aloud, while the men smoke cigars and drink all the brandy. My fingers ache from playing the piano to entertain them. It's so tedious that His Grace usually pushes the clock forward an hour to hasten our retirement. Then we kiss each other good night, light our tapers, and stumble up the staircase to our chambers in the pitch dark, praying we don't trip on a step and break our neck."

"No gaslight? But, why? Mama just had it installed in her flat. It smells funny, but now, at the turn of a lever, *voilà: la lumière.*"

"*La lumière* here is wax, like everything else." I felt myself grimace. "I cannot wait for the hour when we depart for London. Randolph tells me the renovations are nearly complete. I can't imagine why it's taken this long, except that I insisted on two working bathrooms. As it stands now, my own jug is getting plenty of use."

She came to a halt. "Are you passing much water?"

"Why?" I lowered my voice, though the duchess and her daughters were in their rooms for the mandatory nap, Her Grace having sniffed when informed that my sister and I would take a walk outside rather than be separated until dinner. "Is it unusual?"

"It might be." She let her gaze trail over me. "You do look particularly radiant. And you've gained weight, haven't you?"

"All those cakes at tea and sauces at dinner," I said quickly. "I'll get fat as a cow at this rate. They won't eat anything not smothered in butter or cream. When I asked for a fresh apple the other day, they looked at me as if I'd lost my mind."

She grasped my sleeve. "Jennie. This isn't about apples. What aren't you telling me?"

I cast another surreptitious glance toward the palace, though we were far beyond earshot. "I missed my menses. I think . . . I may be with child."

"How wonderful!" She started to embrace me, then stopped. "So soon? It's only been a month since you . . ." Her eyes widened. For what seemed an interminable moment, she looked unable to speak. Then she breathed. "The meeting at the café . . . ?"

"I'm afraid so." Now that I'd admitted it, I was quite certain of it. The nausea had only worsened, especially in the morning; I couldn't keep blaming the change in my diet for the continuing upset.

She went so pale now, I thought she might swoon. Instead, she composed herself enough to rebuke, "You certainly took an enormous risk. Imagine the scandal had Mama denied you her approval. You'd have been forbidden to ever set foot in society again."

"Yes," I said, with what I hoped sounded like sincere repentance. "But I'm married now. Is a month after marriage really too soon?"

"How would I know? You'd have to consult a midwife." She paused again. "Have you told Randolph?"

"Not yet. He's been so busy with our home in London and preparing for his first speech in the House—"

"*What* are you waiting for? If you conceived before the wedding, he was certainly party to it. Let him break the news to his family, though from what you've told me, it won't go over well if they discover the time of conception."

"Lady Frances has borne eleven children, eight of whom survived," I said glumly. "I should think she's well-informed as to when a babe ought to appear after marriage."

"She also wears bonnets from the last century." Clarita hooked her arm in mine. "She doesn't seem to be someone who cares to notice what doesn't please her."

"What am I going to do? The child is due a month before it should be."

"You'll figure that out later. Right now, you must tell Randolph. The sooner he announces the joyous event, the better it will go— for all three of you."

HIS GRACE TOASTED us at dinner, and Randolph flushed with pride after his brother George, already well into his cups, drawled, "It should be recorded in Burke's *Peerage* as the swiftest consummation of an aristocratic marriage in the history of such marriages." He and Albertha had two daughters and a son of their own, who shared the nurseries with Sarah; I'd not seen much of them, as children in Blenheim were restricted in their nursery, but I'd heard them rampaging upstairs, threatening to crack the frescoes on the ceilings. Neither Albertha nor her husband seemed to have much time or care for them.

The duchess congratulated me with a murmured "Motherhood is a blessing," but I detected the frost in her tone—though, as Clarita surmised, she'd never bring herself to mention it. Moreover, it had become apparent to me that Randolph was her favorite, the son on whom she'd pinned her expectations of exalting the family name, seeing as his dissipated older brother must inherit the title. A grandson by Randolph would be welcome, no matter when he'd been conceived, as Clarita's quick look in my direction confirmed.

Randolph tiptoed to my chamber that night in his full-length bed shirt and a preposterous tasseled cap, a candle cupped between his palms. After having startled the maid who slept on a truckle in the antechamber so she could be ready in the morning for my toilette, he sent her away as I laughed to see him looking so foolish.

"Take off that ridiculous cap. What are you now, an errant schoolboy?"

Tossing the cap aside, he set the candle on the bedside table. "Would my lady Randolph accept the pleasure of her errant schoolboy's company this evening?"

I pulled aside the sheets. "Lady Randolph would."

It was the first time I experienced the passion I feared we lacked. My body had become very sensitive, as if every inch of my skin had grown extra nerves; he had me gasping and clutching him as he brought me to climax. Afterward, as he lay with his chest heaving and arms outstretched, he said, "This will be a rather close call."

"Do they *know* when it was conceived?" I said in alarm.

He put a finger to my lips. "Hush. They suspect, but they'll never speak of it, not even among themselves. You're my wife. What is there to question?"

"Albertha might question it," I said, recalling her resentment at our meeting. I'd taken care since then to avoid her whenever possible, and in a house this size, it wasn't too difficult. "And if she does, your brother might see fit to voice it."

"No one would give credence to anything that comes out of that stupid woman's mouth, George least of all. He barely tolerates her. Come here." He snuggled me into the crook of his arm. "With that said, we should still be careful about how the birth comes about."

"Something we've not been successful at thus far," I grumbled. "Wasn't that contraption you wore supposed to prevent this complication?"

"According to the Prince's secretary, it was." I felt his chuckle under my hand on his chest. "I was assured HRH relies on them religiously to prevent him siring bastards by the dozens. Her Majesty refuses him any part in her royal business, for fear her state papers might end up between one of his numerous doxies' thighs."

"I'd have settled for one prevention," I said.

He went silent. Then he said, "Are you not happy about it?"

I had to gather my thoughts. I hadn't taken time to decipher my feelings about it, being too engrossed in averting the scandal. Was I happy? I supposed I should be. It was part of the expectation of marriage: to bear children and start a family. But now that it was upon me . . .

"I might have hoped for more time," I said at length. "We're going to London. It will be my introductory season as your wife. I'd rather not be received with my belly jutting before me."

"All those fine silks from Paris can be adjusted." He chuckled, kissing my forehead. "You'll be spectacular regardless. You'll devastate society. Look at the impact you've already made here, under these strenuous conditions."

"Hardly reassuring."

Randolph cupped my chin, lifting my face to his. "You'll be a wonderful mother, Jennie."

"Will I?" Sudden fear gripped me. "I don't know anything about raising a child."

"You will learn." He kissed me again. "You didn't know anything about how to make a child either, and look at us now: we've done the job rather nicely."

FOURTEEN

1874–1875

My first season in London began with catastrophe. It was a long-standing tradition for an established female member of the aristocracy to introduce new family arrivals by attending the queen's annual "drawing room"—a euphemism for official presentation to Her Majesty, ostensibly out of her thirteen-year mourning for her much-mourned consort, Prince Albert, though Victoria had made clear her resentment of the public outcry that obliged her to return to her duties by donning unrelieved black and a white veil to obscure her face.

Nevertheless, meeting her required a luxurious appearance, despite her disregard for her own, and Lady Frances was adamant that we must attend. For the season, I'd ordered a new wardrobe; the fine silks couldn't be adjusted, and Papa was experiencing a sudden boost in his fortunes, his newspaper stocks soaring. He sent me extra money, with a letter demanding I show everyone in England how an American lady ought to appear before the queen. I'd splurged accordingly.

But Lady Frances drove me to distraction with her critique of everything I wore, down to the stockings under my buttercup-yellow silk dress. She didn't think its color or the matching ostrich-plumed bonnet at all appropriate for a woman with child, even if I was too delighted with my new house on Curzon Street to pay her any mind. I'd used some of the extra income to furnish it to my taste, a cozy relief after the gargantuan antiquity of Blenheim; it had the functioning water closets I'd demanded, though the plumbing tended to back up in heavy downpours—all too frequent in London—and the racket of hansoms passing in the street, of itinerant merchants shouting out their wares, and of organ-grinders was constant. Still, it was my and Randolph's abode, where we could do as we pleased, prompting my defiance of my mother-in-law's demand for less ostentatious apparel. I reminded her that she should count herself fortunate if I didn't throw up during the presentation. Even though my nausea had abated, being trussed up in a corset to attend the queen was hardly ideal for a woman in my state, and I was only undertaking the effort for my mother-in-law's sake. In truth, I couldn't have cared less about meeting Her Majesty.

We arrived at Buckingham Palace under one of those epic downpours that turned my water closets into sewers. The crush of carriages disgorging ladies of quality, with new daughters-in-law, cousins from abroad, and aspiring nieces in tow, turned the prolonged delay in the audience hall into an ordeal. I was sweating under my garments, sick with the heat, for while Her Majesty was expected to make her way into the hall to greet us, she chose to remain ensconced on her throne, obliging her officials to undertake a hasty reorganization.

We were ordered to queue in order of precedence at the Throne Room door. Lady Frances's rank positioned us at the front. Once the door was opened, the hours of waiting spurred the ladies to frenzy. Those obliged to stand at the rear of the line shoved forward as if they might be left stranded, propelling those of us in the front over the threshold, staggering against our skirts and grasping at each other's mantles to keep from tumbling onto our faces before the queen. It was all I could do to fend off the onslaught, more concerned at the moment by not bringing injury upon myself than by how I appeared.

That evening, after Lady Frances left for Blenheim in humiliation, Clarita listened in dumbfounded dismay while Randolph burst into laughter as I described the finale to the fiasco.

"You can imagine our dishevelment," I said, sipping a brandy. "I lost a shoe and my hat in the stampede, and could scarcely find air to breathe, much less curtsy. Her Majesty took one look at us and retired without a word, stepping past the cloaks, gloves, and various items the ladies had shed in their desperation. I'm certain she'll never deign to receive any of us again."

My husband had to wipe tears of mirth from his eyes. "Oh, my darling. You should write it down for publication. The newspapers would have a field day with this."

"Not how one would hope for one's first appearance at court to go," I replied.

"Don't worry," he said. "It's been well-established that Her Majesty would prefer to never receive anyone again, so this only gives her another excuse to delegate such responsibilities to Their Highnesses of Wales."

Clarita said anxiously, "Does this mean we're barred from the season?" She'd expended Papa's money on a wardrobe, too, missives volleying between her and Mama in Paris, detailing fabrics and styles, and rumors of other ladies who might appear in similar designs—a calamity that must be avoided at any cost.

Randolph lit a cigarette. "Have no fear on that account. After my maiden speech in the House, we'll be invited everywhere. London will vie to welcome the fabled Jerome sisters. Leonard's hard-earned gains expended on Worth will not go to waste."

His maiden speech was so well-received, in fact, that Disraeli commended him and invited himself to dinner. I labored for days with Clarita on the guest list, the table settings, and the menu. In my eagerness to excel, I hired a French-trained chef, whose disdain for British cuisine proved too challenging to overcome. In addition, Disraeli was almost seventy, with an ailing liver that forbade more than a single cognac, so champagne was out of the question.

Regardless, I found the satiric prime minister charming; born Jewish, he'd climbed to the highest rungs of power, and his keen wit proved equally attractive. He complimented my menu's incomprehensible mishmash, my chef having pitched a fit at recipes that offended his sensibilities, and after Clarita and I played the piano to his appreciation, he took me aside and murmured, "His Highness has expressed eagerness to share your company. Do have a care, Lady Randolph. Bertie's appetites often exceed propriety and, I fear, your chef's Gallic capabilities."

I must have turned pale, for he patted my arm. "Providing you establish what you will and will not condone, you'll find him delightful. I'm told most ladies do."

As I entered my fifth month of pregnancy, I suddenly felt like my old self again, full of vigor, and was delighted when the invitation arrived to attend a gala hosted by Their Royal Highnesses, in honor of Tsarevich Alexander of Russia and his Danish wife, Marie, who'd come to visit England. The tsarevna and Princess Alexandra were sisters, and the gala would be held in Stafford House, residence of Their Graces of Sutherland.

It was the culmination of the season. I commissioned Worth's atelier for a black velvet dress, with a cunning set of panels to disguise my enlarged stomach, accessorized with Papa's diamond star in my coiffure. To complement my ensemble, Randolph wore his black tails with a starched wing-collar shirt and piqué vest, emerald cuff links, and his opal lapel pin. Clarita donned a blue-silk gown with an extravagant bustle that enhanced her generous figure.

Amidst the peacock excess of the other ladies, I stood out in my sobriety. The tsarevna, whose own expenditures on Worth were renowned, exclaimed as I curtsied before her, "How charming. Like

night herself, with a single star in her hair: I must take note of it."
Her husband, the burly and towering Russian heir, gibed, "Is this
the American girl we've heard so much about? Here so soon?" al-
luding to my recent marriage, I assumed, as if I should still be at
home taking pleasure in my husband's bed.

I thought him as coarse as his wife was enchanting.

Bertie of Wales was flown with drink by the time he weaved his
way through the crowd toward me. He hadn't changed from the
only time I'd seen him, in Cowes, still disconcertingly cherubic
with his bushel beard and pale, lascivious eyes as he said, "Lady
Randolph, do you mean to avoid me all night?"

I'd been conversing with the Duchess of Sutherland, whose exceptional character disproved my assumption that Lady Frances
epitomized the breed; as I turned to the prince, she laughed. "Your
Highness, I fear Lady Randolph must avoid further pursuit. Every
gentleman present save the tsarevich has charged at her as if she
were the fox at the hunt."

"I am not every man." He seized my hand. "We shall dance, my
lady. I have it on excellent authority that you waltz as exquisitely
as you play the piano."

He waltzed quite well himself, despite his portliness. As we
soared across the dance floor, I saw his wife turn away. In contrast
to her lively sister, who was clearly in love with her Romanov bear,
Alexandra had the impassive countenance of long-suffering regal
endurance.

"Yes," breathed Bertie of Wales in my face at the end of our dance.
"I wasn't misinformed. I would experience more of your charms,
Lady Randolph."

"Perhaps dinner at my home next month?" I stepped back, fan-
ning away the heat of the waltz and odor of his overindulgence in
wine.

"Will your husband be there?" he growled.

"Where else would he be?" I replied, taken aback but careful not to show it. Was he so drunk he'd failed to see how pregnant I was? "My charms are not exclusive, Your Highness, but they are limited in their availability." As I dared to turn to where Randolph observed us with a laconic smile, the prince guffawed. "The devil himself couldn't resist you. Dinner it is."

I glanced at him over my shoulder. He wagged his finger. "See that your chef procures truffles and kidney beans. Disraeli warned me, my lady. I'll not digest soufflé."

During our carriage ride home, I voiced my dismay. "He made advances in front of everyone. Before his wife. To a woman visibly with child. What kind of gentleman does that?"

"No one ever accused His Highness of being a gentleman." Randolph slid mordant eyes at me. "The fact that you're with child only increases the attraction for him. You're most definitely married, and it's a prerequisite to adultery."

"I'm married to you, who was also right there. Has he no sense of propriety?"

"Why should he? When he can eat at any trough and no one dares refuse him?"

"Well, I most certainly shall refuse him."

Randolph chuckled. "I'm counting on it. He'll chase after you in frustration, and all his circle will follow in his wake. We'll find ourselves invited into his company, while others compete desperately for an invitation. What did I tell you? Belly or not, you've just devastated society in your first season."

"You're not jealous?" I asked, surprised by his calculating equanimity.

"Should I have reason to be?" he replied.

"Of course not." I paused. "He wants the menu changed for dinner," I muttered, for lack of anything better to say.

"Indeed. No propriety, and the appetite of a serf. Truffles and kidney beans on toast. Long live the empire, though I fear it shall perish of colic."

DESPITE MY MISGIVINGS, Bertie was well-behaved during our dinner. It was a small occasion, only him and a few elite guests, including Lord Lionel de Rothschild, the first practicing Jewish member of Parliament. I also invited Disraeli, who arrived wearing a plum-velvet waistcoat and a sardonic grin. Perhaps the presence of the venerable politician kept Bertie on his best behavior. He expressed approval of both my menu and my entertainment, departing with a polite kiss on my hand and not a suggestive word uttered, to my relief.

Following the races at Ascot, a thrilling experience for me with my love of horsemanship, and then the annual regatta at Cowes, where I enjoyed returning to the scene of Randolph's and my courtship, the season finally came to a close, and everybody retreated to their country estates to languish and gossip about what everyone else had worn and done.

Randolph and I went to visit Mama, who'd turned her salon into a modest occasion. The bohemian delights of Paris invigorated me; despite my advancing pregnancy, I went riding in the bois and shopping with my sisters. Now in her fifteenth year and recently graduated from her boarding academy, Leonie was eager to make her debut. I promised to introduce her once she turned eighteen, as her prospects in France were uncertain at best.

Leaving Clarita in Paris, we returned to England in early November to spend the holidays with Randolph's family. I dreaded Christmas in the confines of Blenheim, but there was nothing I could do to avoid it. Upon our arrival, Lady Frances took one look at my prominent stomach and declared, "So large, with the due date still months away. It must be a boy."

I clung to the hope that my babe would take its time, at least until after our return to London, even if the increasingly urgent kicking inside me warned otherwise. Still, I made light of the sleeplessness that now plagued me, though Lady Frances's restriction of all unnecessary activity should have caused me to lapse into somnolence. Instead, while Randolph took up grouse shooting, I went for restless ambles in the gardens, his sisters seated on the terrace watching me like sentinels, and suffered prolonged teas where Lady Frances plied me with cake as if I were starving her grandchild of essential British nourishment.

Finally, I couldn't bear it another minute. Rising early one morning after Randolph left for one of his shoots, I ordered a cart hitched to a pony and took myself for a drive into the countryside. Recent storms had left the grounds lush with grass, and the late November wind buffeted the oaks as I urged the pony to a canter, delighting in the gusts of air against my face. I knew I'd be severely chastised upon my return for such flagrant endangerment of my delicate state, but I was with child, not an invalid. If I didn't do something, I feared I might give birth out of sheer defiance at one of Lady Frances's teas.

I laughed to myself as I envisioned it. In her world, childbirth must be scheduled like everything else, without any deviation from the ordained time line. To have one of her sacred teas so rudely interrupted would be the height of poor manners—

A sudden pang caused me to let go of the reins. As it cut off my breath, I drew the cart to a halt and stood panting, feeling another, stronger pain crest inside me. It doubled me over. I couldn't even gasp from the intensity of it. As I felt water splash between my legs, horror overcame me. In my heedlessness, I'd traveled far from the palace. I'd have to make it back quickly, lest I deliver my child in this cart.

Yanking at the pony, who intuited my distress and retraced the route we'd taken, I was clamping back on a howl of helpless agony by the time the stables came into view.

The stable hands rushed to assist me. The entire palace staff was alerted as I was bundled through the nearest entrance into the family chaplain's bottom-floor room. Lady Frances arrived, exclaiming in dismay, "But it's not time yet. How can this be?"

"Send for Randolph," I hissed at her through my teeth.

"Surely we'd do best to send for a midwife," she replied, the color draining from her face as the maidservants, all village girls with more presence of mind, stripped me to my shift and propped me on pillows upon the narrow chaplain bedstead.

"*Fetch my husband,*" I shrieked. Even through my pain, I took pleasure in her recoil and swift retreat, her daughters following in a fluster at her heels.

I doubted Randolph would make it in time. But if his mother was occupied elsewhere, she wouldn't be here, gauging every breath I took. If I must give birth with only maidservants to attend me, so be it.

LADY FRANCES DISPLAYED initiative by dispatching urgent word to London for the family physician. The local village doctor was much closer, however, and once word reached him, he arrived within the hour. My doubt concerning Randolph's timely appearance was also disproved. He was pacing outside the door by my third hour of labor; by my eighth, the entire family held vigil. I didn't know it at the time, nor would it have mattered if I had. After refusing chloroform, determined to marshal through with my wits intact, I now lay in pummeled exhaustion. I could barely lift my eyes, let alone my head, to the swaddled bundle the doctor set in my arms.

"A healthy son, Lady Randolph. See for yourself."

He had a scrunched-up face and wisps of reddish hair; at my touch, he let out a wail.

"Those are, without a doubt, our family lungs," declared Randolph. "Darling, he's already enraged and not an hour since his arrival. What shall we call him?"

I smiled weakly. "Leonard. For my father." I rather thought he had Papa's lungs.

Randolph gave a tight smile. "Mamma insists on a proper dynastic name. He is, after all, an heir to our duchy. She suggests Winston, after the first Duke of Marlborough's father. Would Winston Leonard Spencer-Churchill be agreeable to you?"

"Yes." I was having trouble staying awake, barely feeling the babe taken from my arms. "It sounds very distinguished . . ."

LADY FRANCES INSISTED on a wet nurse, obliging me to undergo the painful binding of my breasts to dry out my milk. The palace nurseries were well-stocked, though like most everything else, the items were timeworn and old-fashioned. She was so appalled when Mama sent congratulatory shifts and stockings from Paris, along with Clarita, that to ensure her new grandson wouldn't start out life in foreign garb, she ordered replacements from a British clothier.

He'd be raised at Blenheim, of course. London was much too unsanitary, she declared, and Winston would have everything he required at the estate. Though it was apparent by his weight and robust temperament—he took to the wet nurse with greed and slept through the night at once—that my child couldn't possibly be premature, she swept this inconvenient fact aside in her joy at a grandson she could mold to her specifications.

I submitted to her authority. As enchanted as I was by my son's sturdy little body and fist clenching, now that he was here, motherhood terrified me. I felt myself entirely unsuited to the immensity of the task and relieved to let his overbearing grandmother take charge. Winston would indeed lack for nothing, while I couldn't imagine assuming permanent residence in the palace, forsaking the life in London I'd only just started to enjoy.

"We have plenty of time," I told Clarita after the New Year celebrations of 1875 and my twenty-first birthday in January, as we prepared to depart Blenheim. "I can visit him here as often as I like. For the time being, I leave him in capable hands."

My sister nodded. "You do, indeed. You'd think Lady Frances gave birth to him herself, the way she carries on. And she has all this mysterious maternal experience you claim you lack."

"Do you think it selfish of me?" I paused in the oversight of my packing. "Should I stay, regardless? I could always learn, I suppose. Mama had no experience at first yet she managed to raise the three of us."

"In New York City," replied Clarita. "With Dobbie and plenty of other occupations besides her children. What does Randolph say?"

"He has his obligations in the House. In a few weeks, we must prepare for the season. He needs me in London more than Winston does here."

"As do I." Clarita handed me my jewelry case. "And don't forget that Leonie is visiting for the season, so she needs you in London, too. Whatever would you do here if you stayed? You can't even burp the child without Lady Frances present to supervise it."

I let out an uneasy laugh. "True. He'll be spoiled by an excess of attention."

Yet after I kissed my child goodbye on his milky brow and our carriage pulled onto the road to London, I kept looking through the rear window, wondering if I was making a mistake that I would come to regret.

FIFTEEN

1875

My lingering doubt over leaving my infant son prompted me to seek a nanny whom I could trust to report on his welfare. While I had no doubt Winston would enjoy his privileges, I didn't want Lady Frances inculcating in him the same traits displayed by George, who idled his time in vain pursuits while waiting to inherit the title. My son was half Jerome; his maternal grandfather worked for a living, and Winston mustn't forget it. If I couldn't be there to remind him, I must have a substitute to do so for me.

Lady Frances protested she was perfectly capable of hiring a nanny when the time came. I went ahead, regardless. Making inquiries of my American friends in London, several of whom had followed in my footsteps and wed into the aristocracy, I located one Mrs. Elizabeth Everest of Kent, who resided in the home of a widowed reverend, where she'd overseen his brood of six. She came with impeccable references and, most important, a sensible attitude, neither punitive nor indulgent. Hiring her on the spot, I sent her to Blenheim with the warning that she'd face opposition but must remain firm in her charge, as I was the one paying her salary.

Just before the season started, I attended one of Randolph's speeches in the House, curious to hear him declaim. Crowding with the other wives in the suffocating upper Ladies' Gallery of the Commons, known as the parliamentary cage, I took note that while he had a distinctive presence and voice—he stood out in his pencil-thin attire and dramatic cravat—he was also much younger than the majority of his peers, so he adopted a haranguing tone to mimic them.

When he expressed discontent later over the obdurate rejection of his measure, as well as the lack of newspaper coverage, I said, "Perhaps a change in delivery is required to sway them."

He eyed me over his cognac. "Such as?"

"A bit more flair. I read the newspapers; much of what's debated in the House makes no sense to the average person. A less ponderous tone would attract attention. If you like, I can help compose your speeches. Clarita always tells me my letters are fit to be published."

He snorted. "Letters to one's sister are not a literary qualification." But then he sipped his cognac thoughtfully. "You do write well, however, so I suppose there's no harm in having you revise my next speech. But only between us. I can't have it said my wife does my work for me."

He liked my revision so much that it became our secret, especially after he received his first round of applause and approval on his measure. A mention in *The Times* praising his fiery delivery ensured that he submitted all his subsequent drafts to me for editorial changes, which in turn helped gain him notice as a skilled and modern orator.

With the season upon us, Leonie arrived from Paris bursting with excitement to partake of whatever she could. I flung open the doors of our house to entertain Bertie of Wales and his exclusive set, whose influence could bolster Randolph's career and bring my sisters into notice.

In return, I was expected to appear at every major event held by others, which demanded unceasing variety in my wardrobe. Papa had suffered another reversal of fortune, with funds suddenly limited, so I had to resort to altering my seasonal dresses at home, Clarita and I switching out bodices and trims to freshen styles. I made a statement of my diamond star, and regardless of their outdated settings, employed my Marlborough gems to spectacular effect by pairing them with simple dark attire, eschewing the new fashionable dyes that gave gowns flaming hues and left searing rashes on their occupants' skin.

When the prince announced that he'd been appointed to tour India as Her Majesty's representative, a belated effort to instill some duty in his sybaritic lifestyle, Randolph and I held a spectacular bon voyage gala for him, with a menu satisfying his peculiar culinary preferences. This time, as I was now without the belly, he flirted shamelessly while I held him at bay, ensuring he left England with a very satisfied impression of his association with Lord and Lady Randolph.

I was looking forward to a much-needed respite in Paris when disaster struck.

RANDOLPH BURST INTO the parlor to tell me, leaving me aghast as he frantically lit a cigarette.

"But this isn't anything in which we can be involved," I said. "George has gone and done the unthinkable, abandoning his wife to carry on with this Lady Aylesford, who's married to His Highness's best friend. No good can possibly come of it."

My husband raked a hand through his hair, cracking its pomade. I'd never seen him so disheveled. "We're already involved. George demands a divorce. In order to obtain one, he must have royal consent. We can hardly fault him for wanting to be rid of Albertha, after having put up with her inanity for as long as he has."

His defense of his brother took me aback; he'd never had a kind word for George, often referring to him as a blight on the Spencer-Churchill name.

"Be that as it may, they have children together," I said. "It is their marriage to sort out. We cannot think to interfere."

"Their marriage is over. If I don't interfere, George threatens to hand over the prince's letters to the newspapers. The letters are to

Lady Aylesford from Bertie, her husband's best friend. She was his mistress. George thinks he can force royal consent to his divorce by threatening to publish the letters."

I clutched at the back of my chair. "Has he lost his mind? It would be our ruin."

"Though I doubt it'll come as any surprise to Lord Aylesford," said Randolph drily. "I did tell you that Bertie eats at any trough. But he likes his aperitifs separate from his main meal; he's opposed to divorce, particularly within his circle. Divorce complicates things for him, as unattached mistresses are more difficult to manage. For that very reason, he's dispatched his best friend from India forthwith, as it falls upon the husband to bring the wayward wife to heel lest it turn into a royal scandal. But the voyage takes well over a month, and George isn't about to wait."

"It will be a scandal anyway, if His Highness learns she gave over his private letters to her new lover," I said in growing panic.

"Which is why I must undertake the negotiations on my brother's behalf and present the letters directly to Alexandra," he replied, to my horror. "She'll have no wish to see incriminating evidence of her husband's philandering made public. Let her persuade Her Majesty to grant the divorce. Before Lord Aylesford arrives or Bertie can lift an objection, it will be done."

"You would go to the princess with letters written by her husband to a mistress? Why would you do such a thing?"

"Why else?" he said impatiently. "She'll never receive George under these circumstances, nor will the queen countenance any request for divorce. He gave me the letters with the understanding that I would take care of it. Jennie, he's our future duke, whether we like it or not. I'm his brother. This situation could adversely affect our standing. If I show Alexandra the letters, she'll see that both George and Lady Edith have their divorces, to keep it quiet."

"Randolph, you mustn't. It's too great a risk. What if she thinks you're trying to blackmail her? Inform your father at once. Let him instill reason in your brother."

He guffawed. "Since when has anyone instilled reason in George? He wed Albertha over everyone's objections and has now absconded from Blenheim to elope with that woman, leaving his wife in a puddle of woe. He's gone mad as Byron. The only way to put an end to it is to use the situation to our advantage. Those who most stand to lose are Bertie, his wife, and the queen."

I didn't agree. I saw all too clearly what we stood to lose. I doubted Princess Alexandra would appreciate delivery of letters confirming her husband's debauchery, and Bertie would be outraged. We could destroy everything we'd set out to accomplish.

In my desperation, I said, "At least let me accompany you. Her Highness may be more inclined to react favorably if she feels she has a sympathetic ear in the room."

He considered me. "Very well. But, Jennie, she must be thoroughly terrified by the implications if we have any chance to succeed."

HAVING BARELY SPOKEN three words to the princess before, I felt cold sweat break out under my gown as we were ushered into her drawing room in Marlborough House in St. James's, Their Highnesses' London residence. With the season over, Alexandra should have left for Sandringham, the Norfolk estate she preferred. In fact, as her head matron informed us, she was due to depart next week. She'd agreed to receive us only because Lord Randolph insisted it was an urgent matter.

When she entered the room, in a gray gown without jewelry, her lack of expression forewarned she was aware of the urgent matter. Such things couldn't be kept secret. Gossip traveled faster than fire; by now, the scandal of Edith Aylesford and George of Blandford must be on everyone's lips. The affair itself wouldn't have excited much comment. Infidelity was rife, even expected, providing those involved behaved with discretion. But it was deemed very poor judgment to cast aside one's social standing over an extramarital dalliance.

Thinking of how many dalliances she herself must have overlooked, and how her husband had made advances on me while she was in the same room, I was acutely uncomfortable and barely able to meet Alexandra's eyes as she ordered tea served. I held on to the delicate china cup as if I teetered on the edge of a scaffold. Once she told her ladies to withdraw, I braced myself. She would not have seen to privacy if she hadn't known what was afoot.

Randolph withdrew the parcel of letters from his jacket, setting them on the table between us. She took a cursory look at them. "How do these concern me?"

I had to admire her indifference, as if nothing beneath her warranted notice. Even as Randolph explained why she should be very concerned indeed, I already knew we'd made a terrible blunder. To me, his proposal sounded exactly as I'd feared, like blackmail, even as he said, "I think Your Highness will agree it would be better for all concerned if none of this came to light. Her Majesty will no doubt also concur that divorce is the only remedy."

It should have conveyed his dutiful willingness to turn the letters over so they couldn't be published. But then, to my disbelief, he did the unthinkable: he reached over to retrieve the parcel, indicating he wasn't prepared to surrender the evidence to her until she acted accordingly.

Her hand, on which only her wedding band shone, came down on the parcel, stopping him cold. "Thank you, my lord, for bringing this matter to my attention."

Only then must he have realized his error. He'd forced her to contend with a situation she had long pretended didn't exist. Her husband's mistresses might be legion, but her marriage depended on a decorous ignorance now torn asunder. Obliging her, the Princess of Wales, to bring her husband's infidelity before her mother-in-law, the queen, was unconscionable—a direct affront to her dignity and rank.

She rose to her feet, concluding the audience. As we made to depart, Randolph had gone visibly pale. Alexandra said, "Lady Randolph, a moment, if you please. You may wait in the antechamber, my lord."

The drawing room doors closing after him echoed in the stillness.

"I'm of the firm mind that you cannot possibly be a willing party to this unpleasantness," she said. "I realize that as an American, you were not born into our way of life, but even so, whom among us would countenance another's humiliation?"

Lowering my eyes, I murmured, "Your Highness, I cautioned my husband against it."

"Indeed. Yet it is our lot to bear. We must always stand by our husbands, even if we suffer for their poor judgment. I will not hold you responsible."

She motioned that I could depart. Feeling as if the polished floor under my feet had broken apart, I heard her add, "Unfortunately, I cannot promise the same for Lord Randolph."

"DUBLIN?" CLARITA STARED at me as if we'd been exiled to a penal colony in Australia. "But isn't Ireland beset by a dreadful famine?"

I tried to conceal my own distress. I'd returned to Paris after a three-week sojourn in New York with Randolph to visit my father, fleeing the purgatory in London after his failed attempt to coerce the princess. Alexandra immediately notified her husband; upon his precipitous return from India, Bertie declared Randolph "a knave and blackguard," in whose presence he'd never be seen again. He'd arrived too late, as had Lord Aylesford, to stop Lady Edith, and he was enraged that not only had she given over his letters, but they had been used against him. He persuaded the queen that under no circumstances could she consent to divorce. Not surprisingly, society was alerted to our disgrace, and the prince, in no mood to restrain his public remarks, declared that it would be a cold day in hell when he permitted even the son of a duke to coerce him. The Aylesfords agreed to separate, and George fled with Lady Edith to Holland, while the doors of all those we'd cultivated shut in our face.

"Under the circumstances, His Grace thought it wise to accept the viceroyalty when Her Majesty offered it," I now said. "It's considered an honor. Randolph will act as his father's secretary when not obliged to be in London for the House, while Lady Frances and I will . . ."

My voice faded as Mama said from her settee, "An honor? I hardly think that's the reason. More likely, Her Majesty decided in her wisdom that the Churchills must be sent away to allow for time to pass and tempers to soothe. What do you intend to do, precisely, in a savage country, where the English are thoroughly despised? I should think neither you nor Lady Frances will accomplish much of anything."

I'd been dreading her rebuke ever since Randolph's letter with the news arrived.

"We'll find a way to occupy ourselves," I said. "And if I have more spare time than expected, I'll spend it with Winston. He scarcely knows who I am."

Mama sniffed, conveying everything she wouldn't voice. Here was my comeuppance for ignoring her warnings, for plunging into marriage with an impulsive man, whose impaired reason due to his privilege had now been laid bare for all to see.

"Is there society in Dublin?" asked Clarita. "I'm having new dresses made for the season. Where shall I wear them if not in London?"

"I imagine there must be," said Mama drily. "Savage as it must be."

SIXTEEN

1876–1880

Ireland was indeed wild and dangerous, with murderous Fenians intent on establishing independence from England and the peasantry plagued by poverty, but it was also breathtakingly beautiful. Though Their Graces bore the expression of those who must endure the unthinkable, I found myself enthralled by the isle's rugged vales, its namesake emerald hue, and bracing, sea-laced air.

Clarita would have been relieved to discover there was indeed society, too; and as viceroy and lord lieutenant, the duke was expected to entertain it. But my sister, intent on securing a husband, accepted Fanny Ronalds's invitation to stay with her in London for the season instead, while Lady Frances and I organized receptions at the Viceroy Lodge, a drafty pile of stone that to my eyes possessed all of the stately discomfort of Blenheim.

I chose to live apart in the Little Lodge, an adjoining manor in the protective acreage of Phoenix Park. Mrs. Everest and Winston stayed with me; now in his second year, my son was determined to stand on his own and left us both breathless as he teetered about. I could see my father, as well as myself, in his persistence. While he physically favored Randolph's side of the family, in his heart my son was a Jerome.

"He'll need a firm hand once he reaches the age for school," Mrs. Everest told me after an afternoon spent keeping him from trampling or choking down the army of painted tin soldiers

Randolph had bought for him. "I fear he'll not be amenable to being told what to do."

"I wasn't amenable either," I said, smiling at my son as he lay curled in a blanket, exhausted from his struggle to decimate his soldiers. "I detested school."

"Well, like every child, he must learn." Mrs. Everest gathered him up in her arms, heaving a sigh as he nestled against her chest. "But all in good time, my lady. He has years yet to expunge his temper."

I felt a pang of jealousy at how he molded to her ample form. I'd taken pains to assure him that I was his mother, nearly bursting into tears when one night, as I saw him to bed, he exclaimed, "Mamma," and grabbed at my pendant. I couldn't tell if he thought my pendant was his mamma, but the very fact that he'd uttered the word filled my heart. I was determined to create a lasting bond with my child.

And I had plenty of time to do so. Randolph's career had been damaged by his actions, but he wasn't about to surrender. He threw himself into bolstering ties among his party, none of whom were particularly fond of the prince, and he was therefore often absent, either traveling with his father on an obligatory assignment or attending the House. It was the most time we'd been apart since our marriage. To fill my days, I went riding in the mornings, accepted invitations to tea, and dedicated the rest of my hours to Winston.

Then, in a fit of either boredom or compassion, Lady Frances announced that we must address the dire state of the peasantry, whose conditions, she'd been told, defied comprehension. She arranged a visit to Connaught, where we arrived to find hamlets of mire-sunken huts, populated by hollow-eyed women and emaciated children.

I'd never seen the like, even in the squalor of London. Lady Frances was dismayed as we descended from our carriage and nearly stepped upon the rotting carcasses of sheep left to decay where they'd fallen. Most of the men had immigrated abroad to find work, following the devastation of famines, abrupt shifts in land division, and the heedless rush to breed cattle, which croup and the unforgiving Irish winters had felled. Entire fields lay fallow, given over to makeshift graveyards. The doctor accompanying us advised caution, as typhoid, cholera, and consumption were endemic. The Irish peasants' life span, he grimly informed us, rarely exceeded thirty years, with hunger being the least of their afflictions. But when he extended masks soaked in medicinal preventives for us to wear, the duchess thrust him aside.

During our return to Dublin, her skirts crusted in mud from walking the hamlet and speaking to everyone she encountered, she said, "It's a disgrace." To that end, she set up her Irish Famine Relief Fund, funded by charity galas where the very landowners responsible for their tenants' misery were obliged to contribute. Word spread to London, abetted by Randolph, who made a speech saying that he was repulsed to call himself an Englishman after reading what I had described. My American friends and Lionel de Rothschild donated substantial sums. Armed with the money and her clout, Lady Frances dispatched her relief to the most stricken areas, winning praise for her dedication to the unfortunate.

All of which helped lift us from our disgrace, though not quite as much as perhaps Lady Frances had hoped, as Fanny Ronalds informed me when she came to visit.

I assumed her affair with my father was over, as she'd taken full-time residence in London, along with a new lover, the composer Arthur Sullivan. Yet she remarked that she'd visited Papa in New York just before the season, bewildering me, though I had no time to question her as she launched into a voluble account of the season's galas while we walked in the lodge gardens.

I feigned polite interest, concealing a stab of resentment that I'd not enjoyed the like, until she said, "I fear His Highness can't abide the Spencer-Churchill name in his presence." She watched me trail my fingers over the rosebushes. A thorn nicked me, making me recoil. "I don't mean to pry, Jennie, but the question on everyone's lips was, whatever got into your husband?"

"He thought he could resolve the matter," I said. "For all the good it did."

"Yes, it seems the remedy was more injurious than the offense. I fear there was much talk of it."

I went still. "People *know*?"

"Oh, not the particulars. Bertie has made no bones of his displeasure, but he's been surprisingly spare on the details. Yet seeing as Lady Edith Aylesford was once his mistress and he refuses to receive anyone associated with the Churchills, you can imagine the speculation."

"About Randolph? I hardly see why. He didn't leave his wife to take up with Lady Edith. George did that all on his own, putting us in this predicament."

"Yes, but George will inherit the title, so no one cares to criticize him. It's much easier to direct offense toward Randolph, given their considerable envy."

"Envy?" I felt the sting of blood on my fingertip as my hand bunched up.

"Why, yes. You had society at your feet. Everyone wanted either to be invited to Lady Randolph's home or to entertain her in theirs. An American, wed to a British lord, who attracted the prince's attentions. Come now, you can't be so naïve. And now this"—she looked about with a bemused air—"it's lovely, I suppose, if you like rustic charm. But hardly the place for you."

"I don't mind it. At least no one here condemns me for my husband's mistake."

"Indeed, though perhaps it will come as some consolation that if there's one name in your husband's family that His Highness will still tolerate, it's yours."

I'd always admired Fanny's candor. I'd been looking forward to her visit, but now I wished she hadn't come. Her conversation had broken apart the idyll I'd built around myself, the reasoning that Bertie simply needed time for his temper to cool. "Randolph only did as he thought best. His brother was determined to cast us into scandal, as Bertie surely knows."

"Yet I do not see Randolph with you, enjoying the dubious fruits of his endeavor. Is he often away these days?"

I paused. Something in her query plunged a blade down my spine. I thought in sudden alarm of his frequent absences, his humiliation at having to act as his father's secretary prompting him to depart for London at any excuse. I knew he had his obligations, that he attended his gentleman's club and dined with close friends, because he told me so in his letters, but I assumed he was restricted by the impossibility of gaining entrée anywhere the prince might be.

"He's not here at present because of his obligations in the House," I said, but I heard my uncertainty, as if I were suddenly trying to convince myself.

"So many obligations? Last I heard, he wasn't our prime minister."

I hardened my tone. "Fanny, if you have something to tell me, please do so."

She hesitated. "I don't wish to upset you. These things are unfortunately common. Only after his brother's disgrace, he should have a care . . . To him, it's no doubt meaningless. With husbands, such transgressions invariably are."

Her words struck me like a blow. "Transgressions?" I stared at her. "Are you implying that Randolph has strayed in some way?"

She sighed. "In one particular way. No man is immune to it. Believe me, I know."

I had to step back. Everything darkened around me, so that I stumbled against my skirts as I turned blindly toward the lodge. When I failed to contain my shock, Fanny took my arm and drew me to a nearby bench, sitting me down as if I were still that bewildered girl in New York, learning of her parents' estrangement.

She'd kept the truth of it from me as long as she could, but in the end, she hadn't lied. Smelling her cologne in the handkerchief she pressed into my hands, which brought back vivid memories of that tumultuous time, I had to bite back a scream.

"You have to compose yourself," she said quietly. "I thought you must have suspected by now. If there's the opportunity and the means to indulge it, few husbands will deny themselves."

"Does he . . . ?" I choked on the words.

"Oh, no. Nothing like that. From what I understand, there's no mistress. He merely indulges himself with whatever is available when he's away from you."

"With whatever is available . . . ?"

She averted her gaze. "Must I spell it out?"

"Brothels?" I said in disbelief.

Fanny nodded. "And some dancers in music halls. Quite meaningless, as I said."

"Since when?" I had to wrench my words out, reeling as the cascade of events that had led me to this moment overwhelmed and sundered me. It made sudden, horrible sense, Randolph's reckless offer to assist George, putting us in jeopardy: he'd done it because he understood the compulsion behind George's affair. Because he, too, had been unfaithful.

Fanny gave me a sad smile. "Probably not long, if my experience is worth noting. Husbands tend to stray after the first child is born, once the woman they married becomes more than their wife. They feel they must turn to others to satisfy their baser needs."

I drew in a jagged breath. "I will not tolerate it. I refuse to be my mother."

"Clara is actually whom you should emulate," she replied. "She not only tolerated it but accepted it until Leonard was accused of financial misdoing. She understood she could do nothing to prevent it, so why make a fuss?" Fanny paused. "Your mother and I were always in perfect accord. I knew my place while she was with him, and I never overstepped it. And despite everything, your father loved her. He still does. I was never the love of his life."

I couldn't speak.

"Be that as it may," Fanny went on, "not all of us can move to Paris to set up our salon. As I've told you before, Clara has my deepest admiration. She also has an annuity from Leonard, ensuring her comfort. Few women share that luxury."

Life will upend us if we don't have the foresight to prevent it—something you've clearly yet to learn.

Mama had known this day might come. She'd lived through it. Had all of London known it too, as I preened in my Worth gowns and Marlborough jewels? An icy wrath unlike anything I'd felt before rushed through me, leaving me sick to my stomach. Whispers behind my back, in the very drawing rooms where I'd entertained and fended off Bertie for my husband's sake.

"Are you suggesting I should *ignore* it?" I asked, trembling.

"I'm saying you don't have another option. You did marry a British lord—"

"Who promised to love and cherish me."

As Fanny reached for my hand, I yanked it away.

"Jennie," she said. "Your father tried to warn you. He understood how men are. He told you, to marry for love is a dangerous affair. You cannot think to stage an uproar over this."

Hearing her speak of it as if my husband had imbibed too much wine at dinner, I had to curb an urge to strike her. I'd known these things happened, more often than not. I remembered after my father's stay with us in London how I'd begun to see marriage as an unpredictable snare. I had my own parents as my example, but in my rush to marry Randolph, falling in love without thinking it through, I'd forgotten my misgivings. I'd never imagined it could happen to me. Even now, it seemed impossible.

"He has a wife," I said. "A son. A family."

"Indeed. And none of it can survive another scandal. You saw what happened when his brother tried to divorce his wife. George fled the country and remains unhappily married. Randolph has no intention of suffering the same. You must adapt. Your marriage is for life."

"Is it?" I came to my feet, dropping the crumpled handkerchief at her feet.

And before she could detain me again, I marched away to the lodge.

IN THE NEXT months, I accepted every invitation that came my way, riding myself to exhaustion at hunting excursions and splurging on a new wardrobe I could scarcely afford, prompting Lady Frances to chide me for my "intemperance." When I retorted that she could hardly expect me to stay cloistered at home until Randolph saw fit to return, she went tight-lipped. I suspected she knew as well, and that only incensed me more.

Then Randolph sent me a berating letter—from Germany, of all places. His mother had informed him of my behavior, and he sternly advised me to take into account our uncertain standing. He failed to mention when he might be returning or why he was abroad.

Unable to sleep at night, I replayed how we'd met and fought to marry, overcoming obstacles that would have felled a less devoted couple. I seethed at the thought that while I'd supported him without hesitation, even as his brother's fiasco plunged us into disgrace, he still enjoyed the freedom to come and go as he pleased, making us a laughingstock, another bit of malice for the gossip mill. More than just his infidelity outraged me; it was the betrayal of my loyalty and my trust. I wanted to turn back time, erase everything that had led me into this delusion. I'd believed our love could conquer anything.

Knowing how wrong I'd been, I vowed to take my revenge.

SEVENTEEN

Opportunity arose where I might have expected it. Dublin might not have been as sophisticated as London, but society was quite the same everywhere. Yet when it happened, I wasn't prepared. I'd been invited to the estate of Derrick Warner Westenra, Baron of Rossmore, who'd inherited his fortune after his brother's tragic demise in a riding accident. An accomplished equestrian himself, he hosted weekend hunting parties to which everyone flocked because he kept the best preserve in the region.

I soon became aware of his intention when I saw him astride his enormous charger, his eyes the color of dusk and tousled black hair falling about his forehead in unruliness, his jaw clean-shaven, disdaining the current fashion for oversized mustaches and beards.

We took to the hunt together, his daring glances spurring me to keep pace. I covertly admired his command over his mount, his thick thighs encased in skintight jodhpurs, flexing as he chased the fox, getting far ahead of the hounds. It was all I could do to keep up, and something in how he kept looking at me, as if in challenge, compelled me to it. I'd had enough of decorum. I could ride as ferociously as any man and wasn't about to languish behind.

When he cornered the fox, he leapt from his saddle, seized the poor creature in his large hands, and slashed its throat with his knife, spurting blood across his jacket. It was an act of pure savagery. He should have killed it with his rifle, but he smeared its death on his cheek, then severed its ear and brought it to me.

I found him as irresistible as the land that spawned him. And unlike Randolph in every way. Powerful and assertive, virility exuding from every pore. It actually made me feel a thrill of dread and excitement, as if he tendered the forbidden apple of desire rather than a severed ear.

"I would see more of you," he said, without preamble, as the other riders approached over the hill, the hounds baying at their heels. "Alone."

This, too, excited me. A man who didn't care to mince his words. It reminded me of my father. With the fox ear dripping in my hand, I heard myself reply, "You have guests."

He met my eyes. "Guests leave."

The rest of the weekend was layered with innuendo, though I made sure to stay close to the ladies in the evening and avoid contact with him. After the hunt, as he'd roamed his antler-festooned dining hall in his gore-spattered jacket, I suspected he must be a consummate rake. Unwed and wealthy, with those looks, he couldn't be anything else. I found him all the more magnetic because of it.

If I wanted to exact revenge on Randolph, with whom better than him?

When he sent a note a few days later saying that he was coming to see me, I dispatched Mrs. Everest with Winston to visit Lady Frances, who complained I was keeping the child too much to myself. As soon as they departed, I dismissed the maid and butler as well, sending them on time-consuming errands in town, insisting I had a headache and wished to rest.

Then I spent an hour at my mirror, trying on gowns without a corset and avoiding my eyes, thinking I must be mad to contemplate such an outrage. If he were seen entering my house in mid-afternoon while I was unattended, there'd be no avoiding the scandal and Lady Frances would surely hear of it. That alone spurred me, like his daring looks during the hunt.

Scandal was what I wanted. It was the only thing that would

force Randolph's return, short of imploring him, which I had no intention of doing.

Once I heard his horse pounding up the driveway, I closed my eyes, breathed deep, thrust jeweled combs into my coiffure, and went downstairs to greet him.

He strode into my drawing room as if he'd been there before. He seemed even larger inside my house, like a chiseled monument, his body straining the seams of his clothes.

"Here?" He gave me a sardonic arch of his thick eyebrow.

"It is where tea is served," I said, though as I'd sent the maid away, unless I brewed it myself, I had none to offer. "Or would you prefer something stronger?"

I started to move to the sideboard, to Randolph's favorite cognac. I hadn't yet reached for the glass decanter when he strode up behind me, those big hands of his grasping me about my waist, much as he had the fox he'd slain.

"I'd prefer you," he breathed in my ear. He turned me around, stared into my eyes for a moment before he crushed his mouth against mine.

My heart hammered in my throat. This wasn't at all how a gentleman behaved, even one with illicit purpose; we'd barely spoken a dozen words to each other. I put my hand against his chest, somewhat breathless as I drew back. "Might some conversation be in order first?"

"Why?" His eyes narrowed. "You're married. I'm not. What conversation should we have? If we like this, we can see to the niceties afterwards."

His brazenness ignited rebellious fire again in me. I let him shove me against the wall. Raveling my fingers in his mane, I felt his might, so strong he could crush me to dust.

I wasn't afraid of that.

I was afraid of how much I wanted him to.

We didn't speak again. The occasion apparently didn't require it. Lowering me to the carpet, he rucked up my skirts to lower himself between my legs, spreading them apart and using his mouth to pleasure me, making me writhe and clamp down on my gasps. Randolph had never done this to me. I'd never done it to him. As fleeting memories of our sedate lovemaking cut through the growing heat in my body, my climax crashed over me. I couldn't stop from moaning at the intensity of it.

He looked up at me, his lips wet. "I like a woman who enjoys it," he rasped. He released himself to thrust into me. I gasped again at the girth of him, and he grinned, moving rhythmically as if he were on the saddle. My cries as he moved faster, deeper, sending tide after tide of brutal sensation through me until I thought I would drown, must have carried all the way to London.

Then he moaned, went taut, and started to pull out, spattering onto my skirts. As I thought we'd gone too far, beset by terror that he may have spent some of his seed inside me, he sprawled beside me, panting. "It's true what they say. You're more animal than woman."

Shame washed over me. Pulling down my disheveled dress and pushing back my tangled hair as I sought for the buried combs, thinking I'd have to wash off those milky spots on my dress before anyone came home, I asked, "Who says that?"

He chuckled as he watched me attempt to put myself to rights. "That effete diplomat D'Abernon attended one of the banquets at Viceroy Lodge. He commented you had more of the panther in your look, dressed all in black with a star in your hair."

I wasn't sure if he meant this as a compliment until he added, "Next time, I want to see the panther undressed and in a proper bed."

"Next time?" I gave him a look. "Is this the nicety that comes afterwards?"

He uncoiled to his feet with a limber fluidity that made him seem like an animal himself.

"If you don't wish to see me again, you need only say it. I'm not in the habit of begging."

"No." I gazed at him. "I . . . I do wish it."

He smiled. "As do I."

WE CONTRIVED TO meet as often as possible, at my house, when I could manage to send the servants away and Mrs. Everest with Winston to his grandmother. But I couldn't make up excuses every time, so we also went riding at his estate, seeking secluded groves where we made love on the loam. The more I had of him, the more I craved. My original intent to wreak vengeance transformed into something more insidious, uncontrollable. At night when I undressed myself, refusing my maid's assistance, and beheld the bruises on my body from his enthusiasm, I feared I'd lost my reason. We still rarely spoke after our encounters, as if satiating our flesh was all that mattered. The niceties were relegated to not being caught.

It unnerved me, that I could experience such passion for a stranger. I'd never felt anything like it with Randolph, whose bedchamber visits had been courteous and brief—almost, I realized now, perfunctory. Was Fanny right? Did he think because I was his wife, the mother of his child, he must resort to others rather than request what he wanted of me?

Regardless, I risked catastrophe. Rossmore could do as he liked, while I ran the peril of extreme censure should our liaison become public. Though I'd set out to achieve that very end, I now took pains to avoid any discovery of our affair, not wanting to end it yet unable to admit as much to myself.

Until the day when I returned from an afternoon with him to discover Lady Frances in my drawing room with Winston. As I entered, she said coldly, "There you are. I happened upon Lord Rossmore several days ago. You and he seem to be seeing rather a lot of each other."

I unpinned my hat, noticing a rip in its veil from snagging it on brambles as he'd taken me on the ground. "He owns the best-stocked hunting lands in the region," I said, casting a quick smile at my son, where he lined up his soldiers on the rug, having learned that toys were for playing, not eating. "He's very hospitable. I see no harm in it."

"Well." She sniffed. "You must be unaware of his reputation. He's in debt and squanders whatever he has on iniquities. It's indecent to seek his company. You must not do so again."

With what I hoped was sufficient detachment, I said, "Lady Frances, with whom I choose to spend my time is not your concern."

"Is it not?" She rose to her feet. "Rest assured that while you may not think it my concern, it most certainly will be Randolph's."

"And who is he to reproach me?" I riposted. "Given what he does in his absence?"

She paused. "Your morals are deplorable. I told him not to marry you. Not only are you of lesser family, but you have no decency." Before I could reply to her insult, the first she'd dared utter aloud, she added, "Your son will not grow up with these outrageous notions. If necessary, I shall see to Winston's upbringing myself. Entirely."

Infuriated, I threw my caution aside. "Leave my house. This instant."

After she departed, I looked again at Winston, who continued to play with his soldiers, oblivious to the confrontation. Mrs. Everest bustled in moments later. "Forgive me, my lady. I did try to tell Lady Frances you had an engagement, but she insisted on returning before you."

"Never mind. Please take Winston upstairs for his bath."

I sank into a chair as Winston wailed that he didn't want a bath. My reckoning was upon me.

EIGHTEEN

Is it true?" Randolph stood before me, his overcoat dripping on the carpet. He'd arrived unannounced, startling me where I sat at the piano; it was storming, the isle beset by a winter tempest that preempted any outdoor activities.

I would have secluded myself regardless. I'd not seen Rossmore again, nor had I offered him any explanation, so I kept expecting him to burst into the house instead. He had not, making me wonder if he'd deliberately accosted Lady Frances. It would have been unspeakably boorish, even for him, so it was also possible she'd inferred our affair from some careless remark he'd made, as it wouldn't have required much deduction on her part, given my comings and goings. Whichever the case, my yearning for him yawned like a pit in my being, even as I resolved that our liaison could not continue. Lady Frances's threat had stayed with me. I wouldn't risk my son. Should Randolph elect to sue me for adultery, I'd be denied any contact with Winston.

Randolph now stared at me as if I were a stranger. I felt the same about him. After six months without seeing each other, he looked impossibly frail. I wanted to show compassion, understanding how shocked he must be, but all I felt was contempt that he'd dare express outrage over something he himself had precipitated.

I met his eyes. "It is true."

"You—you let that rake take liberties with you? Do you know how many others he's ravished? He makes a vice of it. They call him the Cad of Dublin. He's—"

"He didn't ravish me." I went to close the drawing room doors, though by now the entire household must have been alerted to our altercation. "I did it willingly."

"*Willingly?* Are you mad? You're my wife. You cannot bed whomever you like."

"You didn't seem so perturbed when Bertie was making advances on me. As I recall, you thought it quite desirable for him to chase after me if it could bring us into his circle."

"That was different. You didn't take him as your lover," Randolph flared.

"While you went off to bed whores." As he stared at me, I went on. "Fanny Ronalds informed me." I marveled at my calm as I spoke. I didn't feel calm at all. "Did you think you could keep it a secret? If she heard of it, so has most of London."

"Fanny Ronalds had no right." He drew himself erect, unbuttoning his coat and tossing it onto a chair. "If you must know, I had to abandon my upcoming speech in the House about the appalling situation in this country to come here and contend with your appalling behavior. You're supposed to uphold me," he said, raising his voice against my protest. "It is your duty as my wife to ensure our name remains above reproach, not turn us into a scandal."

"Your brother did that already. And you helped him," I said coldly.

His face darkened as he took a menacing step toward me. I didn't recoil, even as he said, "I could divorce you for this. By law, adultery in a wife is an intolerable offense."

"Do so," I retorted. Though if he did, I had no idea how I would survive it. I couldn't rely on Papa's support, with his uncertain fortunes, and moving in with Mama was out of the question. I'd never hear the end of it, after she'd warned me that by my own actions I'd forced my parents to submit to the duke's terms for our marriage, leaving me without financial security should something untoward occur. I might return to New York, but how could I leave my son here? They'd never allow me to take Winston abroad to live.

Randolph made an exasperated sound, as if he read my thoughts. "I'm not so cruel as to cast you out into the street. But what I do when we're apart is my own affair. It has nothing to do with us. When have I denied you anything? Your expenditures exceed all limitations and not once have I reproached you."

My calm shattered. "This isn't about money. What I lacked was you at my side. How could you leave me here alone, at the mercy of your mother for months on end, while you went about your so-called affairs? Had you been faithful I'd never have gone so far."

"Faithful?" Without warning, raw laughter erupted from him, followed by a hacking cough. He extracted his cigarette case from his waistcoat, lighting one of the cigarettes and blowing smoke toward the ceiling. "I'm as faithful as any husband can be. I don't keep a permanent arrangement, though I'm the rare exception. Wives better than you put up with it."

I started to reach for a nearby vase and had to stop myself from flinging it at his head. "How dare you? I am *not* an aristocratic wife who will put up with it."

"You will. I don't owe you—" All of a sudden, he swayed, the cigarette slipping from his hand as he grappled for the armchair. I rushed to assist him before he collapsed, alarmed by the translucency of his skin, the veins in his temples visible like blue-tinged webs.

"Fetch me . . . a cognac," he whispered.

I watched him gulp it down. His face was drenched in sweat. I now saw how his shirt collar gaped about his neck, how his frock coat hung like an oversized wrapping on his diminished frame. He had lost too much weight. He'd always been very lean, but now he bordered on gauntness.

"Randolph, are you ill?" My voice caught in worry.

He winced. "It's nothing. Some fatigue. This bloody cough . . .

They tell me I must partake of dry air and avoid the damp of this infernal place. That is why I stayed away for so long. It was recommended I repair to a spa in Bad Homburg. Apparently, the Prussians have a cure for everything."

"A cure?" I thought of consumption, that dreaded ailment that attacked out of nowhere, draining its victims. Decades could pass before this thief finished its grisly work.

"For this fever I can't seem to shake." He scowled. "I've been assured it's not fatal, so stop looking at me as if it were. I simply needed time away to recover."

"You don't appear recovered to me. Randolph, you look very unwell."

"Don't say that." He reached again for his cigarette case until he saw my stare and thought better of it. "My nerves are shot. I'm besieged on all sides. This blasted disgrace that keeps me from the prince. My brother's recklessness—Edith Aylesford has borne him a bastard son in Holland, if you can believe it—and it seems as if Gladstone will be our new prime minister. Now this." He avoided my eyes as he spoke. "Jennie, what you've done is disastrous. Mamma insists that we remove Winston from your care."

"Never." My voice turned icy. I was very concerned to see the suave man I'd married returned to me, in less than a year, a specter of his former self, but I wouldn't abide such a threat. "I'll take my son to America before I ever let her assume charge of him. She'll turn him into a colossal waste. Like your brother."

Randolph's arid chuckle took me aback. To my disconcertment, it also defused the fury between us. "You never were one to do things halfway. I should have known that if you decided to take a lover, you'd choose the most reprehensible lout in Ireland."

"He didn't mean anything to me," I said, repressing a pang at my dishonesty. It *had* meant something, but not enough to destroy my life over. "I did it out of anger."

"No doubt." He paused, once more taking out his case. This

time, I let him light his cigarette, the smoke wreathing his colorless face. "You must put an end to it, however, lest I'm obliged to call the man out to a duel."

"I already have."

"Good. Then let us speak no more of it. Unless . . ."

I went still.

"Unless you no longer care for me," he said. "I can forgive an indiscretion, but if it means you're so unhappy in our marriage, we should decide how to proceed. Divorce is out of the question, but we can always live apart. I'll do my utmost to keep my mother at bay."

"I don't want to live apart." I clasped his hand. His skin was clammy; he still had this mysterious fever, no matter what he said. "Randolph, I love you. I've never stopped loving you."

As soon as I spoke, my voice choked. I'd been so angry, so determined to make him suffer, yet he was the man I'd fought to marry, for whom I'd defied everyone. I wanted to hate him for what he'd done to us, but I couldn't. Despite everything, I still loved him.

"And I love you. You're engraved in my heart." A thin smile curved his bloodless lips. "You must forgive me. All those gentlemen whose favor I have to cultivate in the House as if they were reluctant virgins, they invite me to these places and I am obligated to go along. I don't want it said that Lord Randolph is a reluctant virgin himself."

"Your fellow MPs invite you to discuss politics in brothels?" I said drily.

"You'd be surprised how many of our governmental affairs are decided under those tawdry eaves. We should reward every whore in London with a patriotic pension." He sighed, twining his fingers in mine. "We needn't explain ourselves, providing we understand one another. I am so tired, Jennie. I missed you so much. Forgive my impudence. I detest quarreling with you."

I didn't think it the right time to question him further. As I helped him to stand, I could feel his bones under his clothes. After guiding him upstairs, I undressed him myself, hiding my dismay at the sight of his incised ribs.

As I drew the coverlets over him, he whispered, "You must never leave me. I'd be lost without you. Life would cease to hold any meaning for me."

I kissed his brow. "Rest now. I'm not leaving you. Ever."

UNDER MY MINISTRATIONS, and after I sent for larks' tongues from London and oysters from Paris, both of which he relished, Randolph slowly regained the weight he'd lost. I presided over every meal, insisting he finish his plate. Perturbed by his appearance, Lady Frances refrained from mentioning the matter that had brought him home, but I wouldn't forget. Though I couldn't deny her time with her grandson, I knew how she felt about me and would remain on my guard.

Once Randolph recovered, we undertook a tour of western Ireland so he could witness firsthand what I'd described in my letters. The call for Home Rule, or Irish self-governance, had turned vicious, with attacks on British ministers culminating in a wave of murders that enraged Parliament. Tory MPs called for the execution of every Irish terrorist in custody. The duke wisely refused to institute such barbaric reprisal, and won himself little favor by doing so.

As a staunch monarchist, Randolph opposed Home Rule on principle, but neither of us believed the only way to contend with the Irish was to crush their spirit. He asked me to help him write a speech calling for independence in Irish affairs—a controversial stance that might not gain him allies in his party but would garner him prominence. As Bertie still refused to receive us, we had to raise attention on our own. The newspapers would take note, perhaps sway public opinion in Randolph's favor to ease his upcoming reelection.

In the midst of this, I discovered I was again with child. Randolph had come to my bed unexpectedly one evening. Though our sedate lovemaking roused stark memories of Rossmore's ardor, I took solace in the fact that he still desired me. I found myself thinking that perhaps his dalliances truly did have nothing to do with us, that I should count myself fortunate he strayed only on occasion, sparing me the humiliation of an ongoing situation, like Papa with Fanny.

Then, as he fastened his dressing gown to return to his room, he said, "I didn't mention this before in my delirium, but I've had time to consider. Should you feel the need to take a lover again, I want you to know I do not oppose it. Only, choose someone who appreciates discretion."

"I don't feel the need," I said at once, startled by his equanimity. "Do you?"

"Not at the moment. But we should have an arrangement in place." His voice softened. "Jennie, I've seen too many failed marriages to believe in fidelity. Our very nature is inconstant; whom we love and whom we wish to bed are not always the same. I don't wish to deny or curtail you. Nor do I wish to deny myself."

His statement unsettled me, even if I had to concede its sensibleness. If insufficient freedom was how marriages inevitably corroded, worn down by familiarity and routine, perhaps he was right, I thought, recalling my mother's warning that marriage could be for a very long time.

"Very well," I said at length. "How do we go about it?"

"I have no idea. I've never done this before. I will say this much: I don't like complications. I have no desire for a mistress, nor can I afford one, so I prefer to pay for my pleasures when required. That, however, isn't an option for you, so I suppose we'll have to muddle through as best we can. The risk is mostly mine," he added, with a smile. "I'll never fall in love with anyone else. From the moment we met, I knew there was no other woman in the world for me.

We can't be everything to each other; no one can. But I am yours forever."

"As long as we are honest above all else," I said. "I detest secrets."

He smiled. "You know all my secrets now."

He left me in contemplation. After the turmoil caused by his deception and my affair, if it could be called that, I didn't care to repeat the experience. If we were to proceed as he thought best, we must protect our marriage. An arrangement seemed reasonable enough; I'd rather not be taken again by surprise, which was unlikely if I knew what he did while he was away.

And for the foreseeable future, extramarital activities were the last thing on my mind. As my pregnancy advanced, I plunged into irrational panic over my child's paternity, plagued by terrifying visions of my babe roaring into the world with coal-black hair and eyes that proclaimed his illegitimacy, though I knew it was impossible. It had been well over two months before I became pregnant, and I'd had my menses; the child could only be Randolph's.

On February 4, 1880, after six hours of labor, my second son arrived with scarcely a whimper. As far as I could tell, he bore only a marked resemblance to Winston at his birth. He was well-formed and healthy, the doctor assured us, and appeared to be full-term.

We christened him John Strange Spencer-Churchill, for the first Duke of Marlborough and the duke's lifelong friend, John Strange Jocelyn, fifth Earl of Roden, who happened to be in Dublin at the time. Because I'd gone into labor while the earl was in residence, he offered to stand as godfather and Randolph suggested the honorific use of his middle name. In the family, my son became known as Jack.

I thought him unusually docile, lacking the vociferous outbursts Winston had displayed. When I expressed my concern to Mrs. Everest, she chuckled. "Your firstborn is headstrong as a mule, so it's to be expected the second will be the opposite. Consider yourself blessed, my lady. Imagine the trouble if they both had the same temperament."

"You're certain there's nothing to worry about?" I said, holding Jack to my breast. I'd insisted on nursing him myself, despite Lady Frances's dismay. I'd not suffer again the excruciating process of drying out my milk.

"He's suckling as he should," Mrs. Everest pointed out. "If he suffers less colic than expected, it's indeed nothing to worry about. He'll find his voice soon enough, if Winston ever lets him get a word in edgewise."

I laughed. Winston was very curious about his new baby brother, peeking into the cradle in the nursery and staring fixedly as I nursed. He demanded that I let him nurse at my breast as well, to which Mrs. Everest retorted, "If you want milk, fetch a cow."

It comforted me to think my boys would have each other growing up, as I'd had my sisters. I dreaded relinquishing them. But by mid-April, our time in Ireland reached its end. Elected prime minister, Gladstone persuaded Her Majesty to recall the duke and appoint a replacement who wouldn't balk at bringing Ireland to heel.

During our carriage ride to the ship that would convey us to England, the disgruntled populace of Dublin pelted us with fetid lettuce and fistfuls of mud. Their ugly chants of "English, go home!" followed us all the way to the deck, where Lady Frances, with tears in her eyes, whispered, "God save this wretched country." She gave me a hard look. "I trust this has been sufficient for you and Randolph to refrain from further scandal."

It was, if nothing else, a fitting epitaph to our departure.

PART III

THE DIPLOMATIC WIFE

1881–1895

*The magic of first love is our
ignorance that it can ever end.*
—Benjamin Disraeli

NINETEEN

1881–1883

Mama says he's completely unsuitable because he has no money or family name. I don't care about any of that." Clarita lifted her chin in the drawing room of my home in Connaught Place, as if I was the one who must be persuaded. "Moreton Frewen might not be titled or rich, but I'm about to turn thirty. All I'll ever be is alone if I refuse him again."

"Again?" I rang the bell for tea. "How many times has he proposed?"

"Three." Her accusatory tone indicated I'd been remiss in not keeping abreast of her situation during my time away. "Shortly after I met him at the season, he claimed he was besotted. I couldn't indulge such a precipitous declaration, but he followed me to Paris and proposed again. Naturally, Mama dispatched me forthwith to Papa in New York. He showed up on our doorstep there, if you can believe it. He's acquired land in Wyoming and has plans to build a ranch. Apparently, there's a cattle boom in the state. He talked it over with Papa, who told me he admires Moreton's adventurous spirit and gave us his blessing."

"I see." I decided not to remark that Papa's blessing was hardly decisive, given his own erratic financial trajectory. "And in all of it, do you have any care for this Moreton?"

"Of course," she said at once, though I heard the falter in her voice. "He's handsome and ambitious. He says he loves me, so I suppose I should love him in return."

"You can't suppose yourself into love." I paused as the maid entered with our tea. "Clarita, trust me. Love is the beginning. Maintaining the marriage is what tests our forbearance."

As I poured tea into her cup, I felt her stare. "Why would you say that? You fell in love practically overnight and look at you now: esteemed Lady Randolph, with two sons, a rising politician husband, and position in society. Whatever has tested you?"

I lifted my gaze. I thought of confiding in her, only doing so wouldn't make me seem any less culpable. "You know how trying my life has been since our falling-out with Bertie. Only the Rothschilds have stood by us, and by virtue of their fortune, they can afford to. Otherwise, we may as well have stayed in Ireland or removed ourselves to Blenheim. No one else dares incur His Highness's wrath by receiving us."

She took up her cup. "He can't stay angry forever. Randolph is making quite the impression with those fiery speeches of his in defense of Ireland. He's been in all the newspapers. The prince will have to come around eventually, if only for diplomacy's sake."

"One can hope. Still, none of this comes without its cost. I had to canvass Woodstock for votes to help Randolph re-win his seat, and Lady Frances was furious that I was out courting the people like a vendor. And after he drafts his speeches, I must revise each one to ensure he doesn't stray too far and anger the prince even more."

"Well, Moreton won't be giving speeches to cattle, so we needn't worry about angering anyone," she huffed.

"Except Mama," I said.

Her face turned plaintive. "Can't you write to her, or better yet, go visit and tell her that you approve? She might pretend your marriage wasn't to her liking, but I've heard her in her salon, boasting to everyone about how her daughter married into the Spencer-Churchill family and started a trend for others to follow."

"A *trend*?"

"Didn't you know? They're publishing a quarterly in America

listing prospective titled bachelors. Mama has a copy of it. You're cited as being one of the first: Jennie Jerome, the New York millionaire's daughter who enraptured a British lord."

"Honestly." I had to laugh. "How absurd. Do these American girls check off potential prospects in the quarterly before setting sail with their trousseaus at the ready?"

"They do." She set her cup down with a determined clink on the saucer. "And all of them come with family names and, more importantly, reams of family money. Jennie, I can't keep attending the season year after year in hope someone better will take notice of me. Moreton is who I have. I want to marry. Start a family. It's time."

Looking at her voluptuousness, which was tending toward Mama's portliness, though for now she was too young yet for it to merit remark—I saw that I had indeed been remiss. My older sister, whom I'd so often envied, was on the verge of desperation. Told since childhood that she must make a superb marriage that had failed to materialize, she now faced the unthinkable: spinsterhood. In my current predicament, I couldn't do much to help her. I hadn't lied. Since our return to England, I'd barely been received, though I'd redecorated my new townhouse and ordered new gowns for the season. Bertie of Wales's displeasure hung over us like a scythe; without entrée into his coveted circle, I couldn't present either myself or my sisters to anyone of importance.

"Jennie, must I beg? I supported you when you wanted to marry Randolph. I need your support in return. Mama will heed you; I know she will."

I had my doubts about that, but I smiled anyway. "I should probably meet him first. Bring him here for dinner next week."

MORETON·FREWEN WAS indeed handsome and well-built, with an impressive mustache and a head of thick auburn hair. He reminded me of Papa, with his grandiose assertion that in America he would make his fortune. I didn't fail to notice how he kept glancing adoringly at Clarita and how she returned his gaze in limp-eyed awe. It would have taken a far stronger character than hers to resist such a man, even if I feared she might be in for a disappointment.

Randolph shared my misgivings. "I'm afraid Moreton is known for these harebrained schemes," he told me after they left. "I've made inquiries. His father once served in the Commons, but the family has no pedigree to speak of. Moreton is a superb sportsman, however, with a passion for all those outdoor pursuits we revere, so he's admired. Unfortunately, he also has a knack for investing in ventures that come to nothing."

"Clarita doesn't seem to care," I said. "She's quite determined to marry him."

He inserted a cigarette into his mother-of-pearl holder, an absurd concession to his doctors' advice to curtail his intake, as he smoked just as much. "I suppose she could do worse. He hasn't incited any scandals, to my knowledge. Everyone seems to like him well enough to receive him."

"Unlike us." I watched him turn to pace the drawing room. "My darling, when shall our disfavor end? We can't possibly further ourselves without the prince."

Randolph scowled. "Believe me, I'm very much aware. Bertie refuses to hear a word in my defense, much less anything from me in person. When Gladstone approached him to suggest a rapprochement after my last speech, which brought the entire House to its feet, Bertie gave him an earful. I'm afraid we're excluded indefinitely from His Highness's favor."

"But Her Majesty invested your mother with the Royal Order for her famine relief. If the queen can forgive us, why can't His Highness do the same?"

"Because Bertie makes a point of countermanding anything his mother does. His obstinacy is equaled only by his perversity." As Randolph smoked his cigarette to its stub, I recalled what Fanny had told me: *If there's one name in your husband's family that His Highness will still tolerate, it's yours.*

"Perhaps I could bring about a rapprochement," I said.

He went still. "Absolutely not."

"Why not?" I stood, wincing. I had ordered my maid to lace my corset too tight, in the hope of restoring my sixteen-inch waist, which childbirth had widened to an unacceptable twenty-four. "Her Highness has always been very courteous to me. I might be able to persuade her to——"

He held up his hand. "Have you forgotten how our past attempt at persuasion went?"

"This is about your career," I told him. "Everyone is taking notice of you, including Gladstone. He once espoused Home Rule. In time, he might champion you as his successor." I set my hands on his shoulders as he regarded me warily. "Randolph, you might be prime minister one day—but only if we have Bertie's support."

"Gladstone's espousal of Home Rule tore a breach in our party that lost us influence for twenty years. And now you think I could be his successor?" He chuckled, breathing out the acrid scent of his tobacco. "Jennie, as always, I'm enthralled by your ambition, but I'm beginning to think it knows no bounds."

"Not where we are concerned." I kissed his cheek. "You must allow me to make the attempt. I've nothing to lose, save an uncomfortable meeting with Her Highness."

As I turned to go upstairs and release myself from the torment of my corset, he said from behind me, "I can't imagine she'll receive you. She must despise us as much as Bertie does."

"Women have other ways of finding accord," I replied. "Trust me in this."

MAMA HAD GROWN stout and complacent in Paris, where she exerted absolute independence in her affairs. In contrast, Dobbie was visibly stooped, moving slower, but as devoted as ever to her Miss Clara. She was also overjoyed to see my sister and me, chiding me for not writing more often. I hugged her and promised I would, though she snorted, knowing I most likely wouldn't. She asked after my boys, wanting to know when she'd meet them, too; I offered to bring them once they were older or bring her to England for a visit. She nodded, but it was evident to me that unless Mama came with her, Dobbie wouldn't budge from her side. She'd gone from being our nanny to Mama's sole companion.

And unfortunately, Mama hadn't changed one bit, even if the world was moving too quickly for her to keep up. Those brides of means Clarita had mentioned were now arriving in droves—brash, young, and very rich, baiting impecunious lords eager to shore up their brittle lineages with an infusion of American wealth. The quarterly should have been published monthly, so swiftly did its listings go out of date.

"Moreton has nothing to commend him," Mama said. "A few acres in Wyoming and a proposed ranch do not a future make. Whatever will Clarita do there as his wife?"

"Raise a family. She loves him and he loves her. Isn't that enough?"

She glared at me from across the tea table. "Since when has love been a requisite for marriage?"

"It was for you and Papa," I countered, darkening her face. "Clarita is no longer of age to compete for a title. We're no longer the toast of Paris or London."

"Certainly not after your husband's disaster. Leonie's debut can't even be considered, held as it was under a storm of royal displeasure. And now, she too thinks to marry for love." Mama directed a censorious look at my younger sister, whose sable-lashed eyes and quiet demeanor belied her iron will. She had entered her twenty-first year, and while not outwardly as striking as Clarita or me, she had my talent for the piano and had attracted the affection of Sir John Leslie, heir to an Irish baronet, during her season in London.

"John is serving in the Grenadier Guards," Leonie said. "He'll inherit a prosperous estate, including Castle Leslie in County Monaghan. I don't see why you should oppose him."

"Lest you forget, his family opposes you. God save me, one wants to go live in the wilds of Wyoming and the other in the wilds of Ireland. Must I contend with two headstrong daughters at once?" Mama redirected her furor to me. "This is your fault. Had you not rushed to marry in the heat of passion and set this impossible example . . ."

Her voice faded as she took in my silence.

"I can't be blamed for the fall of an empire," I said. "I wed the man I loved, and Clarita and Leonie now wish to do the same—with or without your approval."

Mama motioned Leonie from the room, then said to me in a flat voice, "I'll not have you fill her head with nonsense. Clarita may be a lost cause, but Leonie isn't engaged. Should the Leslies have their way, she never will be. She shall go to New York instead to stay with your father. Leonard will see her presented in society as she should be."

I gave an exasperated sigh. "Papa has moved back into our mansion because he couldn't afford to keep his room at the club. His payments on my dowry are nine months in arrears. Do you think he's in any position to tend to Leonie's welfare?"

"Better than you are. You see to your affairs and let us see to your sisters."

I left Mama ensconced in her salon, returning to London to inform Clarita of the result of my trip. My sister's jaw set. "Moreton is waiting for me in New York. I have Papa's approval. I don't need hers."

She booked passage. Before she left, I helped her acquire her trousseau, for which Papa sent funds, and promised to attend the wedding. Then Lady Frances informed me by letter that the time had come to enroll Winston in school. I had to visit Blenheim before my departure for New York, once Clarita wrote that she and Moreton had set the date. To emphasize her disapproval, Mama refused to bestir herself from Paris. But Leonie had gone to stay with Papa, so Clarita would have both her sisters and our father at her side on her wedding day.

I found Winston plagued by a bronchial cough and his combative nature. Now in his eighth year, he'd taken to questioning any authority save that of Mrs. Everest, prompting Lady Frances to undertake his enrollment in St. George's School in Berkshire, an exclusive boarding academy that, according to her, would hold him to impeccable standards.

"I don't want to go," roared my son as Mrs. Everest clasped her hands in distress.

"My pumpkin." I sank to my knees. "Every boy must go to school." My nickname for him had been coined in Ireland, because of his perfectly round head, topped by a disarray of coppery curls, but his scowl deepened at my endearment. Crossing his arms over his narrow chest, he spat, "Jack is a boy. He isn't going."

"Jack is only a year old. When he's your age, he, too, must go to school." I held out my arms. "Come here. I promise you, nothing bad will happen."

Mrs. Everest clucked her tongue. "Heed your mother, pet. She's come all this way."

My chest tightened at the imploring look he cast at her. "Will you come with me, Woomany?" That was what he called her—his beloved nanny, who'd tended to his every scrape and ailment. I had only myself to blame. Since Ireland, he'd not set eyes on me. I'd not had a moment to visit him, with the demands of Randolph's career and my own family imbroglios.

"I'm afraid not," said Mrs. Everest. "Nannies can't accompany their charges to school."

"If Woomany isn't going, neither am I." Winston returned his scowl to me. I expected him to stomp his foot or fling a nearby object. If there'd been any doubt as to whose temperament he'd inherited, there couldn't be now. I saw myself at his age, debating every order my mother gave, causing Dobbie no end of trouble. I saw my father, cracking his whip as he careened through New York like a demented renegade.

"Woomany must stay here to care for Jack," I said. "Don't you want to become a learned man? They'll teach you everything you need to know at school. And on the holidays, you can visit us in London."

"I can?" His scowl eased.

"I promise. I'll visit you at St. George's as well."

He took a hesitant step toward me. Just as I started to think he'd not budge another inch, he plunged into my arms, nesting his chin on my shoulder. He was so small, so vulnerable, despite his ferocious temper. "I'm afraid, Mama," he whispered, and over his shoulder, I saw Mrs. Everest turn away, fighting back her tears.

I caressed his nape. "There's nothing to be afraid of, my love. It's just school." He clung to me, suppressing a cough. It reminded me of Randolph, overwhelming me with concern that my son might fall ill from the tumult of leaving the only home he'd known. "Now, you must help Woomany pack your things," I said. "You have to choose which books to bring."

He loved to read. Mrs. Everest had taught him the basics and he'd taken to it with alacrity, poring over old tomes that had been gathering mildew for decades in Blenheim's library, enthralled by the fables of Camelot.

"He'll be fine," said Mrs. Everest as he went to peruse the stack of volumes by his bed. "After he adjusts, he'll be the first in his class. He's extremely bright."

"I hope so." I regarded my older son doubtfully, his brow furrowed in concentration as he contemplated each of his books. "His health concerns me."

"It's not as serious as it seems. He stews himself into these fits;

he has all this energy, all this curiosity, with nowhere to direct it." She lowered her voice. "Her Grace can be too strict. It's her way, but she's not wrong in this. Much as I'll miss the lad, he does need to be in school, where he can put his mind to good use."

"And you did warn me he'd require a firm hand when this day came," I said.

She sighed. "I fear we'll need a footman or three to get him out the door."

Leaving them to their task, I went down to the drawing room, where Lady Frances waited for our inevitable tea. "And how did you find him?" she asked, still in her oversized crinolines and dowdy cap, as if current fashion had no influence over her.

"Is he eating enough? I found him too thin." I took the seat opposite her, feeling that seam of tension that was now always between us. I'd told myself I couldn't visit because my husband and sisters needed me, but finding myself alone with her, I couldn't deny that I'd mostly kept away to avoid this: another thorny exchange with my mother-in-law.

"He eats well enough, when the mood suits him. He doesn't like this or that; he constantly debates our menu, as if this were a restaurant. I vow I've never contended with a more contrary child . . ." She let her insinuation linger. Of course my son's inconformity must be my fault, the unfortunate legacy of my inferior bloodline.

"St. George's is a fine institution," she went on, as the overladen tea carts were rolled in. She still spent a ransom on cakes and pastries. "The headmaster will not tolerate these tantrums. He will teach the boy how a gentleman must conduct himself."

"Winston is a child. He has years yet to learn to be a gentleman."

"It's never too early to learn proper manners," she exclaimed. "At this rate, he'll trespass beyond all civilized norms."

I heard Miss Green in her voice and gripped my teacup so hard, I wondered it didn't crack. "I won't have my son harmed," I said.

She made a moue of surprise. "One should never spare the rod if it's required."

"No." I stared at her. "If they lay one finger on him, I'll remove him from your fine institution myself. Is that understood?"

Her mouth pursed. "You must do as you think best, as you always do. Only permit me to say that Winston has obligations. Indulging him will do him no favors."

"At the moment, his obligation is to learn. No child needs a rod for that."

We resumed our tea in silence. As soon as enough time had passed for it not to be considered rude, I stood, taking up my bonnet and wrap.

"Must you leave so soon?" she said. "You only just arrived."

"My sister is getting married in New York. I've much to prepare before I depart."

"Randolph told me." She might have sniffed, had she not sensed my own unpredictable temper brewing. "To Moreton Frewen, I believe?"

"Yes. What of it?"

"Nothing at all. I understand he's an excellent huntsman. I'm quite sure he can round up cattle in your country with equal aplomb."

Hatred boiled in my veins. "Clarita is very happy with him," I said.

"Is she? Then please give her my regards for her continued happiness."

As I marched out to my carriage, I understood exactly what she meant. My older sister had married precisely where she should, while I had overstepped myself.

I WAS OVERJOYED to be back in New York, even if our family mansion looked threadbare from the absence of Mama's meticulous oversight. Papa had grown grayer, with a hint of jowl, not that the years could contain his exuberance. He escorted Clarita, Leonie, and me to his beloved concert halls and operas, and on carriage rides about the city. One day while Leonie and Clarita went shopping, I asked him how he fared. He waved aside my concern.

"The stock market is fickle. She wants this, then she wants that. We must adapt to her volatility."

"No, Papa." I set my hand on his. "How are *you*? You're living on your own here. Isn't there anyone . . . ?"

He chuckled. "Since Fanny left me for her temperamental composer? I'm afraid I've no time for it. Your mother is settled in Paris now, but Clarita's dowry. Her wedding. And Leonie's will come soon enough. Who will pay for all of it, if not me?"

Guilt knotted my chest. He'd worked all his life to support us as Mama demanded, but he was at the age when other men retired. With his family flung across the ocean, I suddenly realized Papa was indeed all alone in New York, shackled to his work with no end in sight.

"You could come to England," I said. "Stay with us."

"And do what? I'm not made for bouncing grandchildren on my knee. Bring your little ones here, if you can. They should see New York. They're half American."

"Yes," I said, biting back tears. "I will. And you mustn't worry about me, Papa. See to Clarita and Leonie. Randolph and I have our annuity from Blenheim. We'll make do."

He sighed. "I intend to honor my obligation to you as well. After I pay for the wedding."

I warned Clarita not to overspend, but we'd paid visits to our fellow pupils from Miss Green's Academy, all those imperious girls with whom she had vied. She regaled them with tales of our life in Europe, investing it with an exaggerated glamour that left them, as she noted in satisfaction, "pea-green." Most of them had married well, though none could claim her husband had a title. And while Moreton didn't have one either, the mere fact that he was British made him a catch, and my sister wanted her wedding at Grace Church to be a grand occasion.

She looked beautiful as Papa led her down the aisle, in her white gown and rosette-studded veil, the same one I'd worn, my gift to her. Beside her broad-shouldered groom, she was everything a bride should be. For the first time in her life, she also looked fulfilled. I still wondered how she'd adapt to life in the middle of nowhere after all the expectations inculcated in her, but she assured me she would do as she always had: strive to make the best of it.

"Who would have thought?" she said, as we finished packing her trunks for the train journey to Wyoming. Moreton had gone ahead after their honeymoon in Newport to prepare the ranch. "I still remember that day at Miss Green's when you recited Baudelaire. And look at us now. Both married to Englishmen, and with the last one"—she darted a glance at Leonie—"about to follow in our footsteps."

A blush crept over our younger sister's cheeks. "Not if Mama has anything to say about it. Poor John doesn't know what to do, caught between her and his family."

"You must marry him anyway," declared Clarita, though a trace of sorrow marred her defiance. Mama's refusal to attend her wedding had hurt her. Our mother hadn't so much as sent a congratulatory gift, underscoring her disapproval.

"Mama will reconcile herself to it in time," I told Leonie. "She's not entirely heartless. She just has this firm notion of who we ought to be and——"

"We've been a disappointment," said Leonie. Clarita and I stared at her in surprise, considering how rarely she ventured an opinion. "Well, we are, aren't we?" she went on. "We've certainly not done anything as she'd prefer it."

I burst into laughter. "We certainly have not. We might not be the toast of two cities anymore, but we're still Madame Jerome's troublesome daughters."

In the ensuing silence, as we gazed at each other from the twin beds Clarita and I had shared as girls, Leonie said, "We'll never forget it, will we? No matter where life takes us, we'll never forget we are sisters?"

"Never." I enveloped her under one of my arms and held out my other hand to Clarita, whose blue eyes turned watery.

"We must always care for one another," I said. "Let us make the promise now. Should one of us ever be in need, the others will rush to her aid without question. Agreed?"

"Yes." Clarita's voice caught. I felt Leonie nod in agreement against my shoulder.

"In sorrow and in joy," I said. "Sisters to the end."

SHORTLY AFTER WE saw Clarita off, a telegram arrived. I'd been hoping to spend the summer with Papa and Leonie. My father needed our company. But as soon as I opened the yellow wire with Randolph's message, I let out a moan of despair.

His father the duke had died.

TWENTY

1883

Black banners hung on Blenheim's façade, adding a funereal touch to its calcified air. His Grace had passed suddenly of heart failure in London; after his casket was brought to the palace to lie in state in the chapel so the tenants could pay their respects, he'd been entombed in the family mausoleum.

"He looked as if he were asleep," Randolph whispered as we gathered in the drawing room. "You wouldn't have thought—" His voice snagged.

I took his hand in mine. He was pale from the shock, though he and his father had never been on good terms. Still, the duke had been in his sixty-first year and shown no sign of illness, and the loss of one's father was a tragic inevitability I couldn't imagine suffering.

At least I'd been spared the grim funeral. Although I'd done my utmost to make haste, by the time I crossed the ocean and reached Oxford, His Grace was already in his tomb and oppressive silence shrouded the estate. Lady Frances had secluded herself in her rooms, unable to endure the pressing necessities, while those of the family with vested interests congregated in the drawing room, much like ravens over the open grave.

Confronted by their somber expressions, I realized how pressing those necessities must be. All around us, the walls were bare. I hadn't noticed it during my prior visits, but it seemed His Grace had sold off most of the artwork. I wondered how many paintings survived in the gallery, all those masterpieces no one took a second look at. Blenheim required endless funds for its upkeep and without the duke to see to it . . .

"Where's your brother?" I asked Randolph, in a hushed voice. "Why isn't he here?"

He grimaced. "He's been delayed in Holland. Not that there's need for concern on his behalf. He'll inherit the entire lot. Or whatever is left of it, which I daresay isn't much."

My apprehension at his words, after having assured my father in New York that we'd make do, made me feel more acutely the damp that had settled into the palace. July sunshine speckled the grounds outside, but heavy rain had fallen earlier, and the drawing room was dank. As I returned my gaze to the assembly—Randolph's sisters with their husbands, along with the eldest, Rosamund, who'd recently become engaged—I caught sight of Albertha, swathed in a voluminous mourning gown, her baleful stare cutting toward where Randolph and I sat.

Even as I avoided staring back at her, her strident voice rang out, startling everyone to attention. "Until my husband sees fit to make his return, I shall assume charge over this house. My son is now its heir, so it's only fitting."

Randolph tensed beside me; I marked his restraint in the precise manner he drew out his cigarette case, although Lady Frances never tolerated smoking in her drawing room, claiming it smudged the frescoes. "Isn't it premature to stake one's claim? My father is scarcely cold in his winding sheet and his wife, the duchess, lies prostrate with grief—right upstairs, mind you."

"She's the *Dowager* Duchess now." Albertha's cheeks turned red. "George is the duke and I'm still his wife, no thanks to you."

And here it was, the unpleasant truth none of us cared to hear: this malicious woman was the new duchess—not that anyone could conceive of her taking Lady Frances's place.

As this thought went through my mind, Randolph said, "Fitting as you may think it, let me assure you that you're fit only to launder my mother's stockings, were you capable of distinguishing between soap and venom."

One of his sisters let out a stifled gasp. Albertha lunged to her feet, stabbing her finger at him. "You—and this—this vulgar American of yours. You'd have seen to my ruin. My destitution. You schemed to have my husband cast me aside. You are to blame for all of it!"

"All of it?" Randolph remained seated, to his credit; I had to clutch the edge of my chair to avoid catapulting myself at her. "I rather think you bear the brunt for the hideous state of your marriage. George endured more than any husband should. My sole regret in that unfortunate affair is that he didn't succeed in ousting you entirely from our existence."

His sister Georgiana hissed in a tone that would have done Lady Frances proud, "Randolph, that is enough."

"I think not." He rose to his feet. Albertha was inchoate, straddling the carpet with her finger aimed at us, hatred blazing in her eyes. With icy contempt, he said, "But by all means, Albertha, do your best. You never could manage much before, so perhaps you'll surprise us."

"*Leave this house at once,*" she shrieked. "Leave and never return. *I forbid it!*"

Randolph smiled. "Gladly. I'll take my American back to London forthwith. Oxford never did agree with us."

He had to tug me up by my hand. I resisted, thinking of my son Jack upstairs in the nursery. I couldn't leave him here. Sensing my tumult, Randolph turned to the aghast assembly to declare, "My father sacrificed his entire life to this estate. My brother is now its master, so far be it from me to question his purview. As usual, George is tardy in assuming his obligations, but he'll be here soon enough. And who else can he hope to rely on, save his flesh and blood?"

He directed himself to Albertha, draining the fury from her

face. "My brother will see this matter put to rights. Until then, Lady Frances maintains her charge here. I'll broach no interference with my mother's authority."

Not until we were in the carriage did my rage overcome me, making me tremble as we rattled under the massive gateway onto the road. "We should have brought Jack with us."

Randolph brooded out the window. "In a few years, Jack will be in school like Winston. Jennie, we can't deprive my mother of her grandson at this time. She's always doted on the boys. She'll not let any harm come to Jack. Nor, I should think, will that formidable nanny of yours. Our son is perfectly safe."

"And us? Are we safe? You must have seen the empty spaces on the walls. How much more has been sold behind your back? How much will your brother auction off? We rely on your estate annuity for our expenses."

"Yes, well. We can hardly rely on those dowry payments your father promised, can we?" He met my stare. "Quite the conundrum. And, I fear, difficult to resolve."

"What do you mean by that?"

"What I mean, my darling, is that judging by those empty spaces, there's no longer enough to go around. Albertha isn't the problem. Indeed, her unwarranted high opinion of herself and my mother's determination to keep her at bay may be all that stands between Blenheim and ruin. Should he be given free rein, George will sell the house and grounds."

"Randolph." My voice quavered. "We have our home. Mrs. Everest's salary. Winston's tuition. How are we to pay for all of it?"

"It's incumbent on us to find a way." He lowered his gaze. "The prince's inner circle can gain us more than political influence; his friends also have access to exclusive financial investments. With them on our side, we could patch together sufficient income. So, your offer to persuade Princess Alexandra . . . Perhaps now is the time to request an audience."

THERE WAS NO question of what was required if we sought reconciliation with the prince: we had to first storm the gates. To achieve that goal, I suggested a new speech for Randolph, decrying his party's opposition to an economic bill benefiting Ireland. This time, he wrote it entirely by himself, accepting only a few of my revisions, and on the day of his speech, I crowded with the other wives in the Ladies' Gallery to behold him in his flamboyant cravat as he delivered my condemnation—a rallying cry for Irish aid that brought half the House to its feet in applause and set the other half to hissing at his effrontery.

The newspapers printed his speech on the front pages, liberal editors declaring Randolph a much-needed voice of reason and conservatives caricaturing him as a gnat in Gladstone's ear. Only then did I dispatch my request to Marlborough House.

The response was returned within the day. Her Highness would receive me.

Alone.

SHE WAITED FOR me in the same gilded drawing room where Randolph had subjected her to humiliation. Whether it was deliberate or merely the protocol to receive visitors thus mattered little once I beheld her. Dressed in a blue silk gown and magnificent pearls that highlighted her unrevealing eyes, she sat against a backdrop of painted screens, as if posed for a portrait. Despite her resplendent attire, I thought she looked wan, as if she'd recently been ill, but her demeanor forbade my solicitous inquiry as she stated without preamble, "I would have you know, Lady Randolph, that this meeting was not my choice."

I thought she'd keep me standing as a sign of her displeasure, but she motioned to a chair, as if she were braced for an inevitable function. After giving birth to a son and two daughters, she'd assumed the tiresome public duties the queen no longer cared to undertake. Beloved by the British people, everything she wore emulated by the masses, for all her status, Princess Alexandra had always struck me as a deeply unhappy woman.

And I was about to request a favor of her that she'd probably reject outright.

"Randolph regrets his actions," I said into the frigid silence.

She hadn't called for tea. She sat with her hands folded in her lap, allowing the uncomfortable moment to extend before she replied, "Does he? I can understand his imprudence, given his temperament, but it seems you've learned that none of us are immune to the indignities imposed on us by our husbands."

My throat constricted. She knew about Randolph's infidelity. For a moment, I was tempted to riposte that any betrayed wife could do what I had done, but Alexandra of Wales couldn't. Nor would she ever consider taking a wild Irishman to her bed out of revenge.

"In any event," she went on. "You are here. I assume you have a purpose."

My voice sounded forced to my ears. "Randolph and I wish to make amends."

"It's not necessary. I told you, you had my forgiveness." She paused, gauging me with her opaque eyes. "Or is it my husband's forgiveness you seek? Bertie's wrath must be felt more keenly than any of mine. If so, you might ask him instead. I believe he still holds you in affection, Lady Randolph, despite your husband's behavior."

The air seemed to solidify between us. I made myself sit more upright, if it was possible, seeing as my spine scarcely grazed the back of the chair. "Wives can find accord that husbands rarely share," I finally said. "I wish to extend an invitation to our home. If you would agree to accompany His Highness, perhaps he'd see fit to accept."

One of her hands twitched in her lap, the sole indication that I'd skinned a nerve. "May I assume this invitation also has a purpose? The duke's death, perhaps? We were very saddened to hear of his passing. He was most esteemed by Her Majesty and by all those who had the good fortune to know him. I imagine his loss must be hard on his family."

I'd underestimated her, imagining her a prisoner of her circumstances. Yet even immured behind palace walls, Alexandra wasn't ignorant of what went on beyond them. If she'd heard of my marital troubles, she also no doubt knew that the duke's death had put Randolph and me in a desperate financial and social position.

"Yes, it was a dreadful shock," I said quietly.

"And an unfortunate one for his estate, I imagine. I understand his eldest son hasn't his late father's exemplary sense of duty."

As silence once again settled over us, making me despair that I had failed, she added, "I shall speak with my husband. It so happens I believe the Spencer-Churchills have done sufficient penance. Your husband acted indefensibly in his brother's interest, without family consent. Yet seeing as said brother is now the duke, we can hardly allow this discord to persist. Her Majesty concurs. Indeed, it was she who encouraged me to grant you this audience."

I went still, half out of my seat. "Her Majesty . . . ?"

"You must know how highly she regards Lady Frances. Your own efforts to relieve the suffering in Ireland also didn't go unnoticed. My husband can be immovable when it comes to his honor, but . . ." Her voice lingered as I stood there, like an animal caught in a snare. "He is not unreasonable."

"Your Highness." My curtsy was clumsy; I was too taken aback by the turn of events to pay mind to my posture. "I'm indebted to your kindness."

As I stepped to the double doors, she said, "It is not kindness, Lady Randolph. It is necessity. Even wives must do their part for the empire, albeit in our small ways."

She didn't need to say more. One day, her husband would rule over said empire, and her small ways of influencing him might be essential to maintaining his favor.

Yet as I reached for the latch, which wasn't needed, as at an unseen cue the doors were parted by the footmen, I heard a muffled chuckle from behind the screens framing her. I didn't look around as I stepped out, but I knew that derision couldn't be hers.

To my ears, it carried the distinct ring of male satisfaction.

TWENTY-ONE

1884–1885

At over seventy years, William Gladstone was experienced in the vagaries of the political life, having had the distinction of serving as prime minister for three prior terms. Disraeli had mockingly dubbed him "God's only mistake"—a fanged pun on his humorlessness—and in his severe black frock coat with its high collar, Gladstone might have been mistaken for a prosperous undertaker. Until he began talking. He held wide-ranging interests in myriad subjects, from recent archeological discoveries in Egypt to the challenges of Victoria's reign.

I engaged him in conversation as the other guests mingled in our drawing room. Clad in his inimitable silk cravat and black tie, Randolph spoke with the Rothschilds and members of the Liberal Party who supported our PM, mandatory inclusions on the guest list. Like me, he refrained from looking toward the entry every time our butler announced a new arrival, but we were both on edge, fearing Their Highnesses might fail to appear.

We'd orchestrated the entire evening to cater to the prince. A menu composed of his favorite dishes and selections for my after-dinner piano recital by his preferred Prussian composers. At Randolph's insistence, as he was advocating a bill in the House to adopt the invention, we'd replaced our gaslight with electricity—a costly endeavor with drawbacks, as the new lights tended to flicker out at a moment's notice, obliging us to keep candles and lanterns at the ready. For tonight, I'd insisted on candlelight alone to avoid any mishap, though if the prince failed to show, electricity or not, we'd be the laughingstock of London. We'd never survive it.

"You mustn't worry, my lady," Gladstone said in his melodious voice, an instrument he'd honed to perfection and one I suspected Disraeli must envy. "I'm told His Highness has every intention of attending tonight. Alas, punctuality has never been his virtue."

I waved my fan with a careless air. "Is it so obvious, my lord?"

"Not at all." His keen eyes didn't waver from my face, though I'd caught him at our greeting taking assessment of my person. For the evening, I'd spent an exorbitant sum at Worth's London atelier for a gown of exquisite green watered silk, with a bodice overlaid with iridescent African beetle shells upon the fabric like chain mail. The effect was dazzling, the crystallized shells capturing the light, but it was somewhat rigid and fragile.

"As always," Gladstone added, "you appear to be in perfect composure. But"—he lowered his voice—"I'm aware of the significant effort expended on His Highness's behalf."

He glanced at Randolph, who was busy charming a group of wives. "Your husband merits as much. Should he persist in his present vein, he might rise high in our ranks."

"Might?" I echoed.

He returned his gaze to me. "He must curb his tendency toward intemperance. He can be erratic, when the mood overtakes him, as no doubt you are aware. Those rousing speeches of his in defense of Ireland, I suspect you have a hand in them."

Unease went through me. Randolph and I had connived to keep my involvement strictly between us. "You think a mere woman capable of such?"

He chuckled. "All those clever foreign ladies invading our shores: I should think they'll soon be pulling the strings in half the chancelleries of Europe." He reached for his brandy. "Not that I disapprove. Few thought Her Majesty capable at first, yet she's ruled over us for more than forty years and weathered storms that would have felled a lesser constitution. Mere women, as you say, are often anything but."

I inclined my head. "I daresay, your open-mindedness isn't widely shared."

"It is not. But progress is unstoppable. None of us can hope to detain it."

At this, a sudden hush came over the assembly. As I turned to see what the matter was, the butler declared, "His Royal Highness Albert Edward, Prince of Wales, and Her Royal Highness, Princess Alexandra."

Everyone dropped into obeisance. As I painstakingly curtsied, I saw Bertie take a dramatic pause in the entryway. His beard had turned silvery and his paunch discernible. Good living was his vice, and he made no effort to curb it. Alexandra stood glacial at his side in a muted blue gown and diamond-clasped pearls; I now marked the slight bulge of her stomach. The pallor I'd noticed at our audience wasn't due to illness. She was again with child.

"Now, now." Bertie made a dismissive gesture. "Off your knees. No monarch here." Even as he spoke, he disengaged from Alexandra to make his way toward me. His cheeks were flushed as he said, "Gladstone, you sly devil. Monopolizing the hostess, I see. Off with you. I would have the pleasure of Lady Randolph's company to myself."

Randolph eyed me as the PM went to greet the princess. I'd left orders with our staff that dinner should commence within fifteen minutes of Their Highnesses' arrival, so I accepted Bertie's kiss on my hand with the thought that I could weather him for the brief time required.

"May I interest Your Highness in a cognac before the meal?" I asked.

"Is the cognac French?" he retorted, and when I nodded, he grimaced. "I'll drink French wine at dinner." Then he broke into a sudden smile, as if a mischievous boy peeked out of his fleshy face. "Quite the circus you've assembled. You needn't have gone to the trouble. After your bravura at my palace, I'd have accepted any invitation you cared to make."

My blood froze. The chuckle behind the screens . . .

"I wasn't about to let my wife endure alone what could have been another questionable request from the Churchills," he added, his smile widening. "And I confess to insatiable curiosity as to how you intended to extricate your husband from his imbroglio."

My faltering composure flared into temper. "Eavesdropping is beneath Your Highness."

"Is it? After the indignity suffered at your husband's hands?" He took in my chastised expression. "You could not think I'd enjoy being branded a faithless dog. Your family wasn't the only one who had to make reparations."

Alexandra's pregnancy. A princess's timeworn defense against scandal.

"I am sorry," I murmured. "It wasn't something I condoned."

"I did not think you did. You're not cut from the same cloth as my aristocracy, always seeking advantage through my downfall. Tonight's event is a necessity brought on by your father-in-law's death. Otherwise, you wouldn't have spared me a second thought, would you?"

All of a sudden, I found him more appealing. The vulnerability under his royal guise was unexpected, reminding me that, like all of us, he concealed parts of himself, only he had the crown hovering over his head. Royalty was an imprisonment, for all its privileges.

"I don't know you," I said at length. "I know the Prince of Wales."

"Would you be interested in knowing the man?" he asked, with almost childlike eagerness, as well as expectation of rebuke.

"Perhaps," I said, surprising myself. "If I'm not obliged."

He let out a chuckle. "I'm not in the habit of forcing myself on anyone. If you're willing to entertain a private occasion at a later date, and should we discover mutual accord, perhaps we can find a remedy to your predicament. Not that I'm of any mind to assist your husband, but I'd not see you suffer for it. Society has been all the poorer for your absence."

Sensing every pair of eyes in the room, including those of his wife, on us, I smiled. "Then we must see to it, yes?"

"I look forward to it." He hooked his arm in mine and gave me a wink. "I'm famished. Have your meal served and I'll hear you at the piano. No use in letting this trouble go to waste."

"SECRETARY OF STATE in India." Randolph set the official appointment letter on my dressing table, where I sat brushing out my hair before bed. "Quite the honor. Can His Highness have been so impressed by our little gathering?"

I smiled at him in the glass, my hand gripping the brush handle. "Our dinner party had nothing to do with it. That was months ago. Lest you forget, you helped defeat the Liberal budget resolutions by crossing the aisle to declare support for the Conservatives."

"Which made me a traitor, seeing as Gladstone was ousted from office."

"He retired with his dignity intact, having served in exemplary honor. And you made an ally in our new PM, Lord Salisbury. Perhaps he suggested you for the post?"

"Salisbury claims he had no knowledge of it." My husband contemplated me with a hint of suspicion. "Bertie, however, must have."

I made myself shrug. "If he had something to do with it, should we question it? After all this time under his disfavor?"

"I suppose not." He went quiet as I finished plaiting my hair. I had a sharp moment of unease that he'd inquire further or exert his marital rights, though we'd not been together since Jack's birth. I had requested honesty between us, no secrets, and now I was breaking my own rule. But he only said, "I'll have to travel there without you. There's too much unrest in India at present, with those wogs calling for their independence along with our heads."

Much as the idea of seeing India appealed, I was relieved. "It's not the right time, in any event. My sisters and I plan to attend Ascot together this year; as you know, Leonie wed Leslie and is in Ireland meeting his family. And I've received word from your mother that Winston is having a difficult time at school, so I must visit him, and then check in on Jack at Blenheim."

"Very well." As always, Randolph expressed no interest in our sons' welfare. "Then I'll see to my arrangements." With a kiss on my cheek, he retreated to his room down the hall, leaving me alone with my charade.

I should have told him the truth, and I had trouble deducing why I couldn't. After the prince made his offer, I'd accepted the invitation he extended. My curiosity got the better of me; I'd heard so many tales of his prowess not to wonder how much of it was true, and the chance of forgiveness for Randolph couldn't be ignored. I went to his private townhome in Belgravia prepared to decline more than dinner, until he welcomed me into his sumptuous abode, every room redolent with flowers and decorated with his priceless collection of art.

Bertie showed me each painting, explaining its provenance with obvious pride. "For many, these are but adornments. To me, they're pieces of an artist's soul that must be treasured," he said, as I admired a darkly religious painting by the Spaniard Velázquez. I couldn't help but recall all those masterpieces moldering in the gallery at Blenheim, nor wonder how many remained. Not once had anyone in Randolph's family expressed the slightest interest in them.

The dinner the prince served was intimate, an exquisite French menu that made me smile. I was flattered that he sought to impress me, though I knew he was a practiced voluptuary. But given his rank and the harem of mistresses at his disposal, I'd surmised he saw no reason to make an effort. Only then did it occur to me that he truly wanted to be liked for himself.

I ended up accepting more than dinner.

Once he saw me to his bed and stripped himself bare, his rotund, hirsute body and broad grin under his beard were so effusive, I burst out laughing. Without his regal panoply, he was a man like any other, albeit with the power to indulge his every whim—until my mirth turned to smoke in my throat when he fixed his gaze on me and said, "Did you know that in Japan, pleasure is also an art? Their geishas practice it like curators. So dark and enigmatic."

I had to smile. "Unlike most artists, aren't geishas compensated for their performance?"

"As shall you be." His manhood grew erect before me. "I shall see your husband dispatched on empire business—to defend our vital interests in India, no less."

He employed that odd prophylactic device that Randolph had botched in Paris, only he was adept at ensuring its utility. The next time we met, he gave me a pale-blue silk kimono, acquired during his time in Asia. He had me serve tea while nude underneath it, my hair upswept with combs that he removed like butterfly wings, unraveling my tresses as his ardor built. He might not have cut an impressive figure naked, but what he lacked in physicality he made up for in agile expertise. Playful and inventive, intent on my pleasure before his, he explored my body like uncharted territory, making me understand why so many women capitulated to him. I'd felt pleasure before, but with Bertie I experienced fulfillment.

Still, it wasn't an affair, I told myself. Even after I returned home at the preordained hour, to be present when Randolph arrived, I could feel his fingertips on my skin, his quickening as he plunged into me, his teasing whisper, "Not before you, my geisha. You must have your release first."

Yanking my coverlets over my head, I buried my face in my pillows, as though they might douse my shame. I couldn't admit the truth because I'd trespassed over that threshold I'd vowed never to risk again after Ireland. It bewildered and excited me that I still had this depth of passion. While I remained devoted to Randolph, as in all other respects we were perfectly matched, he didn't have the enthusiasm for the intimacy I relished. If I told him as much, it would only hurt him. And as he'd said, whom I enjoyed bedding and whom I loved were not the same.

And I was doing it for us. His post in India could be our stepping-stone to greatness, if he managed his duties as expected.

And he would. If nothing else, I would see to it.

I FOUND WINSTON too thin and pale; most disturbing, he was uncharacteristically subdued. His school was an impressive collection of weathered buildings about a courtyard where the boys could expend their energy in sporting activities, but my boy didn't appear to be enjoying any of it. My inquiries revealed no discernible cause either, other than prolonged homesickness. He kept muttering that he missed Blenheim, Woomany, and his brother.

"I don't understand," I finally exclaimed. "The headmaster sent a letter to your grandmother claiming you fare very poorly in your studies. My pumpkin, how can this be? You love to read and learn. You're very intelligent. Don't you want to succeed here?"

He let out a forlorn sigh, but as I reached out to touch him, he shifted away.

"What is it?" My voice caught. "Winston, please tell me what's wrong."

Without a word, he clutched my hand. His mouth quivered, as if he were holding back tears. Only then did he say, "Don't make me stay here. I want to go home."

"Darling, your term isn't over yet. You must finish out the year. I can't possibly—" Horror rose in me as I started to caress his back and felt him wince. As he tried to pull away again, I took hold of him, easing up his uniform jacket, his rumpled sweater and shirt, to find a lattice of welts across his back.

"What in God's name . . . ?" Fury stoked my voice. "*Who* did this to you?" If Miss Green had been able to beat me with impunity, I would have suffered just as many stripes, if not more. He was defenseless, a child, as I'd once been, but unlike mine, his parents, who were supposed to protect him, had been miles away in London, leaving him helpless.

As his tears broke free and he wept in my arms, I gazed in anguish across the courtyard. A lean figure in a flapping black robe was striding toward us. I came to my feet, my hand nudging Winston behind me on the bench.

"Lady Randolph," intoned the headmaster. "I expected to welcome you in my office."

As he glanced in distaste past me at Winston, I said coldly, "Do you not maintain any discipline here?"

He blinked. "I assure you we enforce the most rigid standards of behavior at all times. I fear your son has failed repeatedly to comply with them."

"How so?" I was having difficulty keeping a civil tone. "Because it looks to me as if someone who complies with your rigid standards has taken a cane to my son's back."

"Lady Frances authorized us to see to his discipline. Winston believes he's above the rules; he's stolen sweets from our pantry to barter with the other boys. He refuses to follow our schedule and questions his instructors without cease. Only yesterday, he dared contradict his history professor—"

"Perhaps his history professor needed contradicting," I cut in, my voice razoring.

"I regret to say this, Lady Randolph, but should matters persist, Winston will be deemed unsuitable for further instruction at this academy."

I took a step toward him. "Did *you* cane his back?" When he failed to reply, I had my answer. "He's a child," I snarled. "A little boy. You'll see his belongings packed this instant and sent to Blenheim. I'm removing him from your establishment, and rest assured, I shall tell everyone I know of your intolerable standards."

He went ashen as I swerved to Winston, who gazed at me in desperate gratitude. Taking my son by the hand, I marched with him across the courtyard toward my carriage.

"Lady Frances gave us authorization," the headmaster called out after me.

I did not pause, but once Winston and I sat in the carriage, departing through the school gates, I looked at him through my own furious tears.

"Never again," I said. "Do you hear me, my darling? No one will ever hurt you again. I promise you, on my life."

LADY FRANCES EXPRESSED incredulity, citing St. George's unimpeachable credentials until I yanked up Winston's shirt to show her his welts.

"He must have done something to merit it," she said, though her own color drained at the sight. "Such punishment is only reserved for the unruliest."

It was how she saw the world. In the minds of those like her, reared on the notion that children must never be indulged, corporal punishment was required to mold them into adult compliance. But much as my mother hadn't tolerated our insubordination, she'd never raised a hand to us nor permitted anyone else to do so. Her punishments had consisted of extra chores, no dessert at dinner, and other deprivations. I couldn't imagine how Lady Frances could see her grandson in such a state and not be as outraged as I was, but she'd given over the raising of her offspring to servants. It made me wonder if this was why Randolph was so indifferent toward our sons, because he'd never had affection in his childhood.

In any event, I couldn't abide her exculpations and went up to the nursery with Winston, who flung himself with a wail of joy at Mrs. Everest. Now in his third year, Jack was walking and chattering up a storm, healthy and happy.

After Mrs. Everest saw Winston bathed and put to bed, she sat with me in her little parlor off the nursery with a pot of tea, where I poured out my fury. Once I was spent, she sighed. "It's been one of my lasting disagreements with Lady Frances. I don't believe the rod can accomplish anything but instill fear in a child. And fear can breed a very difficult temperament once they grow older."

I gulped my tea, thinking Lady Frances would require smelling salts once she learned I'd sunk so low as to partake of refreshment with the nanny, forgoing her inviolate ritual in the drawing room. "I'll not see him in another of her fine institutions. Perhaps I should take the boys to America and let my father see to their education."

"Must the remedy be so drastic?" said Mrs. Everest in dismay.

"Of course, you must go with them. You may find New York to your liking."

"I'm quite sure I would, but I daresay at my age, I wouldn't know how to adjust to living abroad." She paused. "I do know of another school. It's not as prestigious as St. George's, nor, I should think, as costly, but perhaps Winston would do better there."

"Oh? Well, less cost will be welcome, seeing as St. George's charged us a ransom to cane my son," I said. "Tell me about this other school."

I trusted her implicitly. She'd been the sole bulwark between my sons and the Spencer-Churchill legacy of ignoring children until they were deemed worthy of notice. If she knew of a suitable alternative, no doubt it was worth considering.

"I'd suggested it to Lady Frances before," she said. "But she thought Brunswick, which is near Brighton, not any sort of place for her grandson. Yet it has an excellent reputation, with a renowned music curriculum. Perhaps my lady might consider enrolling him there for a term?"

I realized she was doing her utmost to be helpful, while restraining her concern that she'd be left without a position. To my shame, I knew nothing personal about her. I suspected that, like most women without prospects, she'd never married, inserting the "Mrs." before her surname to dispel the taint of spinsterhood and devoting herself to other people's children. I couldn't deprive her of employment, and in truth, my father, with his erratic finances, wasn't the wisest choice to oversee their schooling.

"I suppose it's worth a try. He couldn't possibly be more miserable there."

"I believe he'll be less so. If my lady would permit it, I can ease him into the idea, seeing as the remainder of this term is lost and he'll stay here with us until next year."

I yearned to reach over and take her hand, though I sensed I shouldn't. "I am very grateful for your kindness, Mrs. Everest."

"Oh, my lady. Your boys have claimed my old heart. I think of them as my own."

"And they love you as much. I'm envious of their affection for you."

"My lady, envious of me?" She gave a startingly merry laugh. "Why, Winston thinks the moon and stars of you. To him, you're the most beautiful woman in the world. His eyes light up whenever I tell him his mother is coming to see him."

"The moon and stars," I said quietly, "can be very distant."

Now, it was she who reached over to pat my hand. "If you'll forgive my forwardness, that is why my lady hired me. London is no place for a child. They'll grow into fine young men and appreciate that you gave them plenty of fresh air and room to run about."

"Do you think so?" My throat tightened. "How can Winston ever forgive me for sending him to that wretched place? I promised we could visit on holidays, but we never sent for him; we were always too busy. And on our carriage ride here, after that awful incident at his school, he told me he'd planned out the trains he needed to take, in case I didn't arrive to see him . . ." My voice drifted off as she nodded sadly, but didn't make any remark on what all of a sudden had become terribly clear to me. My son, a little boy, had taken the time to mark out his routes of escape to London, to reach his mother. What did that say about me?

"He spent holidays here," Mrs. Everest eventually said. "Blenheim is his home. My lady mustn't fret. He's at that age when the challenge seems overwhelming, but if it's any consolation, he has never once complained to me about your absence. As I said, he thinks the world of you."

"Thank you again." I was deeply touched by her reassurance. "Randolph has taken a post in India, so I'm on my own for the foreseeable future. Perhaps you and the boys can come this year to celebrate Christmas in London with me."

"We'd be delighted," she said. "I'd much prefer London to traveling all the way to New York. Now, how about another cup of tea, yes?"

TWENTY-TWO

My sisters and I reunited in Paris, filling Mama's overstuffed flat with our chatter and mounds of boxes from our shopping excursions.

Dobbie promptly assumed charge of Clarita's baby son, Hugh, tartly informing us she might be getting on in years, but she hadn't forgotten how to change a swaddling cloth. In the aftermath of her pregnancy, my older sister had grown slightly careworn, though she declared herself content and said that Moreton was making headway with the ranch. I'd heard otherwise. Papa confided in his letters to me that a surfeit of cattle in the state had caused the price of beef to plummet, and he'd had to loan Moreton extra capital to stay afloat. I did not mention it, however, taking Clarita for an afternoon at Worth's atelier. She protested the extravagance, saying she had no place at home for French gowns, but her entire person transformed as she beheld the latest styles.

Leonie radiated newlywed joy. Mama begrudgingly accepted the fait accompli after hearing how warmly the Leslies had received her, despite their initial opposition to the marriage. In private, however, my younger sister confided she'd have to go out of her way to earn their respect, inciting mutual complaints of our intransigent British in-laws and murmured confidences over Papa's inability to cover our dowry payments.

Traveling across the Channel, we met up with Fanny Ronalds in London. She'd decided to join us for the races, as she was in one of her innumerable separations from her composer-lover, their affair as tempestuous and mutually unfaithful as ever.

Fanny refused to age. Still slim and exquisitely dressed in the latest fashions, she had us model our new Parisian acquisitions for her. I reveled in her company, until as we rode in our hired carriage to Berkshire she said, "I understand that among your many notable accomplishments, you've enthralled the prince. I must admit, I'm quite jealous."

"What?" I turned to her in dismay. We rode together, my sisters taking to a second carriage behind us, but my alarm was such that I feared they might overhear.

She laughed. "Don't bother to deny it. Pursuit of Lady Randolph has become a covert assignation among London's most well-heeled gentlemen."

"I'm entirely unaware of anyone's pursuit, save Bertie's. He was hardly subtle about it."

"Yes, well. No one will dare seek to usurp HRH's place in your bed."

"HRH is *not* in my bed," I retorted.

"No?" She arched a skeptical eyebrow.

"No. I was in his. For a very brief time."

"Which is how it should be. A lady should never soil her own sheets." She paused. "Did he not please you?" she asked, with a lack of judgment I had to appreciate.

"He did, for the time it lasted. But he has his obligations, as I have mine. He also has other women. Neither of us expected a long-term arrangement. It was an enjoyable dalliance, and in truth, I'd rather be a fleeting conquest than a permanent addition."

"Of course. He's always held you in the highest of respect." She kept her eyes on me. "If you don't mind me asking, is it true he's as insatiable as they claim?"

"He is. And very skilled," I said, unable to resist a teasing smile. "Surprisingly so."

She sighed. "Oh, my. What I wouldn't give to be ten years younger . . ."

I shifted on my seat. "Fanny, he made it clear that he'd consider forgiving Randolph if he and I found mutual accord. He didn't force me; I was perfectly willing, but should gossip spread, it might reach Alexandra's ears. I betrayed her confidence."

"She'll never hear of it," replied Fanny. "As you say, he has others. And he's never spoken of you in that manner. I only inferred it by how he speaks of you in general; I can tell when a man is besotted. I do find it curious, however, that you're not concerned about it reaching Randolph's ears. India may be across the world, but it's part of the empire. News does travel."

I swallowed. "He already knows." Her eyes widened as I went on. "His posting in India came directly from Bertie; he can't have failed to notice the timing. I suspect he decided to turn a blind eye. After Ireland, we reached an agreement."

"How very civilized. I didn't think he had it in him." She patted my hand. "My lips are sealed. I can't vouch for others, but no one will ever hear a word of it from me."

Ascot was attended by the most well-bred, both animal and human; a celebration of excellence, as well as the unofficial opening volley of the season, where everyone took stock of the competition on and off the racecourse. Constricted by a punishing corset under her new gowns, Clarita shed her pioneer air to wade into a sea of former admirers. Watching our sister assume command of the milieu, Leonie remarked drily, "You'd think she'd never seen cattle, much less lived among them," forcing me to contain my laughter.

In turn, I reveled in the races. The sheen of horseflesh over fine-tuned musculature, the swell of excitement as the trumpets blared and the jockeys tensed on their mounts, the thunder of hooves on the earthen racecourse. It returned me to my childhood, to Papa and his wild carriage rides. Clutching my parasol as the riders vaulted forth, I had to hold back my shouts of encouragement, as it was deemed in poor form to bellow at Ascot.

One competitor in particular caught my attention. Lean as the crop he wielded with an insouciant air, the bones of his aristocratic blood molded like Gothic architecture under his defined cheeks, aquiline nose, and tense-lipped mouth, highlighted by a trim mustache, he couldn't go unnoticed. After winning several races with exceptional ease, he basked in admiration. When he removed his riding hat, his cascade of dark hair was a poetic seduction.

"Count Karl Kinsky of Wichnitz and Tettau," whispered Fanny in my ear. "Greatly admired by Empress Sisi herself, who knows a thing or two about men and horses. He hails from a distinguished lineage and stands to inherit his father's estate, yet remains entirely unspoken for, to the consternation of countless ladies throughout the continent."

I watched him stalk with feline grace through the crowd toward the stables; as he passed under our box, he raised his piercingly dark eyes to us and executed an impeccable bow.

Fanny chuckled. "It appears he hasn't failed to take note of your appreciation, either."

I forced out a smile. "I'm certain he's very aware of his impact."

"Are you of yours? Jennie, you have an arrangement. Randolph isn't here at present."

"I'm still a married woman," I said sharply. "I can't simply—"

"Whyever not? Do you honestly believe your husband is keeping to himself in India? Come now. Allow me to arrange a proper introduction."

"Absolutely not," I said, even as I wished she would.

He found his way to me anyway. At the evening ball, he materialized before me in crisp white tie that turned his complexion to alabaster; he requested a waltz and I found myself caught in his arms as he swept me across the floor, his practiced grace denoting an impeccable education in all the required social graces.

"I fear we'll start a rumor," he said, his English flavored by a slight accent.

"With a dance?" I smiled, aware that his prestigious lineage had marked him as prey by every matron in the room with an unwed daughter.

"I've been warned that Lady Randolph often excites talk."

"And gossips often talk about those they know nothing about. As I'm certain you must know, it being quite the same everywhere."

His smile deepened. "Gossip bores me. I prefer firsthand experience."

As his laden suggestion enveloped us, I sought a hasty change in subject. "You're an expert horseman. Have you always wanted to race?"

"My father's master of horse was English. He had two great passions: his native land and the steeplechase. He taught me to ride, and I've preferred to be on a saddle ever since. Horses will never betray you. People, on the other hand . . ."

I went quiet. He was so handsome and privileged, I'd assumed he would be unbearable in his conceit. Yet he seemed almost nonchalant, as if his suave exterior were a shield. It made him more attractive. It also made me wary, for it was the same quality that had attracted me to Randolph.

"You, too, are an expert horsewoman," I heard him say. "As well-regarded for your equestrian skills as your musical talents and superlative beauty."

I laughed. "Must you flatter me, too?"

"Do I offend?" he said.

I paused. "You do not."

As he escorted me from the floor, I felt the pressure of his gloved fingers on mine and then the card slipped into my palm. "After Ascot," he murmured, "I'll be in London for a time, attending to business interests." He walked away, besieged at once by all the overdressed matrons eager to display their simpering daughters.

With his card in my hand, I thought he could be dangerous to my well-being.

LEONIE, CLARITA, AND I proceeded to Cowes for the regatta, crowding into a hotel suite and bickering over the wardrobe space, as sisters are wont to do. For the final gala, Bertie invited us onboard his yacht. With so many others present, I found it easy to evade him. Alexandra greeted me courteously, inquiring after Randolph. If she knew of my indiscretion, she'd never deign to mention it, and it cemented my determination to keep her husband at bay.

Then I had to say goodbye to my sisters. We promised to meet again soon, tearfully embracing on the docks as Fanny tapped her foot. I felt bereft as their ship departed. The distance separating us seemed too vast.

During the return to London, Fanny said, "I hoped to see more of the gallant count in Cowes. How odd he wasn't there, considering everyone else was."

I thought of his card, tucked in my purse.

"He must have other obligations," I said, avoiding her stare.

"No doubt." With a complacent sound, she settled against her seat.

UPON MY ARRIVAL in Connaught Place, I found an enormous vase of yellow roses waiting for me. Tucked among the thornless stems was a handwritten note:

If you are so inclined, I'd be honored to offer an invitation.

It wasn't signed. There was no need.

Bending down to inhale the roses' heady fragrance, I knew I shouldn't encourage further liberties. It could only lead to one outcome.

I also knew I couldn't resist the temptation.

TWENTY-THREE

He invited me to Covent Garden. I'd had little occasion to attend the opera since my marriage, our social schedule having been made up of dinner parties and other functions to benefit Randolph's career. I was reluctant at first to appear in public with him, but he persuaded me that an evening of music couldn't be construed as anything untoward. To ensure it did not, I invited Fanny to accompany us; as we entered the marble-faced opera house foyer with its Romanesque statues of revered composers, I recalled Papa's joy in music with a pang. I also took note of the new electric lighting, instituted after a conflagration sparked by an errant gas flame had shut down the house for an entire season.

"Oh, Randolph would be so delighted," I said, without thinking. "He championed the wider use of electricity in London, and look—here is his cause, on full display."

Fanny gave me an exasperated look. The usher rang the bell announcing the curtain's rise, prompting Kinsky to escort us to his reserved box without a word. Only then did I wonder if I'd somehow offended by mentioning my husband. While Fanny ignored us, unleashing her opera glasses to scan the crowd, we took to our seats. When the auditorium's magnificent chandelier dimmed, Kinsky leaned to me to murmur, "Do you miss him very much?"

I paused in my retrieval of my own opera glasses from my wrist bag. "He's been away nearly seven months. Letters take too much time, if they arrive at all."

"He's serving as secretary of state in India, yes?" he asked, startling me, though all he'd had to do was make inquiries. As if he sensed my perturbation, he added, "Lord Randolph was mentioned in the newspapers; there's been civil unrest in Burma. I trust he's not in any danger?"

"I don't believe so," I said as Fanny continued to ignore us, too engrossed in seeing who was here and who wasn't. In truth, I had no idea; my most recent communiqué to Randolph had been sent in haste from Cowes, after encountering Mina Boyer, companion of Alfred de Rothschild. Lord Alfred had been named director of the Bank of England, and Mina advised me that the hostilities threatened Rothschild interests in the region's ruby mines; they urgently required that Burma be brought under British authority. In return, she suggested the bank would look favorably upon any personal settlement Randolph and I cared to make. Seeing as our debts continued to mount, I'd informed Randolph, asking that he do whatever he could to assert British dominion. The bank extended an interest-free loan that helped me reduce our debts, but I hadn't stopped to consider whether my request might jeopardize my husband's safety.

"Burma will fight annexation," Kinsky went on, turning his attention to the stage. "I fear these civil revolts invariably turn violent."

The opera was Handel's *Agrippina*, not one of my favorites, and I found myself drifting into unsettled contemplation. Randolph had never suggested he was in any peril, complaining only of India's intolerable cuisine and heat. Still, I might have asked. To distract myself from my belated guilt, I directed my glasses toward the audience; it was a baffling habit in England to converse freely during performances, but tonight, everyone seemed intent on the opera—until I espied a well-upholstered matron with her own glasses fixed on me.

I recoiled. Despite Fanny's presence in the box, the rumor mill would be churning before the second act. While her husband was abroad, defending the empire, Lady Randolph had been seen about town with an eligible foreigner.

Setting aside my glasses, I glanced at him. His long-lashed eyelids had shut in appreciation of the music, his profile etched in shadow; I suddenly longed to trace his angular cheek with my fingertip and let that matron see me doing it. Alarmed by my urge, I abruptly lurched to my feet, startling him from his reverie.

Fanny hissed, "Jennie, the aria is about to start."

"Forgive me," I said. "I . . . I'm not feeling well."

Kinsky hastened after me as I fled the auditorium, holding up fistfuls of my cumbersome gown. In the fog-bound street, where the smoke from the factories accumulated like a sulfuric miasma, I looked for a cab, the sooty mist coating my bare arms and shoulders. I'd neglected to retrieve my wrap from my seat.

His voice fell on my chilled skin. "What is the matter?"

"Nothing." I didn't look at him. "Everything. This was a mistake."

"A mistake? How so? We're attending the opera. It's hardly a crime—"

"You know what I mean."

As my words broke between us, he lowered his head. "Please," he murmured, "let me call for my carriage. I will see you home at once."

I should have refused and found my own way home, if only to quench the gossip. We'd left Fanny stranded in his box. But the opera had just begun and there was no available transport, so when his carriage pulled up, I stepped into it, shivering from the damp. He offered me his cloak. Enfolded in its velvet depth, I smelled his unfamiliar cologne, a hint of citrus and verbena.

"If I've put you in a compromising position, I ask your forgiveness. It wasn't my intention. I thought an evening out . . ." A rueful smile surfaced under his mustache. "It seems I've been a bachelor for too long."

"It's not your fault." I shuddered as warmth returned to my limbs. "It was my error in judgment. When you asked me about Randolph's safety, I realized—"

"What?" He regarded me intently.

"How little thought I've given it," I said.

"Ah. When I asked if you missed him, you merely explained the separation was long and letters unreliable. I assumed you did not wish to say more."

His perceptiveness lodged a pebble in my chest.

"Marriage can be complicated," I said haltingly.

"Indeed. It's why I've resisted it. I'm afraid it's made me a disappointment to my family, but to insist that I wed a titled gentlewoman who can bear me heirs and carry on our name, without ever suggesting she should be someone I care for . . . I find it unnatural." He paused, the silence lengthening. "Do you still love him?"

I hesitated. I hadn't confided in anyone save Fanny about my private life. "I was so young when we wed. I knew nothing of love. Or marriage, as it turns out. He was so different from anyone I'd met; he fascinated me with his defiance, his eccentricity. He persisted despite both our families' opposition to our engagement. That made me love him."

"And now?"

"Now . . ." A tremor crept into my voice. "The demands of his career, of our children and families . . . it changes you. It changed us."

"I am sorry to hear it. I wish only happiness for you, especially in your marriage."

His graciousness made me want to cry. "And I thought differently of you."

"Most people do." He smiled again. "They only see what they wish to see. I've always preferred it that way. Until now." Though he didn't reach for my hand clutching his cape about me, I felt the ghost of his touch like an invisible caress. "I'd heard much talk about the American wife of Lord Randolph. Many here admire and respect you. Many others are envious. But when I first saw you in person at Ascot, you seemed sad to me."

I was taken aback. "Sad?"

"Not to those who don't care to look. But I've been concealing myself for years, and I thought I saw the same in you. Am I mistaken? Do you not hide who you are, to suit the world's perception of you?"

Was that what I was doing? It troubled me that I didn't know.

"I suppose everyone must hide something. If we displayed our true natures, what kind of world would it be?"

"A less civilized one, perhaps," he said, "but more honest."

The carriage came to a halt before my house. We sat in silence, grappling with the unspoken. I loathed leaving him this way. As I started to remove his cloak, he shook his head. "Please, keep it. You can send it to my hotel tomorrow if you wish. This way, something of me can stay with you tonight."

It was a goodbye. He'd not intrude again. He would depart London to return to Austria, and we would never cross paths. He would see that we did not.

And as the sensation of losing something I'd never known overwhelmed me, I surrendered to what I'd yearned to do from the moment I set eyes on him.

I leaned to him and pressed my mouth to his.

"Jennie," he said thickly, as our breath turned molten. "If we do this . . ."

"I know," I said.

APPRISED OF RANDOLPH'S order to invade upper Burma in the name of the empire, Mina Boyer arranged for an intimate retreat at Lord Alfred's country estate, far from the prying eyes of society and equipped with a magnificent stable and discreet staff. The house exuded privacy, the ideal hideaway, making me wonder if it was true what some whispered, that Mina and Lord Alfred had an arrangement, as he preferred those of his own gender and necessitated the outward façade of female companionship.

We went riding every morning, galloping into the mist-steeped heath. To my surprise, Kinsky wasn't competitive beyond the racetrack, declining my suggestion that we race each other. In meadows still damp with morning dew, he took me on the grass. He had the sculpted musculature of a centaur, pared to his bones; as he mounted me while the rising sun gilded the sky, I recalled the savage ardor of Ireland and felt like Persephone, emerging from the underworld to bloom anew. It entranced me, the way his magnificent body molded to mine, the tension in him as he arched toward his release. He was so beautiful that I found myself fearing he might dissolve, like an impossible dream.

In the afternoons, we embarked on aimless walks in the manicured gardens and idled away the evenings in the library until the servants retired. Then we indulged on the Persian carpet before the fireplace, my ecstatic cries escaping me as he took his time. We never spoke of tomorrow. Perhaps because we knew there could be no such thing for us—I was married and he was expected to find a bride of means after having evaded the obligation for as long as his family would tolerate it—we were free of the petty treacheries that illicit lovers face. We needn't worry over how we'd next meet. The present was all that mattered.

Yet as the time drew closer to our departure, I was beset by this very anxiety. I couldn't imagine saying farewell to him without hope, though when I finally mentioned it, in a furtive voice as I lay in his arms, he let out a sigh.

"I don't know. I shall return to England. I wish to ride the steeplechase once I've acquired the right horse. So, we'll see each other again."

"But when?" Despair yawned in me. He hadn't said he loved me, and neither had I said the same to him; but I did love him, God help me. I'd fallen into the very trap I'd known he presented.

"Let us not make any promises." He kissed my forehead. "Jennie, we each have our lives. If we start making promises that we cannot know we will keep, we'll become disappointed. I don't want us to ever disappoint one another."

I drew back. "Does this mean anything to you?"

His face took on an abrupt solemnity. "More than you imagine, apparently."

"What do you think I imagine?"

"I'm not sure. That you're another conquest for me?"

"Am I?"

He slipped his hand through my tangled hair. "What is it you wish me to say? That I'm in love with you? You must know that I am. I think I fell in love from the moment I first saw you at Ascot, perched in that box like a bird in a cage. But you belong to another and I must respect that. No"—his fingers stifled my protest— "you mustn't say in the heat of the moment what you don't mean. You can never leave him; it's unthinkable. And you still love him. Maybe not as you once did, but I see it in you. I hear it when you speak of him. He is your first love and always will be."

A lump filled my throat. I couldn't deny the truth in his words and his humble acceptance of our circumstances ashamed me.

"Why?" I whispered. "Why now?"

"Because love is cruel." He gathered me back in his arms, resting my head on his chest. "Yet we found each other. We must be grateful for it, when so many never do."

ON THE DAY he departed for Austria, I shut myself in my house, sent the servants away, drew all the drapes, and mourned in self-imposed seclusion. Outside, the autumn wind carried the fang of winter. I'd have to bestir myself soon, prepare the house for Yuletide. Winston and Jack would be joining me, though at Lady Frances's insistence, they would return to Blenheim for Twelfth Night. Jack was too young to discern any change in me, but Winston was attuned to my moods; he might sense my despondency. For his sake, I must be the mother he'd always known.

Yet even as I contemplated it, all I could think of were fragments of mist burning on the heath, incinerated by a passion that had turned me inside out.

TWENTY-FOUR

1886–1890

When Randolph sent word that he'd been recalled to England, I determined to confess everything. I had gone beyond our arrangement by falling in love with another man, and if I attempted to carry on behind his back, it would only bring misery to both of us. Upon his arrival after New Year's 1886, he was showered in accolades for his triumph in ensuring Britain retained its stranglehold on India and for the conquest of Burma, prompting his fellow MPs to herald him as a champion of imperial supremacy.

But after his absence of nearly a year, my first sight of him was deeply alarming. His cough, exacerbated by his smoking, was now accompanied by pronounced jaundice. He'd lost weight again, appearing years older than his thirty-seven. He waved aside my concern, insisting he'd been unable to digest what passed for food in India, and plunged into his demanding schedule. I couldn't find a spare moment to sit him down and tell him the time had come for us to separate.

Then, to my surprise, the queen sent word that she wished to bestow upon me the Order of the Crown of India—an honor I found bewildering until Randolph remarked, "It's only given to women. Her Majesty must have been informed that you encouraged me to embark on that bloody mess, so she could gain a new province in her raj. You must accept her offer."

Days before the event, he collapsed during his speech in the House. As his valet undressed him, I gasped. A spidery rash latticed his entire torso. He muttered that it didn't hurt him, and it wasn't palpable, more like a malign pentimento lurking under his skin, but it was enough for me to order him to immediate bedrest.

"No doctor," he said feebly. "If word gets out, they'll cancel our reception at court. Ever since she lost Albert to typhoid, Victoria has a mortal terror of sickness."

While he convalesced, I kept occupied with fittings for my court gown and a surfeit of additional worries. Clarita wrote that Papa had fallen ill with pneumonia and had been advised to take a sea-side cure, but she was with child again and couldn't oversee his care. Might he come to England? There was a spa in Brighton, where Winston was enrolled in school, though I'd yet to pay my son a visit. Our Christmas together had been lovely, and my son clung to me when we parted, begging me to let him stay in London. With months gone by since then, I returned word to Clarita that of course Papa must come. Winston would be overjoyed to see his grandfather.

Then I awoke one night to restless pacing in the corridor. It paused by my door, as if uncertain of its destination. Flinging a shawl about me, I went out to find Randolph drenched in sweat, nude and dazed on the landing. He jolted at my touch, seemingly disorientated as I led him back to his rooms, where his valet, who slept in an adjoining chamber but had failed to wake, apologized for his lack of oversight. Together, we put Randolph to bed and tried to lower his fever, which rose so high that he became delirious, mumbling of monsters lurking in the corners and devils crawling inside him.

I sent word to Dr. Cheever, who'd served the Spencer-Churchills for decades. After enclosing himself with Randolph for well over an hour, he emerged in grim silence into the corridor where I waited anxiously.

"What is it?" I asked. "This fever isn't new, but it's always come and gone. Has he contracted some malady during his time abroad?"

Dr. Cheever's refusal to meet my eyes spiraled my worry. "My lady, I fear Lord Randolph must be the one to inform you of his condition. If he does, I advise you to make an appointment with me at your earliest convenience. I can assure you of my utmost discretion."

I had to resist seizing hold of his sleeve. "Is it so serious?"

He cleared his throat. "Again, I must insist that you speak with your husband. It's unheard of for me, as his physician, to divulge my patient's confidence."

I found Randolph seated in his robe by the fireplace. The shadows of the flames played across his hollow face; at my approach, he said, "Did he tell you?"

"No." I came to a halt, my wedding band indenting my palm as I clasped my hands. "He said you must be the one to inform me."

Randolph kept staring into the fire as if he might find an answer there. As I took another step toward him, reaching for his shoulder, he said, "You mustn't touch me."

My hand hovered between us. "Randolph, what on earth—"

"I'm dying." His declaration cut off my air. Turning to the opposite chair, I fell into it.

"You can't be," I said into the dreadful silence. "It's just one of your fevers. You told me India was unsanitary. You'll improve under the proper care. You always have before."

"Not this time." He shifted his gaze to me; the stoic acceptance masking soul-quenching fear in his eyes terrified me. "It's syphilis. I've had it for years, according to our physician."

I couldn't utter a word. I could barely draw a breath, my entire existence darkening. I knew of the malady, of course—not that it was ever cited aloud in society, nor was it a subject upon which any woman should be conversant, but I'd heard whispers nonetheless, as something terrible that must be avoided, if not a concern for those like us. I'd never heard of anyone in our circle who had it or of anyone who knew someone who had. Even as I thought this, I realized, of course, I would not have. Who would dare admit it?

"It's . . . not possible," I said faintly.

"Cheever thinks otherwise. I have all the signs: the canker that first bedeviled me but then went away, these ongoing fevers, the eruptions on my skin, and now blood in my water . . ." His sudden laughter was harsh. "All that time resorting to spas in Germany and posts in tropical climes, when it seems what I needed was a prolonged dose of mercury."

"It can be treated?" I grasped onto this fragment of hope.

"In its early stages. Though as you can imagine, mercury is not without risk and there's no guarantee of success. And I'm past the early stage. My kidneys are compromised." His voice didn't falter. "You must be examined. There's a possibility you may have contracted it."

A primal scream roiled inside me. "I've never had any signs," I said, thinking of Ireland, of Bertie. Of Karl. Had I unwittingly brought this nightmare into our lives?

"I told Cheever as much. He believes your likelihood is remote, as children born of afflicted mothers are often crippled or perish in infancy, while both our sons are hale."

Despair overwhelmed me as I mentally calculated the last time that we'd been intimate; it had been well over a year, and I hadn't been seriously ill a day in my life, but my skin crawled at the thought that I, too, might harbor this disease inside me.

"I'll make the appointment with Cheever," I managed to say. "But we must seek out treatment at once. Randolph, we'll find a sanatorium abroad. You're not dying yet—"

He held up a bony hand. The firelight seemed to show through the tendons, as if his flesh were translucent. "I won't spend whatever time remains to me chasing false hope. Jennie, listen to me." His resolve riveted me, a sole anchor in the howling disbelief clouding my senses. "It ends in madness. I shall die a lunatic. I'll endeavor to fulfill my obligations until I no longer can and then announce my retirement. Once my time comes, you must see me to my tomb. No one can ever know. Will you promise me this?"

He already had a plan. While I still struggled with the horror, he'd begun to plot our course, as if it were a political campaign in which I'd always played a vital, if unsung, part.

"How?" I heard the fissure in my voice. "How can we hide such a thing?"

"We can. Moreover, we must. Imagine the disgrace, should it become known I perished of this sailor's bane. The humiliation would be unbearable. For everyone."

I felt myself nod. I didn't know what else to do, confronted by something so terrifying, so surreal, it eclipsed my ability to think past it. My husband had an illness I barely understood. And I must keep it a secret.

He looked away as I stood and lurched to the bedroom door, wanting only to flee from the sight of him, melting like a specter into his chair.

At the door, I paused. "What about the boys?"

"What of them?" he replied. "I see no reason to involve them in any of it."

KNEELING ON THE velvet cushion before the queen, I scarcely heard her, missing my cue to rise until someone hissed and I looked up to see her aged hand extending the satin-ribband badge of the order, set with her cipher in diamonds and pearls.

As she pinned it to my breast, I met her filmy gaze, recalling the previous and only time I'd encountered her, at my disastrous introduction with Lady Frances. She appeared ancient; I wasn't certain if it was a smile or a grimace on her bloodless lips as she nodded and stepped back.

Bertie gave me an insouciant wink as I made my way into the hall
for the gala. I'd caused a stir by arriving unaccompanied. Charged
with overseeing the festivities so the queen could retire, Bertie had
me seated near him. Leaning to me, he said, "I trust Randolph isn't
too unwell. We were very sorry he couldn't be here."

I forced out a smile. "He's exhausted. The trip from India and
taking up his duties in the House so soon . . . He sends his regrets." I paused as Bertie's gaze stayed fixed on me in contemplative
silence. "Was it you?" I finally asked, to deflect further inquiry.
"Did you recommend me to Her Majesty for this honor?"

He smiled. "Alexandra petitioned on your behalf. She said you
had earned it for advising your husband to intervene in Burma."

I couldn't tell if he was being facetious. He must have heard
by now that it had been the Rothschilds who first advised me of
the situation in Burma and settled my debts, the safeguarded ruby
mines adding millions to their already immense fortune. I also had
the disconcerting sense Bertie suspected more than he let on, especially when he said, "Should you ever require my assistance again,
you need only ask."

"Thank you, Your Highness." I swallowed the taste of ash in
my mouth. What should have been a moment of pride for me, the
first American woman to receive this royal prize, was tainted by
the knowledge I now carried inside.

Hours later, after I'd feigned interest in the innocuous banquet,
the banal inquiries as to my plans for the summer, which I answered with a false smile—yes, I would attend Ascot and Cowes,
as usual—Bertie escorted me to my carriage. As he took my hand,
he murmured, "I meant what I said, my geisha. You need only send
word."

I knew then that the rumors must be spreading. Randolph had
collapsed in full view of the House, giving rise to unavoidable
speculation. While it was unlikely anyone would discern the precise
cause, we couldn't escape the talk, especially among his political

rivals. Like blood in the water, they would scent his weakness and seek to take him down.

A week later, I submitted to my examination by Dr. Cheever, arriving at his office swathed in a veiled bonnet to avoid notice. After I emerged from behind the modesty screen, he relayed that given my overall state of health and history, which he'd annotated in detail, there was every indication I'd been spared. He encouraged me to ask any questions I might have. There were so many, and all so unspeakable, I couldn't articulate a single one, so he took it upon himself to inform me that going forward, all marital relations must cease. He went on to elucidate that while it was impossible to establish exactly when Randolph had contracted the disease, he believed it to be advanced, so my husband must have had it for a number of years. The end result was "full incapacitation," and it remained contagious. I mustn't risk myself.

I must have shown my anguish, for he gave a troubled sigh. "I've seen many victims of this ailment. It's impervious to class and gender, and fatal in the majority of cases."

"Is there no hope at all?" I asked, my voice fracturing.

"I fear not here. I'm of the firm belief that it's not in our interest to malign the patient, considering how many suffer the consequences. However, as I informed Lord Randolph, on the Continent there's less inclination to condemn one's moral fiber. I understand your husband's need for privacy, but if you could persuade him to consult with my colleague in Berlin, you may find hope there. Herr Ehrlich has made a name for himself in his study of the disease."

I didn't inquire further, my mind too awash in hideous imagery. Leaving his office in sickening dread, I thought it wasn't only our privacy I had to protect. Our very legacy hung in the balance. I must take charge of the situation and organize a trip to Berlin. Once everything was in place, I would inform Randolph of it as a foregone conclusion.

I would not stand by and watch my husband die.

RANDOLPH GAVE ME an incredulous stare. "Berlin? I'm organizing opposition to upcoming measures in the House and have important meetings planned. I can't possibly absent myself on holiday. And lest you've forgotten, you agreed to accompany your father to Brighton."

"Papa isn't coming until October. We'll be back by then." I took in the chaos of his study, the leather-bound statutes by his desk, visible detritus of his determination to focus on what was still within his control. "It's not a holiday. Herr Ehrlich is an expert in—"

"There are no experts." He removed his spectacles, rubbing at the tender spot on the bridge of his nose. "Besides, I haven't had a fever in weeks. The rash is nearly gone."

"You are still ill." I stepped to him. I had to overcome his resistance, but seeing him like this, elbow-deep in his work as if he might maneuver his way out, cracked my heart in my chest. "Randolph, do it for me. I cannot . . . I couldn't bear it if you—if you . . ."

He went still as my voice crumbled. "Jennie," he said softly. "You were the one who told me I'm not dying yet. And while I hold Cheever in high respect, he's not infallible. He acknowledged it might not go as he thinks."

"We still must do whatever we can." I sank to my knees, clasping his hands. He did appear improved. Prolonged rest had restored some color to his cheeks, and he'd been eating enough to put flesh on his bones. What had changed, what I couldn't bear to see, was the muted acceptance in his eyes, the loss of his irrepressible spirit. I hadn't allowed myself to feel it until now, but the thought of losing him before his time, before our time, was a chasm within me, swallowing all the light, all the comfort and trials of our life together.

"My darling." He put a hand to my cheek. "I thought we'd lost this."

"Lost?" I whispered.

"I thought we no longer felt this way about each other." He paused. "Though I fear I must ask, how did you organize it so precipitously? We don't know anyone in Berlin."

I went still, feeling his hand on my skin, his eyes on my face.

He let out a tight exhale. "The Austrian." When I couldn't reply, he removed his hand. "Lady Sandford saw you at the opera with him and Fanny. She's a frightful gossip, so of course she bandied it about. I defended your honor. Not every woman seen in public with a man who is not her husband is a brazen adulteress."

I watched him reach for his cigarette case. "He's a friend," I finally said. "I wrote to request his assistance. I didn't tell him anything other than we required a suitable house to rent for the summer."

He eyed me. "Why not a hotel? It's just a consultation. Or were you planning on a more permanent stay? It would be convenient to have a friend close by, I suppose, while I submit to whatever poison this alleged expert recommends."

I jolted to my feet. "There is no such plan. We need privacy, not an extended stay in a hotel where anyone might see us."

The silence between us grew dense before he said, "Is he your lover?"

For a moment, I wondered if I should deny it. Then I said, "Yes. I was going to tell you about him before . . ."

"Rather inconvenient," he said drily. "To have one's affair interrupted by a fatal disease."

"Randolph, he owns a townhome in Berlin. He's agreed to put it at our disposal. We won't see each other. He resides in Vienna."

He crushed out his cigarette. "He sounds like a gentleman. You should see him, if you like. As I've told you, I don't oppose it, providing it's done with discretion. Attending the opera in his company was hardly prudent, but I'm in no position to cast any stones."

"I have no intention of seeing him," I said again, even as my blood leapt. Karl had returned word that he could travel to Berlin if I needed him; while I hadn't explained the reason for my request, he must have sensed my unvoiced tumult.

Positioning his spectacles back on his nose, Randolph returned to his papers. "Very well. For you, I will go. But, Jennie," he added, "Cheever might be fallible, but he was succinct. There is no cure. We must proceed accordingly."

TWENTY-FIVE

1894

We arranged to meet in Berlin's Tiergarten, a vast woodland park in the heart of the city. Statues of German composers and monarchs punctuated the pathways, their marble reflections wavering in placid lakes where well-fed swans glided like pagan gods.

Berlin belied the Teutonic aggression that the kaiser's bellicose nature had sown throughout Europe. Sophisticated restaurants offered international cuisine, and music threaded the air from the city's beer gardens. The Germans loved to sing, making it part of their daily routine. While I'd come to detest them after their brutality against France, I couldn't hold on to my prejudice; I found them boisterous and welcoming, not at all like their harsh reputation.

However, Randolph's examination by Herr Ehrlich confirmed that both his kidneys and his liver were failing. Mercury could be administered even at this late stage and might provide some relief, but he advised Randolph to put his affairs in order.

Though he'd warned me as much, the diagnosis plunged Randolph into brooding. We had the townhome for the summer, and he agreed to undertake his treatments under Ehrlich's supervision, but waved me off impatiently when I suggested a carriage ride along Potsdamer Strasse or a visit to the museums. And he wouldn't condone me accompanying him to the hospital, declaring it unnecessary for me to bear witness to his ingestion of poison.

Finally, I sent a wire to Karl. I told myself I shouldn't, but I hadn't anticipated the profound loneliness of being in a city where

I knew no one, where my husband was ailing and I had to confront our grim future. In the end, I needed someone to confide in, and Karl returned word that he'd come see me on his way to England, where he'd acquired a champion horse for the steeplechase.

The sight of him walking toward me from Beethoven's monument, in a charcoal gray suit fitted to his elegant form, his silk top hat clasped in his kid-gloved hands, struck me like a blow. We'd had only the one previous public outing. All of a sudden, I felt short of breath as I tilted my parasol over my face, thinking absurdly that we might be recognized, remarked upon, even if there wasn't a soul in the Tiergarten who knew us.

"Oh, Jennie." His greeting was low, imbued with sympathy.

"Is it so plain?" I asked, a sliver in my voice.

He reached for my arm, guiding me into the garden. The wing-swoop of larks and plash of fountains, the cries of children chasing each other as nannies scolded, drifted about us like a distant mirage.

"You look as if you've been through an ordeal," he said.

"Randolph." I took a shallow breath. "He's very ill."

A shadow crossed his face. Before he could ask, I blurted out, "It's syphilis. We came here to consult a physician, but there's no hope. He's dying."

I wasn't certain what I wanted to hear from him. Perhaps in some unacknowledged part of me, I longed for him to say we would still have a future together, once I saw Randolph to his end. It was un-speakably callous of me, but I'd become desperate, envisioning the years ahead of me closing in like a prison—the widowed mother of two sons, excluded from society, relegated to my husband's memory until my own end came. I was forty years old, not yet of any age to be relegated to the confinement of widowhood. I'd never imagined my life could be so savagely disrupted or upended.

He let out a fraught sigh. "I'm so sorry."

"The doctors assure me I'm well," I heard myself say, feeling repulsed by my haste to stake my distance. "By some miracle, I do not have it. But Randolph . . ."

Karl squeezed my hand on his arm. "It's a dreadful fate. You must be beside yourself." I heard by his tone that while he might not have considered my possible contagion, I'd unwittingly broken some elusive spell. While he spoke appropriate comfort, my revelation discomfited him.

I drew back, bringing him to a standstill. "Is that all you can say?"

"I do not know what else one can say to such terrible news."

"My husband is dying. Does it not concern the both of us?"

Though he didn't look away, the distance between us widened. "How so?" he asked. When I didn't speak, he sighed, longer this time. "Jennie, you cannot possibly think . . ."

"Why not?" I whispered.

Now, he did avert his eyes. "Because it's impossible. A widow with children," he said, voicing my private fear. "I'd be disinherited. What kind of life would that be for us? You are understandably distraught over losing your husband. Marriage is all you've ever known. But you would not be happy as my wife."

Mortifying clarity came over me. Marriage had indeed been my refuge. Randolph had rescued me from the only expectation inculcated in me, by allowing us a union that proved both liberating and safe. Because he truly loved me as I loved him. While with Karl, the spell I'd broken was the illusion of an object of desire that could never be claimed. He'd pursued me because I couldn't be anything but an affair to him. And while I'd thought myself in love with him, I now realized that I, too, had fallen for the illusion, seeking to recapture the ephemeral passion that my marriage had faded, to recover the past and not contend with the terrors of the present.

"I am still here for you." The apologetic note in his voice turned my blood to ice. "I will do whatever I can to help you through this awful time."

I raised my chin, blinking back my sorrow and rage. I would not surrender my last shred of dignity. "I appreciate it. However, you must allow us to pay you for our stay in your home."

His eyes dimmed. "Is that necessary? At least allow me this much."

"Very well." I forced out a brittle smile. "It was good of you to come see me, given your schedule. I hope this racehorse in England brings you luck."

He nodded in pained understanding. "The empress wishes to experience the steeplechase for herself. I've been invited to be part of her retinue. I'll be in England for an extended time during her visit, so perhaps . . ."

"Naturally." I tilted my parasol to shield my expression. "You must send word." Even though we both knew he should not send word.

He invited me to tea. I declined, citing my need to return to the house before Randolph came back from the hospital. Accompanying me to my carriage, he said, "My feelings for you haven't changed. I hope I did not deceive you about my intention."

"No," I said quietly. "Rest assured of it."

I'd deceived myself. As my carriage pulled away, I watched him recede under the park gateway, and recalled what he'd said:

Love is cruel. Yet we found each other. We must be grateful for it.

In that heartbreaking moment, I clung to that small gratitude.

RANDOLPH SAT ENVELOPED in a shawl by the fireplace. He gave me a wan smile, a handkerchief clutched to his mouth, wiping away saliva.

"I don't think I can find relief here," he said. "The remedy is worse than the cause."

I sat by his side. He looked at me for a long moment before I felt his thin hand reach out. His touch was papery; he seemed to be dissolving before my eyes.

"Was it ghastly?" Somehow, he knew.

I swallowed. "It's unimportant." I enclosed his hand in mine. "Once I see Papa settled in Brighton, I'll ask Mama to come tend to him. You and I shall travel to New York; they have expert physicians there, too. We mustn't cease until we—"

"Jennie." I flinched at the weariness in his tone. "If your ardor for life could save me, I'd already be cured. It cannot. I would very much like to see America again. Travel is precisely how I wish to say my goodbyes. But, please. No more of this."

I lowered my eyes, tears falling down my cheeks.

He whispered, "Do not weep for me yet. You are engraved in my heart. Not even death itself can make me forget you, Jennie Jerome."

TWENTY-SIX

1895

"Jennie, it's time." Clarita stood on the threshold of my bedchamber at Blenheim. I sat before the mirror, trying to affix a cameo to my black collar. I couldn't seem to make any sense of the latch, pricking my fingers repeatedly until Clarita came to me and clicked it into place.

She gave me a tired smile, submerged in mourning. Averting my eyes from my reflection, in which I saw the same, I stood, swaying for a moment before I started across the room for my veiled hat.

I heard her say, "Are you wearing any shoes?"

I hesitated before hiking up my hem to reveal my black-stockinged feet. "Apparently not." My voice choked. "My husband's burial and I'll be branded a Godiva."

Clarita hastened to fetch shoes from the wardrobe, kneeling so I could slip my feet into their contours. She used a hook to fasten the buttons. "Scandal averted." She stood. "You always look wonderful in black. Remember how he used to say no other woman could wear such an unbecoming hue and appear draped in midnight?"

"Yes," I whispered.

"You must remember him as he was, Jennie. The man who refused to take no for an answer. To bid him farewell is a mercy. He suffered so much, yet to the very end, he was fighting to stay with you."

Despair coiled in my chest, bringing back sharp memories of our peregrination from America to Singapore, Madras to Egypt, and finally back to London when it became apparent his end neared—a yearlong blur of seas and misplaced luggage, of hotels with cracked ceilings and suffocating changes in climate; and, inescapably soul-rending, Randolph with his decaying teeth and ulcerated skin, the tip-tap of his cane on ship promenades and the chipped marble of ruined temples, his haunting desire to take in every sight of our final voyage together. Though Dr. Cheever had predicted insanity, Randolph clung to his lucidity until the very end. He did not die ranting and oblivious. He died exhausted, his body too ravaged to endure any longer.

"What will I do now?" I said haltingly. "How do I live without him? I never thought . . . I never imagined we would end like this."

She linked her arm in mine. "You will find a way. I'm here. Moreton is selling the ranch and I've rented a house in Aldford Park. Leonie is not far in Ireland. You have Mama, too. I know she's no comfort, but she's mourning Papa; she understands what it means to lose a husband. And you must be strong for your sons. They've lost their father. We know how painful that is."

Papa had died the previous year, felled by weakness from his pneumonia. At his burial in Kensal Green in London, my sisters and I were distraught, unable to conceive that our irrepressible father was gone. Mama insisted he'd wanted to be interred in Brooklyn, where they'd acquired their first home, and we must see to the transfer of his remains. I'd been bereaved by his loss, forewarned by it of what was yet to come as Randolph succumbed to his illness. Now I longed to launch a vociferous grief that would shatter this palace, crack its frescoes and unhinge its last remaining masterpieces from their frames. But I couldn't weep, as if the flood behind my eyes was held back by an intangible wall.

How could I not shed a tear, as if I'd lost any capacity for crying? As my sister led me to the staircase and I saw my sons waiting in the foyer below, the funeral cortege gathered in the outer courtyard beyond, I balked.

"I can't," I whispered. "I can't watch him be put in a tomb."

Winston was gazing up at me, stalwart in his black frock coat. Now in his twenty-first year, he bore a shocking resemblance to Randolph when we first met. Beside him, fifteen-year-old Jack was lanky, too mature, already an adolescent without my having taken notice of it, while Lady Frances and my mother flanked them like decaying artifacts.

Clarita paused. "You must. You're not the distraught widow who must keep to her bed lest she faint. Would you be like Lady Frances?"

I snorted. "She only deigned to keep to her bed after she oversaw her husband's funeral like a general. And not for long, once she heard Albertha plotted to seize the estate."

"Well, there you have it. The British can't abide self-indulgence." She released my arm so I could descend alone. "Show them what Lady Randolph is made of."

MY LONDON HOUSE was too large. Too empty. Countless times, I started in my seat, my book shifting in my hands, imagining I'd heard the front door open, the wet sough of his umbrella, his grumble about the dreadful weather and his party's indecisiveness. It had the eerie feeling of the time he'd been in India, as if he'd return, except I knew he never would. The silence was too immense as I wandered through rooms decorated to exalt our prestige, populated by memories of our parties, the intrigues of our guests. The table in the foyer overflowed with bouquets and condolences sent by everyone who'd known him; I couldn't bear to open a single one until my butler took it upon himself to set the most pressing before me, alongside preaddressed acknowledgment cards I must sign. Even in death, appearances had to be maintained.

Bertie wrote to me in genuine affection, again offering his support in whatever I might require; his missive so warmed my heart, I sent him one of Randolph's watches as a token of appreciation.

Karl also conveyed his condolences in a perfectly composed letter that included the offer for me to visit Vienna, where he had a
house at my disposal. It kicked up the passion for him that I was
determined to put behind me. I knew he had toured England and
Ireland with his exuberant empress and champion horse, winning
the steeplechase, and I'd been abroad with Randolph in Egypt
when I read in *The Times* that Karl had wed a titled heiress, as ordained by his family. It came as no surprise to me.

Much as I wanted to, I did not reply to him.

Then Winston came to see me, on leave from his regiment to
visit his beloved Woomany, whom Lady Frances callously discharged
upon Jack's entry in school. She'd barely given Mrs. Everest notice to
pack her bags, enraging Winston, who posted to me furious grievances that arrived months after the fact, as his father and I were
traveling. Upon his graduation from the Royal Military Academy
Sandhurst, he'd been accepted into the 4th Queen's Own Hussars.

Now my son strode about my parlor in his braided red and gold
military dress, a lock of his thick hair, turned darker in adulthood,
escaping its pomade to furl across his forehead.

"We must give her a proper severance for her years of service.
She was devoted to us and now she's living as a tenant in her sister's
North London home. It's appalling."

I nodded in commiseration. "Yes, I agree her discharge wasn't
handled well at all, and I do feel for her. But we've nothing to offer
her. Your father's testament—"

His quicksilver swerve to me took away my breath, it was so
like Randolph's. "What of it? You were named joint trustee of his
estate. I was present at the reading of his will."

I met his indignant stare. "Yet you apparently failed to hear
that after his debts are paid, the capital share of his estate is held
in trust for you and Jack until you both wed, with the profit from
the proceeds provided to me for my expenses. Winston, we're not
wealthy. How do you expect us to help Mrs. Everest?"

"We have that pile in Oxfordshire full of treasures no one cares about," he retorted.

"Blenheim and its neglected treasures went to your cousin Charles upon your uncle George's death." I refrained from adding that Lady Frances had also seen to Charles's engagement to Consuelo Vanderbilt, the New York heiress—an irony not lost on me, except this time, my mother-in-law had made certain the American fortune was intact and sufficient to shore up Blenheim. After losing her husband and both her sons, she'd resolved to keep the estate where she believed it belonged, which was nowhere near her half-Jerome grandchildren.

Winston went still. "Are you . . . ?"

I made myself shrug. "I'll make do. I'll have to sell this house and find a smaller residence. A widow doesn't need so much space, or so your father's solicitor has informed me."

He scowled. "That ferret. How could Papa leave us in such a state? And it would seem poor Woomany must suffer for it as well."

"Your father," I said quietly, "often failed to think matters through. In any event, we must get on with the business of living. I am very sorry about Mrs. Everest, but unfortunately there is nothing we can do. I must put this house up for sale and travel to America to rent out our mansion. It will bring in extra income, which your aunt Clarita sorely needs. She's living here now, with three children to raise, and—"

"A ne'er-do-well of a husband," cut in Winston, his scathing insight once more reminding me of his father. "Did Moreton's expedition to mine—what was it again, diamonds in Australia?—fail to yield the fortune he anticipated?"

I had to curb sudden laughter. "I'm afraid so." As silence fell over us, he sat on the sofa opposite me, folding his long hands. He had refined fingers, like mine. Fingers made for the piano, which he'd never taken to, despite the vaunted music curriculum at Brighton.

"I must seek employment then," he said. "Work for a living, like any honest man."

I started in my chair. "What of your military commission? You can't abandon it. Winston, it took three separate attempts for you to gain admittance. I won't hear of it."

"I can't drill and march forever. I need some experience in this business of living, as you say. I may as well start now. Spencer-Churchill men tend to die young."

"You cannot live in fear of that," I said. He didn't know the truth about his father. I'd kept it a secret as promised, telling everyone my husband had suffered from a brain tumor. Still, Randolph had only been forty-five and his brother George forty-eight at the times of their deaths, so I couldn't truly fault my son for believing his lineage was short-lived.

"Perhaps not, but it's still advisable not to waste time. Cuba is fighting for its independence from Spain. I wish to go there, but I need an official credential."

"Credential?" I echoed. War was the last thing I wanted him to pursue, but he had both the virtues and the defects of his bloodlines. Like Papa and Randolph, when he set his mind to something, nothing could dissuade him.

"As a journalist," he explained, betraying that he must have been considering it for some time. "I could then travel to Cuba to report on the conflict."

I was surprised. "Do you wish to be a journalist?" Even as I spoke, I recalled his numerous letters to me over the years, the ink that kept us bound. I'd read some of them aloud to Randolph as he sipped his cognac before the fire. Though my husband never had much praise for our sons, he remarked that Winston had apparently inherited my talent for words. "He writes like you, my darling. Perhaps we should hire him to compose speeches for me."

As I recollected this, Winston said, "Yes, I think I'd like to write for a living. And you know all the newspaper editors who supported Papa."

"Are you asking me to find you a job?" I asked wryly.

"Would you?" He leapt to his feet. "It would mean so much to me."

I melted at his eagerness. "I suppose I owe you as much, after my years of neglect."

"It wasn't neglect." He bent down to kiss my cheek. "I understand how much you had to contend with. Just allow me the introductions and I'll do the rest."

He sundered me where I sat. My little boy, who had never faltered at speaking his mind, was now a young man, who should have had a litany of reproaches to lay at my feet for the years I'd left him to fend for himself in Mrs. Everest's care, at the mercy of his intolerant grandmother. Instead, he was comforting me, and it prompted me to say, "I have a little reserve in case of emergencies. It's not much, and not nearly sufficient to change her living situation, but you must take it to your Woomany, Winston. We do owe her at least that."

"Mama." He blinked against sudden, uncharacteristic tears. "Are you certain?"

"I am. It's not enough to make any difference to me, but it might be for her." I smiled back at him through my own threatening deluge. "We are not Spencer-Churchills who think the world owes us," I added quietly. "We must never behave as if we are."

AFTER CARING FOR Papa in Brighton, Mama had declared her decision to stay in England. We tried to persuade her otherwise, seeing no reason for her to upend her life—she'd never expressed a desire to be closer to us in her old age—but she insisted on selling her flat and renting a house in Kent. She hired a local day maid, as

Dobbie had grown suddenly very frail, her years of stoic devotion melting flesh from her bones. She passed away one morning while preparing the tea for delivery to my mother's room, a task she'd refused to relinquish; her heart gave out, so that in her final moment, she must have been outraged that death had had the poor taste to take her then and force her to leave an unfinished duty behind. I was grief-stricken, my mourning for her so sharp and deep that I felt as if I were drowning. Mama was beside herself as well, but when I insisted that we must send Dobbie's body for burial next to her family, my mother said, "How? We can't afford it, if we could even locate where her family is."

"You . . . you don't know?" I was aghast. "*How* can you not know? You were the one who first hired her. Surely, you must have some idea of where her family might be."

"Honestly." Mama plucked at the blanket across her knees. "I hired her when I was about to marry your father. She kept in touch for a time with her family, but I never inquired or intruded in her personal life. It was not my place."

"Then we must search her belongings, see if there are any letters—"

"There are not. When we left Paris, she had only one bag, with her clothing and her Bible. She'd stopped corresponding with her family after I gave birth to you and your sisters; three girls to raise while your father was establishing his business was more than enough for the two of us."

"Then we must acquire a plot for her in New York. And don't tell me we can't afford it," I said, cutting off her immediate protest. "You sold everything you owned in Paris to move here, though I still don't understand why, save for that ridiculous imperial porcelain. We can sell that to cover the expense."

"Never." Her face shut like a trap. "How I dispose of my belongings is my affair. Dobbie would never want me to sell something so precious to buy her a plot. Enough, Jennie. We shall bury her right here. Her soul is with God. Her earthly remains do not care where they rest."

I thought her heartless and cruel, and it hardened me even more against her. But I couldn't undertake the expense on my own to send my nanny's body overseas, and when I rallied my sisters, they demurred, not selfishly but in genuine regret. None of us were solvent enough to do it, even if we pooled our resources, so Dobbie had to be buried in Kent.

Much as I resented my mother for refusing to honor our nanny in death, she visibly and rapidly declined without Dobbie at her side. It soon became apparent to us that our mother alone in Kent, with just the day maid to tend to her, wasn't safe or sensible at her advancing age.

"Why not come live with Leonie or me?" Clarita pleaded during one of our visits. We always went to see her together since Dobbie's passing. In addition to our argument over her remains, Mama had still never fully reconciled herself to my rebellious marriage, though she'd allegedly boasted of it in her salon. Even now, she eyed me askance in my black mourning, making me brace for her terse reminder that she'd foreseen this hour when I'd find myself in precisely the situation I faced—a widow, desperately short of income.

Swathed in a shawl in her armchair, her hair gone completely white, she was diminished, a shadow of the formidable woman we'd known, but her reply was firm as ever. "I have no interest in dying in an Irish castle, and most assuredly not in London with children underfoot. I'm perfectly fine here."

"She's given up," said Clarita sadly as we returned to London. "She misses Dobbie and Papa too much. She lived since she was a bride with Dobbie at her beck and call, and she never stopped loving Papa. She left him, but in her heart, she always saw herself as his wife."

We were not with Mama when she passed, Clarita weeping in anguish when news came that she'd died alone, as she'd determined to live in her final years. She left her last word in her testament, dividing her remaining estate between my sisters; according to her, my late husband had provided for me. She bequeathed minor sums to Winston and Jack, as well. Only then did we learn that to ensure our New York mansion remained ours, she'd used the bulk of the proceeds from the sale of her Paris flat and belongings to pay all of Papa's outstanding debts. She requested burial in Brooklyn, beside Papa (she left a specific sum for it) and that her porcelain remain in the family. I dispatched it into storage, along with my belongings, as my house was under contract to be sold. I detested that porcelain with every fiber of my being, but Clarita almost wailed when I suggested we auction it off.

While Clarita saw Mama embalmed for transport to America and arranged the transfer of Papa's casket from London, I scraped together funds with Leonie and Winston to purchase a mausoleum in Brooklyn. I thought of exhuming Dobbie, putting her in the mausoleum, too, but Winston counseled me against it, citing we only had enough to see to my parents.

Leonie accompanied me to New York. Just before we boarded our ship, Winston sent a letter. He'd been hired by the *Daily Graphic* and was on his way to Cuba. He would meet up with us in New York; he longed to see America with his American mother. And he enclosed the last letter he'd received from my mother. To my surprise, it appeared he'd kept up a regular correspondence with Mama and she'd always encouraged him, citing her maxim that nothing worthwhile was accomplished without endeavor, as she must have done so many times with my father.

As the ship departed England, I didn't look back at the receding cliffs, gazing instead into the tumultuous waters, reflecting my year of loss and reconciliation, of seeking a way back to who I had been, even if that girl no longer existed. I was the widow Lady Randolph now; and if my circle continued to include Bertie of Wales, I'd still been cast adrift from the anchor of marriage.

I must learn to fend for myself, without Randolph at my side. And I'd have to be bold. Much like those of my sons, my destiny was mine alone to forge. I would not end my days like Mama had, a cantankerous captive in death's antechamber.

No matter the cost, life was meant to be lived.

PART IV

CHURCHILL'S WIDOW

1899–1921

*Life is not always what one wants it
to be, but to make the best of it as it
is, is the only way to be happy.*
—JENNIE JEROME

TWENTY-SEVEN

1899

"Traveling abroad was all very well," I told Bertie as we dined in the ostentatious great hall of Warwick Castle. "But I was starting to feel aimless. One can't depend on the generosity of one's friends forever. I needed my own home again, something useful to occupy my time."

"Hence, your magazine?" He smiled at me through his voluminous mustachios; he'd grown increasingly stout in his late middle years, if no less enthusiastic. "It's not the preferred occupation for an aristocratic widow, is it?"

His tone was jocular, not condescending, though other reactions had been less conciliatory. "My *Anglo-Saxon* is a distinguished quarterly dedicated to culture, featuring articles by our most accomplished writers," I replied. "Not just a magazine."

"And quite the undertaking. You must know it'll cause a stir, launching yourself as an entrepreneur. Some might even say it's not fitting for a widow of your station."

"Perhaps." I sipped my wine, holding his gaze. "This particular aristocratic widow, however, would prefer to do work rather than mourn."

As soon as I spoke, I feared that he might interpret my remark as an aspersion cast upon his mother, the queen, who'd dedicated herself to her mourning, but he burst out laughing instead. "Well, don't let your passion for the written word overshadow our dire need for single women who know how to dance. We've far too few of you as it is."

I had to smile. "I've no intention of putting away my dancing shoes."

His gaze turned carnal. He never missed an opportunity to make his advances, but to his amusement and frustration, I kept citing my work on the review—a time-consuming endeavor that I'd plunged into after two years abroad, wandering from Paris to Cairo. Upon my return to London, with no idea of how to get on with my life, let alone replenish my finances, Winston came to see me, on leave from assignment in India to consult with his publisher. He'd written a well-received account of his experiences fighting rebels and grumbled that England sorely lacked for a reputable literary review. He encouraged me to try my hand at it, so I scraped together the initial investment through various loans from friends and called upon my writer contacts, most of whom leapt at the chance to deliver original essays and cultural reviews. After painstakingly editing the content, I launched the debut issue with a cover of classic art from the British Museum. While there'd been disdainful sniffs from those who thought a widow should confine herself to gardening or needlepoint, its poor sales couldn't be solely attributed to that. More likely, as Winston remarked, the quarterly needed time to cultivate its readership.

Although Bertie detested anything more onerous than a newspaper, I dispatched a copy to him and then had to accept his invitation to this weeklong stay in the ancient seat of Henry Beaumont, Earl of Warwick, and his socialite wife, Daisy. Being seen in his company would generate publicity, and Bertie complied by taking us on an outing in a new motorcar about the castle grounds—a thrilling novelty for me that was photographed for the newspapers. He also unleashed his habitual arsenal of seduction, until he took notice of the ardent focus on me by a fair-haired member of his Scots Guards, who'd been circling me all weekend, and now watched intently from his post at the wall.

Bertie shot him a glare. "That misty-eyed pup is starting to make a nuisance of himself."

"Who?" I asked, feigning nonchalance.

"You know very well. George Cornwallis-West, heir to Ruthin Castle. He might boast of noble lineage, but he's expected to marry wealth, like his sister before him. He's also twenty-four," he added pointedly. "The same age as your son. How is Winston these days, by the way?"

I took up my glass, hoping my sudden flush went unnoticed. I'd smiled and encouraged Cornwallis-West without taking into account the disparity in our age, his attention a welcome reminder that I could still attract notice beyond the prince. With Bertie, it was a given, something he almost did by rote and I laughingly but firmly fended off; I was no longer under any obligation to him, and while I'd enjoyed our intimacy, bedding him entailed additional complications I'd rather not invite in my widowhood.

"Winston is doing well," I said, to hide my discomfort. "Rather too well, one might say."

Bertie guffawed. "Yes, I heard talk of some extraordinary Savile Row debt he ran up. Do journalists have need of expert tailoring?"

"Young men like to impress, even if they lack the funds to do so." Not that I'd been at all pleased by my son's outstanding bill, which had fallen upon me to cover.

"And is he still in Calcutta, writing for—what was it again?"

"He's in the Sudan at present, reporting on Kitchener's campaign for the *Morning Post*."

Bertie grimaced. "A nasty business. And not likely to improve."

A pang of worry went through me. Since his time in Cuba, Winston had taken to the pursuit of war reporting with fervor. But rather than compose dispatches from the safety of a desk, he was plunging headlong into conflict, causing me no end of anxiety.

Bertie gestured at the servitor to refill my glass, another obvious attempt to intoxicate me enough to gain entry to my bed. When I glanced to where Cornwallis-West was standing, I found him gone. A pity. I enjoyed how his adoration crept under Bertie's skin.

"I trust Jack doesn't intend to follow in his brother's footsteps? Having two sons trotting about with pen and rifle would wreak havoc on any mother's nerves."

I sighed. "Unfortunately for me, Jack has been commissioned into the Hussars. He's mentioned the possibility of deployment to South Africa."

"He mustn't." Bertie's stern reply took me aback. "The Boers have discovered diamonds in their republic and vow to repel any attempt we make to seize control. War is inevitable." He grunted at my silence. "Have your son steer clear of those savages."

"I hardly think Dutch Calvinists can be called savages."

"Fie. You think like an American. The Boers overthrew their own East India Company and resisted our abolishment of slavery, much like your ravaged southern states. We've tangled with them before. Believe me when I say, they can be exceedingly unpleasant."

"But if Jack's regiment is deployed . . ."

"Send word to me. I'll see he's kept safe." Bertie patted my hand on the table, in full view of those about us. From her place beside her husband, Daisy, a longtime friend of mine, gave me an amused look. She was Bertie's most recent mistress, with whom I'd shared confidences of his inexhaustible vigor, though it fell upon her to keep him sated during this visit.

Stifling a yawn, I came to my feet. "I fear I'm exhausted. By your leave." As I started to make my exit, Bertie snarled, "Must I come knocking at your door like a schoolboy? Or shall I find that Cornwallis pup barring my way?"

He sounded genuinely frustrated, as well as jealous, both of which took me aback. Until now, I'd assumed he shared my belief that we'd had our time together and casual flirtation was all we should expect of each other. And his unwitting echo of the time at Blenheim, when Randolph had done just as he described, roused abrupt sorrow in me.

"You're here for someone else," I reminded him. "Honestly, Bertie, you don't think—"

He grunted. "And it would seem that you, too, are here for someone else."

Was he *pouting*? I didn't linger, weaving my way from the hall and pausing to roll my eyes at Daisy. Let her sort him out.

Once I was in the dank corridors leading to the guest wing— like Blenheim, the castle was a monstrosity demanding constant stamina and upkeep—I tugged at the combs in my hair, unleashing my coiffure in relief. My feet ached in my satin shoes and my corset was too tight, despite my reluctant acceptance that my days of a sixteen-inch waist were over. I'd kept up my strict regimen of horseback riding, determined not to succumb prematurely to corpulence, but I was no longer the svelte girl of my youth.

Still, as I navigated the dimly lit corridors under the mildewed eaves, I couldn't resist a surge of melancholy. I had my independence and my literary review, my new house in Great Cumberland Place, by Marble Arch. I didn't mind so much that my income remained perennially scarce, but I did mind the solitude; I missed a life together with shared goals. Though I'd filled my time with travel and friends, Randolph's ghost haunted me. To my consternation, I found myself resisting taking a lover because, perversely, now that he was gone, I didn't want to betray my husband's memory.

Most of all, I missed being in love, the heat of skin upon skin that transcended the flesh. And for a woman of my age, such longings were absurd. I was pining like a lovelorn adolescent.

I almost failed to hear him coming up behind me. When I discerned the footstep at my rear, I turned about, half expecting to encounter Bertie, soused and grinning. Instead, to my simultaneous dismay and delight, I was greeted by the ardent hazel eyes of my admirer.

"My lady Randolph," he said, somewhat breathless, as if creeping behind me had cost him effort. "I was hoping we might have a moment alone."

We had, in fact, not had such a moment due to Bertie's presence. And now that we did, I saw he was indeed a pup, as the prince had called him, with the flawless complexion of youth, evanescent color, a high unlined forehead, and moist lips under his wax-pointed mustache. His dark suit adhered to an almost too-slim frame. He was, I realized, a gilded reflection of Randolph—the same polished façade, with a furtive vulnerability in his gaze untried by maturity. Though he was far more angelic looking than my late husband, the resemblance was still unsettling, as if we already knew each other.

"You . . . you do wish the same?" he asked, his voice quavering.

"To share a moment alone? For what?" Of course I knew what he wanted. I'd seen that look enough times to recognize it. But he was very bold to have ventured this far. Few men would have dared, with the prince under the same roof.

"So we might know each other," he said. "I've done nothing all week but try . . ." His plea drifted into uncomfortable silence when I said nothing. He bowed his head. "Forgive me. I intrude on your privacy. It is late. Another time perhaps."

As he turned heel, I heard myself say, "I've learned that time shouldn't be squandered."

He paused, glancing over his shoulder.

And I smiled.

TWENTY-EIGHT

My Missie, I'm always thinking of you. I cannot help but build castles in the air about you and I living together, you in your lovely Japanese gown and me in my old slippers. I have been so forlorn since we last parted, fearing all our little plans for our future might burst, like a bubble . . .

Clarita glanced up in astonishment from the heap of ribbon-tied letters I'd handed her. "Little plans? Lovely Japanese gown?" she echoed. "Jennie, has he *proposed* to you?"

I had to stop from yanking away the letters from her. "Not in so many words, but yes, I believe he does hope for us to marry. I wanted you to read his letters for yourself so you can see it's not what they're saying. He does truly love me."

She thrust the parcel onto the side table. "Do you even know what they're saying? He's young enough to be your son is what they're saying. It's a scandal of the highest order is what they're saying. From his parents to Bertie himself, everyone has expressed disapproval of it."

I laughed. "Of course Bertie must disapprove. He sees no advantage in it for him if a woman should marry for love."

She gaped at me, momentarily speechless. She'd come to London at my behest from her new home in East Sussex. Moreton had acquired the property from his older brother, at my sister's urging. She was expending money on rent when the neglected estate guaranteed an annual income, and, while sorely dilapidated, it could be restored. After Moreton bought it, Clarita had it bound in trust as a legal inheritance for their son, Hugh. She then set herself to repairing the manor, relieved to have a roof over her head that her husband couldn't squander on his foibles.

"You should have a care," she said at length, "because everyone who disapproves will also oppose marriage. Jennie, you must end it at once. How could you—"

"End it?' I exclaimed. "Why? Because they don't approve? Yes, George stands to inherit a title, but it's not as if I'm preying on his wealth. He's no innocent."

As her color drained—every year that passed, she resembled Mama more, encased in a fortified corset that failed to contain her disapproval and overflowing curves—I thought she would have an apoplexy if she knew everything I had done.

How on that night in Warwick Castle, I'd invited him into my chamber, taken George's face between my palms and kissed him, thinking to leave him in a sated puddle, only to discover he wasn't as malleable as he appeared, his rush to divest himself of his attire revealing taut flesh. How I'd felt embarrassed to show myself to him and he'd removed my clothing as if I were a long-awaited goddess, worshipping between my thighs until I had to sink my teeth into his shoulder to keep from crying out. How we spent the rest of the summer trailing each other at the various estates where Bertie made his rounds, conspiring to meet in secret at night, brewing such a tempest it was a wonder we didn't bring the very eaves crashing down upon our heads.

"If he marries you, his inheritance could be forfeit. It would be a terrible scandal . . ." My sister's declaration faded as she took in the expression on my face.

"No one approved of my first marriage," I said. "Why should my second be different? I'll not allow society to dictate my life. We satisfy each other. That is all we need care about."

As my sister sank into the settee, I felt sudden remorse, knowing how difficult her marriage to Moreton had turned out to be. "Clarita, I love him, too. He makes me feel so young again. So alive. You cannot imagine it."

"No," she said. "I surely cannot."

I had started to reach for her hand when she said, "But it is not love."

"What?" I stared at her. "Would you presume to tell me my own mind?"

"You did ask for my opinion. The fact that he'll inherit a title can't be disregarded. You are in dire need of funds. To become his wife would resolve, at the very least, your financial constraints."

"Not if he's disinherited," I retorted.

She sighed. "Be that as it may, it's an infatuation brought on by your circumstances. You first fell in love with Randolph when you were very young, only to lose him before his time. Now you've reached a time when you fear you'll not find that love again. But it's not the same." She softened her tone. "He can never be Randolph."

"Don't you think I know that? I was married to Randolph for twenty-one years."

"Then why do it all again? You tossed caution to the wind for him, yet surely you must know better now. Mama always said your passion overwhelmed your reason—"

"Mama was wrong. I had to be very reasonable with Randolph. Anything we achieved in our marriage, we only did so because of it."

"That may be true, but, Jennie, you can't thumb your nose at the world this time." She went quiet for a moment. "His family has expectations. Conceiving at your age may be impossible. Would you deprive him of children, of a legacy, because of how he makes you *feel*?"

I bit back another protest. I hadn't wanted to contemplate this unavoidable fact.

"We haven't discussed children yet," I said. "It's much too early for that."

"If it's not too early to be discussing marriage, you must broach the subject." Clarita sighed. "One of you has to."

I abruptly felt very foolish. "I suppose I'll talk to him, then."

She nodded. "Do it as soon as possible, before this gets entirely out of hand."

TWO DAYS LATER, George burst into my house in his Scots Guards uniform, which I thought devastatingly attractive with its blue wool tailcoat and black-braided epaulettes. Before I could catch my breath after his exhilarated embrace, he cried, "We are going to war against the Boers! The announcement will be in every paper tomorrow. War, my love," he said, as if it were a pageant. "At last, I'll have a chance to prove myself at something other than guarding the palace gateway."

As he poured a measure of French cognac—like Randolph, he relished its expensive taste—I struggled for the right words. My thoughts immediately went to my sons. I'd persuaded Winston to campaign for his father's parliamentary seat—a time-honored Spencer-Churchill tradition, as I took pains to remind him. His journalism was costing me too much anxiety, not to mention expense, and while he hadn't been pleased, he'd heeded my advice. But Jack was still in the Hussars, and as I recalled Bertie's warning to steer him clear, I thought that given the prince's temper toward me, he might not be willing to make good on his offer.

"Have you nothing to say?" George removed his coat, his starched shirt sweat-dampened under his arms as he gulped down his cognac and regarded me in unfettered enthusiasm.

"Must you go?" I immediately asked, with concern, but not so much as to be cloying.

"Naturally. Every Englishman must. I'll put in my request, as shall others in my regiment. You might put in a word for me as well."

"A word? To whom?"

"To His Highness. A palace recommendation would secure me a posting."

"Bertie isn't likely to give us anything at this time. He's quite cross with us."

"He also knows that to defeat the Boers, we'll need as many able-bodied men as we can muster. If Winston is going, why should His Highness deny me?"

"Winston is *not* going. He's no longer employed as a journalist. He's in Oxford, preparing for his campaign."

George eyed me. "I've heard otherwise. It's no secret you and I are about to be engaged; my mates in the Guards have done nothing but tease me about it—all in good sport. One of them knows Winston and tells me your son intends to report on the war."

This wasn't the right time; I was too alarmed by the news of Winston, but Clarita was right: it had to be broached, especially as George believed we were already engaged.

"Have you considered children?"

He frowned. "I don't intend to wage war on the Boer—"

"Not *their* children. Yours. George, I may not be able to give you any."

"Oh." He went still. "I suppose we'll have to try and see."

"What if we try and I can't? I'm not . . ." My voice faltered. I found it impossible to say that, besides my age, there was my disinclination toward it. I had two boys. I wasn't interested in another pregnancy or the trials of rearing a babe. Moreover, I couldn't afford it. I'd had Blenheim and Mrs. Everest before to see me through.

"I don't care about that," he said. "My sister will have children."

"You're the only son. The heir. Your parents expect it of you."

"Well." He shrugged, with what seemed to me more defiance than conviction. "They'll have to adjust their expectations. I love you and want you to be my wife."

I sighed. Perhaps it was best to leave it for now. With war looming over us, marriage was far enough in the future that we could
discuss it at a later time.

"What else have you heard of Winston?" I asked.

"He's not lacking for offers from the newspapers." George turned
to help himself to more cognac. "It's a matter of national pride.
Everyone must do their part. Jack, too," he said, oblivious to my
mounting consternation. "They'll requisition the Hussars for the
cavalry."

"Just like that? Must I resign myself to seeing all of you risk
your lives?"

He chuckled. "It's hardly so dramatic. The Boers are no match
for us."

"Yet the empire needs every able-bodied man it can muster?"

He returned to my side, putting his arms about me. "Oh, my
Missie. We must put on a show of force, but most of us will likely
sit idle in some infernal outpost."

"Then it sounds like a colossal waste," I muttered, feeling his
lips at my throat and the urgent press of his arousal against me.

"That isn't the point." He began tugging at my stays. "Our
honor is at stake. Great Britain must show the world that we remain
invincible."

What could I say? Men regarded war as a rite of manhood, and
to question Britain's honor was unthinkable. While they indulged
in carnage, women were expected to pine for their safety. I wasn't
interested in doing what was expected of me anymore, but I kept
my feelings to myself, submitting instead to his ravenous desire
even as I wondered if Clarita had been right in more ways than I
cared to admit. Perhaps he was simply too young for me.

After he fell asleep, arms akimbo in my disheveled bed, I gazed
at his face in repose, his unblemished skin still flushed by our
exertions, a hint of the golden beard he couldn't yet fully grow
darkening his jaw.

Now you've reached a time when you fear you'll not find that love again.

Was I trying to recapture what had been lost? His entire life lay ahead of him, while mine was half lived. Could we survive the burden of time, of the sacrifices we'd have to make? I did want to marry again, to belong to someone and know that he belonged to me, yet as I watched my lover bask in dreams of battlefield glory, I couldn't help but also wonder whether losing him now might be less painful than losing him later.

AS THE ENTIRE country exploded in patriotic fervor, with demonstrations demanding the annihilation of the Boers, Bertie agreed to receive me at his office in St. James's. As soon as I entered his chamber, with its Tudor wainscoting, he waved his secretary out with a scowl.

"I'll have you know, Lady Randolph, that if you're here for a favor, I am not pleased."

I dipped my head under my hat. "Your Highness did promise to assist me, should I ever have need of it. I haven't asked until now."

He reclined in his upholstered chair, a hand tugging at his beard. "I did."

"This war," I said. "I need reassurances."

"As do we all. Alas, war rarely affords them."

I hardened my tone. "I must know my sons won't be put in harm's way. I'll not lose them to some silly spate over diamonds."

His mirth faded. "It's more than a spate. As Winston would be quick to tell you—"

"He cannot tell me because he already left," I said, making Bertie's eyes widen, as only I would have dared interrupt him mid-sentence. "He sent a telegram to inform me he's on his way to South Africa as a correspondent for the *Morning Post*." I couldn't contain my ire. "He didn't consult me beforehand because he knew I'd never consent to it."

"He's a grown man. If we did everything our mothers wished, where would we be?"

"Not waging war in South Africa," I riposted.

He smiled. "Jennie, your son has your will. You cannot fault him for it."

"I fault whoever started this war. Winston has just won his seat in the House. He should be here, taking up his obligations as MP."

"Yes, your suggestion, I presume? I commend him for it. But he can serve us as a journalist as well, seeing as everything we do is played out in the newspapers. Unfortunately, I've no control over where editors choose to assign their writers."

"Can you find out?" Panic edged my voice. "If letters are delayed by the war, it could be weeks before I hear from him again."

"I'll make inquiries. Anything else I can do?" he purred, savoring my predicament.

"Jack. At least he accorded me the courtesy of informing me his regiment will be deployed. They're awaiting official orders."

"I'll see what I can do on his behalf. I cannot guarantee desk duty, however. Jack is in the Hussars, which by their very nature involves riding on horseback into battle."

My hands tightened in my lap.

"Yes?" said Bertie.

"George," I finally said. "He wishes to secure a posting."

"Our eager pup would brandish a rifle, delaying the wedding bells?"

I met his sardonic stare. "Can you help him?"

"I could. Your question should be, will I?" He pointed to the sheaf of papers on his desk. "You see all this? It's but a fraction of the deluge of petitions I'm receiving daily from every hot-blooded man in our regiments eager to spill Boer blood. If I cared to address each one, the war would start and end without us. And Her Majesty is most put out by this inopportune foreign engagement. We cannot deprive her of our entire Scots Guards, as well."

Drawing in a steadying breath, I said, "I'm asking you as a friend to keep George safe. We still have a friendship, do we not?"

He went silent. "Do you intend to marry him?" he abruptly asked. "I must have your assurance first, before I can consider whether to give you mine."

I hesitated. "Not at this time."

"Not at *any* time. Jennie, we'll not stand for it. His family has besieged me with pleas to intervene. They're beside themselves at the thought that their son and heir will marry a widow twice his age—and one not of his blood or status." He held up a hand before I could erupt. "I do not share their lofty ideals. Far be it from me to say who is worthy to dust the lintels of Ruthin Castle. But neither can I consent. Moreover, I will not. Not now. Not ever." He paused, allowing his denial to carry its full weight. "This is about precedents."

"I see," I said stiffly. "In other words, my sentiments are of no account."

"You cannot possibly think your sentiments would go any other way. He is—"

"Too young for me," I cut in again. "Too well-born. Too everything, apparently." I forced out a smile. "Others have warned me as much."

"Then do us a favor and heed their advice." He shook his head. "I've always admired your spirit; few women can rise from a husband's demise as you have. But you go too far even for my admiration. I cannot set the aristocracy against me over this."

I rose to my feet. For the first time in as long as I'd known him, he appeared uncomfortable as he said, "I'll see to his posting for your sake. But you must promise to put an end to it. He'll survive the heartbreak. Young men always do."

"Thank you, Your Highness." As I turned to the door, without having promised anything, I heard him quip, "I'd prefer to see you on your knees under less trying circumstances. Perhaps once this silly spate over diamonds is over, we might tend to it, yes?"

I burst out laughing. "You never can resist trying, can you?"

He gave a chuckle, patting his enlarged paunch. "For all the good it does me. Now that you know both the prince and the man, you're no longer impressed by either."

"I like both very much," I replied. "I consider that quite good, indeed." I left him with a smile on his face, knowing I could always rely on him never to change his ways.

Just as I had no intention of changing mine.

TWENTY-NINE

Bertie had George appointed as aide-de-camp to the 1st Division, under the venerable Lord Methuen. He went equipped with his polo pony, of all things, and an eighteen-bottle case of Scotch whiskey—which to me exemplified the absurdity of it. George was very enthused, however, expressing his intent to hunt down the Boers "like rabid dogs."

I accompanied him to Southampton, bringing Fanny Ronalds for support. As he clicked his heels with militant formality before his commanding officer, all around us the docks clamored with weeping women as their uniformed men boarded ships, cranes overhead disgorging loads of foodstuffs and enough spirits to inebriate Africa.

"Do they plan to win the war with Rothschild wine?" Fanny remarked, regarding the stamped crates in amusement. She went quiet when George lifted my hand to his mustachioed lips (he'd spent a month nurturing his facial adornment) and declared, "I will return a hero. Then we'll see how they stand on our marriage. I don't mean to back down from either fight."

I caressed his cheek with my other hand, desolate as he mounted the gangplank to his vessel, where he saluted from the deck, standing among the proud young men of his division.

"Oh, dear." Fanny hooked her arm in mine. "He's very determined, isn't he? Whatever shall you do if he returns unscathed? You may have to do the unthinkable and elope."

"Do you doubt he will return?" I asked. "Everyone has said this war will be over soon enough. The Boers don't have our expertise or resources."

"Don't they?" She paused. "They might act as if the Boers pose a negligible, if unconscionable, threat to our honor, but don't you think it odd that no one save Winston has expressed concern that the war might turn out to be more than a skirmish? They're all so intent on triumph, they've neglected to consider the alternative."

"Which is?" I glanced over my shoulder as horns blared and George's ship lifted anchor. I couldn't see him from that distance, but I knew he was still there, watching me walk away and probably thinking I did so to conceal my despair at his departure.

"Defeat." She tightened her hold on my arm. "According to Winston, the Boers are not only well-armed but fully prepared to meet us head-on. Haven't you read his dispatches? They've been featured on the front page of the *Post* every week."

"I most certainly have. He's doing me no favors. Jack has yet to be deployed and Winston's contesting of our advantage has so incensed Bertie, he refuses to receive me."

Fanny chuckled. "Are you still smarting because Winston went off without your permission? Or because you, too, fear all this imperial pomp will end in catastrophe?"

I felt myself grimace. I did fear our much-vaunted advantage might be our undoing, but with both my son and my lover now engaged in the fight, I couldn't bear to contemplate it. Already, the days stretched ahead, desolate without my sons and George. I'd miss George terribly, for both his reckless confidence and his romantic determination. I could try to keep busy with my literary review, but if few copies had sold before, with the country in fever pitch over the war, even fewer would sell now. And I still needed to safeguard Jack. My younger son was too eager to join the cause, and I held out hope that Bertie, despite his current petulance toward me, would see that he did not. Jack turned twenty this year, too young in my opinion to do more than parade about with the Hussars in full dress uniform.

Upon my return home, as Fanny unpinned her hat in the foyer and I went into the parlor to ring for tea, I found Jack waiting for me. At the sight of him—unlike Winston, he took after me, with his darker hair and crystalline blue-gray eyes, and the slender build of my youth—I faltered at his expression. He held a yellow wire paper in his hand.

"Mamma." He spoke quietly. Despite our physical resemblance, he had a docile temperament, unsullied by my and Winston's volatility. "I've received news."

"I'm so sorry." I jolted toward him with my arms outstretched, even as relief flooded me. He'd been denied a posting, thank God. Or thank Bertie, who'd no doubt tease me about showing him my appreciation with an afternoon tea performance.

"It's not about me." He extended the wire. "Winston is missing."

As Fanny's gasp broke the sudden silence, I couldn't take another step, staring at the wire in my son's fingers while he said, "He was reporting from the border of the Transvaal and due to depart. His train never arrived. The Boers derailed it. Captured everyone onboard."

I felt but didn't hear the horrified moan that pealed from my lips. Jack took hold of me to bring me to the settee. As Fanny rang the bell to order my maid to fetch tea, Jack sat beside me.

"You must petition the prince. I've sent word to the *Post*, but it's doubtful they'll know more than what this wire says. His Highness must, however. Taking a British journalist as a prisoner of war is a grave international offense. Winston isn't serving in a military capacity and should never have been detained."

"Are we certain he is detained?" I struggled to unknot the tangled breath in my throat, my heart hammering in my ears.

"It's the most likely scenario. Knowing Winston, he's giving

264 C. W. GORTNER

them such an earful right now they'll release him just to shut him up. He knows the rules of engagement during war."

"Rules?" I was aghast. "Do the Boers care for such things? Bertie told me they are savages! He warned me to steer you clear of them—"

Jack stood abruptly. "I'm going to enlist. Don't think to stop me. I don't want you or the prince interfering. My brother is now a captive of the so-called savages and your lover has gone off to fight. Would you have me be the coward who stayed behind?"

"You mustn't." I grasped his hand. "Jack, please. I need you here."

"England needs me more." His face softened as he kissed my cheek. "I'll send word as soon as I know my posting. In the meantime, please ask the prince. Winston is very resourceful, but he might require our help."

As he walked out of my parlor, the reality of what I'd sought to deny crashed a black wave over me. War. War and death, with those I loved caught up in the thick of it.

Then Fanny said, "You cannot keep your sons under your skirts forever. You raised them to be self-sufficient men. Now you must fight for them."

"How?" I cried. "I can't take up a rifle and go to war, though I wish I could."

She had the temerity to smile. "Of course you can. Not with a rifle, perhaps, though I've seen you shoot a pheasant dead at twenty paces during the hunt. But women can still go to war with other weapons. All you need to do is find yours."

MY WEAPON, IT turned out, was in Winston's published newspaper reports, which I pored over in my anguish. He'd condemned the surfeit of ale and beef bloating our military encampments, without an ambulatory ward to be found. Where were the medical facilities, he asked, the doctors and nurses? Did we believe we'd suffer no injuries or casualties?

If such care was needed, I could provide it. I could fill a ship with bandages, antiseptic, and morphine, along with a team of physicians. Who would protest? It would be not only a patriotic endeavor but one that those in charge had apparently failed to address.

I wrote to everyone I knew. The millionaire founder of the Boston Atlantic Transport Company offered one of his retired ships, the *Maine*, though it required extensive renovations. And Clara Barton, founder of the American Red Cross, had certified medical personnel.

"We need one hundred and fifty thousand dollars to refurbish the ship and hire a crew," I told Fanny. "I can't possibly raise such a sum here. Some have confided to me that they don't approve of the war and won't be seen contributing toward it, not even for a medical ship. Others who support the war claim funding my enterprise would admit we have a vulnerability."

"And President McKinley has stated the Boers' cause is just," said Fanny. "They're being hailed in America as upstarts fighting against imperial aggression, much as we did during our Revolution, so our American friends may not wish to contribute either."

I went silent, considering. "Unless an American of impeccable standing here stepped forth. Then everyone would fall over themselves to follow her example."

"Is there an American of standing here, other than you—?" she started to say, and then stopped. "You're not thinking of . . . ?"

With a smile, I inked my pen. "The new Duchess of Marlborough is a fellow New Yorker, isn't she? And I'll wager she's about as bored and itching for a spoil in Blenheim as I was. If I can gain her support, doors will fling open. No one can say no to a duchess, especially one whose wealth far exceeds theirs."

FOLLOWING RANDOLPH'S DEATH, I'd vowed never to set foot in Blenheim again. Lady Frances had died the previous year, after devoting herself to preserving the estate for her grandson, Charles, the ninth duke, and his wife, Consuelo Vanderbilt. Albertha had died years before, after gloating in satisfaction that her son had inherited the title, though she'd remained estranged from her husband, Randolph's brother, until his own death. Gossip had kept me apprised of the birth of Consuelo and Charles's two sons, the restorations funded by her money, and inevitable rumors of dissatisfaction in the marriage. Strangely enough, however, our paths hadn't crossed; I hadn't attended the season since Randolph's passing, while Consuelo was very selective about where she appeared. I knew her only by repute and was very curious to meet her when I returned to the place where I'd spent my first months as a wife and had given birth to Winston.

At first glance, nothing seemed changed. I did note the splendid new fountains in the gardens as my carriage took me through the grounds, but within the palace itself, everything still felt imposing and inert.

Until I was escorted into the drawing room, where Lady Frances had presided over her epic teas, and saw the evidence of renewal, the empty spaces now covered by new masterpieces and the walls freshly covered in blue-and-white silk. Chinese porcelain vases brimming with fresh-cut flowers cluttered the sideboards, and the service on the table was an exquisite Sèvres porcelain, with the signature interlaced *L*s—something Lady Frances would never have tolerated, it being the product of a foreign country.

Then the duchess glided into the room. She was willowy, her classic oval-shaped face dominated by arresting black eyes, her mass of dark hair piled in a disarrayed chignon that highlighted her slim neck.

"My dear Lady Randolph." She held out her hand. "After all this time, I feared we'd never meet in person."

"I might have come sooner, had I known I was welcome," I replied without thinking.

Her laughter was a delicate chime. "I'm afraid your name was anathema to Lady Frances, which naturally made me desperate to make your acquaintance. I met Winston several times when he came to visit his grandmother, and I plied him with questions. He's so very proud of you. Please, sit down. We now have all the time we need to get to know each other as we should."

After we took our seats, she poured thick brown liquid from the pot. "I hope you like coffee. I have it imported especially from Cuba. I find English tea insipid."

I laughed. "I adore coffee."

"I thought you might." She motioned to the sugar bowl. "It's bitter if you don't sweeten it." She did not add any sugar to her cup. "I prefer it this way. It reminds me of home."

"Do you miss your family?" I asked, savoring the unsweetened brew.

"I miss New York," she said.

The muted catch in her voice gave me pause. "Not your family?"

Her fingers tightened on her cup. "May we dispense with the formalities? Forgive me, but I feel as if I already know you, after hearing so much about you."

"None of it laudatory, I imagine. Winston might be proud, but Lady Frances and your own mother-in-law, Albertha, did not think highly of me at all."

"Which is why I think the contrary. When women express such malice toward another, I always suspect they're the ones at fault." She paused. "To answer your question, I do not miss my family. My mother and I . . . we have a difficult relationship. All this"— she looked about the room, her tone encompassing the palace—"is her doing. Had I been given the choice, I would never have consented to live here."

"It's not an easy place to live," I said. "And I know about difficulties with one's mother. I rarely got along with mine."

She poured more coffee into my cup. She was serving me herself, which I found very charming and modern. "Were you happy in your marriage?" she suddenly asked, startling me. "Or am I being too forthright?"

I hesitated. In that moment, I realized no one had ever asked me this question before. Everyone had assumed my happiness with Randolph as a matter of fact.

"Most of the time," I said. "But being married to a Spencer-Churchill, as you know, isn't easy, either. Randolph could be like this estate. Rooted and immutable."

She lowered her eyes. "Yet happiness at times must be preferable to none at all."

We sat in silence. I could see she wasn't only unhappy in her marriage but also lonely; I recognized the signs, having experienced them myself.

"Is Charles often absent? Randolph's career always took precedence, so I had to find ways to keep myself occupied."

"My husband now resides in London. We both agree it's for the best." A tenuous smile crossed her lips. "Now, tell me why you are here. I was so delighted to receive your letter."

Once I detailed my enterprise, she exclaimed that she couldn't imagine my desperation, not knowing if Winston was safe and with Jack about to deploy. She expressed concern for George as well, without any hint that she questioned the suitability of our match. "If our men must risk their lives, we cannot possibly sit idle," she declared. "I don't condone this notion that women must stay at home to darn stockings. I only wish I could set sail with you."

"Me? I was only planning to raise the necessary funds. Do you think I should accompany the ship, as well?"

"Who else? If I'm to contribute, I want you at its helm to ensure it arrives where it needs to go. Now," she went on, as I grappled with this unexpected development, as well as the realization that she must have maintained control over her money in her marriage.

"Forgive me if I'm the one who's being forward now," I ventured, "but don't you need to consult with your husband before offering me a contribution?"

She frowned. "Why would I consult with him? Charles has no say over it."

I forced out a smile. It would seem Lady Frances hadn't been able to drive by herself the hard bargain that her late husband had leveraged over my father.

"It's my money," Consuelo went on. "My mother agreed to an annual sum to maintain the estate, but we retain ultimate control of my finances. Or rather, she retains control. But she'll have no issue with this. She's been encouraging me to do something useful. It's how we behave in New York. To contribute to worthwhile causes isn't the exception there; it's the rule."

"Yes," I said quietly. "No one in New York has an ancient title to hold up."

"Titles are useless without the means to fund them. I personally find them absurd, given the exorbitant cost." She reached over to take my hand. "We can use this weekend to draw up a list of all those titled ladies best equipped to be on your planning committee. We'll need matrons of impeccable standing, whose own means can sway others like them to your cause."

Once more, she took me by surprise. "I haven't brought anything with me."

"Just tell me what you require; I'm certain I can provide it. It'll be only us and my staff. We needn't dress up for dinner."

I burst out laughing. "Did Lady Frances still insist on it when she was alive?"

"Every night. Now I absolutely refuse to wear a corset when I can avoid it."

"A dreadful contraption," I agreed.

Her smile turned eager. I'd been right in my assumption. The duchess was bored and itching for a spoil. And she had both the money and the clout to take it on.

"We'll eat buffet and keep to our dressing gowns all weekend," she said.

CONSUELO'S PARTICIPATION BROUGHT London's upstanding matrons stampeding to our American Ladies Committee, where they devised a schedule of musical galas, featuring me playing duets with various well-known musicians. Every event sold out in advance, the novelty of a hospital ship patronized by the Duchess of Marlborough reaching as far as Windsor Castle, where the queen gave us her blessing, providing the ship didn't fly the Union Jack, as it was a private vessel on a private undertaking. Nevertheless, she appointed a British major of distinction to accompany us.

In the midst of this, a tattered letter finally arrived from Winston. He was unharmed, to my immense relief, but in Boer custody. His jocularity shone through—he complained about the "abominable leavings" he was being served, as if he'd booked an inconvenient stay in an overrated hotel—and while I was still terribly worried for him, at least I didn't have to set sail without news of his whereabouts.

Other news was less fortuitous. Jack had enlisted in the South African Light Horse and had been dispatched to the front. And George sent an urgent cable; he'd suffered severe heatstroke and was being sent home to recover. With both my sons in South Africa and my ship at the ready, postponement was out of the question, prompting George to barrage me with reproaches. His petulance was so deeply upsetting to me that Leonie offered to look after him in my house in London while he convalesced.

On the evening before I left, Consuelo and I dined together onboard in my refurbished cabin-suite. As we said our goodbyes, she pressed my hands in hers. "Don't ever give in to what people think or say. Royal approval or not, you must marry your young man upon your return. How often do we get a second chance?"

"Be well, my friend." I embraced her. "I wish you were coming with me."

"As do I. Send me a letter as soon as you can. I want to hear all about it." She moved toward the gangplank and paused, smiling at me over her shoulder. "And hoist whatever damn flag you like. After all this time abiding by their rules, you've earned the right."

THIRTY

1900

I had both the Union Jack and the Stars and Stripes hoisted and celebrated the new century, along with my forty-sixth birthday, on the open seas. As we crossed the equator, the men underwent their ritual shave—a tradition among sailors, which I enthusiastically captured with the box Brownie I'd purchased for the trip.

But the voyage was nearly three weeks, and my cabin's refurbishment had consumed most of the ship's promenade, giving rise to the male orderlies' grumbling at my indulgence. I had no patience for complaints from the personnel I'd hired, even less so for their zealotry; when I heard that some of the American nurses had smuggled religious tracts onboard, as if they were going to convert pagans rather than care for wounded soldiers, I ordered the tracts dumped into the sea. The nurses were so outraged that the British major suggested I make amends. I reluctantly ordered the boxes of sweets unearthed from the cargo hold and distributed, declaring sugar more conducive than prayer to our well-being.

The nurses were not appeased.

By the time we reached Cape Town, I was eager to disembark. Emerging into the searing South African sunlight in my wide-brimmed hat and crisp linen suit, I gazed in wonder at the imposing flat-topped mountain rearing over the city's crescent-shaped colonnade—a sliver of British formality framed by an achingly blue foreign sky. The air was laced with sea salt and the aroma of fried shellfish; my stomach growled, sour from weeks of salted rations. Lowering my gaze to the quay, I found my son Jack waiting for me, flanked by a distinguished reception of the British High Commission, all in full-dress uniform despite the unbearable heat.

A kilted group of Scotchmen piped up "God Save the Queen," as if I were an arriving dignitary. Obliged to endure the long-winded welcoming ceremony, I couldn't keep from darting my eyes in concern to Jack. His left leg was swathed in a bandage.

"You're injured," I said, once the major had escorted the committee onboard to tour the ship and I could proceed to my accommodations in the Cape. "Is it serious?"

"It looks worse than it is. A clean shot through my thigh," he said as I helped him hobble up the stepladder into the carriage. "I was in the battle to relieve Ladysmith. Others weren't so fortunate. You cannot imagine the carnage."

"Have you any word of your brother?" I asked anxiously. If the war had taken a turn for the worse, my elder son might face reprisals in a Boer prison.

Jack paused. "Don't you know? Winston has escaped. It's been in all the newspapers; I thought you must have heard by now. He was very daring. They're calling him a hero."

I sagged against my seat. "I hadn't heard. I was at sea."

"Well, Winston will be eager to tell you everything himself." Jack went quiet again for a moment. "You should also be aware that despite the grandiose reception, many on the commission oppose your ship. No one can seem to agree whether it's authorized under military law, and some insist it must be filled with the injured and return to England forthwith."

"After we've come all this way? My ship has a modern operating facility, a convalescent ward, as well as expertly trained staff. We even have a major appointed by the queen. What on earth is there for anyone to oppose?"

"You'll need to state your case before our governor, Sir Walter Hely-Hutchinson. Winston is staying at his home." Jack smiled.

"If you can charm Sir Walter as you do everyone else, you'll have nothing to worry about. I'll stand by you. Winston and I have both seen how our soldiers are perishing as much from gangrene as from Boer cannon fire."

AFTER SCARCELY ENOUGH time onshore to regain my equilibrium, we set sail for Durban.

At the governor's mansion, I reunited with Winston, who was underweight from a mild bout of dysentery—"The swill they gave us would sicken a hog," he said with a grimace, reminding me of Randolph's disparaging remarks about India—but otherwise, he appeared none the worse for his ordeal. As he regaled me with his "bold adventure," as he dubbed it, I went through the pile of newspaper clippings featuring his covert escape. After keeping meticulous record of the guard patrols, he'd managed to climb the fence by the prison latrines and sneak into Pretoria, getting as far as the train station, where he jumped a carriage, riding concealed to the Transvaal border.

"Once we were across the border, no trains passed at night," he told me, making me tremble at just how perilous his adventure had been. "For the next five days I had to go on foot. I managed to scrape up food from the natives, though I don't speak their language. Following the railway line, I arrived in Middelburg, where there was a through service. It took me nearly sixty hours to reach Komatipoort, and I spent the entire time among coal sacks. The Boers stopped and searched the train periodically, but"—he laughed—"they obviously didn't dig deep enough."

The Boers also set a bounty on his head, alerting everyone to his exodus. Enthusiastic crowds cheered his arrival in Durban, lifting him onto their shoulders to convey him to the town square, where he delivered a rousing speech, after which the governor invited him to his home. He'd spent his recovery writing about his escape for the *Post*, which featured it on the front page.

"And here we are, together again," he concluded cheerfully, as if it had all been a lark. "Tomorrow, I must return to the front to continue my assignment."

"Tomorrow?" I exclaimed. "But I've just arrived—"

"No, no." He held up his hand. "I have my charge and mean to see it through. Just as you have yours." His voice turned somber. "Your assistance is desperately needed."

I turned to Sir Walter, a distinguished man with slick black hair and a huge mustache, whose weary countenance betrayed the toll of overseeing the war. He gave me a nod. "Your help is indeed most welcome, my lady. We have thousands of injured and far too few to tend to them. Given the dire conditions, we cannot quibble over the details."

Winston guffawed. "And as every stiff upper lip on the High Commission knows, pulling rank is the only way to get anything done."

Ignoring his levity, I said to Sir Walter, "I'll put my ship to whatever service you deem necessary. But I should like to see these dire conditions for myself."

Sudden silence fell. As Winston's mouth quirked in an attempt to curb another outburst of mirth, Sir Walter replied, "My lady, I fear it is no place for a woman."

I had to stop myself from rolling my eyes. "Half of my staff are female nurses. We also brought extra supplies, which my subscribers, the majority of whom are also women, personally charged me to deliver."

Jack said, "I could accompany her to Ladysmith. It should be safe enough now."

"Not that our mother needs anyone to keep her safe," interjected Winston. "She just came all the way here on her own ship."

Sir Walter hesitated. "I suppose I can make an exception. The injured must be transported here for care, so I'll put a train at Lady Randolph's disposal."

EQUIPPED WITH A khaki uniform and my box Brownie, I embarked with Jack and a military convoy to Ladysmith, where my son had been injured in the battle to take back the city from Boer incursion. I found the landscape stunning in its parched beauty, trying in vain to snap photographs of brightly colored birds startled by the train's passage from their perches in the umbrella-like trees, and herds of graceful impalas bolting off into the shimmering distance.

As we approached Ladysmith, the earth turned charred, the air acrid with a pervasive stench that Jack told me was rotting horseflesh. Carcasses began to appear alongside the tracks, horses shot down with their saddles still on their backs, festering. I had to avert my eyes, though within the city itself, there was no looking away. Ladysmith had been retaken at a terrible toll, most of the city in ruins, with makeshift infirmaries erected amidst the rubble, where the exhausted medical staff could barely summon gratitude for the supplies we'd brought.

An agonized litany lifted from endless rows of cots holding men who'd undergone amputations without chloroform. While the nurses accompanying me helped prepare the most badly injured for transport, I went among the men with Jack, pausing to clutch beseeching hands, to murmur words of comfort—all those desperate faces merging into a mosaic of despair. In every pair of eyes, I saw my sons. I saw George. I saw every youth whose zeal to serve Britain could be reduced to this maimed helplessness.

By the time I returned to the train, I was fighting back tears. "All of this," I said to Jack. "So much suffering and loss. For what?"

"Imperial honor." I met his eyes, marking his unvoiced contempt.

"It's not worth the lives of so many," I said.

"No," he replied. "It is not, though nobody in charge cares to hear it."

IN DURBAN, THE ship physicians operated on the urgent cases. Six thousand injured soldiers from Ladysmith awaited transport home, with many in urgent need of rehabilitation. Under the circumstances I couldn't deny Sir Walter's request that my ship convey the first three hundred to England. By now, I was eager to return, my wires to Leonie having gone unanswered, leading me to fear George had taken such umbrage at my refusal to stay and wait for him that he'd forsaken me. Profoundly affected by my experiences, I was determined to do as Consuelo advised. I would marry George and persuade him to seek a living outside the military, just as I'd begged Jack to do. My son reluctantly agreed, his leg injury deemed sufficient to qualify him for discharge from the Hussars. He'd seen enough of this war, he told me.

Before I left, Captain Percy Scott, commanding officer of the HMS *Terrible*, invited me onboard his vessel to view his 4.7 naval gun, which he wished to christen in my honor. His crew gave me an empty shell as a keepsake, and we took a photograph together by the massive gun. Winston was so delighted that he included the photograph in an essay he wrote about my war efforts for the *Post*, published under the headline LADY BOUNTIFUL.

When we docked in Cape Town, the High Commission made its displeasure known. They sent orders for me to discharge every patient onboard to the woefully understaffed hospital there and wait for others from the fronts, endangering those who'd undergone recent surgeries and must reach England in time for further treatment.

"I will not," I informed the commission's medical officer. "The *Maine* is here solely because of my determination. We shall depart as scheduled and return once we've delivered those currently under our care. If need be, I'll cable HRH himself to back me up."

The officer sniffed. "And seeing as the *Maine* would be the first to deliver the wounded of Ladysmith home, far be it from us to interfere in my lady's bid for glory."

"Glory?" I echoed in revulsion, suddenly perceiving the envy behind the command. "You think such flagrant sacrifice holds glory?" He went white at my tone. "Some of these men will never walk again. Never have children or enjoy a day without pain. How can any of it be glorious for me or the empire?"

Turning heel, I stormed back to the ship. At dawn, we lifted anchor.

During the voyage home, the staff performed several more operations. We lost only three patients. The rest were delivered in Southampton, where I disembarked on April 30 to a pounding rain and a resounding welcome. Winston's essay had captured popular admiration, with new funds pouring in for the *Maine*, though as I caught sight of Leonie waving from the quay with George glowering at her side, I knew I'd not sail to South Africa again.

I would be Mrs. Cornwallis-West now if it was the last thing I did.

THIRTY-ONE

Under a warm July sky, I wed George at St. Paul's Church in Knightsbridge. I'd chosen a blue silk chiffon dress with lace sleeves and diamond-ornamented headdress. George wore his military dress in defiance, as his commanding officer, upon learning of our wedding, had discharged him. I had wanted George to quit the military, but not by force, so I called upon Bertie for support.

With the Boer War careening into disaster and my voyage on the *Maine* lauded throughout England, the prince wasn't inclined to contest me. He granted his consent, though George was denied reinstatement and Bertie warned me via private letter that we risked extreme censure should we proceed to the banns and the altar. George's family was so distraught they refused to attend the ceremony, so the Spencer-Churchills and my sisters turned out in force at my urging. Consuelo prevailed upon her estranged husband, Charles, Duke of Marlborough, to give me away, and Winston volunteered to be George's first man.

It was certainly unprecedented. A bride twice the age of her groom, and a best man the same age as the groom. I told myself it didn't matter. I'd spoken with both my sons at length about my decision, and while they cautioned that incurring social disapproval would make it difficult for us, neither questioned my love for George or his for me.

Winston finally said, with one of his dry smiles, "Even if we opposed it, would that deter you?" When I replied, "No," he laughed. "I didn't think so. But, Mamma," he added, "we must see to it that your finances are kept separate. You never know what the future will bring."

Wise advice, even if it rankled me. But my income from their trust mustn't be jeopardized and Winston had the legal agreement drawn up stating as much. Should George and I ever separate or divorce, he couldn't lay claim to my assets. George signed it without seeming to read it, which both reassured and perturbed me. So delighted we were finally marrying, after two years of courtship, he didn't ask why my sons required a prenuptial agreement. We hadn't discussed our financial situation, much as we'd neglected to settle the matter of children, but that changed during our honeymoon in Scotland and France.

Winston wrote to tell me that Jack was going to New York to train as a stockbroker, inspired by my father. Disgusted by what he himself had witnessed in South Africa, Winston was seeking reelection in Oldham, resolved to make an impact in the political arena.

"He didn't fulfill his first term due to the war," I told George, showing him my son's letter. We were at Broughton Castle, where he hunched over the box of unpaid bills that he'd insisted on lugging along, sorting them into piles on the floor and raking a hand through his hair as he tallied the sums. "Unlike his opponent, he's not married, so a female presence is vital. I campaigned in Oldham for Randolph; I know the populace well. He's requesting that I join him on his campaign. Would you mind terribly if I went to assist him?"

George made a despairing gesture. "Jennie, are you aware that your literary review is running up an astronomical deficit? Or that nearly every one of these house bills is in arrears? We must do something, lest we end up without a roof over our heads when we return to London."

I bit back my exasperation. "Can't we ask your sister for a loan? She is married to the wealthiest man in Prussia, after all."

"Daisy already provided me with a significant sum upon our

marriage," he retorted. "Considering I had to sign that agreement devised by your sons."

"So, you did read it?" I was taken aback.

"My sister did. She was most insistent that I send her a copy. She found it highly irregular for marrying the woman who will, after all, be the mother of my children one day."

I went still as he scowled at the mounds of paper. "I might not have been so quick to sign it either, had I known this situation." Taking up one of the bills, he went on, "Look here: an unpaid repair receipt for your barouche, which Randolph acquired shortly after Winston's birth. Why on earth haven't you sold it yet?"

"How would I get about London? It's the only carriage I own. Given my apparent penury, I could hardly afford a better one."

He let out a sigh. "I don't know how to contend with this. We're mired in debt."

"No, *I'm* mired in debt. We'll see to it later. They're just bills. Now, about Winston—"

"We're on our honeymoon. If your son could escape a Boer prison on his own, surely he can manage his political campaign without you."

I didn't fail to mark the resentment in his voice. "His reelection is uncertain. He'll be very disappointed if he loses, as shall we. My darling, you don't want him kicking up his heels under the roof you're so afraid we might lose, do you? Think of our expenses then."

George sat back on his heels. "For how long? We're due to leave for Paris in two weeks."

"I don't know. More than two weeks, I should think. But I'll be back as soon as I can and Paris isn't going anywhere. The important thing is for Winston to win his seat. He's gained popularity because of his war reporting, so this is his time. He tells me he's been offered a lecture tour abroad if he wins. It will earn him significant fees."

"Then perhaps he can give us a loan," George muttered. "My

sister will only show me the door if I ask her to pay for an old barouche."

I leaned down to kiss him. "Forget the barouche. Come with me to Oldham instead."

He drew back. "I think not. We've raised enough ire as it is. If we show up together, he might lose the election and end up living under our bed."

It felt strange to leave my new husband stewing in complaints, but I traveled at once to Winston's side. Inspired by my presence, he took to the challenge. He was a gifted orator, as Randolph had been, and his slight lisp lent him a boyish charm. He played to the audience as if he were an actor onstage. Politics were much like the theater, in truth, with all the illusion and panoply. As for me, I'd forgotten how much I enjoyed the thrill of it, the pompous rallies with cheering crowds and grandiose promises to secure their votes.

At the age of twenty-six, my son was reelected as the Conservative Member for Oldham. Since he wouldn't assume duties in Parliament until the New Year, I encouraged him to pursue the lecture tour. His tour manager asked that I accompany him, citing my renown in New York. I refused, seeing Winston off on his ship and racing back to George, who expressed relief that my older son was now gainfully employed and an ocean away.

It should have been my warning. Motherhood and a new husband were always an uneasy match. With George perturbed by his aimlessness, cast adrift from his regiment, and unsure of his future livelihood, I might have taken note of his dissatisfaction.

But as Mama would have said, passion clouded my judgment.

ONCE IN PARIS, I insisted we indulge ourselves. It was, after all, our honeymoon. He might complain when the accounts came due, but George was eager enough to have new attire tailored for him and to risk his hand at the gambling tables as we reveled in the city's joie de vivre. I took pleasure in showing him all the sights, regaling him with tales of my youth here with my sisters, though I avoided any mention of Randolph. His mood could sour if I spoke of my late husband, as if he felt he had to compete. But he was still young and overly impressionable; I had to smile to see him swagger when we appeared at the Opéra and everyone looked askance at us. I rather swaggered myself. No woman present could boast of such a prize, with their paunchy husbands stinking of an excess of brandy and cigars.

At night, he took me with such fervor that he left me bruised. He refused to use any precautions. While the odds were in my favor, I dreaded the possible outcome.

"Perhaps we should be more careful," I said.

"Why? Didn't you say we should try and see?" He regarded me with an expression I couldn't decipher. Was it suspicion or hopefulness? "Don't you want to bear a child?"

"Yes, of course I do—" My lie stuck in my throat. "Just not right away."

He rose from bed to throw on his robe. "My sister advised me to start a family as soon as possible. My parents may be more inclined to accept our marriage if we do."

"Your sister *advised*?" I echoed, a cold shiver creeping up my stomach.

"It's what married people do, isn't it? Have children. Raise a family." He stalked out onto the terrace to smoke a cigarillo, a disgusting habit he'd taken up while gambling.

I began to think I'd indeed let my passion get the better of my reason.

In a desperate attempt to remind him that I already had a family, when Winston's letter arrived, detailing his American tour, I read it aloud, as I'd often done with Randolph.

"He dined with Mark Twain in New York before going on to

Washington. President-elect Roosevelt gave him a standing ovation. Isn't it marvelous he's making such an impact?"

George eyed me. "Providing he doesn't forget he's an Englishman."

His censure gave me pause. "He's also half American. I'm his mother. I'm not British."

"Yes, but he is. He's also an elected member of Parliament. America did not support our war against the Boers, as he well knows. Courting favor there will do him no good here."

"But . . ." I swallowed. "The war has become a disgrace. We are losing it."

His face hardened, confirming my fear. He was envious of Winston. I tended to forget they were the same age, and George had done nothing to exalt himself either in war or outside of it, while my son had won acclaim.

"Have you given further consideration to the quarterly?" he abruptly said. "Jennie, you must resign yourself to the fact that it will never be profitable."

"I thought we agreed to set that fact aside for now," I replied.

"*We* did not. You may not wish to speak of it, but upon our return, I must insist you see to its dissolution. A lady of your standing shouldn't be involved in such tawdry dealings."

Such tawdry dealings . . .

"I see." I folded Winston's letter into a precise square. "And what should a lady of my standing do instead? Organize flower arrangements and dinner parties?"

He clipped off the tip of his cigarillo. "We'll soon have plenty to do. Daisy sent me a wire to tell me that our sister Constance has become engaged to His Grace the Duke of Westminster. The marriage will take place next year. It'll be a major social event."

"And it won't come about if I'm publishing my quarterly?" I said drily.

"It's no longer fitting." The flare of his match punctuated his tone. "You are the future Lady Cornwallis-West. My family thinks it a very unsuitable enterprise."

"Do they refer to my magazine? Or our marriage?"

He went still, smoke drifting from his nostrils. I had to soften my voice. "Instead of shutting it down, why don't we manage it together? It would be an occupation for you."

"Me?" He laughed. "Artistic dabbling is no occupation for a gentleman."

I could actually feel our joie de vivre withering, thickening with ice like the Seine outside our hotel as early snow preluded incoming winter.

"Very well," I said at length. "Then I shall see to it on our return, as you insist."

WE ARRIVED IN London under perceptible discontent.

After shutting down my magazine, I was plagued by restlessness. Jack was in New York apprenticing in a brokerage firm. Winston joined him for the holidays, compounding my misery. I missed my boys desperately. I longed to be with them, away from the gloom in England, where the sudden death of Victoria's favorite son, Alfred, had plunged the country into mourning. When George left for Wales to celebrate the season with his family, I refused to accompany him, despite his exhortations. Quailing at the thought of Christmas among disapproving in-laws, which I'd thought I had left behind with Randolph's death, I accepted instead Consuelo's invitation to Blenheim, where I took much-needed comfort in our friendship.

"Give it time," Consuelo advised, after I poured out my distress. "It's a new marriage. There are bound to be obstacles along the way."

"He's different somehow," I said. "Like he's become someone else."

She went silent before she replied, "Or perhaps he's simply showing you who he was all along. Jennie, he was born into an aristocratic family. He's behaving just as you'd expect."

"Yes," I murmured. "Perhaps he is. But I don't want to be an aristocrat's wife again."

Consuelo sighed. She didn't say more about it, and though I couldn't admit it aloud, less than a year into my marriage, I feared more than my magazine might require dissolution.

THIRTY-TWO

1901–1902

The new year began with the death of Queen Victoria. It came as a national shock, grieving crowds weeping disconsolately over the black-edged special editions of the *Evening News* announcing her demise. Though she'd been eighty-one and ailing for months, no one, it seemed, was prepared for the inevitable loss. After she had ruled over the British Empire for nearly sixty-four years, her absence was inconceivable. Now her eldest son, Bertie, who'd been her primary cause of reproof and despair, was our new king, Edward VII.

I personally thought it high time. Victoria had steered us through innumerable crises, but Bertie had lingered in her shadow long enough, and he had a more modern outlook. The old queen had held back progress with her antiquated notions, and toward the end, she hadn't seemed all that pleased to be on the throne. I suspected she might have handed over the reins long before, had it been permitted. The question was, could Bertie rise to the challenge and set aside his errant ways?

Winston arrived home on the very day her funeral procession passed through London on its way to her burial in Windsor Castle. After the official period of state mourning, he prepared to deliver his maiden speech in the House—a plea for accord with the Boers, whose cause, he argued, was justified. He came to my house to rehearse his speech, requesting suggestions for improvement. As he paced the drawing room declaiming, George suddenly appeared in the doorway, his valise in hand.

He hadn't sent word of his impending arrival from Wales, where he'd stayed to comfort his grieving family, bereft by the queen's death. When I caught sight of him, I took immediate note of the tension in his posture. Winston was oblivious, even as icy discomfort seeped over me, until my son paused in mid-sentence to turn to my chair.

"What?" he asked. "Is it too much—?"

"Entirely." George's voice rang out.

"How so?" Winston's arid tone roused a glower on my husband's face.

"You would heap dishonor on your first day of office, barely two months after we've lost our queen?" George planted himself with his shoulders squared, as if he braced for battle.

"I would," said my son. I'd marked this subtle change in him, a maturity tempered in newfound confidence from his time in America. "We have a new sovereign. A new reign. To persist in this war is the only dishonor I see."

"Thousands of our soldiers have perished for it." George took an infuriated step forward. "While you were gallivanting about writing articles and getting yourself imprisoned, those far braver than you sacrificed their lives to defend the empire."

As I started to rise in alarm, Winston gave George a peculiar smile. "I'm well-aware. My brother took a bullet for it. You did not."

George lunged. I almost cried out in irritation, thinking it ridiculous they'd actually come to blows, until something inflexible in Winston's stance stopped George in his tracks.

"I must still act according to my conscience." Winston took a laden pause. "Rather than hoist your petard for a lost cause, perhaps you should find some way to make yourself useful. You are not lord of Ruthin Castle yet."

"Winston," I exclaimed. "Really, that is uncalled for—"

George's hiss cut me off. "Get out. I'll not abide a traitor in my house."

"It's not your house," said my son. "It's my mother's. Only she can throw me out of it."

"*Enough.*" I delivered my rebuke as if they were two bullies in a schoolyard. I knew in that instant that I had made a terrible mistake in marrying George. It wasn't only that he had inflated notions of his lineage. He was too young and immature, about to toss my son out on his ear for being better than him.

George whirled to me. "I warned you that should he forget his place, he'd do himself no good. Would you condone him casting aspersions on our very dead?"

"He's an MP," I replied in astonishment. "He was elected to speak his mind. Randolph defended Irish interests when no one else dared and—"

"So, you *do* condone it. Rather than instill respect in him for his country, you'd encourage his appalling shamelessness."

Before I could reply, Winston said, "It is my shamelessness to atone for. Should you ever speak to her in that manner again, it shall be I who sees you from this house."

George narrowed his eyes at him before swerving back to me. "If this is where your loyalty lies, I'll have no part in it." Turning heel, he strode out. Moments later, the slam of the front door announced his departure.

I looked angrily at Winston. "Was it necessary to provoke him so?"

"Unfortunately, it was." He met my stare. "You're not happy with him. I read it in your letters from Paris. I can see it in you now."

All of a sudden, I had to blink back a surge of tears. I wanted to deny it, even as I heard myself say, "He—he's not who I thought he was."

"No?" A dry smile creased his mouth, reminding me with a pang of his father. "He seems to me to be entirely himself. Like most of his ilk, he thinks too highly of himself while failing to take into account his rather precarious position."

I swallowed. "You're one of them, too. The grandson of a duke."

"In name alone. Without the title or the fortune, not that Papa's family ever had much of the latter. I'll not uphold their self-indulgence. To bring about lasting change, we must strive for a more equitable world."

"An equitable world? Since when has that been a Tory principle? Do you plan to cross the aisle like your father and declare yourself a Liberal?"

His smile faded. "Don't change the subject. You never took the time to discover that man's nature because you were so determined to marry him, no matter the cost."

"He told me that he loved me. I love him. Don't I warrant the right?"

His smile faded. "You do. It must be very disappointing to find you have so little in common with the man you love. But you've never been one to look the other way."

I started at the finality in his voice. "What are you saying?"

He sighed. "Jack and I feared this marriage would be a mistake. We bit our tongues and hoped we were wrong because you were so resolved. We wanted to see you happy. But he'll never change. He'll go about as he always has, spending what he doesn't earn, while you shut down your quarterly to satisfy his pride. He has no desire to earn a living while he can enjoy the fruits of our trust as your husband. He believes it's below a gentleman's dignity to earn a wage."

"Are you suggesting . . . I should leave him?"

Winston chuckled. "Couples separate. Grandpapa Jerome and Grandma Clara did."

"I don't want to be like my parents. What of the scandal, after we defied everyone to marry?"

"I don't think you need to worry on that account. His family has no relations with us, and your friends, including our new king, will stand by you. Hasn't he invited you to his coronation?"

"Yes, of course." Desperate for a distraction, I plunged to my desk, fishing through my correspondence. "He sent me this note with the invitation—" As Winston took it from me, I abruptly remembered what the note said and reached to snatch it back when he let out another chuckle.

"Has George seen this? His Majesty has reserved a special box for his friends who are not titled peers. Japanese attire optional." He lifted an amused expression that froze me where I stood. "I'm assuming George hasn't seen it."

"I told him we'd been invited," I said, trying to collect myself. "He insists we must decline. He says Bertie lacks all moral decency."

"Be that as it may, he's still our king." Winston returned the handwritten note to me. "Given the circumstances, how can you possibly refuse such intimate appropriation?"

"You know," I breathed in dismay.

He smiled. "Mamma, I'm in Parliament. Some of the calcified lords were very eager to give me an accounting of your impact on both Papa and our then-wayward prince."

I swallowed. "I was assured it would never become public knowledge."

"By whom? Fanny Ronalds?" Winston had to fight back another smile. "Rest assured, it's more gossip than fact. Bertie was often seen trying to charm his way into your good graces, and, given his nature, it was assumed that at some point you gave in. But no one, I daresay, knows anything about the Japanese attire."

I felt myself flush. "You don't think less of me?"

"Why should I? I've no doubt you did what you had to do for Papa's sake. But you needn't do the same for George. We must strive to keep ourselves in the king's favor; we know what his displeasure can do." He took my hand in his. "You needn't decide anything right now. But when you do, you can count on our full support. Neither Jack nor I wishes to see you so unhappy." He paused. "It's a good thing we had that agreement drawn up. George wouldn't make this easy on you otherwise."

I embraced my son, holding him close. Then I drew back with

a forced smile. "Now, recite your speech again for me. From the beginning. I think the opening lines could be improved . . ."

Afterward, I sat with him to make the corrections. I thought his speech would prove controversial enough to earn him notice, even as in the back of my mind, the question lingered.

What was I going to do now?

It unnerved me that I didn't know.

UNSEASONABLE HEAT SWAMPED London on the day of the coronation. I opted for a white silk gown without jewels. Newspapers had foretold the event wouldn't be lavish after the expense of Victoria's funeral, but when I arrived, I found Westminster Abbey brimming with all the excessive pomp only such a historic royal event could justify. Alexandra was present, garbed in ermine to be crowned queen-consort beside her husband. Consuelo was also present, seated with her husband, but I wasn't slated for a place on their pew.

I came alone, George not having returned since his altercation with Winston, who left his Barton Street bachelor flat to move in and keep me company. I received a brief note from my husband that he was spending the summer at a friend's country estate, where I was welcome to join him. He must have known I wouldn't. Our waning passion had been pulverized by his confrontation with my son. While I kept telling myself that some time apart would do us good, I now had to accept that the chasm between us was too wide. I kept hearing Clarita in my mind.

He can never be Randolph.

I never missed my late husband more than upon my entry into the abbey, where the usher inspected my invitation before escorting me toward the tier Bertie had set aside for his friends. I felt all eyes turning to me, almost heard the whispers volleying between the high-ranking ladies who'd attended my dinner parties, vying with me, emulating my style, flattering me to my face, and rejoicing behind my back whenever I tripped into disgrace.

Lifting my chin, I let my attire attract their frowns. I'd put on weight in the wake of my discord with George, forgoing my abstention for repasts with Winston, so I'd been obliged to don a corset, which pinched my waist. But the discomfort was worth it. I felt statuesque, an avenging figure in my inappropriate garb as I braved the gossips wasting no time in spreading word that Mrs. Cornwallis-West dared appear by herself—and dressed in white like a bride, no less.

Winston had expressed disappointment that he couldn't witness the event firsthand. The invitations were limited. I thought he'd be very sore indeed when I neared the pews to find them occupied entirely by women in garish gowns and lavish hats, perfumed and bejeweled to their teeth. I recognized Lillie Langtry, the famed actress Bertie had long admired; as I took my place beside her, she gave me a furtive smile, as if we shared a secret.

I supposed we did. Apparently, our king had reserved this special box for his favorite mistresses. Taking out my painted fan — the same one Eugénie had gifted Mama so many years ago—I concealed my smile. Trust Bertie to taint his anointing with a touch of scandal.

And in truth, it was where I belonged, among his notorious outsiders.

I SPENT THE last days of summer at Compton Place by the seaside of Eastbourne, with my sister Leonie and her third son, Seymour, who'd taken ill with a consumptive paralysis that confined him to a wheeled chair. Physicians had advised that the sea air might restore his health, so we'd decamped to the spacious estate of the Duke and Duchess of Devonshire, where the poor boy gazed longingly from the terrace to the distant shoreline.

I took it upon myself to lift his spirits by reading Jack's and Winston's letters aloud; both of them sent fond regards. Seymour admired his Spencer-Churchill cousins, and their words rallied him to submit to the painful daily massages prescribed by his doctors. When I relayed Winston's request that I set down my recollections of Randolph for a biographical work he hoped to write, Seymour's eyes lit up. "Oh, Auntie Jennie, you must! I've heard so many stories about Uncle Randolph. I wish I could have known him."

"He wasn't much for praise, but he would have liked you," I said, smiling. "You must help me. Your legs may be impaired, but your fingers are not. If I dictate, will you write?"

He gave an enthusiastic nod as Leonie gazed at me in mute gratitude.

Winston's request kept me busy, precluding any inclination to brood over my continued estrangement from George. I thoroughly enjoyed gathering my recollections of Randolph, even if I had to be editorially circumspect for Seymour's sake.

After delivering four sons, the last of whom was only a year old, and beset by anxiety over Seymour, Leonie also required my attention. She refused to be parted from her boy for any length of time, so in the afternoons, while he underwent treatment, I had her join me in the duke's motorcar for excursions along the coast, where we could share time alone.

"Marriage didn't turn out as we imagined, did it?" she said one evening as we sat in the car, admiring the sunset. Shimmering copper burnished the sea, ebbing fire turning to embers upon the chalky cliffs. The chauffeur stood a distance away, lending us privacy.

I sighed. "I think it rarely turns out as any woman imagines." I glanced at her profile, the wind lifting tendrils of her auburn hair, lighter in hue than mine.

"I suppose not." She fingered her wedding band. I knew she and Leslie had mostly gone their separate ways, remaining married only because it was expected. "Arthur says he's in love with me," she abruptly said. "He asked me to be his mistress."

"Oh?" Her admission startled me. Leonie had always been very reserved about her private life, even if it wasn't a secret that, since her introduction at court, she'd developed an intimate association with Arthur, Duke of Connaught, Victoria's third son. They'd even traveled abroad together, accompanied by the duke's often sickly wife, Louise.

"I told him it was impossible," she said. "We're both married."

"Do you love him?" I asked. She was only forty-two and shouldn't deny herself. I highly doubted Leslie was shunning his extramarital opportunities.

She turned her long-lashed eyes, her most becoming feature, to me, reflecting her innate warmth. "Yes, I love him. But I haven't slept with him. I could never betray Louise's trust. I remember how hurt Mama was over Fanny, and Louise has been so kind to me."

"Mama wasn't so much hurt over Fanny as she was over Papa's disregard for how it appeared," I said. "She ended up leaving him because of a financial crisis, not Fanny."

"Still, I could never be the other woman. And Arthur can't ever leave Louise."

"No, I suppose he cannot."

She paused, taking in my expression. "Were you ever unfaithful to Randolph?"

I averted my gaze, looking toward the scarlet-stained horizon. Incoming dusk chilled my skin. "Yes," I said at length. "And he was unfaithful to me."

"Yet you were so grief-stricken when he died. I've heard you dictating your memories to Seymour. Your entire person changes when you speak of him."

"I'm starting to realize I was happier with him than I thought I was at the time," I said. "We truly understood each other. Our dalliances were never stronger than our love for each other." As I spoke, I remembered Kinsky. I'd thought my love for him might have been stronger, but he had apparently not felt the same toward me. "Marriage doesn't turn out as we imagine, but it can surprise us."

"And it can be good to see the past as it really was, not as we think it should be."

I found myself caught off guard by her perceptiveness.

"And George?" she said. "Will you divorce him?"

"How? No woman of our class has gone so far. I risked enough by marrying him."

"But if you're no longer happy with him? Wouldn't it be better for both of you?"

"Would you divorce Leslie?" I asked, more sharply than intended.

She flinched. "He won't hear of it. He says his family would never condone it and our boys are too young."

"While my boys don't care for George." I heard the catch in my voice. "Winston has indeed urged me to do something."

"Clarita should do something, too. Shackled to that estate, determined to safeguard it from Moreton, with the roof falling in on her head. She's not happy, either. How can the three of us have so misjudged our marriages?"

"Mama did warn us. But then she also misjudged hers. Perhaps Papa was right. Perhaps when we fall in love, it's a dangerous affair."

Leonie sat silent for a long moment before she said, "Maybe it's not that we misjudge, but that as we grow older, we change. We want different things. Men do not."

I leaned over to kiss her cheek, cold from the spindrift rising from the darkened sea.

"When did my little sister become so wise?" I murmured.

During the drive back, she said, "You mustn't let fear of scandal stop you, Jennie. You always were the bravest of us. If you must leave him, do it without regret."

THIRTY-THREE

1908

"What do you think of her?" Winston leaned to me, his eyes fixed on a young woman dancing with an older gentleman on the floor.

We were at the estate of the Earl of Abingdon, attending my son Jack's wedding reception. We had been much surprised when Jack, as circumspect as Leonie, had announced his proposal to Lady Gwendoline Bertie, the earl's daughter. He was working as a stockbroker in London, making a name for himself, but none of us had anticipated his acceptance by a titled family, given his choice of career. When I queried him, concerned, he assured me his "Goonie" (a ridiculous nickname for such a quiet young woman) loved him as much as he loved her. Her father, albeit reluctantly, had granted his consent. Winston later informed me that Jack had confided in him months before his intent to marry her, delaying his proposal to build up his resources and swearing Winston to secrecy. Goonie, it seemed, possessed every aristocratic requisite save one: money. The earl consented because Jack was earning plenty of it.

Now, I followed my elder son's gaze to the woman in question. I recognized her at once. A radiant, dark-haired girl with wide hazel-green eyes, thick brows that seemed painted upon her alabaster skin, and a slender gracefulness like her mother's.

"Why, that's Clementine Hozier. Daughter of Sir Henry and Lady Blanche. Blanche is a friend of mine, she helped raise funds for the *Maine*." I paused, seeing the intense interest on his face. "Why do you ask, pumpkin?"

"Because I met her at a ball in Crewe House four years ago," he said. "A few months past, we met again at a dinner party hosted by Lady St. Helier. I think I like her very much."

As he spoke, she glanced over at us, her eyes lowered shyly.

"She seems to like you as well. Oh, my darling. How wonderful. She's perfect for you."

"Is she?" he said.

"Why wouldn't she be? You know how much I want you and Jack to be happy in your marriages. I've been very forthright about it, haven't I?"

"You have. Warning us to take our time to find the right match, to not rush into anything. To take you as our example, the rich girl who never made the effort to think it through."

I pinched his hand on the table. "Don't be cheeky. I found happiness with your father. I only wish the same for you."

As I spoke, I thought of how difficult things were with George. He'd suffered a nervous collapse following the failure of a business venture, repairing to St. Moritz to recover under Fanny's covert eye, as she was vacationing there as well. He'd made a calamitous investment after seeing how well Jack and Winston fared; the publication of Winston's biography of Randolph, in particular, had been so well-received that it spurred George out of his indolence. He ended up in debt, some of it to my sons, who'd loaned him capital in a futile attempt to show support for my sake, as I still balked at an official separation.

Winston paused. "I've heard rumors."

"Rumors?"

"Of Clementine. Her father." He swallowed. "People can be despicable."

I'd heard the rumors, too. Who hadn't? Lady Blanche was a very carefree woman who'd lived in France, befriending intellectuals. Passionate about the arts and notorious for her innumerable affairs, after Sir Henry found her in flagrante with a lover, she had averted his suit for divorce by citing his own indiscretions, but they still separated.

"Sir Henry raised her as his own," I said at length. "Pay no mind to rumors."

"If you can call what he did raised. He didn't show Clementine any affection growing up, according to her. As if he knew."

"Knew what?" I asked, though I was aware of what he referred to.

"That her father is Captain William Bay Middleton, one of her mother's lovers."

"Clementine told you this?" I was taken aback. "It is so serious?"

He nodded. "We've spoken at length. I'm thinking of inviting her to Blenheim, to show her the old pile. She likes Consuelo. Maybe I'll propose to her there. The setting is idyllic."

"Oh." I couldn't curb my stab of surprise that he'd planned so far ahead, without thinking to inform me before now. "As serious as that."

He gave me a stern look. "Don't start. I know how much you like to boast about me to your friends. I don't want it bandied about society. She's not aware of it. She may turn me down."

"She won't." I returned my gaze to her. She was laughing as her dance partner escorted her off the floor. As she moved past us, she cast a quick smile at Winston. "Don't underestimate a woman's intuition."

"So, you approve?" he said, eager but uncertain, like when he was a boy and wanted to rush up to hug me, but held back because of his need to be shown first that he'd been missed as much as he missed me. I was abruptly saddened by it, knowing this reluctance in my sons was my doing. I hadn't been present for most of their childhood. Although they loved me, I still retained the aura of the glamorous stranger who'd swept in on occasion to brighten their world, the distant moon and stars they admired but couldn't claim as their own.

"If you like her enough to ask her to be your wife, yes, of course I approve," I said. "Winston, I'd never stand in the way of your happiness."

"It's not that." He furrowed his brow. "My undersecretariat for the Colonial Office did not go easy on me, as you know."

"Yet you can still boast of success," I said. "Drafting a constitution for the Transvaal, overseeing the new government in the Orange Free State—you ensured equality between us and the Boers after the terrible conflict."

"But my proposal that we desist importing Chinese indentured labor in South Africa was refuted because of economic concerns for the colony. And relations with the Africans remain very tense. The Zulu Rebellion in Natal was a butchery of the native population by us. I want to do more but lost my reelection to the Conservatives in Manchester North West by a mere handful of votes. We're resolved to remain an empire at any cost, even though we can't continue to bully the world. We must learn to stand for something greater than our pride."

"The Liberals supported your seat in Dundee," I reminded him. "Not all is lost."

"Yes, but the struggles ahead . . . You know better than most what's at stake. What it's like to be a politician's wife." He tugged at his collar, an impatient gesture that reminded me of how Randolph would adjust his cravat in Parliament, a distraction to prime his assault. "Clementine must be prepared. This life I'd bring her into, I'm not sure she'll want it."

"Prepared for what?" But this, too, I already knew. He'd written Randolph's biography relying on my recollections. He'd gleaned through the edited prose my aborted aspirations for his father, the ultimate ambition that never came to be.

He didn't speak for a long moment, as if saying it aloud might negate it. "I hope to be prime minister one day," he finally said. Before I could react, he went on. "I'm only thirty-three, the youngest member in the House. I've much to learn, like the empire itself. But I'll do whatever it requires. It will take years of hard work and disappointment. I may never succeed. Clementine must understand this, if she's to marry me."

I blinked back tears. Just when I thought I was an outsider to him, he'd disclosed an intimacy deeper than his attraction to a young woman. A revelation of his inner soul.

"And what do you wish me to do?"

"Talk to her. Help her. She hasn't had much of a mother. Or a father, for that matter. But a mother, most of all. She needs one now. I need you to be one to her."

I clasped his hand in mine. "It'll be an opportunity for me, to make up for where I failed with you and your brother."

He smiled. "You mustn't say that. We do not fault you. We never have."

"I fault myself. Go. Dance with her. Invite her to Blenheim. I won't hear of diffidence. You are Randolph Spencer-Churchill's son. He never backed down from a fight."

Winston stood, passing his palm over his thinning pate, a legacy from his paternal grandfather that he detested and therefore ignored. Pulled down his rumpled jacket.

Then he said, "I'm also Jennie Jerome's son. She, too, never backs down."

As he walked over to where Clementine Hozier stood sipping champagne, the delight on her face when he neared moved me so much, I had to turn away to hide the tears on my cheeks.

When I least expected it, I had found redemption.

THIRTY-FOUR

An affair," I said.

Fanny nodded. "I'm afraid so. I am so sorry, Jennie. I did debate whether or not to tell you, considering the last time I brought you such unpleasant news."

As if to punctuate her discomfort, she smoothed a hand over her smart travel suit from Paris, cut in the latest style. I'd complimented her on it. No fripperies or gewgaws. Hats were still enormous, crowned by plumes or fake fruit, like dining-room adornments, but dress lines had become tailored and trim. Hers was mauve wool, with velvet piping on her knee-length coat, her high-necked blouse pinned by a tiny bow, the skirt narrow, without bulky petticoats.

Though she neared seventy, she still looked as fresh and modern as she had during my childhood, as if she were immune to the passage of time.

"You're certain?" I shifted on the settee, feeling gargantuan in my flowing day gown, a relic of the fading era.

"I'm afraid so. They were seen coming and going from his hotel in St. Moritz. She has a husband, naturally, so you needn't worry on that account."

"Is it serious?"

She picked up her coffee cup, eyeing me over it. "Is it ever, with him?"

I heard my halting laugh, like a nip of teeth in my ear.

"Jennie." She hesitated.

"I know. I just don't know how."

"How else? There's no other solution."

"No? We don't have children together. Separate households. Mutually-agreed-upon terms. It can be arranged without any fuss."

"You don't want that." Her voice turned firm. This was the woman who'd always been more of a mother to me than my own, my adviser and sometime instigator, and at moments like these, the one willing to utter truths I'd rather not hear. "You have years ahead of you—"

"I turned fifty-four in January. I'm a matron, Fanny, not a debutante."

"You must think me ancient! It's a new century. We have women marching in the streets, calling for our right to vote. It's not our mothers' epoch anymore. We can, and we should, divorce unfaithful husbands."

"Not in Britain. Not someone like me."

"Well." She paused. "Then you must be the first, mustn't you?"

"Fanny, Jack has recently married. Winston is planning to propose to Clementine and has high ambitions for himself. For their mother, the widow of Randolph Spencer-Churchill, to divorce her second husband—imagine the uproar."

"Oh, they'll blast you from the floor of the House itself." She made a dismissive gesture. "Condemn you in society columns from here to New York. What of it? They'll huff and puff, and never speak of it again. Because that is how these things are done."

"He has to consent," I reminded her. "He must sue for divorce first."

"According to whom?" She reached for the coffeepot, pouring herself another cup. "You don't require royal consent if you're untitled. Why not sue yourself? If the rules are not to our liking, it behooves us to change them. Blaze the path for others, as you've done before."

I sat in silence, turning it over in my head, warming to the notion, as I always did when faced with a challenge. Then recoiling as I envisioned the outcome.

"He may fight it," I said.

"Let him. He betrayed you. If he were Randolph—" She cut herself short, giving me an apologetic look. "We both know that was different. And he has no standing on which to protest, and too much to lose if he does. His mistress, for one, won't appreciate being dragged into public notice. Nor, I daresay, will her cuckolded husband. If George knows what's best for him, he'll sign without any of this fuss you fear."

"And if he doesn't?"

"Let Lord and Lady Ruthin take him to task. They never approved of the marriage to start. They'll be relieved to see it come to an end, even if it ends with their son worse for the wear."

I found myself nodding. "We cannot go on like this." Yet even as I recognized the inevitability, I recalled his uncertain eagerness that night in Warwick Castle, how his passion had roused the youth under my skin, resurrecting a desire I'd thought lost.

Now, lost again.

Fanny started to rise, moving to my side as I whispered, "We did love each other."

She sighed. "Yes. I'm afraid that's the most difficult part to forget."

CLARITA AND MORETON were living apart, her struggle to safeguard the estate having created an unbreachable rift. He'd moved to New York, in pursuit of another unfathomable scheme. Leonie was caught up in her love triangle with her besotted royal duke. None of us were happy in our personal lives, but when we reunited for the holidays at Clarita's manor, we decorated the great hall with mistletoe and trimmed the tree, burned the Yuletide log, and shared stories by the fireplace of our childhood in New York, of Papa's mad carriage rides and Mama's opulent parties. We laughed and drank too much mead, ignoring the gray in our tresses, the aches that made rising from a chair more cumbersome.

When I told my sisters that I was considering filing for divorce, they were both sympathetic, though Leonie was more outspoken than Clarita, declaring it overdue. After our younger sister retired, Clarita stayed with me by the hearth. Her hands were chafed, as if she'd been chopping wood. She caught me staring. "This house doesn't clean itself."

"But you have staff. Surely . . ."

"I maintain a housekeeper, the cook and groundskeeper. Otherwise, we'd be overrun by weeds and mice. No chambermaid or butler. You've seen as much."

I nodded. While the manor was historic, situated in a forested area in the parish of Rosher, I could imagine the effort required for its upkeep, with so little help.

"Why not be done with it? Is it worth so much sacrifice?"

She gazed into the fire. "I suppose to most, it's a troublesome old house with a leaking roof. But it's all I have. In the spring, the gardens are so lovely. I feel at peace. At home."

"Do you?" It wasn't just her hands. She'd aged in her countenance, too. Still beautiful, because my sister couldn't be anything else, yet no longer the butterfly of society, who'd ridden in the royal hunt at Compiègne and enchanted a French viscount.

"As much as I can be," she said. "I must leave something of value to my children. To make ends meet, I'm taking on a tenant in the summer. An American writer, Stephan Crane, friend of Mark Twain. He promises to invite others for gatherings." She attempted a smile. "My own *petit salon*. Mama would approve. If she could see me now, she'd turn over in her tomb."

I reached over to take her hand. "I will help you, if I can."

"You?" She rolled her eyes. "How can you possibly help, with that husband of yours bleeding everyone dry? He puts my Mortal

Ruin to shame. They should join forces to dig wells in Africa. It's all they're good for. And no doubt, they'd make a catastrophe of that, too."

Mortal Ruin was her nickname for Moreton; it always made me laugh.

"Aren't we a pair?"

Her hand tightened in mine. "Yours isn't worth the sacrifice, Jennie."

"Yes," I said. "You did warn me."

"And you didn't listen." A hint of reproof notched her tone. "None of us ever listened. We were too determined to do it our way. The Jerome sisters, charting our path to glory. Only to find ourselves manning our own ships."

"In my case, quite literally."

"At least you did it. You took a ship to South Africa. You survived Randolph. And you'll survive George. It's who you are." She turned her eyes to me. I had to swallow against the sudden lump in my throat. "I've always envied you," she said softly. "Oh, how I envied you."

"Me?" I couldn't believe it. "I was the one who envied you."

"And I took satisfaction in it. But in the end, you refused to give in. While I—well, you might say I have. You grow tired. You reach a time in life when you must decide whether all the struggle can change anything."

We sat in the hush, in the crackle and hiss of the flames.

"I sometimes wonder if it does," I said. "Look at me. Falling for a man young enough to be my son, throwing my caution to the wind again, only to have him—"

"Never." She didn't look at me. "I envy that, too. Your endless desire for life. Never think it's not worth it. It is, Jennie. It's all there is before we die."

THIRTY-FIVE

1909

Winston had been appointed home secretary. During dinner at his new home in Eccleston Square, where he'd settled in with his Clemmie, pregnant with their first child, he declared his intent to put the Irish question to the House.

"It did not go easy for Randolph," I told him. "It's still mired in contention."

"I'm aware." He had his napkin tucked into his collar, like a laborer at a pub, digging into his roasted quail.

I was pleased to see his appetite. He'd always been finicky about food, and Clementine had proven salubrious. Her graceful delicacy belied a will to match his own. Like Randolph, he was prone to immersing himself in work and forgetting to attend to his needs. He'd taken up smoking cigars, too, which she detested. She refused to let him skip meals and had their tidy household under strict order. I admired her efficiency and lack of vanity, especially in her advanced pregnancy. Her upbringing had clearly taught her that if one wanted things done as one preferred, one must do them oneself.

"Papa still espoused it," my son went on, as she reached over to dilute his glass of wine with water. "He remained committed to it. My conversations with Asquith and several others indicate the time is right. We need a proper legislature, with an Irish executive to oversee domestic affairs. Parliament will be reserved for matters pertaining to the Crown, but Ireland must be allowed to dictate its internal policies."

"An ambitious plan. It goes farther than Randolph ever dared."

"Do you think it ill-advised?" he asked.

I glanced at Clementine. I'd positioned myself as a loving but not interfering mother-in-law, having discovered that, contrary to Winston's initial fears, she wasn't intimidated by his ambition or the challenges he faced. She seemed to relish it, a kindred spirit in this respect to me. Though not as instrumental as I'd been to Randolph, given Winston's innate gift for rhetoric, she was still capable of advising him. I took care to not intrude or overshadow her, though my son still turned to me, as he always had, for counsel.

She gave me a quick nod of consent.

"No," I said. "I'm in agreement. But I caution you to advance in stages, not rush legislature through without nationalist support. I witnessed how quickly matters can turn for the worse there. You don't want another outbreak of violence."

"That's the last thing we want." He gnawed his quail to its bone and sat back, scratching his chin. There was a hint of fleshiness about him now. I liked seeing it, after his painfully slim youth. "I've drafted a speech for our next session. Would you review it?"

"I'd be delighted," I said, rising to help clear the table as he lit a cigar and went into his small parlor-study.

Clementine was on her feet, her belly jutting out. They had a day maid, and Winston was hardly parsimonious. But she hadn't enjoyed the privileges of a ducal palace, so she took hold of the purse. With a babe on the way, she told me, economy was only sensible. It was the sole time in our relationship when I'd sensed her disapproval, as if she faulted me for having instilled too much indulgence in her husband.

After I saw the dishes to the kitchen and Clementine refused my offer to do the washing, I joined Winston in his study, waving a hand to clear the air of his smoke, though it took me back to Randolph's cigarettes, his working area always clouded by their smoke.

"Here." Winston thrust the pages into my hand. As I settled into the armchair to read, deciphering his intent through scratched-out lines and inkblots, as his first drafts were invariably chaotic, he chewed on his cigar, waiting impatiently for my reaction.

I looked up. "Perhaps moderate this section about a united Ireland."

He frowned. "It's what we ultimately desire, is it not?"

"Yes, but this is not the time for such a sweeping statement. Irish separatists in Ulster oppose anything that doesn't entail full independence."

He grunted. "Indeed." Leaning to his desk to score out the paragraph, he said abruptly, "Mamma, why aren't you writing anymore?"

"Me? You don't need me to write any speeches for you, pumpkin."

"I meant in general. At least finish your memoirs."

"You think so?"

"You have a standing offer from the publisher." He glanced at me.

"Yes, but you advised me to take care not to hurt anyone's feelings."

"I still advise it." He set his pen aside. "You should still finish them."

"Perhaps I shall." I saw the knowing glint in his eyes. "I already have. Do you want to read all my unmentionable secrets?"

"Naturally." He smiled.

"Just to see that I don't offend anyone." I laughed, coming to my feet. "Don't smoke too much, darling. It's not good for your voice. You must be in excellent voice for this undertaking."

"So Clemmie keeps telling me." He paused. "Are you very lonely these days?"

I went still. He had this unerring capacity for sensing what I refused to say.

"Not in particular. I have Jack's baby son to coddle, and soon enough your child as well. Doting grandmothers should have no time for loneliness."

"That's not what I asked." He held my gaze. "It's not enough. Not for you. I'll not see you turn into a doting grandmother before your time."

"Well." I gave a shrug. "What else is there for me to do?"

"Find yourself another occupation."

"Such as?" If he had suggested it, he must have an idea. He always did.

"You published a literary review. Why not write a play?" he said, to my surprise. "Finish your memoirs, then stage a play. Our theater could certainly use your American wit."

"A play? And you think anyone would pay to see it?"

"I would." His tone was jocular. His expression wasn't. "It could take months, Mamma. Years, even, before you're free of him, if you ever decide to file that suit."

"So, put on a show in the meantime," I said.

He winked. "We know how to do that much, don't we?"

MY PLAY, TITLED *His Borrowed Plumes,* was semi-autobiographical, lighthearted in tone: the story of a celebrated authoress who discovers her husband, resentful of her success, has embarked on an affair. My memoirs, redacted "to protect the guilty," as Winston remarked, had been published to unexpected enthusiasm, so I mined details for the play not included in my book. Despite my affinity for speeches, I found literary writing challenging and despaired of ever mastering it. When a London manager offered to produce the play, I had the suspicion Winston was behind the offer, his impetus for me to complete the work. The manager assured me the public had taken to my memoirs and would surely flock to a play by me. All we required was a suitable venue and an actress for the lead role.

I had only one in mind: Mrs. Patrick Campbell, famed actress of the London stage, pursued by George Bernard Shaw and admired by Bertie. Known affectionately as Mrs. Pat, she'd recently become her own manager, performing to acclaim in New York. Though she was several years younger than I, we bore a marked resemblance, both raven-haired and of generous figure. I could readily envision her playing the part.

I invited her to tea at my home. She arrived with her dark hair upswept in an elaborate coiffure, her generously cut striped walking suit accessorized with a silver-handled cane I suspected was mostly for effect. Queen Alexandra had suffered a fever that resulted in her use of a similar device, making it instantly fashionable. Mrs. Pat wielded hers with commanding presence; she was arresting and magnetic, but of course she had to be. An actress must attract attention, both on the stage and off. She earned her living from it.

"Oh, Lady Randolph," she exclaimed when I told her of my proposal. "I'd be honored. To play this part would be such a privilege for me."

"Not to mention, it would establish you as an independent talent. You left your previous management over disagreements in how they were handling your career, did you not?"

She paused, with dramatic emphasis. "Have you been making inquiries about me?"

"Must I? It seems to me that we have something in common. Two women of a certain age, trying to make their way in the world without meddlesome oversight."

"Well, yes. I won't deny that being in your play would bolster my prestige. But the role itself is so delicious. If I may ask, just *how* biographical is it?"

I laughed. "Biographical enough, embellished for public consumption."

"As all biographical material should be. The unvarnished truth is so tedious."

I liked her. We were actually too alike. Ordinarily, we should repel one another, but I wasn't going to be the one onstage, so who better to play the part, embellished as it was?

Rehearsals commenced in my drawing room while the manager secured a venue; it was to be a limited engagement, to peak attendance and not overstrain our resources.

Opening night at the Hicks Theatre on Shaftesbury Avenue attracted the finest of society; as the curtain rose, the boxes were filled with aristocracy and several crowned heads, including Grand Duke Mikhail of Russia, who was visiting England. Bertie sent me a bouquet of roses with his regrets that he couldn't attend due to a prior engagement, but Winston and Jack were there, alongside George, who'd returned to London unannounced when he caught wind of the event. He arrived on my doorstep in mid–dress rehearsal and was charming to a fault, complimenting Mrs. Pat on her performance and seeming oblivious to the fact that the play mirrored our relationship. He took up residence in the guest bedroom and attended opening night in the tailored black tie we'd acquired in Paris, even if I took note of his red-veined cheeks and sallow dissipation. Winston refused to even greet him.

While the notices for the play were laudatory, they didn't justify more than the predetermined run. The manager withdrew, his obligation fulfilled. Mrs. Pat insisted we must find the means to continue. To my disconcertment, George chimed his agreement, saying that after so much effort, we couldn't think to abandon the enterprise. Plays needed time to mature, like wine. The first taste was never the finest.

Winston growled, "Of course he has no care for the expense. Forget the wine. Books that don't sell and plays that don't play are like dinner guests. They should always depart before outstaying their welcome."

I vacillated, torn between my son's mandate and my hope to

devise a graceful exit from my marriage. George was back at home; he had no current enterprise to speak of, and his proprietary interest in my play seemed to me the perfect opportunity to settle our differences. If we could reach agreement, he might be persuaded to file the divorce suit. Living apart while remaining married was no longer an option for me; I wanted my freedom. Nevertheless, when he suggested he could canvass his friends for donations to fund the play, I saw no harm in him doing something other than wasting his time gambling and drinking, and maybe reap some ancillary benefits that would keep him gainfully occupied. He might take it into his head to become a theatrical producer and move out voluntarily to set up his new business enterprise.

In the meantime, upon learning that the house next door to mine in Great Cumberland Place had come up for sale, Winston suggested we acquire it and have me redecorate it, then sell it for a profit. The turnover would be extraordinary, he said, more than most cabinet members earned in a year, and I had exquisite taste. Everyone said so.

Clementine encouraged it as well. I sensed they had connived to lend me a new endeavor after my failure to become an acclaimed dramatist. In July, she'd given birth to a baby girl named Diana. I was overjoyed by the babe's arrival but also keenly aware that with a child to rear, they had familial obligations of their own. I mustn't become a burden.

I earned a tidy sum on the house sale, a portion of which I invested in the play. I might have kept on doing it, living out of suitcases and boxes as I moved from house to house, throwing up new wallpaper and sconces, had I not discovered what I did.

It shouldn't have come as a surprise. But when I happened upon the parcel of letters on the nightstand in George's bedroom, bold as you please, all signed enigmatically by P., the blow of the discovery was so severe, I had to sit down to catch my breath. I couldn't tell at first if I was more horrified by the banality of it or by my own blindness.

When he returned home well after midnight, staggering in and banging his knee against the crate of my mother's porcelain, piled in the foyer awaiting delivery to Winston, who had requested it, as I couldn't keep hauling it about in my peregrinations, I launched myself down the staircase and flung the letters at his feet.

"No more. It is over. Leave my house."

He drew to a halt, bleary-eyed, staring at the parcel. Then he drawled, "I'm still your husband. Therefore, this is still my house."

"It is not." I paused. "Is it her or merely the thrill of humiliating me?"

"Why should you care?" He stepped past the letters as if they were of no account. "Randolph did much the same. And as I'm told, you did so equally to him."

"I want a divorce," I heard myself say.

His eyes snapped wide. He was drunk, but not to the point of being incapacitated. "Never."

"I will have it." I fixed him with my stare. "I will sue for it myself, if need be."

"You'll never obtain it." He drew himself to full height. "When has it been seen? A woman in your position. And Winston plotting to take over Parliament. You wouldn't dare. You'd destroy his chances of becoming PM—which is all you ever care about."

"Out." I stabbed my finger at the door. "Now. Never come back."

He executed a clumsy bow, meaning to mock me, but managing only to look foppish. As he turned to the door, I added, "And tell your Mrs. P. that the run has ended. She can take the box-office receipts and you, as well, if she likes. Neither is worth my time."

But after he left, as I sank onto the landing, barefoot, my hair disheveled about me, the weight of the years, of the mistakes made and the lessons learned, years too late, pressing down on me—I wept as I hadn't in as long as I could remember. All the tears I'd kept pent up behind the barricade of my heart came pouring forth in chest-heaving despair, until I felt at long last drained of years of grief.

I did not weep for George.

I wept for myself, for the freedom I had so desperately earned, for the youth I no longer possessed, and in belated acceptance that I must now live the rest of my days alone.

THIRTY-SIX

1910–1913

On a bright spring morning in May, Winston arrived unexpectedly at the latest house I'd acquired for renovation, part of my determination not to give in to aimlessness after my official separation from George. As I heard my son enter the disorderly drawing room, where I sat with unpacked boxes around me, I glanced up from my writing desk, where I was penning missives to my sisters.

"Darling! This is a surprise. Are you here for lunch? I'm afraid I've nothing prepared; the house is barely habitable, as you can see. I thought you were in Parliament, contending with the mess." I inclined my face to him as he kissed my cheek. Then I paused, taking in his expression. "Oh, dear. Has the House finally rebelled? Demanded it be returned its God-given right to veto economic bills and serve lifelong terms at our expense?"

He shook his head, removing his hat and setting it carefully on the settee, which was piled with wallpaper samples and decorative books I'd yet to shelve.

"Mamma. We just received word. It's not yet been officially announced. I wanted to tell you in person, before the palace issues a statement. Our king—Bertie. He is dead."

"What?" I froze in my chair. "You can't be serious."

Winston sighed. "I'm afraid I am. He fell ill with severe bronchial congestion; early this morning, he suffered a heart attack. Alexandra is so distraught that she's refusing to relinquish his body. They've sent urgent word to her sister in Russia. The Dowager

Tsarina is on her way here." He swallowed. "I know how close you were to him. It must come as a terrible shock. We are all convulsed by it. The empire, once again plunged into mourning."

My voice frayed in disbelief. "He was only sixty-eight. His mother lived to be eighty-one."

"And he had less than ten years on the throne." Winston sat down suddenly, as if he might collapse. "In the midst of a constitutional crisis, more upheaval. His familial ties to almost every monarch made him not only the uncle of Europe but our national bulwark. Now his nephew Kaiser Wilhelm II will see his path cleared. And our Royal Highness of Wales, Prince George, isn't nearly of the same caliber as his father or grandmother. An untried king at this time, with Parliament in disarray—I fear for our future."

"Wilhelm always resented Bertie for favoring France," I heard myself say, as if it mattered. All other words failed me. Often bellicose and given to his own way, Bertie had wreaked chaos in my life, but in that moment all I could remember was serving tea on my knees, in loose gowns and silk kimonos, and his lascivious grin as he plucked the combs from my hair.

"We'll be invited to the funeral," Winston went on. "I want you there with me; it's important for us to show unity with the new reign."

"Yes. Of course. I—I must say my goodbyes to him." I turned back to my desk. My pen slipped from my fingers, ink spattering the page as I heard my strangled sob. Winston stood and came to me at once, his hand pressing my shoulder.

"Dear God," I whispered. "It's all falling apart. Everything. The very world I've known."

"You must be strong. We all must be. I shall relinquish my current office after the funeral and request transfer to the Admiralty. We have to shore up our naval capacity."

"Capacity?" I said in bewilderment. "For what?"

"What else?" was his grim reply. "Only Bertie stood between us and Prussian aggression."

BEHIND HER VEIL, Alexandra was ashen, already fading into the past. I'd sent her my heartfelt condolences, knowing how much she must be suffering. His death would dictate the rest of her days just as his life had, her family beholden to the same rigid strictures that had regulated her existence. For her, widowhood would be a blessing only for its obscurity.

Following the state-imposed period of mourning, Winston prompted me to file my suit for divorce, saying the time was propitious, with everyone so distracted. It didn't go unnoticed. I was obliged to claim my husband had refused me conjugal rights, the sole basis on which a wife could win a divorce. George responded via his solicitor that he opposed any such claim, never mind that I'd already had his few remaining belongings dispatched to his ancestral castle. And the newspapers took me to severe task, condemning my suit as another symptom of the insufferable disruption in society, with women clamoring for the vote and no one seeming to have a care for propriety. That the widow of Lord Randolph, on the eve of the late king's demise, thought it meet to sue for divorce—it was disgraceful. His Majesty should intervene, lest we saw the empire toppled off its foundation.

Not yet crowned, King George had more urgent concerns, and I thought Bertie must be enjoying a chuckle in the afterlife at my expense. Nevertheless, the courts buried my petition under extraneous mounds of paperwork. I had to hire my own solicitor, at a cost I could ill-afford, to combat the stagnant refusal to advance my suit.

Then, as the dreadful year wound to its close, I found myself perversely inspired. Invitations were arriving on my doorstep from every hostess in London, eager to have me sit on planning committees for galas to celebrate King George's coronation in June. It was as if Bertie had never existed.

"We must do something to honor him," I told Winston in his study, after our Christmas dinner. "Bertie adored the theater. Surely we have many deserving playwrights without sufficient means to stage their work. Why not espouse a national theater, inaugurated in his memory?"

My son nodded, elbow-deep in the perennial stack of papers of his new position as First Lord of the Admiralty. "France has maintained a state-sponsored theater for decades. That we have not highlights our disregard for the very superiority we claim."

After locating a site in Kensington, I set out to raise funds by organizing a Shakespearean-themed ball. Like funding my ship, the effort required expert social maneuvering, as well as implicit support from the royal family. I secured the former in the Rothschilds and Consuelo, who offered generous donations. The latter came from Alexandra herself; she sent a letter thanking me for my condolences and remarking that the only thing Bertie had loved more than his dog was an actress performing on the stage.

I smiled at her dry candor.

The Royal Albert Hall was transformed into the Virgin Queen's court, with costumed players declaiming the Bard's verse. It cast a long shadow over the rote dinner parties devised by the other hostesses, as everyone rushed to don Tudor gowns once they learned our widowed queen Alexandra would attend the opening.

With the down payment secured, I required funds to break ground. After the coronation—which Winston insisted must take precedence—I planned a collaboration with the celebrated architect Sir Edward Lutyens to create an Elizabethan exhibition in the downtrodden district of Earl's Court, replete with a replica of the famed Globe Theatre.

I was in my milieu, overseeing those activities I excelled in, lavish décor and entertainment, when the horrific news struck that the *Titanic* had collided with an iceberg on her maiden voyage, carrying nearly all the men onboard to their doom. The tragedy shut down work on my project, all social events canceled in deference to the lives lost, among them New York millionaire Benjamin Guggenheim. Consuelo was bereft, the Guggenheims being part of her inner circle, and to distract her from her grief, I rallied her to help me complete the panoply at Earl's Court once it could resume.

The exhibition earned front-page coverage, if only for the pathetic tourney where several horses refused to budge and one aristocratic knight-champion lost an eye to his feckless opponent. Attendance was sparse, the novelty unable to overcome public apathy following the sinking of the *Titanic*. But our new Queen Mary offered her congratulations, stating she believed our king would look with favor upon a state theater founded in his late father's name.

In 1913, I celebrated my fifty-ninth year. Formally separated yet still married, I received the final insult when a society column revealed that George had moved in with Mrs. Pat Campbell—a woman closer to my age than his, which only made it sting more. When his solicitor sent a letter retracting his opposition to my suit, I crunched it in my fist.

Let him wait. Clarita's son Hugh was getting married in Rome. I had a wedding to attend.

THIRTY-SEVEN

1914

My nephew had become engaged to the daughter of the duca di Magnano. Hugh had inherited his father's dashing looks but not his wayward nature—my sister made certain to stamp out any vestiges of Moreton's truancy in her children. My nephew served with distinction in the Colonial Service and had found a titled bride, which pleased Clarita to no end. What she'd failed to achieve, her elder son had done for her.

Rome in January wasn't ideal—damp, disrupted by heavy downpours that smeared the grime on the antiquities, but less costly for a social event, the wedding held in a frescoed church on the Via Appia, followed by a reception in the Grand Hotel.

I was staying in the palazzo of the duchessa di Simonetta, who'd been part of the international circle favored by Bertie. She loaned me jewels for the reception, seeing as mine were hopelessly outdated. I paired her exquisite diamond tiara with a silvery silk dress in the new style—a slim full-length skirt and high-waisted green satin sash, its loose, crystal-beaded bodice cut at a cunning angle across my hips.

"Isn't it marvelous that Poiret has retired the corset, freeing us from its bondage?" said Fanny, resplendent in one of the French courtier's latest ensembles. I couldn't fathom how she managed it, but expense never seemed to pose an impediment. She flung money about like bread crumbs every time she went to Paris, a city I could now barely afford.

"At this point in my life, a corset would be welcome," I remarked.

"You're beautiful as ever. And I believe that devastating gentleman who hasn't taken his eyes off you would agree."

I laughed, retrieving my champagne flute. "Must you see secrets behind every door, dearest Fanny?"

"I'm usually correct in what I see, am I not?" A feline smile curved her lips, the hint of crepe under her chin the sole indication that she was at an age when most women would turn a blind eye to such secrets. "He hasn't stopped staring since you arrived."

I'd noticed as well, though I pretended not to. I'd caught sight of him as soon as I entered the reception, late because of the rain, stamping my feet to shake the droplets from my shoes. He stood by the buffet table—of average height, quite lean, with thick dark chestnut hair that had startling threads of white in its pomade, his angular cheekbones accentuating his refined nose, arresting olive skin, and deep-set eyes blue as the sea, which he turned and fixed on me in overt appraisal.

Not at all how a gentleman ought to look at a lady. Especially, as I suspected, despite the gray threading his hair, a lady who was old enough to be his mother.

He now leaned against a pilaster, an untouched flute in his hand, not even feigning interest in the goings-on around him.

"My, my." Fanny chuckled. "At any moment, I believe he might ask you to dance."

"I should hope not," I said. "These shoes are new. They pinch my toes."

In truth, I was in no temper for her tawdry amusement or for the reception. The ceremony in the church had been interminable, the Catholic ritual incomprehensible to me, all that standing and sitting and kneeling. Then I'd had to rush back to the palazzo in the rain to change, breathless, as Clarita demanded I must assist her in welcoming the groom's party. I had no idea whose guest he was; I assumed, given his swarthy appearance, he must be part of the Italian family.

Then he set his flute aside. As the orchestra began to play the opening dance, Hugh and his bride took to the floor and he strode through the applauding crowd toward us.

"Dear God," I whispered.

"Indeed." Fanny gripped her cane—she insisted on calling it a walking stick—and stood, about to leave me stranded at the table as I hissed, "Don't you dare."

She paused. "I don't think he's coming here to talk to me."

"You will stay put. I insist."

"Very well." She assumed that nonchalant air I was so familiar with, still the gracious woman-about-town, unflappable in her confidence.

"Ladies." He clicked his heels, bowing slightly from his torso. Military training, I thought. He moved like Jack. "I was hoping you might honor me with a dance."

His voice was roughened somehow, carrying a trace of laconic humor. And he wasn't Italian, not with that clipped British inflection. All of a sudden, I was plunged back to a night over thirty years ago, when a slightly built, mustachioed young man had requested full charge over my dance card.

"I fear I cannot." Fanny sighed, motioning to her cane. "But my lady Randolph . . ." She gave me a disingenuous smile. "She dances superbly."

His eyes were already upon me. "I thought she might."

I returned his regard. "Surely you can find a more suitable dance partner here," I said lightly, almost adding he might also seek one better suited to his age.

"No." He held out his hand. "I don't believe I can."

With Fanny looking at me in challenge, I found myself coming to my feet, wincing inwardly at the cramp in my toes. My shoes really were too tight.

Everything felt too tight as I accompanied him onto the floor. I thought he must feel the betrayal of my flesh under my dress as he set his hand above my waist, just as I felt the taut strength of his as he guided me into the slow waltz. There was little room to maneuver, the floor filled now by couples, which proved a relief to my feet, if not my overall discomfiture.

For he clearly saw it an opportunity for us to converse.

"Permit me to introduce myself." The roughness in his voice deepened, not amused anymore. He was serious. And sober. I didn't detect the slightest hint of alcohol on his breath. "Montagu Phippen Porch. District officer in the Nigerian Political Service on the Gold Coast. Your son Winston approved my appointment."

"Oh?" I was taken aback. "You know my son?"

"He approved my commission while he was Secretary of State for the Colonies. Both of us, as well as your other son, Jack, served in the Boer War. I was in the Imperial Yeomanry."

An equestrian division, renowned for its ferocity on horseback and skill with the rifle, and also entirely volunteer, sons of landowners and London luminaries who'd furnished their own equipment to fight. Not as young as I'd thought, now that I focused on him more closely. He had telltale creases at his eyes and mouth, the countenance of a man tempered by battle and Africa's unforgiving sun. Perhaps not a youth anymore, but still . . .

"Such a terrible time," I murmured. "I saw the aftermath of Ladysmith."

"I'm aware. Lady Bountiful, as I recall."

I heard my quick laugh. It took me aback. I was sounding flirtatious.

"A ship," I said. "Not a victory."

"The wounded who found succor and transport home on your ship would disagree." He smiled. A scoundrel's smile, ironic and knowing. "I daresay, so would the High Commission."

"You read the newspapers," I said.

"I listened to my fellow soldiers' accounts." His tone hardened, not at me but at the circumstances. "Over half my division perished in that war, either by disease or by the enemy. The slaughter—it wasn't what any of us expected. Our orders to raze entire Boer villages, with women and children wailing in the fires set by our own hands. It was a horror."

"Yes." I lowered my eyes. "Winston was appalled by it."

"Any man of conscience had to be," he said.

"Yet you stayed in Africa," I remarked, as he steered me past Clarita, dancing with Hugh. My sister's eyes widened at the sight of us. "Why?"

"My father was an officer in the Bengal Civil Service. He died when I was a child. My mother remarried, to the Lord Mayor of Glastonbury. She gave him another family. There's nothing left in England for me. I barely know my country anymore."

"But Nigeria . . ."

He grimaced. "Also not expected. I thought serving as liaison between the British High Command and local emirs could incite mutual cooperation. But the emirs detest us and resent our intrusion. I must adjudicate the crimes they commit against us. More horror."

The waltz ended. As he escorted me from the floor, I realized I wanted to keep talking to this man. It hadn't been the banal conversation I'd expected. Not the uncertain fumbling of inexperience or covert prelude to a liaison. A mature conversation, adult and insightful, graphic even, with someone who'd seen our hubris and shared my increasing intolerance of it.

"Will you relinquish your post?" I asked, as he offered me a glass of champagne.

"Eventually." He hesitated. "I'm on leave for this wedding. I met Hugh in Nigeria during his time in the service. There'll be opportunities on the Gold Coast, once the chaos settles."

"Opportunities?"

"Business ventures," he said. "Railroads. Also, diamond mines. That is, if Prussia doesn't force us into more chaos."

Only Bertie stood between us and Prussian aggression.

"My son—Winston. He believes Wilhelm will seek war."

"Your son was never a fool. Prussia is eager to prove its power. All they need is the right occasion."

I sipped the champagne, noticing he again failed to touch his. When the silence lengthened, I said, "It's been a pleasure. Thank you for the dance."

I started to return to the table.

He said quietly, "Is that all?"

I turned to him.

"Because I would have more, Lady Randolph." This time, his scoundrel's smile penetrated my dress. "And I believe you would, as well."

"HE'S THIRTY-SIX. THREE years younger than Winston." Clarita had come racing to the palazzo the moment she'd seen Hugh and his bride off on their honeymoon, and their guests to their various destinations. "You cannot think to—"

I regarded her impatiently, my stole and wrist bag in hand. "It's the opera, Clarita. *Rigoletto.* Not a room in the Marais."

She gasped.

"Honestly." I wrapped my lynx stole, a recent extravagant purchase, about my shoulders. "Every year that passes, you become more like Mama."

"You mustn't. You're not yet divorced. He's not of any pedigree."

"He knows his horses," I retorted. "Pedigree. When has that ever served anyone?"

"So, you *are* thinking it. Have you already . . . ?"

"What a question." I moved to the staircase leading to the foyer from the *piano nobile.* She scampered behind me, grasping my arm before I could descend.

"Jennie." She tried in vain to curb the panic in her voice. "They're already talking. About the midnight motorcar rides about Rome. The weekend at the villa in Florence. Is that what you want? More uproar? More scandal heaped on our name?"

"It's only gossip." I glanced at her hand, obliging her to remove it. "Gossip and disapproval. I've endured it my entire life. They must always criticize something, lest they waste away of boredom. Let them say whatever they like. We're in Italy. No one cares."

"They will care if it turns out to be true."

"The truth would be refreshing for a change. Now, I really must go. He's expecting me. We have orchestra seats." I paused, softening my tone as I took in her dismay. "He departs in three days for Nigeria. You told me you envied my desire for life."

"Yes, but . . ." She faltered. "Not with him. It's not suitable."

"Neither am I. Not anymore, if I ever was." I kissed her cheek. "You fret too much. It's not as if we're planning to marry."

But as I made my way downstairs to the waiting carriage, I could feel her stare boring into my back, and my deception coiled inside me, deceptive as a serpent.

I wasn't planning it yet. Not unless he proposed.

I LAY AMONG the tousled sheets of the bed in his small hotel room, my skin pulsing with waning heat even as one of those icy Roman downpours flung cascades of what sounded like pebbles against the window.

He stood silhouetted by the glass, a long sliver in the shadows.

"Hail," he said. "Like an Arctic monsoon."

"And like a monsoon, it traps everyone indoors. Where they have nothing to do but talk." I pulled the sheet over my breasts. In the moment, I never saw it, my slackened skin, the bluish veins of motherhood, the enlarged nipples. But afterward, once the lust cleared, I always did.

"Of course they do." He turned back to me. It made me catch

my breath, the way he moved, his gait almost feline in its assurance, his musculature chiseled as the ancient statues scattered about the city, which I'd barely admired, too caught up in admiring him. "We expected as much."

"Did we?" I righted myself against the headboard, pushing back my hair.

He gave me a wry glance. "You surely must be used to society's disapproval by now."

"I suppose I ought to be."

"But?" He paused at the night table, reaching for his cigarette case. He smoked like he drank, with extreme discipline.

"My sister came to see me tonight before the opera. She was . . . distressed." I took a moment to fabricate the right tone. "She fears we might intend more than this."

"Do we?"

I met his eyes. "I don't know."

"I do." He put the cigarette down, unlit, and returned to bed, tugging back the sheet, his manhood hard again, defiant as his expression. "I think you do, too."

UPON MY RETURN to London, I received a letter, posted from Rome before he boarded his ship. He chided me for neglecting to give him a photograph, but he'd found tendrils of my hair on his pillow and had sealed them in a locket to wear about his neck.

Do not forget me, he wrote. *I meant what I said.*

I contacted my solicitor to advance my suit. He returned word that he couldn't; a notification had arrived on his desk. My sons had filed against me over their father's trust, which meant the courts would refuse to hear any motion on my divorce until their claim was addressed.

Infuriated, I summoned Winston and Jack. When they entered my drawing room, with their faces downcast, I burst out, "What is the meaning of this? I go to Rome to your cousin's wedding, which neither of you saw fit to attend, and you scheme behind my back?"

Winston was the first to speak. "You did more than attend our cousin's wedding."

I heard my sharp intake of breath. "Whatever do you imply?"

"Precisely what I said." He removed his overcoat, went to the sideboard and the decanter of cognac I always kept there as a memento from when Randolph was alive. He poured three tumblers as I stared at Jack, who still couldn't lift his eyes.

I snatched a tumbler from Winston's hand. "Explain yourselves this instant."

Jack muttered, "Aunt Clarita sent us a letter."

"Telling you what?" I asked, though I already knew. But my fury burned too hot to admit it. Let them say it out loud. I would have words with my sister, the insufferable tattler, later. Some things between us never changed.

"About Montagu Phippen Porch," said Winston flatly.

"The nerve." I gulped the cognac, felt it scorching my mouth. "What business is it of hers? Or yours, for that matter?"

"None. You may do as you wish. Just not with our money."

"*Your* money?"

As Jack shifted slightly on the sofa, Winston removed a sheaf of paper from his overcoat pocket and placed it on the table. "Have you ever bothered to actually read Papa's testament?"

"I'm joint trustee of his estate. Naturally I have."

"Oh?" He cocked an eyebrow—a gesture so like his father's, which I'd always found enchanting. I didn't find it enchanting now. "Then you must be aware of the provision therein concerning you. 'In the event that Lady Randolph should remarry or be deceased, whichever happens first,'" he recited, to my outrage, "'our sons and their legitimate issue are within their legal right to have their capital share advanced to them upon request.'"

"I already remarried." I met his gaze. "Perhaps I should have died in Rome instead."

"Mamma," murmured Jack. "Please."

"Please?" I banged my tumbler upon the table. "Lest you forget, I rely on the income derived from the capital shares to survive. To maintain this roof over my head."

Abrupt silence fell. We'd never exchanged harsh words before, especially not over money, and my outburst seemed to carry, a harsh echo against the walls.

Winston took his seat opposite me in the armchair. I could see his weariness, the sleepless toil of endless hours spent at the Admiralty in Whitehall, where he, Clementine, and their baby now resided, so he could be within walking distance of his office.

"We didn't protest when you wed George," he said at length. "We secured the agreement to ensure that income remained yours. But we can't make a habit of it. Which begs the question: Once you divorce George, will you marry Phippen Porch?"

"I have no idea," I replied, adopting his same matter-of-fact tone.

He let out a terse breath. "Aunt Clarita seemed to think your relationship with him had turned quite serious—"

"It was a week in Rome. Her definition of serious and mine are apparently different."

"Is that so?" He allowed a moment to pass. "If that is the case, if you can assure us by legal writ that you have no wish to marry again, we'll withdraw our suit."

"This is . . . blackmail," I hissed. "I do not owe you any such reassurance."

"Unfortunately, we think you do. As I said, we let it go with George, though we feared the worst, as indeed came to pass. George is on the verge of insolvency, which comes as no surprise to anyone; he's requested a settlement to finalize the divorce. We suggest complying, to have the matter done. As for Phippen Porch, you may do as you see fit, under the stipulation that our trust must revert fully to us. We are within our legal right, as we're both now married. And we can see to your needs."

"My *needs*?" I echoed.

"Yes. To start, we propose you move to my home in Eccleston Square, as it's currently unoccupied. I'll continue to maintain it, of course. It will relieve you of the burden of this house, which can then be sold as intended, with the profit invested for your expenses."

"How tidy for me. You've organized my future like one of your fleets, tucked in the harbor and primed against disaster."

"It's not like that. We've never dictated how you should live."

"No? Because it sounds very much as if you're doing precisely that."

"We are not." Jack turned to me. He'd always been the one averse to emotion, but now I marked a sternness in his manner completely foreign to me. "I can manage your finances, Mamma; it's how I make my living. By investing the proceeds of this house, I'll earn you income. You've no concept of the value of money. You never have. You spend whatever you like, without thought for the future, as if debts pay themselves. While you were away, I reviewed your situation. You owe more than you can ever hope to repay, despite the profit derived from the trust. Indeed, the profit isn't enough, so the capital is being depleted to keep up with your demand. You can't keep drawing on it without consequence to us."

I found myself dumbfounded, chastised as if I were a spoiled child. It didn't fail to occur to me in that moment that this was the legacy of my upbringing. Of my father shoring me up in times of need and my headlong plunge into marriage with Randolph, ignoring its financial drawbacks because, at the time, I'd barely understood them.

"If I never had any concept of money," I said defensively, "it's because no one ever gave me the opportunity to learn."

"Indeed," said Winston. "Women of your generation rarely were. We always understood that and we adapted. But coupled with your private life—"

He couldn't finish. Raking my stare over him, I whispered, "How *dare* you?"

Jack cast a nervous glance at Winston before he said, "We're just concerned. Should you marry this man, he's in no position to see to your maintenance."

"I know what he earns," added Winston. "I approved his commission. Believe me, he cannot possibly see the marriage through for a year, at your current rate of expenditures."

I swallowed, recalling my dressmaker bills in Rome. The lynx stole. The opera and theater engagements. The weekend in Florence. All paid for by me. Except I never actually paid. I forwarded the bills to the trust and assumed whoever was in charge took care of it.

"It happened with George," Jack went on. "He came to me in desperation. He's another Mortal Ruin, but I had to concede his point. He claimed the cost of the marriage exceeded anything a reasonable man could endure."

I forced my voice out. "So, my expenditures are to blame for its failure?"

Winston fixed his eyes on me. "Don't play martyr with us. I'll not stand for it. We've always supported your decisions, no matter what. That will never change. What has changed is our willingness to see what remains of our trust put at risk by another marriage that has no chance of survival under present circumstances. Investing the proceeds of this house, if done wisely, could earn you as much as, or more than, the profit from the trust. We must take control of it."

"And I? Don't I have the right to take control of my life?" I cried, but it came out as a plea, dismaying me with its folly, as if I were still that cornered girl in Paris, deemed unworthy to wed a duke's son.

"You do, indeed." Winston softened his voice; he had the wherewithal to look ashamed, as he invariably did when I was close to tears. "We've only ever wanted your happiness. But you must understand the trust is all we have left of Papa, and we have our own families to support. Leaving things as is will only ensure the trust's devaluation and eventual decimation."

I sat in silence, looking at each of them in turn. "I cannot agree to it," I finally said.

"We feared as much," Jack said sadly. "We must therefore allow the courts to decide."

THE COURTS DECIDED in my favor. It came down to one word: Randolph's testament specified "after" my second marriage took place, not "following" the marriage. The courts deemed this sufficient to signify after its dissolution or my death. As I was still very much alive and not yet divorced, in the courts' eyes this reading nullified my sons' claim.

As we left the courthouse furtively, fearing journalists might be lurking about and none of us wanting to end up splashed across a headline, Jack excused himself to return to his office.

Winston escorted me to the carriage that would convey me to Eccleston Square. I'd submitted to his suggestion. His house was empty and available; I might as well reside there and sell the one I was renovating. I couldn't keep moving about like a Bohemian.

"I trust this won't result in bad feelings," he said. "We did as we thought best."

I understood. It had hurt me deeply, but also exerted its intended impact, jolting me into awareness beyond my own concerns. As in their childhood, I'd failed to take into account how what transpired in my life affected my sons', my failed marriage obliging Jack to lend financial counsel to my errant husband while Winston took charge of my well-being.

I still meant to have words with Clarita over it, but now wasn't the time.

"We should celebrate our defeat," he said. "Our first battle, and we lost resoundingly."

I had to smile. "I wouldn't call it a defeat. When I'm divorced from George, you can refile your suit and I'll be the one who loses resoundingly."

"I think we've had enough of courtrooms, don't you? Let's invest the proceeds of the house and take a family holiday together. Overstrand is ideal in the summer. Who knows how much longer we'll have to enjoy it?"

A shadow slipped across his face, a foreboding I didn't want to give credence to.

"That would be lovely," I said. "Clemmie and Goonie in the kitchen, with the children underfoot. I can play doting grandmother at long last."

He laughed. "May our children grow up to be as ferocious as their doting grandmother, who truly can never back down from a fight."

WE WERE BY the Norfolk seashore when Archduke Franz Ferdinand of Austria was assassinated in Sarajevo by a Serbian rebel—the opening volley in the very escalation of hostilities with Prussia that Winston had feared and done his utmost to prepare for.

With a single gunshot, war was upon us.

THIRTY-EIGHT

1914–1915

The war seemed to erupt overnight. Every able-bodied man was rushing to enlist as Europe divided against itself—France, Russia, and Britain forming the Entente in opposition to the Central Powers of Germany and Austria-Hungary. I could barely make sense of it, this insane avengement of the murder of an archduke, but, as Winston remarked, we needn't understand why war occurred for it to happen.

He was tireless in his oversight of our navy, which he'd wrangled into readiness. As founder of the Naval Air Service, he traveled from port to port, organizing bases near enemy lines. Whenever he returned to London, he was anchored at his desk, scarcely going home to rest or eat. Clementine packed up hampers of sandwiches, walking them over to his office, resolved to provide him with essential nourishment as the world was torn asunder around us.

Unlike the Boer War, this wasn't a distant, foreign uproar. It affected everyone we knew, every family with a son of age to fight. By September, the lists of the dead were being printed in small type in the newspapers, overtaking entire issues; just as Winston had foretold, the kaiser seemed determined to drag us into a horrifying, prolonged ordeal.

When Leonie's favorite son, Norman, left to fight in France, she wrote to tell me they'd parted without tears, but she felt as if he'd vanished into thin air. I encouraged her to come stay with me. The unrest in Ireland had turned violent again, with separatists agitating to seize advantage in the chaos. Her eldest, Shane, had served in the British ambulance corps until he suffered a nervous collapse, while her third son, Seymour, was working in New York, his past illness deeming him unfit for service. Her youngest son, Lionel, was only fourteen and still in boarding school. There was no reason for her to sit and worry in Castle Leslie.

She was with me when news came that Norman had been killed while charging up an embankment in Armentières after fighting for less than two months. As my younger sister collapsed in grief, Clarita made haste to our side. I cabled Winston for assistance; Norman's body hadn't been recovered and Leonie must be allowed to bury her son. Winston returned word that he would do his utmost but thousands of bodies now littered the battlefields in France, the corpses of enemy and ally mingled in the trenches. It was proving a monumental challenge to evacuate the wounded, let alone retrieve the fallen.

"We must do something," I said to Clarita. We sat before my empty fire grate, enveloped in shawls to ward off the frigid cold, fuel shortages having become endemic as every available resource was siphoned to support the war.

She plucked at her skirts, fatigued from tending to Leonie, who'd fallen into a silence more disquieting than her heartrending wails. My older sister had her own worries. Hugh was talking of enlisting, his Italian marriage having soured despite the birth of a son. Her other son, Oswald, was already in the naval forces, his letters describing ferocious confrontations and vicious torpedo exchanges. Her daughter Clare's husband was also about to enlist. At any moment, she, too, might have to confront the unthinkable.

"What can any of us do save pray?" she murmured.

"Clarita." I resisted my flare of temper. "They're shooting at our sons. When the same thing occurred with the Boers, we did something."

"*You* did something. Perhaps you can devise a way to shoot the kaiser." I was startled to hear her chuckle. "I have the rifle. One of Moreton's, from Wyoming."

"And I would use it," I declared.

She lowered her face. As a tear slipped down her cheek, my chest constricted. "Leonie will never recover," she whispered. "To lose a son . . ."

I had to clench my hands to stop myself from succumbing. Winston was in danger by virtue of his position, whether from his ceaseless travel to the fronts or from increasing criticism of his oversight of the Admiralty as we failed to halt Germany's advance. The floundering stock market had led to Jack's decision to enlist; Goonie had begged him to delay for as long as possible, but I knew it wouldn't be long. As during the Boer War, Jack could not stand by while others died.

"Have you any news of Phippen Porch?" Clarita asked unexpectedly.

"Nothing recent." I tried to sound nonchalant. "I'm surprised he still makes the attempt to stay in contact with me, given the war, but he does. In his last letter, he told me he'd been made an intelligence officer. According to him, it entails trudging through jungles to spy on the German colonial forces and pick through their dead for secret documents."

She smiled weakly. "I don't see why you're surprised. He was clearly very taken by you in Rome, as you seemed to be with him."

"Yes, well. Who knows if we'll see each other again?" My voice tightened as I sought in vain not to sound as concerned for him as I was, or to convey my anguish that we might never have the chance to discover if we were meant to be together.

In the ensuing hush, she sighed. "You also can't sail a hospital ship to Nigeria, much as you might wish it."

I nearly started to scoff at the absurdity, then paused.

"No," I said. "But perhaps we can build one here."

THE STOCK MARKET'S precipitous decline had wreaked havoc on my financial stalwarts. The Rothschilds were donating vast sums to war-related causes and in no position to offer more; they referred me to Paris Singer, heir to the sewing-machine fortune, who agreed to acquire a run-down mansion in Devon, which I could renovate to my specifications.

Rallying my social roster—all ladies with sons or grandsons at the fronts, some already wounded in action or killed—and touting the published lists of the injured overwhelming our hospitals, we devised fund-raising galas to refurbish the mansion. The American Red Cross donated personnel; we had the interior of the structure razed in record time. Behind its gloomy brick façade rose a modernized facility, equipped with electricity and updated devices, including gramophones to play music for the soldiers under our care.

We inaugurated it as the American Women's Hospital.

As with my ship, I ensured not a single patient was left unattended. I obliged Clarita to join me on my rounds on the wards, stopping to exchange words of cheer with the maimed, oft-delirious young men, whose limbs had been blown off or who had suffered incapacitating head trauma.

Clarita finally begged exhaustion, absconding with Leonie to her daughter's home. Leonie's oldest son, Shane, risked his life to travel to France to locate his brother's body. He found it interred under planks near the death site, hastily covered by the surviving division. The relief that Norman had been found eased Leonie's mourning, but she soon became distraught again when told that under the circumstances, with every available transport requisitioned for the wounded, the body could not be brought home to be laid to rest.

To distract her, Clarita took Leonie to visit Empress Eugénie, languishing in exile on the Isle of Wight. She remembered us, or so Clarita claimed. Over tea, they reminisced about Compiègne and

Clarita's debut, when she danced with the prince imperial, killed years before by Zulu rebels in South Africa. As I read my sister's letter, marking both her pride in the empress's recollection and her sorrow at Eugénie's diminished circumstances, the empress being the last survivor of Mama's fallen empire, I felt a tinge of exasperation. Being taken to see an old woman who'd lost everything save her useless title could scarcely have been a comfort to our bereaved sister.

And I had no patience for the tragedies of the bygone past. By the start of 1915, the war had taken countless lives, with no end in sight. Clarita's daughter's husband was killed in France, only days after Clare gave birth to their son. Without any influence over our new king, I couldn't petition for the safety of anyone in my family, not that the scale of the war would have allowed it. Clarita and I were in despair when her son Hugh and my Jack enlisted as feared and were immediately deployed to the Dardanelles in Eastern Thrace. The fighting there was intense, a concerted effort to break Turkey's alliance with Germany. Following the catastrophic fall of Antwerp, for which he was blamed, Winston found himself beset by opposition to his repeated demands that air-strike capabilities be diverted to the Dardanelles, and he announced his intent to go there in person to see to it.

I raced back to London.

"I cannot have both of you risking your lives," I exclaimed, as he paced his office, the stacks of paper on his desk and maps with battle lines pinned to the wainscoting evidence of his staunch commitment. "Isn't it enough that Jack is deployed there? Must you go, as well?"

"I must prove I'm not wrong," he said, with a bite of intolerance. "Like you, mothers across Europe are enduring the unimaginable. I stand accused of excessive hubris because of Antwerp, though I warned everyone from the start that the Germans would never stop and Turkey would turn against us. We must persuade the Greeks to help us repel the Germans from the Dardanelles and we must have air support to accomplish it. If I must personally undertake the organization of our air bases, so be it."

"What do your advisers say? Do they even think Greece can be persuaded?"

He grimaced. "My somnolent Room 40? Their intelligence appears to be limited to where one can locate contraband sugar for tea."

"Then it's an unnecessary risk, if your own advisers can't tell you for certain."

"Everything is an unnecessary risk. All of it. All of *this.*" He flung an enraged hand toward the maps. "A colossal and unnecessary savagery. The Continent turned into a charnel house, with the kaiser as its head butcher."

"My pumpkin—" I started to reach to him.

He stepped back, taking refuge behind his desk.

"No." He drew in a shuddering breath. "We *cannot* lose the Dardanelles."

"You also cannot single-handedly fly every airplane there. Winston, you're doing everything possible. You're only one man."

"And I'm never enough." He shook his head. "I refuse to be anything less."

He didn't make it in time. Even as he prepared a circuitous route to avoid passing through enemy territory, we suffered a catastrophic rout at the hands of the Turks. Jack wrote that as he stood on the deck of his ship, he watched men being slaughtered by the thousands. When he finally ventured ashore, he donned shorts and brandished a ducal sword purloined from Blenheim, mincing his way past the dead like a duchess to rally the remaining soldiers, who dubbed him Lady Constance for his humorous valor.

Now, he wrote to me, *we can boast of another Lady Bountiful in our family.*

I laughed through my tears. Jack survived the battle, miraculously, as if he'd been gifted by inexplicable luck. Much like Montagu, from whom I received a long-delayed letter informing me that despite the jiggers burrowing under his skin and bouts of malaria, he was still alive, still trudging through swamps in pursuit of German intelligence. He still thought of me. He still wore the tarnished locket with the strands of my hair about his neck.

I hadn't lost a son. I had not lost my lover.

Even if the worst was yet to come.

CLEMENTINE MET ME at the Admiralty residence door. Though it was early May, spring hadn't touched London. The night was smothered by dense fog that emphasized the misery of a city under curfew, with every window blacked out in case of a zeppelin raid. Several of our coastal ports had been bombed by those monstrous flying machines and newspapers warned of attacks on the city itself. In addition to shortages of everything from tea to meat, and the recent torpedoing of the ocean liner *Lusitania* off the Irish coast, London was gripped by fear, its occupants cowering inside their homes in anticipation of an explosion from above.

I'd been surprised when my daughter-in-law sent for me. We'd not seen much of each other in the past months, with me attending to my hospital while she tended to her children. Following Diana, she'd borne a son, christened Randolph in my late husband's honor, then another girl, Sarah. Raising three children during wartime was enough without a mother-in-law underfoot, so I'd made myself available if needed, but otherwise kept out of her way.

She appeared exhausted, her eyes sunken as she summoned me inside. Toys lay scattered about the parlor. I narrowly avoided crushing a doll on the carpet as I removed my mantle and waited for her to speak.

"I'm sorry to have woken you," she began. "I realize it's late—"

"Not at all." I felt a jolt of alarm. "I sleep very little these days."

"As do I." She managed a wan smile.

"I can imagine. Three mouths to feed must be a full-time occupation."

"And Winston," she said. She paused, as if she needed a moment to compose herself. "He's not come out of his study since—" She started to avert her gaze, then apparently thought better of it. "He blames himself."

"He couldn't have known the Turks would be so well-prepared," I said. "He takes every defeat to heart, though he didn't start this war."

"It's not only the Dardanelles. That ship. All those lives lost onboard."

I gave grim assent. "When history takes stock, the Lusitania will go down in the annals of infamy. Civilians, without a soldier among them. What possible gain can there have been to sink that ship, save to sow more terror?"

Clementine went silent for a moment before she said, "Winston was warned. The Germans sent a dispatch, warning they would attack any Entente ship flying a false neutral flag. Members of his cabinet brought it to his attention, suggested that he authorize armed escorts for any ships at risk. He refused to grant it to non-military vessels."

I stood as if paralyzed.

"The Lusitania departed New York under the American flag," she went on, "although her British provenance was well-established. She carried illicit cargo: supplies of ordnance and barrels of gunpowder, arranged by Winston through diplomatic channels in Washington. The Germans found out; they targeted the ship because of it."

"Dear God," I whispered.

"Over a thousand dead. Lord Chambers in the Commons is saying because there were Americans onboard, Winston put the ship at risk to force the United States into the conflict. The Americans issued an alert before its departure. Chambers demands to know why, if the United States saw fit to warn of potential peril, the Lusitania was denied an escort. Why did we ignore reports of

German U-boats patrolling the Irish coast? He's calling for an official inquiry."

"It—it cannot be. Winston would never have allowed such a calamity."

"No? The supplies would have bolstered our efforts. More important, it was a first step toward American involvement. He didn't assign an armed escort because it would have drawn attention. The cargo was too vital—both as reinforcements and for its political value."

I had to reach for the back of a chair. "How—how do you know this?"

Her smile was tight. "I often write his correspondence for him, from his notes. He's careful about what he lets me see. Since the Dardanelles, he's been less so."

"Does he know?" I asked.

Her smile faded. "It's not my conscience he's concerned about."

"I'll talk to him," I said faintly, moving toward the stairs.

"Jennie."

I glanced over my shoulder. I'd told her to call me Mother, but she never did. She'd replied she already had a mother and preferred to address me as a friend.

"They can never know the truth. To safeguard his reputation, he must deny any knowledge of the cargo, should it come to light."

"Can it come to light," I asked, "with the ship at the bottom of the ocean?"

She turned away. "Not unless he tells them."

THE KEROSENE LANTERN on his desk, like those used in field camps, cast barely enough light to illuminate Winston, hunched in his armchair, a snifter of brandy at his side. His glass looked untouched, but the smoke of his cigars hung thick in the air.

He grunted at my entrance. "Clemmie shouldn't have troubled you."

"You've not left this room in days. My darling, you must eat. Take your rest."

"Must I?"

I came to a halt. "Brooding won't resolve anything."

He shifted in the chair. "I'll have plenty of time to rest later." He reached for his glass and let his hand drop, as though it cost him too much effort.

"You mustn't blame yourself." I wanted to ask if it was true, had he purposefully let that ship cross the Atlantic unprotected, disdaining the warning, the reports of Germans stalking the Irish coast? But what good would it do? True or not, he was punishing himself.

"I blame myself," he said, "because it was my mistake. I knew they'd been agitating against me from the moment I took charge of the Admiralty, claiming an untried stripling with scarce rank in the Hussars should never have been given oversight of the greatest armada in the world. They criticized my every decision, blocked me at any turn they could. Had it not been for them, we might have saved the Dardanelles. But I was still in charge, so I should have foreseen the danger. Never mind that the Huns have trespassed beyond all established rules of warfare. Never mind that they fired unprovoked on a civilian vessel."

I was sundered by the desolation in his voice, a dark resignation he'd never displayed before. It had finally caught up with him, his struggle to see us through this nightmare. I had my answer, even if I couldn't bring myself to accept it. In his desperation to gain ground against the enemy, he'd taken a calculated risk and lost.

"They'll have my head for it," he said. "An example must be made."

"But Asquith is our PM." I was trying to find something to bolster his spirits, to not reveal my shock at what I had learned.

"He would never have appointed you to the Admiralty had he not trusted in your judgment."

"Asquith is also one man. He cannot go up against the entire House." Winston paused; though his face was in shadow, contempt singed his words. "No one wants to hear harsh truths now. Their only concern is to wipe their hands clean of the tragedy and put on a public show of indignation. That we may end up saluting the kaiser is a secondary worry at present."

He seemed to shrink further in his chair as I stood there, not knowing what else to say.

"You should go home," he said at length. "Tell Clemmie not to worry. I'll want my quail pie soon enough."

I started to turn to the door when he added, "And see that the extra bedrooms have fresh sheets. We'll not be long for this residence."

"Winston—"

"Don't say it. I don't deserve it. I'll not have you or anyone else deny me my penance."

THIRTY-NINE

1916–1917

Asquith had no choice but to bow to the prevailing political tempest. While the official inquiry into the sinking of the *Lusitania* put the blame on the Germans, making no mention of illicit ordnance, Winston was removed from the Admiralty. I cringed as I read the scathing newspaper coverage, knowing that after my son had been driven to such an extreme because they'd refused to heed his pleas about the Dardanelles, he wouldn't rest easy, despite his exoneration. He proved as much by requesting the appointment of First Air Lord, intent on raining bombs on our foes. Asquith granted him the chancellorship of Lancaster instead, a futile compromise that plunged him into melancholy.

Adding to this came dire news from Jack, still posted in Eastern Thrace, where he bore witness to another calamitous rout at Suvla Bay. Exhausted by months of combat, plagued by disease from the unclaimed festering bodies of dead friends, our soldiers refused to obey their superior's suicidal order to charge the Turkish guns, stripping naked instead to wallow defiantly in the straits, braving the hail of enemy fire.

There was nothing to be done but for us to retreat, so we repaired to a rented farm in Surrey for the summer, bringing the family together to rally Winston.

It proved an uneasy balm. He trudged about with a scowl that eased only when he donned coveralls and rubber boots to take Jack's son, Jack Jr.; Diana; and his boy, Randolph, to pick berries.

He took up painting, the dusk catching him out in the fields with his palette and canvas, his shabby coat flapping about him as he stared toward the horizon.

When I went to fetch him for dinner, he extended paint-flecked fingers to me.

"My hands have blood on them. All those men dying every day—we thought we'd make short shrift of this war. We might have succeeded, had we reacted in time." He met my eyes. "I cannot keep on like this. Clemmie advises patience, but if Asquith won't grant me a suitable command, I must enlist. Serve in the trenches, like Jack and thousands of others."

Voiceless, I took his hands in mine. The very thought of him fighting at the front clawed talons into my heart, but I knew my wails of protest wouldn't help him; they would just make it more painful for him to do as he must.

"You must watch over Clemmie and the children," he said. "Promise me."

"Don't. Please," I whispered. "Don't even think it."

He smiled, his sparse hair like wisps across his prematurely lined forehead. "It's inevitable. What matters is not the manner of our death, but how we choose to live our life."

We embraced, the summer night engulfing us; as I bit back my tears, I felt him stiffen slightly, drawing away. "Well," he remarked, with a welcome trace of his habitual wit. "It would appear not even the terrors in Nigeria can detain true love."

I swerved about, my breath catching at the sight of the lean figure advancing toward us. As he neared, I raised a hand to my tousled hair, acutely aware of my dishevelment, trying to set myself to rights as Winston chuckled.

"It's no use. You look like a doting grandmother. I doubt he'll notice."

Winston left me to return to the farm, pausing to exchange a few words with Montagu.

Montagu was pared to muscle and bone, his complexion burned copper by the sun, so that his eyes stood out like pools of blue light. As his mouth quirked in a smile at my obvious surprise, I blurted, "How is it you're in England?"

"I've been granted an extended leave for services rendered." He let his gaze pass over me. "They've transferred me to the residency in Zaria. And just in time, I might add. I don't know how much longer I could have tolerated the squalor."

"You're very thin," I said, for lack of anything else. I couldn't believe my eyes. He was here, before me. The last person I'd expected to see.

"Yes, well. The jungle doesn't provide much in the way of sustenance. I trust I can fatten up sufficiently here, though I'm told there's not enough of anything these days."

I burst out in laughter at his wry tone. "I've enough flesh to spare for both of us."

"Not to me." He took a step closer. "Jennie, I find I've missed you rather desperately."

My eyes faltered, dropping to his open collar, to the tarnished chain about his neck.

"I've not taken it off once," he said quietly. "It's my talisman."

His arms wrapped about my waist. He was a sliver of flesh but taut as ever. I wondered if, underneath his plain charcoal-gray suit, he had fresh scars from the war, if his body was as burnished as his face. I wanted to peel off his clothes and see for myself.

"Marry me," he said, his mouth at my throat. "The world might be coming to an end, and I don't want to leave it without knowing you're mine."

I felt the pressure of his arousal, thought he might actually take me right there in the fields, as if I were a milkmaid. The idea bolted a spike of flame through me.

"Yes," I heard myself say. "I will marry you."

HE ATE DINNER with us, relating tales of his time in the Nigerian swamps, causing Clarita to gasp at his description of lurking for hours in fetid marsh, amidst crocodiles, as a German reconnaissance unit searched for him. He'd secured valuable intelligence that helped beat back the enemy's advance in the region, and I noted how Winston's expression clouded over as he heard this. So did Clemmie's. She abruptly rose to clear the table and broke up the conversation, as if silencing tales of Montagu's exploits might somehow make the war cease to exist.

Winston invited Montagu outside for a cigar. I assisted Clemmie in the kitchen while Clarita and Goonie took the children to bed.

"Why is he here?" she asked me, lathering the plates.

"To see me, I suppose. And he knows Winston. They both served in the Boer War—"

She thrust the dishes at me to dry. "Yes, he's very brave. Practically heroic. Has Winston said anything to you about enlisting?" Her question was accusatory, as if I'd connived Montagu's visit to rub the salt of his service in my son's wounds.

I went quiet, avoiding her stare.

Her voice turned thin. "You must dissuade him of it."

"Clemmie." I lifted my eyes to her. "Much as we prefer it, we can't keep him here, under our skirts. His brother is fighting in Turkey. Men he oversaw are perishing daily. You cannot—"

"He has a family. Children. He's not Montagu Porch, with no one to miss him."

I set the dishes aside. "Montagu has me. He's asked me to marry him."

Her face hardened. "You might think carefully about another husband, at your age."

I returned her regard without giving voice to my sudden anger. It was enough to return her to the sink, her hands plunging into suds.

"Tell Winston not to enlist," she said. "Then do as you see fit."

I WED MONTAGU Phippen Porch in June in a registry office on Harrow Road. No extravagance or newspaper announcement; it wasn't the time for it, and, in truth, I preferred to keep the event quiet for various reasons, not the least of which was the war. Montagu borrowed an officer's uniform and Winston acted as our witness, quipping after the ceremony to my new husband, "I hope you'll not regret marrying her."

Montagu smiled. "I doubt I will," he said, and kissed me primly, as if I were a virgin before my wedding night. He was much more enthusiastic during the night itself.

To Clementine's furor, Winston did just as I predicted. He refused to hear any worry on his behalf and enlisted in the 6th Royal Scots Fusiliers, deployed to fight on the Western Front.

His departure was fraught. We refrained from outright tears, knowing they would only upset him. But Clementine wasn't at all pleased with me for having failed to persuade him, and a distinct frost emerged between us that I thought might never thaw, particularly after we learned he'd narrowly escaped death when, during German shelling near Belgium, shrapnel fell inches between him and his staff officer, Winston's cousin Charles, Consuelo's husband. When the Royal Scots Fusiliers merged with another division, my son requested permission to leave active service. I suspected he'd only done it for Clementine, after her barrage of imploring telegrams and letters, reminding him that he had a family at home, desperate for his safety.

America finally entered the war in 1917—a cause for rejoicing and the beginning of the turning of the tide. Back in the Commons but without official office, Winston expounded on the war, citing his personal experience and calling for recognition of our troops' bravery and the urgent need for mass production of steel helmets to protect them. To his outrage, he was still blamed for the devastation in Turkey, especially the horrific massacre on the Gallipoli peninsula, until a published report absolved him of culpability, noting he had in fact argued for an increase in air support to aid our Turkish offensive.

He came to visit me often at my new house near Hyde Park, as he and Clemmie, along with the children, had returned to theirs, necessitating my removal. He admired my transformation of silver watch cases into door handles and the use of yellow curtains to capture the sunlight in the drawing room, while sharing his travails in the House. When Montagu was recalled to service in Nigeria—an event that dismayed me, as it meant another separation while the war continued—he and my son closeted themselves together in the parlor and spoke at length about the situation in Africa. I was relieved that Winston made the effort to form his own opinion, apparently deciding my third marriage might not be the calamity he'd feared, for as he kissed me good night, he said, "A sensible chap. Not at all like—"

"Let's not say his name." I nudged him out the door. "Go home before Clemmie has more reason to be cross with me. I'd like to see my grandchildren again."

He set his hat on his balding head. "She's not cross with you. She's cross with me, but she can't tell me as much, so—"

"I understand." I waved him off to his carriage.

Then I spent the night in my husband's arms before he departed. I did not know when we would see each other again.

FORTY

1918–1921

The war ended in November 1918, by an armistice signed by the major powers. Germany had plunged into upheaval, after entire units of their navy refused to set sail for a large-scale operation in view of the ongoing defeats. The uprising across the country led to the proclamation of a republic and the kaiser's abdication, finally bringing an end to the four-year catastrophe that had taken the lives of hundreds of thousands of young men.

An entire generation lost, over the murder of an archduke.

By the end of the year, Jack had returned home, gaunt from what he'd endured. He resumed his career as a stockbroker. Winston was appointed by our new PM to demobilize our forces; he argued in vain against harsh punitive measures instituted against Germany, further decimating that country's resources for survival, and supported the use of our troops to assist the White Army in Russia, fighting against the revolution that had brought about the downfall of the monarchy. It was rumored everywhere that the tsar and his family had been killed to prevent a restoration of the Romanovs, prompting a tide of aristocrats to flee into exile. I thought of Alexandra, whose sister the Dowager Empress had been obliged to flee as well, without knowing if her son the tsar or her grandchildren were alive or dead.

Montagu resigned from colonial service and returned home. He soon grew restless. Nigeria, he claimed, offered plenty of oppor-

tunity for enterprising men to invest in the cocoa industry and
railroads. Winston supported his venture financially so he could
return there to set up his business. I wasn't happy about it—we'd
spent far more time apart than together—but I'd learned my lesson. I couldn't interfere with my husband's professional pursuits.
He had to work; he always had, and the age of idleness had been
blown apart by the war. If I insisted that he remain at my side, as
Winston pointed out, I ran the risk of souring the marriage by
obliging him to seek an occupation in England in which he had
no interest. We agreed that I should visit him once he established
himself, and he would make frequent returns to see me.

I was sixty-five years old. I had to content myself with the life
I had, which, in many ways, was richer than those of many others
my age. Not many women I knew could claim to have a husband
half as young as they, let alone two sons who had survived the war.

For Christmas 1920, my sisters and I reunited. Clarita had completed her transformation into Mama, plump as a partridge and
unperturbed by it. I found it incredible that the girl who'd once
been the locus around which our family revolved had ceased to
care about her appearance. In return, she chided me for my vanity.

"Who would have believed it? Once I was the one who thought
there could be no life without new clothes, and look at you: done
up like a trousseau in white lace and silk."

"Have a care," I said tartly. "I haven't forgiven you for setting
my sons against me."

She laughed. "You had your way in your end. As you always do."

Leonie hadn't recovered from the loss of her son. Her beauty
grown muted, she ended her complicated relationship with her
royal duke and cleaved to her dignity in the midst of her failed
marriage to Leslie. We rallied around her, Winston amusing her
with outlandish tales of political conniving in the House and, like
the rest of us, making no mention of the war.

For the spring, Montagu and I arranged to meet in Rome, site of our infatuation; ostensibly, I was going to visit my friend the duchessa di Simonetta, who requested my assistance in refurbishing her palazzo. It was a challenging enterprise, the old palace having seen better days, but I took to it with resolve, attending parties with her in the evenings and learning the tango, which I thought very risqué, occupying myself with the redecoration while awaiting word that Montagu had set sail from Africa.

When word came, I was so delighted and nervous to see him again after nearly eight months, I went shopping for a new outfit, the current fashions delightfully freeing in their ease of cut. Enchanted by a pair of black velvet heeled shoes for my olive-green wool ensemble, I purchased them on the spot.

On my way down the duchessa's staircase, eager to be on the docks when his ship arrived—I never could find myself able to keep proper track of time—I felt the soles of my new shoes catch on the denuded marble steps of the palazzo staircase, as I'd had all the old carpeting removed.

The staircase was a sudden chasm as I reached in panic for the balustrade, clutching it with a sigh of relief just before my leg gave way. With a cry of anger at my ineptness, I went tumbling down the stairs, landing in an undignified heap at the bottom.

The duchessa came racing to me with her footmen, assisting me to rise.

"Oh, my dear. How awful. Are you hurt?" she asked, as I stood, swaying and dazed. I felt a sharp jab in my left leg, near the ankle.

"Just bruised." I felt myself grimace. "Honestly, you'd think I'd never worn shoes before. Come—" I limped with as much dignity as I could muster to the cab. "We mustn't be late."

He didn't arrive. Devastated as I waited hours for the ship's passengers to disembark, it wasn't until I returned to the palazzo that his telegram came. He'd been delayed and suggested we meet in England instead, since he was uncertain when he could book another passage.

I finished the palazzo refurbishment and returned home.

By then, the pain in my leg had become so constant I had to resort to a walking stick, like Fanny, which enraged me more.

"Montagu will come home to find me fat as a mare and hobbling about," I grumbled to Winston and Clemmie on our way to my house. "So clumsy of me."

Winston insisted on summoning a physician. He examined me as I lay on the couch, impatient at the cautious probe of his fingers down my leg. When he reached the spot that I'd felt upon rising from my fall, I couldn't contain my yelp.

My son went pale. The physician frowned. "My lady Randolph, you have suffered a severe fracture. It's very swollen and tender."

"Of course it is," I said through my teeth. "I fell down a marble staircase."

"I must insist on complete rest. No walking at all. You mustn't put any weight on it. Warm compresses should help reduce the swelling."

"No walking at all?" I echoed in dismay. "I cannot just wallow here for—"

"Two weeks at a minimum," he said.

"Absolutely not," I told Winston as soon as the physician departed.

He lifted his hand, cutting me short. "I'll send word to Aunt Clarita and Aunt Leonie. One of them can come here to assist you— No, Mamma. It's only for two weeks. You will follow the doctor's instructions to the letter." He passed his gaze over me. "Whatever were you thinking, dancing the tango and running about in high-heeled shoes at your age?"

"Don't you start." I glared. "I'm not ancient yet."

He chuckled, leaning down to kiss my cheek. "At this rate,

you'll celebrate your centenary and still refuse to acknowledge the passing of time."

"I will celebrate it dancing the tango," I retorted.

Clarita hastened to my side—another irritation, as I had to depend on her to take a bath and use the commode. Yet despite my stubbornness, the swelling subsided and I started to feel less pain. I looked forward to mobility and sending my sister back to her own house.

Until the morning I woke, pulled back the covers to yank down my camisole, which had hiked up during the night, and beheld the frightening blackening of my skin.

"Clarita!" I cried out. She hurried in, took one look at the leg, and gasped. "We must summon an ambulance at once."

"Cable Montagu," I said as she raced out. "Tell him not to worry. Before someone"—"probably you," I wanted to add sarcastically—"informs him I'm about to lose my leg."

"IT IS GANGRENE, I'm afraid. We must amputate," the physician at the hospital told us grimly as Clarita moaned and clutched Leonie's arm.

"Amputate?" I heard myself say from across a vast distance, as if it were happening to someone else. "How is that even possible? It was a fall. A pair of silly shoes."

"Is there no other way?" Jack's measured tone instilled some much-needed calm to the situation, as Clarita was already starting to weep.

"None," said the doctor. "The leg must come off as soon as possible."

"How—how much of it?" A tremor snagged my voice.

"To the knee, my lady. I'm very sorry, but we must stop the corruption from spreading. I will prepare the operating facility at once."

Winston turned to me. "Mamma." Tears swam in his eyes, his face suddenly a child's again—the little boy who didn't want to go to school, who'd wept in my arms when I discovered the caning inflicted on him. My beautiful, difficult, and charismatic son.

"No, pumpkin." I made myself smile. "We must put my best foot forward. My only foot." I looked past him to Jack, also so precious to me, as he regarded me with his quiet eyes, not the same since the war, and my sisters, Clarita, disconsolate, and Leonie, who'd yet to speak.

"See that they remove the right leg," I told her.

"It's—it's the left one," Leonie whispered.

"Yes," I said. "Precisely."

HE RETURNS TO me in a dream.

In his navy-blue frock coat and top hat that seems out of place for the moment; but he was always so fastidious about his appearance. The opal pin gleaming like a tiny moon in his cravat, his receded hairline parted in pomaded symmetry, and his delicate features overpowered by that preposterous mustache, waxed to tipped points above his thin-lipped mouth.

A cigarette in his hand. Always his cigarette.

I chuckle. "As you can see, I'm quite the fool."

"My fool." He smiles. He's standing so close that I can smell his cologne.

Lavender.

"I miss you," I whisper. "So very much."

He nods, his eyes holding mine. "I am always with you, my darling."

I'm still struggling to make sense of it as he turns away. In the encroaching darkness, I hear a lament of wind, the susurrus of faded petals, and he starts to turn into a silhouette, ghostly in his slightness. Sudden fear seizes me that I'll never see him again.

"Don't forget me," I call out.

He turns to gaze at me with such longing that it reopens that ache inside me, which I now know must be love.

"You are engraved in my heart. Not even death itself can make me forget you, Jennie Jerome."

AFTERWORD

Jennie died on June 29, 1921, at the age of sixty-seven, from a sudden hemorrhage after the amputation of her leg. She summoned the nurse, complaining she was wet; when the nurse drew back the bedsheet, she found Jennie drenched in blood. Jennie lost consciousness by the time Winston and Jack were alerted. She passed away within an hour of their arrival at the hospital.

She was buried in the Churchill plot at St. Martin's Church, Bladon, Oxfordshire, near Blenheim, beside Randolph, with whom she began her grand adventure nearly fifty years before.

Winston left a wreath of red roses on her casket.

Jennie's last will, dated from 1915, was deemed invalid. It fell to Jack and her widower, Montagu, to sort through her debts, as Winston had been named Secretary of State for the Colonies in February and was embroiled in the political roller coaster that would define his long career.

In her last letter to Montagu, Jennie wrote, "I love you better than anything in the world." It could be said that of her marriages, the third had been the charm, the man most suited to her volatile temperament and sexuality. Montagu remarried in 1926 and retired to the countryside following a successful business career in East Africa. He died in 1964, never volunteering to discuss or capitalize on his romance with Jennie.

John Spencer-Churchill, known as Jack, was awarded the French Croix de Guerre and the Légion d'Honneur, as well as the British Distinguished Service Order for his wartime service. He continued to work as a stockbroker, outliving his wife and losing his home on

Downing Street during the Blitz. He died in 1947, at the same age
as his mother, and was buried near his parents.

In most historians' estimation, Winston became the greatest
statesman of the twentieth century. Plagued by bouts of severe
depression, as well as monumental victories and defeats that he
took very personally, he described himself as "a man of destiny,"
perhaps a trait instilled in him by his mother. His recklessness
could often overcome his reason, again something he likely inherited from Jennie. But his lifelong horror of war and his passion for
Britain cannot be denied. Though he made remarks that can only
be interpreted as racist, he was also known to have expressed genuine intolerance for the subjugation of Ireland and the sufferings inflicted on Africa and India by the British Empire. This afterword
is too brief to extoll Sir Winston's many accomplishments and
drawbacks, but in his greatest hour of steering Europe through
World War II, he exceeded every ambition that his mother had for
him and fulfilled his beloved nanny's belief in him.

Sir Winston died on January 24, 1965. He was laid to rest in
St. Martin's Church after an outpouring of international mourning. Never reluctant to state his pride in his American heritage, he is
one of only eight people to have received honorary U.S. citizenship.

Clarita Jerome Frewen outlived her estranged husband, Moreton,
and died in 1935. She was eighty-four years old and fought to the
end to retain the manor she'd restored as a legacy for her children.
In her later years, she dodged penury, the bane of all three sisters.

Leonie Jerome Leslie died in 1943, also at the age of eighty-
four. Her grandson Jack Leslie inherited his paternal family's Irish
estate.

The Jeromes also had a fourth daughter, Camille, born in 1855,
after Jennie and before Leonie. In 1863, at seven years of age, during
a family vacation in Newport, Camille died of a sudden fever.
Childhood mortality was very high in this pre-antibiotic age, and
her bereaved parents' reaction to the devastating loss was to never

refer to their daughter again. Clara made a specific point of evading any mention of Camille. Due to the constraints imposed by a novel of this size, with so many characters and events to cover, I did not mention Camille either, though her death must have left a lasting effect on both her father and mother. Jennie was eight years old at the time of her sister's passing; it's unknown whether that exerted a lifelong impact on her.

Documentation about Jennie is plentiful. Her memoirs, however, are far less revealing. To protect her family, she published a romanticized version of her life, in which she bypassed various controversies, particularly those concerning Randolph, to whom she remained devoted.

To date, the cause of Randolph's death remains under question, giving rise to speculation about his sexuality. Based on my research, in which most reliable sources concur, it's almost certain he contracted and died of syphilis. I found no evidence to support that Randolph was gay; indeed, it seems vaguely homophobic to suggest that being a closeted gay Victorian made one more predisposed to what was then an untreatable and fatal venereal disease. In reality, syphilis was endemic throughout Victorian society, and Randolph was known to be promiscuous, bedding women from all social classes, including prostitutes. He may have slept with men, too, but exactly when or from whom he contracted the disease can never be known.

Regardless, Jennie Jerome became celebrated during and after his life as one of the first American women to wed into the British aristocracy. Her triumphs and setbacks became fodder for international gossip that cemented her legacy as a daring, often contrary, but always courageous woman who never allowed the era's restrictions to impede her. The daughter of a self-made millionaire who squandered as much as he earned; the wife of Lord Randolph Spencer-Churchill, whose eccentricity, political aspirations, and achievements she encouraged and abetted; and the mother of

Sir Winston Churchill—while others followed in her footsteps, none achieved her level of fame or accomplishment.

As Winston once said of his glamorous mother, "She made a brilliant impression upon my childhood life. She shone for me like the evening star." While he doubtlessly made his declaration with unvoiced pain, given her undeniable neglect during his childhood, they had grown closer in adulthood than they'd ever been while he was growing up, and he remained loyal to her memory. What he suffered as a boy never overcame his abiding love for her.

Jennie made many mistakes in her life. She wasn't a caring mother to her young sons. She could be vain and self-absorbed, as well as insensitive to how her actions affected those around her. In both her faults and her virtues, she laid bare the hypocrisies of her society and the struggle that so many women endured to find independent fulfillment. Thus, Winston's description of her holds true. She was indeed the evening star that personified the brash spirit, baffling contradiction, and evanescence of her era—and in doing so, she transcended them.

While I've endeavored to adhere to the facts and documented personalities, besides those already mentioned, I admit to certain liberties, such as shifts in time or place to facilitate the narrative, as well as the omission of people and events to maintain cohesive pacing. My insight into these characters is my fictionalized interpretation, based on what is known. Any errors I may have made are inadvertent. To depict Jennie's life in its entirety poses a challenging feat for a novelist with a limited word count, and I hope I've done her spirit justice.

I RELIED ON many sources to research this novel. While not intended as a full bibliography, the following list contains the works I consulted most often to portray Jennie and her world:

Goodman, Ruth. *How to Be a Victorian*. New York: Liveright, 2013.

Higham, Charles. *Dark Lady*. New York: Carroll & Graf, 2006.

Kehoe, Elisabeth. *The Titled Americans*. New York: Atlantic Monthly Press, 2004.

Lee, Celia, and John Lee. *The Churchills*. New York: Palgrave Macmillan, 2010.

Leslie, Anita. *Jennie: The Life of Lady Randolph Churchill*. London: Hutchinson, 1969.

Martin, Ralph G. *Jennie: The Life of Lady Randolph Churchill*, 2 vols. London: Prentice-Hall, 1971.

Sebba, Anne. *American Jennie*. New York: W. W. Norton, 2007.

ACKNOWLEDGMENTS

As always, I thank my husband, who supports my endless hours at the computer and forgetting dinner. My cats, Boy and Maus, remind me that missing dinner is not an option. My agent, Jennifer Weltz, has seen me through countless crises as a professional writer and continues to weather the storms with me.

Rachel Kahan first offered me encouragement when I was an aspiring writer. She later rescued me by preempting this book. She's remained steadfast in her support. As with my previous novels, *Mademoiselle Chanel* and *Marlene*, I'm privileged to have her as my editor. I owe special thanks to Isabelle Fields, my insightful sensitivity reader, who made me laugh with her gif comments, and to Susan M. S. Brown, my meticulous copyeditor.

I thank all the booksellers who continue to recommend my books and host me for events, even when only one person shows up for the cheese and wine.

Most of all, I thank you, my reader. Your enthusiasm for my work inspires me to continue this unpredictable career. I hope I can continue to entertain you for many years to come.

Last, please do something every day to help our planet and the unique species who depend, as we do, on its survival. We must never forget that we only have one home, and each of us can make a difference in restoring our Mother Earth to harmony and balance.

Thank you!

About the author

About the book

Insights,
Interviews
& More . . .

Meet C. W. Gortner

Stephanie Mohan

C. W. GORTNER is a former fashion executive. His passion for writing led him to give up fashion for the page; now his many historical novels—including *Marlene* and *Mademoiselle Chanel*— have been bestsellers and have published in more than twenty countries. He lives in California. ↝

Behind the Book

My interest in Jennie started in my childhood. I was a boy living in southern Spain when I first saw the 1974 *Masterpiece Theatre* series starring Lee Remick, based on Ralph G. Martin's monumental two-volume bestseller. Ms. Remick's audacious portrayal in what is now a dated production stayed with me; something about this tale of a girl born in the United States, who was taken to Europe and set out to conquer it, echoed my own childhood circumstances. Over the years, I read everything I could find about Jennie's life, attracted to her fascinating personality. Despite my love for the romance of the clothing and my having written three novels set in the period, I'm not an ardent fan of the Victorian era, because it wasn't one of advancement for women. If anything, despite being the longest reign by a British monarch, exceeded only by that of the present-day queen, Victoria's era was marked by setbacks in most areas where women were concerned. But Jennie defied these obstacles with a bravado that can only have been American. At heart, she was a New Yorker, in everything the term entails.

Writing about the past is a difficult endeavor. The research alone takes years, with sources invariably contradicting one another and requiring educated deduction. History isn't a precise science; it comes with its imperfections. Most ▶

Behind the Book *(continued)*

challenging, however, is to re-create
the emotions of those who knew a
world so vastly different from our own,
both technologically and in our human
liberties. Rights that we now take
for granted, such as the women's right
to vote, were still contentious in Jennie's
lifetime; she herself was recorded as
expressing indifference to the suffragettes,
as did Winston Churchill, until the
suffragettes besieged his home, pelting
it with eggs in protest of his refusal to
endorse their plight. Jennie counseled
him to defer to the prevailing winds,
and he publicly upheld the call for
women to vote. It might seem baffling
to us that a woman as politically astute
and sexually adventurous as Jennie—
and for her time, she certainly was,
helping orchestrate her first husband's
career, becoming an entrepreneur,
marrying two men far younger than
her, and suing for divorce from one—
wasn't immediately on the side of her
own gender. But she, too, was a product
of her time in this respect. Like many
Victorians, she didn't deem civil liberties
to be essential for an equitable society,
though her defiant behavior was
revolutionary for her lifetime.

I often say that I don't choose my
heroines; they choose me. It seems like
a strange declaration, but that's how
it feels. I can't take on my character's
voice if she doesn't invite me. I can't
embody her, interpret her life or her
world through her eyes, if she refuses
to cooperate. It must be a collaboration,

so that whenever I stumble upon a contradiction in the sources that sends me down a research rabbit hole, I'll know, in my gut, where the truth might be. From her reaction to pivotal historical events to her most intimate decisions, regardless of whether I agree with her, I must stay true to what is known of her recorded personality. It's a delicate balance, requiring sensitivity and empathy, and I do my best to reserve my judgment.

Because I don't always agree with my heroines, it never fails to surprise me when I receive an e-mail or social media comment from a reader upset by how she's been portrayed. The women I write about were fallible, like all of us. They made both good and bad decisions. Their complexity is what I seek to reveal; if I find my character incomprehensible or start to judge her for her actions, I'm in trouble as a writer. I must *understand* her, which is not the same as agreeing with her. If I comprehend why she behaved as she did, then I can step into her shoes.

I'm known for portraying controversial women in my work. From Juana, the Mad Queen of Spain, to Catherine de Medici, Lucrezia Borgia, Isabella of Castile, Coco Chanel, Marlene Dietrich, Maria Feodorovna, Sarah Bernhardt, and now Jennie Jerome, I'm attracted to characters who break the rules, who strive, willingly and otherwise, to be more than what's expected of them. It's more interesting ▶

to me to explore our rough edges;
I'm drawn to conflicts in our nature,
and what we do or don't do to overcome
them. Eras tend to matter less to me
than my leading lady, but they are still
vital to deciphering her life, because
society exerts such an impact on us.
We may think that someone like Jennie
wouldn't be considered daring today, and
yet, she would. The wife of a politician
who outlived him; launched herself as
an interior decorator, a publisher, and a
playwright; had numerous love affairs;
and refused to conform to how society
believed she ought to behave . . . It's not
far-fetched to imagine a Jennie Jerome
of the twenty-first century making
headlines, just as she did in the
nineteenth century.

To read and write about the past
is how we learn from our forebearers
and discover that what we've faced and
overcome was often due to our unity
in times of need. To write the past,
as I do, can illuminate the present by
shining a light on how to avoid the same
tribulations we've been through before,
and I consider it an honor. I owe you,
my reader, an engaging and fact-based
story. I owe my characters the
unvarnished truth.

Keep reading and live out loud. Thank
you for choosing my book. ∽

Reading Group Guide

1. Had you heard of Jennie Jerome prior to reading this novel? Were you familiar with this time period? What about the era was most familiar, or most surprising, to you?

2. Jennie says of her father's mistress, Fanny Ronalds: "Mama didn't share Papa's enthusiasms, so I'd assumed she forgave Mrs. Ronalds for doing so in her stead." And indeed, Clara and Fanny have an alliance that might seem unusual to some. What do you make of Fanny's friendship with Jennie and her sisters? How would you have managed the relationship with Fanny had you been Jennie's mother?

3. Early in the novel, Fanny tells Jennie: "Your father is very resourceful. He will overcome this setback, as will you, my dear." Does this foreshadow events in Jennie's own life? What were her greatest setbacks? How did she manage to overcome them?

4. What did you make of Jennie and Randolph's ploy to ensure they'd be allowed to get married? Would you have taken the same risks? ►

5. Jennie's mother tells her: "Marriage brings obligations. Once the passion ebbs, the hard work begins. Those who are ill-prepared reap untold misery." Did Jennie's marriages reflect this? Why do you think she married three times despite experiencing real hardships and even misery in her marriages?

6. What were the advantages and disadvantages of marrying into the Duke of Marlborough's family? Was Jennie's outsider status as an American a liability or an asset?

7. In addition to her three husbands, Jennie has passionate affairs with other men. What do you think she enjoyed about those relationships? How did her sexual adventures contrast with those of the men around her, like her husband and the Prince of Wales, who were both inveterate womanizers? Did her infidelities change your opinion of her?

8. How did Jennie bolster the political careers of her husband and then her son? What are some of the ways that women in her time exercised "soft power" to get results, since they could not vote or hold office themselves?

9. When Jennie's sons sue her in order to protect their inheritance, she admits to herself that her perilous financial situation "was the legacy of [her] upbringing. Of [her] father shoring [her] up in times of need." She tells her sons: "If I never had any concept of money, it's because no one ever gave me the opportunity to learn." Is that true, even though she was intelligent and competent in so many other ways? How have things changed since Jennie's time?

10. One of the part-opener epigraphs has this quote from Jennie Jerome: "Life is not always what one wants it to be, but to make the best of it as it is, is the only way to be happy." Do you agree? Did Jennie seem to find happiness that way? ∼